The Judgment Game

BOOK 1 - THE MASON JAR SERIES

All rights reserved. No portion of this book may be reproduced, stored in a retrieval system, or transmitted in any form or means including electronic, mechanical, photocopied, recorded, scanned, or otherwise, with the exception of brief quotations in reviews or articles, without prior written permission of author or publisher.

Scripture quotations are taken from the Holy Bible, NIV®, MSG®, KJV®

This novel is a work of fiction. All names, characters, places, and incidents are either from the imagination of the author or used fictitiously. All characters are fictional, and any similarity to people living or dead is coincidental.

Published by 3dogsBarking Media LLC

© 2019 by Steven G Bassett

Cover Design by Steven G Bassett

Interior Formatting by 3dogsBARKING MEDIA LLC

US COPYRIGHT Steven G Bassett 2020

ISBN: 978-1-7358159-1-6

The Judgment Game

BOOK 1 - THE MASON JAR SERIES

A NOVEL BY ELI POPE

THE JUDGMENT GAME

DEDICATION

Thank you to my loving wife, my beautiful family, and wonderful friends for their support.

I thank my Mom, who loved this story and pushed me to finish it. I know there are words and parts she cringes when she reads, but real-life stories from real-life hardships are often hard to look too deeply at because they differ so much from ourselves, yet they co-exist beside us.

She dedicated her career to the psychiatric nursing care field.

This story is for those who have lived through the horrors of what abuse leaves behind from every brutal form it rears its ugly presence in even after the actual pain giver is dead and gone.

I was one of the lucky who knew only love growing up and never felt the agony that those less fortunate lived and died.

Hell brings more hell, and stories like these are all too real.

THE JUDGMENT GAME

Acknowledgments

C.A. Simonson-First Draft Editor and Contributor

She is also a person and author whom I hold deep respect.

Candy drove me to deepen my characters and pushed me to make a richer story through description and action. Thank you!

Julie Luetschwager-Final Editing and Contributor

Her insights and encouragement gave me what I needed just when I needed it.

3dogsBarkingMedia LLC -Interior Design and Formatting

Thank you for the many Beta Readers who helped me develop and improve the flow and content of this story. Without your time and attention, this whole process would not have come to fruition.

This creating a story truly takes a village to bring it to life in the best form possible. I thank each and every villager that has belonged to my world created in this story. Without the villagers, the world would be broken and incoherent.

This Story will be available soon at Audible.com

Narrated by Paul McSorely

Music created by Nikki McSorely - nmcmusiccreative.com

THE JUDGMENT GAME

Prologue

1969- Apalachicola, FL

Billy (Jay) Jay Cader and Catrina (Cat) Anne Cader

(Poppa and Momma)

Billy (Billy) James Cader and Darrell (Darrell) Lee Cader

(Sons)

"We had one scraggly old peach tree in our backyard. Momma would take Darrell and me outside, and she would ask me to climb up to pick the ones really high up at the top. It made me real proud. Afterwards, we'd carry them inside in brown paper bags from the Piggly Wiggly, and Momma would preserve em in Mason jars. Somehow, those peaches that were sweet fresh off the tree were even sweeter after Momma canned em.

"One Friday evening, Poppa walked in after gettin' home and went straight to the pantry and pulled out one of them jars of peaches. With the familiar "pop," he took off the lid and dumped em on the kitchen floor.

"He'd discovered another use for the Mason jar, and none of our lives were ever the same."

***

It had been Friday the entire day long. Friday's were bad.

Billy knew Darrell was terrified the moment they both heard the rumble of the diesel truck pulling into the yard. Billy was also scared, and his stomach would grow twisted knots, even though he was usually lucky enough to draw grace when Poppa came home. Those miserable knots would squeeze tighter because he knew for some reason Darrell was rarely as fortunate as he was in Poppa's dang punishment. He hated the fact his little brother usually bore the brunt of Poppa's wrath. It hurt his heart to hear his little brother scream from the other room while Poppa gave his punishment. It made him need to vomit, but he usually held it from fear.

Billy glanced over at Darrell, who was sitting in the corner of the dark living room. The week's dirty dishes that were piled on the coffee table partially hid him along with the trash that was strewn across the floor. Momma hadn't felt well enough to tidy the house up this week. Just like last week too. She'd spent a good deal of time in her bed. It was a change that took over since they'd seen her with the "medicine" bottle she was drinking from more and more.

Life became a blur of dread and fear. Billy couldn't recall how long Momma had been drinking the brown liquid. The poison which stole her away from them.

The summer days, without school to break them up, just melted from one into the next. Until, of course, Friday.

An occasional palmetto bug scampered quickly over the stained and sticky carpet to the safety of the shadows against the wall. It then disappeared back down the heat register opening.

Darrell sat on the floor visibly shaken, his legs bent, close to his chest. In no particular sequence, his knees would bang together nervously, then return tightly clenched together, his chin resting on them before breaking apart and repeating.

Billy looked over again, quietly trying to comfort his brother, "It'll be okay, Darrell—if you don't get grace—and I do, I'll let you have it. I'll take whatever Poppa gives you." Billy smiled at his younger brother, assuring him he would be okay, but what he really thought was that there had to be some dang way to stop that sombitch from hurting him.

Billy lifted his head, peeking over the window sill, spying how close his Poppa was to coming inside, his insides twisting tighter into knot after knot. It was a ritual that came once a week. No matter how many times they'd gone through it, the ceremony never became any easier. The fear was deep inside. So deep, his bones ached. His heart ached. And their momma was nowhere near to protect them. Many times, Billy thought about stealing the bottle of brown liquid for him and Darrell to drink—so they could escape too. *Poppa would probably kill us, though.*

He was working at hauling things outa' the semi, then taking them over to the shop. Billy couldn't see what all he was unloading because the fall sky was dim, and the wind was blowing the rain up onto the porch windows, causing them to blur. He lowered his head back down below the sill as their momma called out, "Billy…is that your Poppa gettin' home?"

"Yes, Ma'am," Billy answered quickly. "He ain't headed in yet, but he's sure enough home."

With the mention of Poppa being home and the words 'headed in,' Darrell could no longer contain his nerves or his bladder. A small wet spot grew more significant in the crotch and seat of his pants until a small puddle formed under him. Billy glanced back at him, "Darrell, I swear I'll kill him this time if he hurts you—quick go and hide those pants before he gets inside!"

With his big brother's words, a terrified, six and a half-year-old, dirty strawberry-blonde haired boy, scampered off around the corner and down the hallway.

His ten-year-old brother stood up to keep Poppa busy from noticing Darrell's absence if he should suddenly come in from the outside.

There were two sounds in both brother's worlds that instantly changed their moods to one of fear. The drone of Poppa's diesel pulling up the drive on Friday evenings, and the sound the wooden tiles made in the Mason jar as Poppa shook it vigorously, mixing them up. The noise preceded their discipline at the end of the evening, before bedtime. It didn't matter if they'd done anything wrong or not. It was just how things were done.

Momma would cry. She would beg Poppa to throw the damned jar away. But Momma's words never overruled the little wooden square tile with a punishment etched on one side. Once it landed on the tabletop, it was law. That tile that Poppa would shake out onto the table from the Mason jar contained an assortment of punishments, each burnt onto the wooden surface.

Neither boy could bring himself to look at the jar as it sat motionless on the kitchen shelf while Poppa was gone. They learned quickly not to touch it and that it "Goddang well better be there in the correct spot" when Poppa went to fetch it. Billy learned the hard way about that rule when he thought he could hide it, so Darrell wouldn't quiver in fear when he would see it.

Billy could never bring himself to touch it again after Poppa beat him senseless for his effort. He knew one day he would make Poppa stop. One day when he was older.

1

(Poppa) Billy Jay Cader-Early days in Ocala, FL

Billy Jay Cader turned forty-four in 1977. He was married with two nearly grown kids and wore his life story, fully tattooed up each arm from the wrist to shoulder. Most of them were of poor quality, done by fellow inmates during a ten-year stint at the workfarm. Cons that fancied themselves artists of the ink. He wore the scales of justice tattooed on his chest, with lady justice dying, a dagger in her heart, and blood-red ink dripped down his chest to form a puddle in his bellybutton.

He hadn't lived a comfortable life growing up. He experienced harshness daily and brutality from those who were supposed to love and care for him.

Billy Jay was the unfortunate boy to have parents who fought like cats and dogs, with their usual form of communication at an angry, screaming level, chocked full of expletives. The word love was nonexistent unless his mother screamed something like, "For the love of God, Billy John, you're gonna kill that f'ing boy one of these days." Billy John Cader was his daddy, and he was one mean "sonovabitch," as Billy Jay would later describe him when pressed to talk about his past. His momma Emma Sue Cader was just a pathetic, beat down, woman from the years she'd been tied to Billy

John. A day filled with violence and vulgar verbal attacks was just another typical day in her life. She could send those same nasty words back with no problems, either.

Young Billy Jay grew up fast and fierce. He'd been kicked out of school so many times and held back in grades, he eventually quit and never returned.

Just days after his fourteenth birthday, little Billy Jay's mother lost her battle with cancer. A hell of a way to beat a hard marriage. She left their cruel world three days after Jay's birthday. There was barely any recognition of either his birthday or her funeral. The only thing his daddy ever gave him was swift punishment from a leather belt, a switch, hairbrush, or anything else within quick reach. There was one time his daddy grabbed a hammer and swung it at him. If he'd been hit, he'd surely have died in a bloody mess. His daddy owned a quick temper. He used to hold Billy Jay's head underwater in the tub as a form of punishment, called dunkin', along with locking him in the dark basement for hours on end. Billy Jay's daddy had his other ways also. All scribed on little wooden tiles and kept in a fruit jar to be shaken and then emptied on the table like a lottery.

With his momma dead and gone, there was nothing left for him at home, but the cruel meanness doled out from his daddy's hand. Billy Jay quickly ran away, leaving his first name Billy behind. He went by Jay from that day on. He didn't want nobody findin' him to bring him back to the evil monster that didn't know nothin' 'cept beatin' his ass.

Jay lived on the streets of Ocala, Florida, for several months. Occasionally in the middle of the night, he would walk by his daddy's house, spying on him through a lit window. His daddy never came looking for him. Not once.

Late one evening, a kind woman found Jay digging in a dumpster out behind a local greasy spoon diner. Ms. Lila Pasternack was the only bright spot Jay ever experienced in his life other than his momma on a good day. Her love was also the only form of genuine love he ever knew up to now, but it was far too late for it to sink into his psyche fully, and he never became comfortable with the feeling. Jay lived in Ms. Lila's spare room for two years, going from small job to small job. He would pay Lila some rent and food money from each paycheck and then stuff the rest into an old Mason jar he'd found out in the shed behind her small house. Jay had big plans to move down to the coast one day with his savings and buy a small fishing boat with a cuddy cabin below. He just knew he could live a quaint life away from the world that dealt him such a painful losing hand.

Ms. Lila would occasionally call him out from his room and guilt him into watching an old movie with her that she liked. They were usually silly love stories, but she just felt better watching with a friend beside her. At times, her loneliness would overtake the usually cheerful personality, and she relied on her new friend to warm her with conversation or quiet company.

Jay would sit through the movies, laughing how they were bullshit in portraying the world, or he would get angry when it painted the father figure as someone who cared about his children. He certainly never experienced anything of that nature in his life.

Ms. Lila tried many times to convince Jay to go to church with her, "Now Jay, we all need to know Jesus. I know you came from bad times, but Jesus can help with those bad memories." Her pleading words were always to no avail.

"What would God give me, but a weak heart for those who took advantage of me and others?" Jay would fire off replicating his daddy—of course, that was the cleaned-up version.

"God's grace can help heal an ailing mind, Jay."

Jay laughed and responded, "I've heard of God and that nonsense about his grace, but Daddy always said grace was nothin' but a game of chance. You'd benefit yourself better by bettin' your last dollar on craps."

One day after a long hard week of digging drainage ditches beside a residential street for the city, he took his pay home to stuff it in the Mason jar. It was getting almost full, and he would soon have to find another. He'd saved several hundred dollars in folded ten-dollar bills crammed tightly inside. When he wanted to count it, he would lay the bills on his bedside table as he carefully unfolded them.

Jay immediately sensed something was wrong upon opening Ms. Lila's front door. Items were scattered across the floor while drawers always left closed were now wide open. He hollered out her name, but no one answered. He rounded the corner; attention perked as he listened carefully for any sounds of Ms. Lila. He tiptoed up to her bedroom door, partially open, which made his heart begin to pound in his chest. Something wasn't right, Jay felt it in his gut. He called out softly, "Ms. Pasternack? You in your bedroom?" He waited for an answer. His thoughts began to jumble as tension built inside of his body, his heartbeat pounding in his chest.

He slowly moved forward as he gingerly pushed her door open. His nose filled with the scent of roses and powder. The fragrance overwhelmed him, making his head spin. He sucked for air, but the powdery smell robbed him of the breath his throbbing head needed to continue. Eyes were darting across the room from left to right; he first noticed her dresser drawers pulled out and strewn everywhere. Frilly lady's garments lay across the floor—things he'd never seen before except in his daddy's magazines.

What caught his attention next would never be able to be unseen or erased from his memory. There lay Old lady Pasternack, fully naked on her bed. There was bright red blood everywhere, and her eyes were wide open, yet an empty stare with no gleam in them at all. Her neck badly bruised while her head lay twisted unnaturally. There were deep, bloody cuts in places he'd never seen unclothed. He knew she was dead. His breath became heavier, and he struggled to take in the air he needed. He moved in closer, seeing a belt or something lying loosely around her neck. He reached over loosening it, even more, pulling it out from under her and tossing it to the floor. Not sure if his stomach was going to hold out much longer, he leaned in to see if he could feel her breath or hear a heartbeat.

That's when the stench of urine and spoiled meat overtook the aroma of perfume, and he began to wretch. Quickly stepping back and covering his mouth, he ran to the bathroom just across the hallway. Jay fell to the floor on his knees, grabbing the toilet with both hands, and began vomiting and choking on his bile. His stomach bursting with pain, his mind overwhelmed by what he'd seen and smelled.

When the shock wore down enough to realize his only friend was gone, a small tear crept from the corner of each eye. It seemed in that tiny moment in his life; he understood what love was. It had come in the form of a sweet old woman who showed compassion for a homeless teen, bringing him into her own home and caring for him. His mind searched for answers to why this could happen to someone so kind. It quickly turned into anger for whoever stole the only good thing he'd ever known. That only love he'd ever experienced was gone. Brutalized and left for dead. What good had she gotten for her kindness? Where was her grace? He pushed aside those feelings momentarily as he ran to his bedroom.

In this moment of reflection, he finally felt how she'd loved him, and quickly returned to more familiar feelings of hate as he entered his room. He looked around and saw his Mason jar broken on the wooden floor, nothing but shards of glass were left. There would be no moving to the coast to live aboard his fishing boat. His hard-earned savings to get to the coast were gone; his dream was dead like his friend Ms. Lila Pasternack.

Once again, he ran and was all alone.

He didn't go far. While Ocala wasn't a large town, he quickly found refuge in an old storage barn about six miles east of town, next to the Silver River.

There was a large field of string beans that he attempted to live on, but within two weeks, he was spotted and caught by the authorities. Jay was too weak from starvation to run.

The owners of the farm saw him from a distance and had heard of the murder in Ocala, Fl. They didn't know the two were tied together but reported a young man who looked hungry and homeless on their property.

The sheriff came out to investigate, arresting Jay for the rape and murder of Ms. Lila Pasternack. He pleaded his innocence, but after a rushed trial to quell the public fear, he was found guilty.

Fingerprints found on a leather belt matching his along with him staying with her at the time—seemed enough evidence for the jury to convict.

Back in 1942, in Ocala, Florida—fear took precedence over facts. Billy Jay Cader or better known as Jay may have been barely sixteen and a juvenile, but he, sure enough, began his adult sentence of ten to twenty years hard labor at the state work farm. He was told by his public defender to consider himself fortunate for such a lenient sentence from Judge James Jefferson, who was ordinarily prone to using the death sentence, adolescent or not.

2

Billy Jay Cader-Early Days

It was a hard ten years for Jay. He was the youngest inmate among hardened rapists, killers, and thieves. He quickly learned to trust none of them and to keep his back to the wall whenever possible. He'd only been in lock-up less than a week before being brutally raped by a group of older men who ran the cellblock. It wasn't the last time such horrible things happened to him. These attacks confirmed that there was atrocious evil that existed in this world, even more than he'd ever experienced before. His daddy had beaten him and treated him terribly, but he never imagined another man would animalize a young boy in such perverted ways. He realized there would be no rehabilitation brought to anyone in this hell. He, who was truly innocent of his conviction, would learn only to care for himself. Jay's feelings of the world became more calloused and hardened by the treatment he suffered. It was not only by the hands of the prisoners but also by the guards who sometimes participated. It helped prove that grace was just a pretty word that contained no truth he could see. He knew he was truly alone in not only this prison but in this world. No one was going to save him from the shitty cards dealt. He had only himself to count on to bluff for survival.

Jay knew what others wanted from him. He learned if he played their game, that life might somehow go easier on himself. Nevertheless, each time his parole hearing came up, he sat staunchly in front of the panel and truthfully answered their questions. They were never the answers the board wanted to hear. He proclaimed his innocence each time as the parole panel made their decisions, shaking their heads in dismay at his claims of innocence. Actual innocence meant nothing in this place. The walls of solitude he built around himself block by block, only became more reinforced with each day.

Prison taught him several lessons in life. First, living in this world was harsh and unfair. It didn't matter if you did the crime or not; you got punished for it. He'd heard of grace from a "religious" inmate while sitting in the prison yard one day, but he'd laughed at him saying he never saw or experienced such a thing. He also kept the memory of how his life and dreams were stolen from him when he had found the shattered Mason jar which had held his life savings, now gone. He learned that helping someone got you nowhere. He pictured his last memory of Ms. Lila lying on her bed, beaten and naked with her perfume bottle emptied over her. *What had kindness gotten her? Dead—was the reward her good deed earned her. Grace was for fools he'd told the preaching inmate that day, a game of chance at best.*

When the end of his sentence finally came, and Jay was able to walk through the front gate and back into an unguarded life, he decided something then and there. *I'll do whatever it takes to put myself first and on top from that day forward, to the bitter end. I'll beg, borrow, or steal to survive and leave grace to all the other suckers in this hellish life.*

***

Jay finally made it to the coast, but it wasn't the dream life he'd made it out to be in his head. He quickly realized no matter whatever geographical spot you planted your feet on, the experience stayed the same. Difficult. He didn't care much about birthdays; his family never celebrated them. They were just another day, but he did remember his twenty-sixth. It led to a change in his life. It was, however, eventual.

He sat by a pier in Apalachicola that jutted out toward the sunset. Jay watched as people strolled by, calculating which one would be an easy take. He was hungry, and the few nibbles of a sandwich he'd found behind a restaurant in the trash did little to fill his growling gut. Looking up from the ground, he noticed a pretty young woman walking down the boardwalk towards him.

She sat down beside him as she brushed the wrinkles from her clingy dress that fit snuggly around her thin waist. She looked him over and smiled sweetly.

He noticed her dress immediately. It reminded him of the beautiful clouds floating overhead. Until this moment, he'd failed to see the beauty in a sky could mimic the dazzle of a woman. Her blue eyes paired perfectly with the thin azure belt she wore around her waist. Her smooth legs escaped the cover of the dress and gave cause for Jay to finger-comb his greasy hair back behind his ears in an attempt to make himself look better. It was a futile attempt to make himself more attractive, and he'd never felt the need to do such a thing before.

Memories of Ms. Lila quickly entered his mind as he suddenly pictured his old friend looking like this woman when she was her age. She beamed with the same warmness as Miss Lila but caused the odd feelings of butterflies in his stomach that he was not previously familiar with.

"Good evening sir, my name is Catrina Anne Dobbyn, but everyone just calls me Cat."

Jay couldn't believe that a woman as beautiful as she was would start a conversation with him. He felt awkward and stumbled with returning the pleasantries. "Evening ma'am. It sure is a beautiful blue sky, matches your outfit perfect-like." He looked down immediately, avoiding any eye contact.

"Usually by this time of the evening, the sky is filling up with oranges and pinks." She tilted her head up slightly as she spoke.

"I don't mean to be forward, but since we're talking—what's your name?"

"Jay—eh, actually it's Billy Jay, but I usually go by Jay. I'm uh, I'm not too used to talking too much. I pretty much keep to myself."

"I'm sorry, Jay, I can stop if you'd like?"

"No ma'am, I didn't mean to say it like that. I'm just not used to such company." He tried dragging his fingers through his hair again as she turned her sight toward the docks. The waves rolled against the fishing boats, rocking them gently in their stalls.

"I haven't seen you here before—are you new to the area?"

"Yes, ma'am…."

"Please, call me Cat. You needn't be so formal."

"Okay—if you insist, Miss Cat."

"Please, just Cat!"

"I'm new to the area—Cat. I am still getting my bearings. It's a beautiful little town. I thought at one time, I would like to own a fishing boat myself. Had my money well started in savings, but…"

"I could see you as a captain of a fishing boat!"

"Well, Miss, I mean, Cat—that is kind of my dream. It's on hold for a bit, but I still have it in my mind."

The sky was beginning to darken as the crowd had thinned out. Once Jay looked around, he noticed Cat was the only target close. He knew he could easily take whatever cash she had, but something inside of him wouldn't let it go farther than just a thought.

Cat smiled at him as she got up and asked. "Do you plan on coming here again soon?"

"I imagine I'll find my way back to such a beautiful spot, why?" he quickly asked.

"Well, I guess I'll keep my eyes open for you—so we can chat again. There's just something about you that piques my curiosity, that's all." She smiled again as she turned to look at his face for a response.

Shame overtook him for his thoughts of robbing such a sweet lady. He toed the ground with his head down and then looked up with a sheepish grin. "That would be nice of you, ma'am. I'd look forward to it."

"Well, I'll too look forward to seeing you again, Jay."

As she walked away, he decided to look elsewhere for a place to get a meal. He didn't want to make this spot one he couldn't return to, just in case he was to see Cat—again.

***

Each day Jay went back to the same bench and waited patiently sometimes, not so at others. Cat showed up most days, and they sat and talked. Jay found himself telling her more and more about his childhood, what little he experienced before going out on his own. Cat seemed intrigued by his stories and often got teary-eyed when Jay described the worst of the bad times. Cat did something most people did not—she showed interest, not the sympathy people faked, but the kind you felt deep down. A feeling Jay never experienced much of, until now.

"My Daddy never cared for me. I could tell. He'd push me outside while he and my Momma would either yell and fight—or do just the opposite—if you know what I mean?"

"That's horrible. A young boy needs their father's love and guidance to be prepared to be on their own." She reached over to cup his hand. At first, he quickly pulled away. "I'm sorry I just wanted to comfort you."

"I'm the one that should apologize, Cat; I'm not used to being comforted by anyone. I've always had to console myself. There is only one other person I've ever spent so much time talking to, and she's gone."

"Someone special in a romantic way?" Cat watched Jay's eyes to catch a reaction.

"No, no, nothing like that, ma'am. Ms. Pasternack was like a real mother to me. She helped me out after I was on my own. My real momma passed away. Ms. Pasternack was the only person that ever showed me what real love was supposed to be like."

"What happened to her? Does she live far away?"

"I'm afraid if I tell you, you might not want to see me again." His eyes began to pool—something which hadn't happened before through all of their conversations, no matter how sad. "I'm not ready to give you up on a chance. You're my one bright spot in life that I look forward to, Cat."

"Jay, I'm here. I've listened and learned a lot about you. I look forward to seeing you." Cat blushed. "You're my bright spot that I hope for each day. I'm not going anywhere. I promise." She blinked several times in a flirtatious way.

"I tell you, Cat, Ms. Lila, was the only woman who ever showed me love…" Jay finished telling Cat the entire story of how he'd found her that day and what the outcome became.

Cat held Jay in her arms after watching him struggle with his story. "I'm so sorry, Jay" She squeezed his hands and leaned in close, giving him a quick peck on his lips.

Cat held a heart of gold and compassion for those who were less fortunate. She'd been blessed by a comfortable life, although her family indeed retained no great wealth. The more she continued to meet with Jay, the more taken she became. She soon found herself inviting him to come to her small apartment to share dinners.

Jay began to put more effort into the way he looked than ever before. Jay found a public restroom and shower by the docks, which he began to use regularly. Doing his best to keep the few sets of clothes clean made him able to appear in different attire. He'd never felt shame in his appearance before, but he now was very aware of cleanliness. The efforts had worked as it masked the fact that he lived wherever he could find. There were some of the boats on the dock which the owners never seemed to use. He'd found two he regularly slipped into when the sun went down.

"So where in town do you live, Jay? I can't believe we've known each other this long, and I've never asked." She started to tell him what part of town she lived but stopped when he began to show signs of not knowing how to respond.

"I—well, I don't…I'm not sure how to…"

"It's okay, Jay. You don't have to tell me if you're not ready. I don't want to press."

"Cat—I should have been honest sooner. I just got so tied up in wanting you to like me; I just didn't know how to tell you. You've heard so much of my childhood; I just figured you probably knew." He began to fidget like when they'd first met. He fumbled with finishing his thoughts.

"I'm sorry, Jay. I hate myself when I make you uncomfortable. It's not what I mean to do."

"It's not your fault. Our worlds are so different from each other. It's what makes me afraid that one time I'll say something that will make them collide in such a way we will not be able to continue with whatever it is we have."

"Look at me." She put a soft hand on each side of his rough whiskered face. She gently turned his head to meet hers squarely. "You are like no one I've ever met. I wasn't looking for anything when we sat on that same bench those weeks back. You—you enthralled me in ways I still don't understand, but it's me who is afraid of losing you. I—I've never met anyone who makes me feel the way you make me feel." She tried to continue without bursting into tears. "I lost the only man in my life I ever cared for, my daddy. My momma disappeared after he passed. Sure, I was grown when this happened, but I've never really had anyone either, since then."

The tears were trickling down her cheeks as she sniffled, struggling to continue. "You are a gift to me. Your friendship has grown to be the only thing I look forward to in this life. I think that maybe—no, I know that my feelings are more than just friendship." Her eyes locked onto Jay's as his face appeared to be attempting to predict what the next sentence Cat would speak might be.

"I'm falling in love with you." She spoke in almost a whisper. The words came out in a quiver of body shakes. She fought looking away in fear, forcing herself to search within his eyes for the emotion she'd prayed to see.

"I'm homeless, Cat. I have nothing to give you. I want to love you, I know I have feelings for you—but, I can't make promises on things I have no experience. I don't want to take advantage of you. That by itself is—a new feeling for me."

Cat's eyes closed, followed quickly by her head dropping. Her hands slipped from Jay's cheeks tracing down his sides until they rested neatly against her own.

Cat felt naïve for not realizing sooner that Jay was homeless. Wrapped up in his unique personality and the stories he'd told, she'd never even noticed why he dressed as poorly as he did each time they met. She just assumed appearance wasn't as important to him as it was to her.

Jay witnessed her spirit shatter before his eyes. He sensed her dreams fall to the ground, much like shards of broken glass might spread out at her feet.

He lifted her chin with his calloused weathered hand and gently spoke. "Cat…" her eyes slowly rolled up to meet his. "Cat, I believe I feel what you call love. It's something I have no experience. I know you are a caring person who I would enjoy spending time with. I just don't know how to respond to something I don't understand? I've had to fight for everything I've needed to survive." His head dropped as he stopped to take in a deep breath. "I've stolen from people, I've hurt people. I can't risk doing any of that to you. The last person I felt love for ended up murdered. A crime I was blamed with."

"I know you didn't hurt your friend Jay. I feel inside every inch of my body that you would never hurt me under any circumstance." She pleaded her case for him to succumb. "Give me a chance. Give love a chance. I won't hold you to staying if you find out it isn't love for you." Her eyes looked into his with a look of desperation. She hung on every breath she took, waiting for him to respond with an answer.

Jay sat silent. He knew he didn't want to lose her. She held the magic to make him happy. He wasn't afraid of a commitment himself. He was scared of hurting her—a situation he never before had to wrestle.

He looked back into her eyes and smiled. Jay pulled back and took her into full view. She was wearing the same white cotton dress she'd worn the day they met. Emotions flooded his mind, and he succumbed quickly. "I don't know what love is—but if it is what I feel when I'm with you, then I am in love."

Cat fell back into Jay's arms the moment she heard his last word. She squeezed him as if she would never let go again, holding him tightly as her body released the tension in wave after wave like the tide rolling onto shore.

"Come live with me, Jay. You don't have to live without a home ever again."

The two of them walked hand in hand, sharing glimpses of each other's eyes as the sun began to set behind them.

They barely made it up the stairs and through her front door before their bodies were one, wrapped in a whirlwind of something neither one knew anything about before today.

***

The first morning after their shared night of closeness, Cat lay there looking at Jay as he slept next to her. She studied his chiseled chin and his sharp nose. His face showed a story of a hard life but still held a certain softness to it. Her eyes studied each of his arms intently at the designs inked into his skin. They seemed to tell a story, although it wasn't a pleasant one. There were demons and anger in them. His chest said the most, though. It spoke of the wrong he was accused of so blindly, at least by the way he told the story in his words.

She then smiled to herself as she re-lived the entanglement that they shared just hours before. Those dark stories on Jay's arms had heated her skin through the night as if the flames tattooed on them could burn. The feelings of satisfaction he'd given her were overwhelming. His awkwardness, like hers, surely meant he too had never been with anyone before. She thought to herself, this must be love, and she hoped when he woke, he would still feel the same way.

***

Jay's eyes slowly opened, he quickly looked over to see Cat lying on her side, facing away from him. His thoughts were so conflicted. Last night had felt wonderful, but it was those feelings he knew nothing about. He felt pleasure and warmth—but he knew pain and punishment of some sort must surely follow. The women in his life always eventually brought those things. He thought surely; he should ease out of bed quietly and run. In his mind, giving her up under his power would sting less than having her stolen away without his consent.

He slowly began to pull away, careful not to wake her, but something changed his mind. He chose to turn and snuggle in close, as one spoon fit into another, deciding to risk what fell into his hands and see what would follow. Jay's heart felt warm, and Cat was a person he could spend hours sharing conversation. *So, this was what people were talking about when they described love? Was this what life in the movies was emulating that I once watched with Ms. Lila and laughed about?* He wondered.

3

Nine months to the day later, he and Cat were still together; they welcomed their first son Billy James Cader. Jay seemed like the young, excited, and proud father it was healthy to be.

"Cat! We have a son! I'm glad you want to name him after me! He is my pride and joy, my chance to be different from the dad I had. I want to be everything in his world!" He assured his wife that little Billy would be his shadow. And that is the way their life as a family of three started. Billy Jay would show Billy James off everywhere. His world was beyond good. It wasn't too long after Jay's son was born that he got a job giving him the financial ability to provide even more for his new family. It would draw him away from his son and his wife through the week but would allow Cat to be at home to care for Billy, and they could find an even better place to raise him. Somewhere on the outskirts of town in the country.

Jay, then hired by an over-the-road trucking firm, earned enough to find a small farmhouse to rent on the edge of town. Their dreams were becoming a reality. They moved out of the tiny apartment into the humble farmhouse on three acres with a small shop. Jay's life took a turn towards normal, or as close as he'd ever experienced.

Life would continue and fall into a pattern of being on the road through the week and home on Friday evenings. Back out on the road by Sunday evening.

More was added to the Cader ritual in the years to come, which became his and Cat's life, together. It seemed to Jay maybe somehow, some kind of grace fell upon his current path. He chose to accept it; it covered his family along with him under its blanket of warmth.

***

Three and a half years later, a second boy arrived. Jay and Cat named him Darrell Lee after Cat's father. He came into the world, much like a screaming banshee, which was hard for Jay to handle. Darrell never slept through the night and woke several times during early morning hours, wailing and shaking.

Jay's patience became shorter and shorter.

"Cat! Can you shut that damn baby up? I can't come home after a week of hard work to a house filled with all that unnecessary, screaming noise!" He yelled louder to match each scream from little Darrell's mouth.

"I'm trying to rock him, Jay. He has a slight temperature, and his nose is running."

"Don't back-talk me Cat, just get that little monster to shut it up!"

Poppa worked in his shop alone, where it was quiet and he could concentrate. No little Darrell crying and being noisy.

He had little square wooden tiles laid out across his shop table as he etched words onto the face of them. Evil words like: SLAP, WHIP, STARVE and DUNK. There would be more when Jay was finished. Just like when he was a child.

The old Mason jar sat stoic on the end of the workbench. It was the one he'd collected from the pantry. The jar he'd dumped its contents of peaches out onto the floor the day the idea popped back into his head. Those memories of his childhood coming back to haunt. The jar still held remnants of dried peaches and sugar inside as it sat waiting to hold its new contents of the tiles. The punishment tiles. Jay kept working at etching the bold black words onto their faces with a wood-burning tool. The odor filled the shop of smoke and pine. His memory of how Cat had walked in with a look of bewilderment from his actions still clung to his brain and made him smile. Then the memory of his own childhood and being reprimanded was quickly becoming the beginning of the end of their "normal" family life.

Jay never even saw the end coming himself, he was too close to it. He just saw the jar as a new necessity. Gotta keep the boys in line, like he was.

As the boys grew older, Jay had already begun to mirror his father's form of administering either grace or punishment to them. He just hadn't re-created his father's game with the jar of chance. The Mason jar held wooden tiles with various penalties etched onto their surfaces and became Jay's Friday night tool to dole out discipline, even if the boys were undeserving. Jay never noticed how his harshness grew as time passed. His demeanor continued to grow darker, and the love of his family slipped farther from reach.

Cat watched Jay slip into another world she could never have imagined, leaving them behind in fear and turmoil. Not knowing how to cope, she began to find comfort in a bottle. She begged Jay to go back to the way they were. "I swear, Jay, if you don't change, I will take the boys and leave!" She knew she didn't have it in her to leave. Something inside kept telling her he would change back into the man she'd fallen in love with. Everything would be fixed between them somehow, and they would be happy again.

Jay found his comfort in being away from his family, upon return, being the judge, jury, and administrator of judgment to his two boys every Friday evening. It was a pattern the two boys quickly grew to fear and dread.

Darrell was too young to remember any of the good times. Billy found it harder and harder to retain those happy memories of what life used to be in their world.

Everything changed after the introduction of the Mason jar.

Cat sank deeper into depression and further into the bottle. Her once pristine kept home became messy and unkempt. Dirty dishes piled up while the food was left out to spoil, enticing palmetto bugs, ants, and mice to infest the house.

The word and feeling called love, soon dissipated into a chasm of chaos and destruction. Momma and her boys didn't know what to do other than an attempt to tiptoe and stay out of Poppa's way when he was home. They learned to endure the weekends. Sunday evening would bring calm with the sound of his diesel disappearing back down the driveway, and into the distance for another five days.

4

As time passed and the years slowly drifted by, the boys both transformed from fun-loving children to children full of turmoil and introversion. Darrell would wake up through the week with night sweats crying uncontrollably. Billy would wake up hearing his brother's whimpering and roll over to comfort him as best he could. Darrell began frequently whispering to Billy, "I wish Poppa's truck would crash, so Momma, me, and you could be happy." He would ask Billy many times throughout the week, "Do you think Poppa's tire will blow today? I wish that sombitch would never come home."

"Now Darrell—you don't mean that—it'll be better this week, you'll see. Poppa just ain't right in his head right now." Billy would say. "If he don't get better, I'll figure out a way to make him stop. In the meantime, I'll take any beatin' tile you get and give you either the grace tile if I get it or the better one."

If Cat ever heard them talk like that when she was sober, she surely would have done something—anything, to fix it. The problem being, she was so devastated from the years of Jay's meanness and unpredictability, the only cure she could find came in a bottle of bourbon. It started with Jack Daniels, but now it didn't much matter what was in the bottle as long as it dulled her senses. She used to daydream of their first night they shared, back when Jay was so clumsy and awkward, yet full of a passion like he'd never felt. Now all she thought of was why she ever sat down on that damned bench and fell for the stranger with the chiseled chin and rough but handsome look. Cat imagined God must be punishing her for sins of her past, but could think of none worth the punishment now endured. She loved her babies, but was mentally beat down and could no longer fathom how to escape with them. Her dad deceased for years and having no clue where her mom was, she was stuck. Cat had no other family. Jay never let her work away from the home, so she had no friends. She felt trapped like a frightened fox in a snare, but not enough grit to chew her leg off so she could run and save her boys and herself.

The young girl who cared and reached out to so many with a smile of encouragement became the person she pitied and tried to help. She was now the victim. Her babies became the collateral damage from the mistake made so many years back.

Cat tried to take the boys to church one Sunday evening after Jay left, but Darrell told Poppa about it the next weekend, and he forbade it ever happen again. She remembered the blackened eye he gave her to remember it by.

"All that Jesus stuff is just about gettin' your money and into your business! I've been told about the grace He supposedly hands out; well, it just don't happen. The only grace given out that I know about is when it shakes out of the jar at my hand's doing. The rest is fairy tales, unicorns, and treasure at the end of rainbows. It's bullshit."

The rage inside Jay's eyes scared them all. He scared Cat so severely she never brought Jesus up again. If Jay would have brought the Mason jar out that night—God forbid anyone would have gotten the newly etched tiles that said WHIP or WATERDUNK. His punishments grew in cruelty as time passed.

The man Cat briefly knew and loved, had long ago burrowed deep down inside himself, becoming a monster who grew more insanely evil with each week he was absent. He would call home at all hours, night and day. If the phone rang more than twice, he would make accusations and threats. His ability to control her even when he was out on the road hundreds of miles away, was uncanny. He would call her and ask her what pair of panties she was wearing, and if it wasn't a pair that he thought she should have on, he would accuse her of cheating on him. "I'll kill the S.O.B. that you're messing around with Cat…is it that young boy at the supermarket?"

It never mattered how she answered—she pleaded with him to stop accusing her of cheating. She begged that he just let her and the boys go if he hated them so much. She always ended up crying uncontrollably, causing Jay to laugh aloud and threaten, "I better not find anything out of place, or you'll be getting to sit at the kitchen table taking your turn with the jar."

***

The arguments usually began soon after Jay came into the house. This Friday, it was different.

"I'll gladly take the boys' place, Jay. They're good boys; there's no need for that damn Mason jar! Why did you stop loving us, Goddamnit...?"

The sound his hand made as it contacted Cat's face was loud, but not nearly as deafening as when her head smacked against the wall as she fell backward.

"Don't you ever take that tone or use those words to me again, Cat! You couldn't live without me, you stupid damned drunk. Don't you forget it? Ever!"

Jay left after the weekend, like every other Sunday night, pulling off with dark black smoke rolling from his truck as he drove off into the distance. Cat, Billy, and Darrell watched, frozen in place from the front porch. Each one's eyes showed relief as the tension rolled from their shoulders. Little did they realize—next week would end differently than all the previous Sunday evenings before.

5

Billy was busy talking trade with an older neighbor boy named Chad. Chad gave his price for the possession Billy wanted badly. Billy had to find a way to come up with it. He thought to himself. A *gosh dang puppy can't be too difficult. There had to be one around somewhere. People always dumped them off along their road.*

"It's gotta be a male, and it better be tough as hell. One like a Pit Bull or Rottweiler. I don't want no pussy dog." Chad glared at Darrell as he stated his requirements.

Billy and Darrell set out on their quest. "What are we tradin' for Billy," asked Darrell.

"Don't you worry 'bout it. That's no concern of yours right now." He couldn't tell his younger brother, because he might spill the beans. The matter was life or death, and he couldn't take any chances.

***

It was two days, and after traveling all over the area, the boys couldn't find one single dumped dog. The clock ticked closer to Friday night with each step they took. Billy was distressed because he figured Chad's trade was the only way he could fix their predicament. The only thing he could do was go back and try to bargain something more accessible than a damned pup that didn't exist.

After returning to Chad's, Billy knocked on the door. It quickly swung open. Chad asked. "You boys get my dog?"

"Well—it seems there ain't no damn dogs for miles around here. I was hopin' there was something else you might trade for?" Billy asked sheepishly.

"No dog, no gun. That's just all there is to it." Chad answered.

Darrell looked up at Billy with shock in his eyes. "Billy! You ain't serious 'bout no dang gun? Poppa would kill us if he knew we had one! You best get that idea right outa your head."

"You babies go back to hangin' on your momma's teets or when you got me a dog. I got no time to be wasting on pussies." And with that, Chad slammed the door with a bang.

"See what you did, Darrell? I was negotiating, and now the deal is off the table! We got three days for me to come up with another plan now. Don't you say a word 'bout nothin'! You understand?"

"We gonna actually kill Poppa? I can't do that. I'm just a kid. You ain't that much bigger than me." He looked his brother up and down and then at himself. "Sure, I wish he'd just crash down a mountain or something—but we dang sure can't shoot him. We'd be murderers." Darrell's eyes grew big and round in his eye sockets. "They hang people for that—even kids."

They turned and walked down the stairs out to the road without another spoken word. Each step taken brought sagging shoulders of defeat. Billy finally spoke, "I got an idea rolling around my head of how to stop the beatings we all get regularly—it dang sure has to stop before he kills one of us. I gotta keep you safe lil' brother, especially from Poppa."

***

It was a shame the terror that their Poppa forced them to endure and how it was becoming an everyday part of their childhood. Surely if a neighbor knew or the police had ever gotten wind of it, someone would have put a stop to it. The problem was, the whole burden rested upon two young boys who knew nothing about the world except the fear they faced from their poppa. Their momma, who'd become a bedroom hermit, was always drunk and remained clueless of their plan. Their lives were a recipe for disaster, and the twine holding it all together was quickly unraveling as two youngsters began planning ways of demise and redemption.

Someone would suffer at a minimum. Someone may feel the irreversible pain of their actions. The water was boiling and would soon boil over if left unattended.

The boys trudged along the road toward home, wishing that if there were a Jesus—He would intervene and save them. Surely Poppa wasn't the only one in the world who could dole out grace.

***

Once Billy's barefoot hit the second step from the top of their porch—the answer came to him. He would keep it to himself and not share it. That way, Darrell would be safe. Billy owned a plan now if he was only brave enough to execute it.

6

Friday seemed to arrive sooner than usual. Billy had noticed all week Darrell's inability to sleep through the night. Darrell spent more time pacing around, ignoring the toys that usually entertained him.

***

It had just been three days since Momma had gotten enough energy to get out of bed and bake a birthday cake for Billy. The fact she was up and doing something other than drowning herself with the brown syrup, made Billy's seventeenth birthday special. They celebrated in an unusual way of having cake outside on the picnic table and enjoying the day. It was almost like Momma knew something would be different after this coming Friday. Even Darrell wore smiles and seemed less troubled. The storm was brewing in the distance, but Billy's birthday was a reprieve from the anxiousness of his preparations.

***

"It's okay, Darrell, everything is going to be okay—I promise." Billy wanted to assure his little brother that he held a plan, and the pain was going to end for good, but he didn't wish to get Darrell's hopes up too high either. It would break his brother's heart if he failed—or he might tip Poppa off by accident, by his mood showing different. Poppa enjoyed seeing fear in Darrell, and as much as he hated this fear living in his brother—he needed it to show one last time to keep Poppa off guard.

"I can't do it again, Billy. I—I'm scared." Darrell looked down as the tears began to roll down his cheeks. He began to shake as his khaki pants started to darken with wetness.

"I'll take care of you, Darrell, you know I will—I promise."

Thinking about the pressure and seeing the fear in my brother's eyes along with the fact he wet his pants was killing me. I have to picture myself without fear and being victorious for Darrell and Momma. I know I can do this. I know I must.

If I fail, there will be hell to pay—for all of us.

***

The anger in Billy grew wild for years. He barely held any memories of when he was happy. At times, a mental snapshot of the way things used to be before his Poppa changed, would edge its way back into his memory. It was usually very brief. *I would sometimes dream about the evenings that Momma and Poppa took me down to the boardwalk with the skeet ball games and the huge Ferris wheel on St. George's Island. On moonlit nights, I walked between my parents, holding each of their hands, tightly. We walked through the edge of the gulf waters with our toes squishing through the sand.*

Darrell never experienced much of those days. He was too young to remember when their Poppa didn't have the monster lurking inside of him.

I always woke up in the middle of my dreams when I had them—always at the point where Darrell entered the scene. It was also the same time Poppa had the monster inside him. Sometimes, it made me wonder if Darrell was responsible for Poppa's rage, but he was too young to be able to cause that. I always imagined it must be a coincidence. The dream would wake me at the same point every time.

Darrell seemed wired differently than he was. He'd always been loud and energetic. He never sat still, and he fidgeted constantly. These actions of Darrell's drew the anger out of Poppa. When Darrell cried or screamed in the other room as Poppa tried to relax from all his driving, his face would grow beet red. Red as a devil, and then the rage would unleash.

I also remember the days' Poppa came home when he was young—before Darrell arrived. Back then, I would sit on Poppa's lap listening to stories about all the places he'd seen on his trips. I remembered how Poppa brought me gifts from different truck stops across the various states. I'd collected them, keeping them lined up across my dresser.

But the poison slipped into Poppa's head, and all those fond memories became traded for recollections of dread, fear, and apprehension. The afterthought of Momma's smile was the hardest to swallow. Her smile withered long ago. It seemed like a time when it started to dry up that maybe a little water and tending like the kind of care you would give a garden could have perked her smile back up and into bloom.

Poppa never cared enough to clear the weeds and nurture her garden with any tenderness. Instead, he seemed to enjoy trampling over it as if it were only briars and thistles—not the wildflowers it once was. Poppa somehow became too blind to appreciate what was disappearing before his eyes. But Billy noticed—even as young as he was.

Why didn't Poppa find a different job? One which could have kept him closer to the garden, he no longer tended. Maybe Poppa kept a better garden in some other town? Did he not love us anymore? There had to be something that kept him away from our home.

It didn't matter now. Poppa had his chance and chose to kill it off, flower by flower falling to the ground unappreciated as he played his game of nastiness. He was too busy Lording above Darrell and me, doling out his game of chance. Those six punishments etched onto those Goddamned tiles of wood. And with only one in the mix that forgave. Those scary words SLAP, WHIP,

DUNK, DARK, STARVE, PINCH, and the one he wished Darrell would receive—GRACE.

Darrell rarely received that tile of forgiveness. There was a time when Poppa would let Billy trade Darrell's tile when he got GRACE. He could take the punishment better than Darrell and endured each of those punishments himself several times. But Poppa soon grew tired of allowing it. He said he knew Darrell was the one who caused the most trouble—just like when he was a baby. He would reap what he's sown. That was the day Billy started thinking of plans to put an end to the Mason jar.

Momma knew it was wrong, and surely Poppa did too. Billy knew that someday he would be able to put a stop to it.

***

Friday afternoon of June twentieth nineteen-eighty began to fade, and the evening would soon fall upon them. It would be a memorable day and Billy knew his plan, and he wasn't a small boy anymore. He was a young man with muscle and mind and, most of all—determination! He turned seventeen only days before, not that there was much fanfare or celebration.

He did receive the gift of a plan and the anger to back it. He held the will to make Momma whole again. She was a flower and deserved a gardener who cared for and appreciated her beauty. Darrell should be able to live without fear of being beaten and verbally torn apart from a man who was supposed to care about him and nurture him. He was the man of the house now, and Poppa was the unwelcome intruder.

Billy paced back and forth in the living room, thoughts of all the harm done, his blood boiling hotter. *I'm hungry to confront the monster that contaminates our lives. I know Poppa must be weak to cave to the pleasures of hurting young boys and a woman. No real man would cower to such a level.* He continued pacing when he suddenly turned to the kitchen.

He stormed in, staring at the shelf holding Poppa's precious 'Mason jar of punishment.' He willed it to slide towards the edge and fall to the ground shattering—when it didn't move, he took steps toward it. Reaching up, he grabbed it and shook it slowly at first. When he heard the sound that he and Darrell learned to fear so horribly, he shook it with more vigor. The sound which engrained nightmares of rattlesnakes ferociously shaking their tails, warning of the impending strike to come, caused him to become red with anger. He shook the jar more violently and watched the tiles bounce against each other in a blur of motion mixing with his rage.

Billy suddenly stopped, and then turning toward the stove, he pulled his hand back holding the jar. The jar which caused years of pain was drawn back behind his ear like Wayne Granger readying a pitch for the Cincinnati Reds. Throwing his arm forward, he hurled the object at the stove with all his might, sending it slamming into the metal surface. The ensuing explosion sent hundreds of shards of glass along with the wooden tiles, splattering like a shotgun blast into the surrounding walls and floor. The silence that quickly followed was as deadly quiet as the crash had been deafening. Billy stood, shaking for a moment, trying to re-focus on what he'd just done.

It must have sounded like a gun going off through the entire house as it not only sent Darrell running into the kitchen doorway but also brought Momma stumbling in from her bedroom with a look of bewilderment and shock. The three of them stood speechless, white as ghosts, taking in what just transpired. Their silence morphed into thoughts of fear. What was going to happen when Poppa walked in from his week-long absence to administer the Friday night ritual?

Momma stumbled nervously to the kitchen pantry pulling out the broom and dustpan and quickly began to clean up the mess before Poppa got home. "I'll clean up the mess and tell Jay that I bumped into the stove and accidentally knocked the jar down—it's okay Billy, I'll explain it." She continued dragging the broom in a hurried jumble of jerky motions, moving the shards of glass and tiles from one spot to another.

Billy put his hands around his momma's hands, enclosing them tightly but caringly and looked into her glazed-over eyes, "No Momma, not this time—I want Poppa to see what I've done. A line's been drawn, and when he crosses it tonight—it'll be over—it'll be over for damn good."

The three of them stared blankly at each other for a moment before they all gathered together, standing in the middle of broken glass and scattered wooden tiles, hugging each other like they hadn't done in years. Momma's tears began to stream down her face as Darrell and Billy hugged her tight between them.

Billy was going to save them all tonight. Life was going to change and be very different from what it had become. Love and hope had just been planted in the Cader family garden. It came in the form of a seventeen-year-old-boy becoming a man, and a broken Mason jar scattered across a dirty kitchen floor.

Their arms quickly fell away from each other as the familiar sound of the diesel engine echoing in the distance grew louder. Their eyes each portrayed the same probable thought—*Poppa's home.*

7

Typically, one takes shelter when a violent storm comes rolling in. The thought of an advancing tornado causes the wise to take heed and run for cover.

Not tonight.

Tonight's impending storm rolled in to the drums of a Kenworth Cummins diesel carrying a monster's wrath worthy of Satan himself.

Billy wasn't running for the safety of cover tonight, and he was ready to face the violent rage and winds head-on.

The three stood still in the middle of the kitchen, peering toward the front door. Heavy footsteps sounded across the wooden porch, and the doorknob slowly twisted to the left. The door swung open, allowing a warm breeze to rush in along with the sight of Poppa.

Entering the living room, he sensed a heaviness in the air. He'd grown accustomed to Cat being absent from the living room to greet him, but Billy and Darrell were always there to see him in. He didn't like the feeling he got. Poppa didn't care much for change. Once he'd grown familiar to certain habits—he desired them to remain.

Surprise rarely brought anything good.

He glanced across the room into the kitchen, and then his eyes caught an unfamiliar sight. Cat, along with both boys, staring blankly at him. Cat and Darrell both wore the look of someone who just saw a ghost, while Billy's eyes held vengeance. He felt Billy's eyes stabbing him like shooting daggers.

"What the hell is going on here?" Spit flew from his mouth as his words echoed across the room. Jay looked them up and down and quickly spotted the broken glass and tiles scattered below Cat and the boy's feet. "Just who the hell is responsible for breaking my jar?"

Billy took a step forward and broadened his shoulders in a display of insurrection. His stature emanated defiance and challenge and was directed squarely at his Poppa. The man he'd once loved dearly. "I did it! And I wish I could have seen your face when I broke it, you fuckin' bastard."

"Well now, what have we here, Billy boy? Are you brave enough to play with the big dog now?" Jay dropped the belongings in his hands to the floor where he stood.

"It's over Poppa. You don't live here anymore. Grab your belongings and get out—now!" Billy never hesitated or stammered.

It got Jay's attention immediately. Standing completely still, he mulled over the aggressive greeting he'd just been served. It hadn't been a reactionary response, but one which was thought over and laid to plan. In a small way, he admired his son's fortitude. It was, however, going to need to be admonished with severity. Painful—lesson learning severity.

Jay then glared over at Cat and Darrell, examining their reactions. Had they been privy to this coup, or did surprise take them? No matter—there would be hell to pay tonight—a painful debt indeed—for all three conspirators.

Jay moved slowly toward the kitchen as Cat stepped boldly in front of her babies, determined to defend them as he marched toward her. The tension surrounding them brought her out of her medicated haze, into defense mode. Her heart racing as her brain sent signals that were long dulled by her alcohol consumption.

It was a moment to make a stand. Something long overdue.

The coup was exposed as she stood there beside her co-conspirators, her two young boys. She fought to force words from her mouth in defiance, but they just tumbled over each other before they could exit, making any sound or sense.

Jay laughed as he witnessed his weak wife trip over her words and emotions, surmising she must be full of regret for her actions. "You're gonna pay for this, Cat. You should have just stayed drunk in the bedroom where you belong!"

"You—you monster! I won't let you hurt these boys! I can't believe I ever loved you." Her voice softened at the tail end, and her fire tapered momentarily.

"You'll be paying a price tonight—after you witness your boys get their just rewards!" His hands began to clench tightly.

And there quivered Darrell, cowering behind Cat's thin frame.

"You, weak little terror of a baby." Jay coldly looked directly into Darrell's eyes. "You filled me with anger from the time you arrived in this world. So weak and cowardly." Darrell withdrew more behind his momma, hiding as best he could from Poppa.

"The crier and screamer who can't even hold his piss at the first sign of trouble." As Jay continued to glare at the small frame cowering behind Cat, he saw the dark spot spread from the crotch of his youngest son's pants. Jay smirked.

"How could he have come from my loins, Cat? He doesn't have an ounce of grit in him. You, bitch, you had to have been cheating on me from the beginning. I knew I'd been right," and now suddenly realizing—"I've been feeding the bastard child of another man's seed." Rage became more instilled in Jay as he turned his concentration back to the defiant one. "Now Billy here—he's mine, Cat!" Jay never took his eyes off of Billy as he spoke to Cat. "Look at the difference between the two! Billy is at least strong-willed. He looks exactly like me!" Jay puffed up. "Why, he even sounds just like me, now that his voice isn't that of a damn baby-boy." He boasted with pride over his oldest. "He's practically my Goddamn twin!" He then turned his attention to his younger boy hiding behind his momma's apron. "Who's could the little ginger- blonde girl be Cat?" He looked up at her. "She sure as hell ain't mine."

Billy's blood boiled with hate from the words he heard.

With Jay's attention drawn to Cat for a moment, Darrell ran to the corner behind the table. He shook in terror and bawled with his eyes closed tightly.

Billy glanced back at Darrell, catching movement in his peripheral vision. He returned his focus on his Poppa. Without a word spoken, Billy ran toward the evil monster that spewed his evil words upon his little brother. As he quickly closed in, he reached behind his back, pulling the freshly sharpened hunting knife tucked in his waistband. He instantly shoved the blade forward as the two made contact. They hit the ground in an entanglement of arms and legs twisting, mixed with fury and violence. The grunts and groans between them continued across the living room floor as they punched and rolled, changing positions of who was on top.

As quickly as it began, it came to an abrupt stop. The battle lasted less than a minute or two.

When Billy rolled to his side, his muscles twitched in reaction to the rage just unleashed. Blood flowed everywhere— on him, his Poppa, and the floor. He looked up at the horrified face of his momma and then collapsed. He knew immediately that the act had ended. The knife had done its job.

Screams of terror filled Cat as she ran to the lifeless body lying on the floor as Darrell stood dumbstruck, frozen in time. "What have you done? What HAVE YOU done?" Her helpless cries filled the room. Her eyes were wild with fear. Cat fell to her knees beside them in anguished weeping with sadness, anxiety, and shock painted across her face.

Out of breath from the struggle, he looked at her and then fell on his back, sucking desperately to fill his lungs. The air was heavy with the scent of fresh blood spilled as he realized the horrific deed he'd done.

She grabbed his arm and looked into his eyes, imploring him through her wrenching sobs. "Baby, run. Leave. Now. You have to get far away and not come back." Cat then looked at Darrell, cowering again in the corner. She eased herself from the floor and wiped her eyes with her hand. She walked over to Darrell and surrounded him with her arms as if to shield him from the scene. With a mind freed from the fuzzy haze of alcohol, she let out a slow breath in resignation to what had taken place. "What's done is done. Grab some things and leave. I won't lose you this way," she choked.

He quickly gathered a few things together and looked back at what was left of his family. Tears flowed from his eyes as he realized he could never come back, nor would he ever see them again. "I'm sorry, I love you, it's over now." He looked down and away. Those were the last words he left with her as he turned and ran down the porch stairs into the darkening night—out of their lives forever.

He looked back to catch one last glimpse from the edge of the road, seeing her leaning on the porch rail crying, hanging on, Darrell clinging to her side. Her troubled face would be imprinted forever on his mind. He then thought of the mess he'd left them with as his strained legs carried him out into the darkness, no idea of where he would go.

He just ran.

8

They say time heals everything. Billy couldn't imagine what fool came up with that statement. He wondered how the year had treated them? He couldn't even bring himself to say their names. It hurt too badly to put any humanness to them. Since he was a murderer, he felt little human feelings anymore. He conformed himself into an enigma—a living form surviving day to day in hiding and guilt. He was afraid to expose himself to anyone, even in a short conversation. He imagined others knew what he'd done just by looking at him. He felt as if the word murderer had been tattooed across his forehead.

That last Friday night turned out far different than he ever imagined it would. That night had changed his world. Fridays were now very different, as were Sundays, all blended in a fog of mere existence. He'd never imagined how different his world could change and how guilt could have such power over his mind as it did. At times he barely functioned with the thought of what he'd done. At other times he felt as if he should carry on and revel in a feeling of virtue the act gave him.

Daily survival, along with being a fugitive made for strange bedfellows. Dreams and nightmares readily mixed, creating confusion of reality and fantasy in his mind. Billy felt he was morphing into insanity. He'd never known anything about God or Satan, yet he felt as if they were more than fiction; they were surely battling for control over his soul. It seemed punishment and pain was all his life had been. Would he ever feel pleasure?

He often thought about the Mason jar and the power it contained. It embodied both pain and pleasure—or at least relief. The madness was surely taking root in him. He never struggled with internal battles like these before. He imagined his wrists strapped to a gurney with an intravenous needle dangling from his arm. An endless drip, drip, drip—as the slow stream of poison entered his bloodstream.

He merely existed until the journey's end.

***

Another year passed, while Billy slowly worked his way up to New York City. Drawn to a colder temperature, it seemed living in the cold kept his mind clearer and the suffering more acute. The frigid weather made a form of self-punishment, which was his answer for when the guilt slipped in. He blamed the world for the predicament he ended up living. He was hitting a new low in life since he ran from the farm. The place he used to call home.

Billy now reduced to digging in dumpsters for food and sleeping in alleyways along beside others who were dealt from a similar deck in life. Resentment grew, and the thought of the punishment he'd known his entire life must be due to a select few like himself. Demons were everywhere—moving in and out through the bodies of the walking suffering and empty souls who wandered the streets by night and sought shelter by day. He felt he'd become a vampire of sorts. A walking dead among those lucky enough to be "normal."

Billy found it odd that among those who had nothing but what they could carry, would talk and befriend you during the night on your forage for food and shelter—but would steal what little you owned as you slept during the day. *Was there no compassion at all in this world? Have I been living the best life offered before I resorted to killing? At least before, I knew fresh food and warmth at night. I could freely roam without fear of being hunted down or victimized. There must be a reason for this world and the lessons learned. More than just to suffer and take it to the grave. Was this life even worth the effort to live?*

Billy continued to hold in his anger, pressing it ever deeper into his heart and soul, if he had one. He withdrew from the other homeless, who seemed only to use him for their gain. His mind became more and more cluttered with memories of his past, of what life became in the present. He constantly waged a war of internal wits, always pitting punishment against grace. Grace was slowly losing the battle—slipping farther from his thoughts, bending and molding his belief in punishment and death. *Maybe death was the real grace given in this world?* "Grace is fake, a game of chance," he spoke aloud as his thoughts continued. *You were either born with fortune and luck or not. There was no asking for grace and just receiving it. You had to reach out and take it from someone.*

9

Billy found himself a beautiful covered stone stairwell one night in the Bronx on the edge of a small community. He usually stayed away from church buildings, but he noticed a sign on the front that stated free lunch at noon on Wednesdays. The stairwell was empty, and he would be hungry by noon tomorrow. Maybe it would be nice to forego dumpster diving for a change. He could put up with a little Jesus talk if the food was tasty. He threw his backpack over the short fence and then climbed over, making his pallet at the bottom of the stairs. He found he was left alone more if he slept at night and foraged during the day. He pulled his coat tightly around him, covering his head with the hood.

Billy's stomach ached from hunger, and his muscles had grown weak from the lack of proper nutrition. It was probably a contributing factor as he drifted off to a cautious dream-filled sleep.

It began with the soft swish in a steady rhythmic pattern. Billy felt a coolness around his ankles as the subtle waves encircled them. There were unfamiliar people around, and it was too blurry to make out their faces. He heard a tiny giggling voice that sounded familiar. As he looked around, circling from behind him to his left and then his right, he caught a glimpse of a woman holding a baby, cuddling him to her bosom, whispering. The small baby answered back in coos and giggles. The two were all alone walking at the water's edge, just out of touch from the gentle waves rolling in. He wanted to get closer to see the smiles they were sharing. But with each step he took, she moved farther away in the opposite direction. Not blatantly as if she were avoiding him; it was casual, but he couldn't catch up. Looking around to see if anyone else might be near, he circled back to where he could face her. They had walked farther down the beach, disappearing into the distance.

He felt sadness flood his entire being, and his ankles suddenly began to warm with the flow of heated liquid around them. It felt odd to go from cold to heat, and when he looked down, the once soothing rolling waves of beautiful ocean water had become blood pumping around his feet. Sudden guilt overtook the sadness that entrapped him. The surge gradually became weaker and weaker until seconds later, the liquid was dead calm and cooled quickly to his touch. He looked back toward the beach and the people he'd seen. He watched as they walked away, soon gone from sight as the sun sank. Foreboding darkness swept across the horizon. His mood changed to anxiousness and a guilt-ridden pain in his chest. He felt the wind of oncoming storms in his face, and he ran as fast as he could, fearing he would be overtaken.

He was all alone.

Billy awoke, shivering from the cold dampness heavy on the ground with an aching pain in his stomach, growling a low rumble, begging for nourishment. It was another day in the life of a fugitive from justice—suffering his brand of punishment.

It was seven a.m. Billy had awoken early enough to do some foraging for breakfast on his own before returning to stand in line with the others at the "Bread Basket Ministry" of Woodycrest United Methodist Church of the Bronx, NY.

***

The sun's warmth arose from the pavement of the streets and sidewalks. Billy was able to scrounge some outdated biscuits from a baker who also gave Billy a clean shirt and some socks because he felt sorry for him. Some days there were people in this world who seemed to outsmart the bitterness of life and pass a little bit of joy on to others. He could keep count of the good days much easier than the bad because they happened so rarely. He took the biscuits and clothing items, stuffing them into his backpack and made his way back toward the "Bread Basket" to get an early place in line.

He stood quietly, trying to avoid anyone else already in line, he caught a glimpse of a little old black lady heading in through the front door. She smiled at him and winked. *She must be a volunteer*. He would try to be extra sweet to her if she were in the serving line so that he might get a little extra for supper later. He'd learned some of the tricks to make his way of living just a little easier for himself whenever he could.

***

Cela Moses smiled again at him as he went through the line. When she noticed him sitting alone at a corner table as far from everybody as possible, she sat down beside him.

Cela was the kind of lady who loved to reach the difficult ones. She could usually "spot em a mile away. They's the ones that need the most love." She told her lady friends who helped alongside, in the serving line.

As she sat down, she immediately started chatting. "Honey, you look like you could use a little extra care and comfort. You doin' okay today, child?"

Billy looked up and nodded as he took a bite of biscuit and ham. "I'm getting by ma'am. Day by day. I don't suppose you'd have a little extra I could take along for the cold night, do you?"

"Honey, I surely do—done already wrapped it up in this bag for you. I got a jar of freshly canned peaches too. Canned 'em myself!"

"Thank you, ma'am, that is mighty nice of you. I appreciate your kindness."

"You don't sound like youz' from round here. Where you from if you don't mind tellin' me?"

"Down south ma'am. I've been up here just a month or so."

"Well, you must be some kinda crazy leavin' the warmth from down south, to come up to this frozen apple!" Cela smiled with a quick chuckle.

"I've been told that before. Of course, not with a pretty smile or laugh." Billy looked out of the corner of his eye, her way.

"Now don't go gettin' your feathers ruffled, I was only making fun and conversation 'witcha!" Cela smiled again. She seemed to know how to back her way out of possible trouble as if she'd done it many times.

"Now Ms.—Cela, is it? I'm sorry. I haven't had many conversations lately, and I'm a little out of practice with it. Truth is, I feel like I probably deserve this cold. I haven't always been the pleasant person you see sitting here right now!" Billy smiled and returned a slight laugh as he gave her a wink.

Cela reached over and patted his shoulder, "You can call me Ms. Cela if you like, or just Cela. I like you. I hope you'll come back and share another meal with us soon, Billy." She pushed the small bag containing the extra food and jarred peaches close to him. "You stay warm tonight and enjoy those peaches, Billy." She tried to say his name several times to ensure him she would remember who he was. "Ya know, you're one of God's valuable children. I'm gonna pray for better times for you, Mr. Billy. God has a plan for each of us. Never know when he'll be gettin' into our hearts and layin' those plans out!"

Billy watched as she walked back through the tables, touching others, and talking to them. Occasionally she would hug some, pulling them close to herself, but he seemed to be the only one who received an extra food bag.

He headed out the door and up the stairs into a sunny afternoon among a bustling neighborhood of people coming and going. Everyone seemed wrapped up in their worlds and thoughts, ignoring everyone else around them. Billy would need to keep his eyes open for another spot to squat tonight. He was sure it would be even colder than last night. Winter in New York was nothing like it was in Florida. *Yes, I must be crazy to leave the warmth to come here.* He smiled to himself as he worked his way through all the others walking down the sidewalks.

10

As darkness began to fall, Billy found an out-of-the-way spot to hunker down for the night. He'd had no luck collecting any other food or valuables, but knew he still held his bag of food from earlier in the day—the one Ms. Cela gave him.

It was harder than where he'd come from to find places away from others for the nights. The streets crowded, and law enforcement was visible everywhere on the sidewalks. The last thing he wanted was to be rousted and either run off or locked up for vagrancy.

He made it just past his birthday on October fifteenth without any real trouble. *Birthdays weren't necessary, they never really were.* Billy didn't want to risk anything or draw attention to himself. He was a Scorpio and very cautious with unknown people keeping them at bay. His motto fits with Scorpio's motto; "You never know what you are capable of until you try." He could easily read a room thoroughly and immediately sense how others felt. It was a gift that so far kept him safe from trouble and in the shadows of the background of the busy city.

He settled in for the night, opening his backpack and reaching for the sack of food. Pulling out the jar of peaches and twisting open the Mason jar, brought on a rush of memories. The aroma of sweet peaches, the smell that engulfed him, and overwhelmed his frazzled mind. He blankly stared at his hand, grasping the glass jar reflecting the glow from the distant streetlight. The words "Ball wide-mouth" sparkled as the light refracted through the raised lettering on the side as he swallowed the peaches down, smelling the scent, tasting the sweetness.

His past just caught up to him in the most unexpected way. He hadn't thought of it for a long time—the Mason jar. It contained peaches tonight, but in the past, it contained retribution.

11

It had taken two long years of recovery. It had also taken the help of many others who followed varied paths to reach the same destination Cat's journey had led. Meeting once a week with fellow alcoholics in the backroom of a Methodist church, they spilled their secrets and shames to each other, trying to mix emotional moments with encouragement to continue the fight and to remain sober.

"My name is Catrina Cader—Cat for short. My addiction to bourbon started with an abusive marriage to my husband. I can't blame only him, though. I failed my children because of my stubborn love for their father. I watched him terrorize them weekly as I poured myself into that bottle to escape the same pain that he doled out to them."

That first meeting was very difficult for Cat, but her youngest son Darrell, now sixteen, stood in the doorway for support. He was ready to run to her side if she faltered. "My only son left from my family's horrible story is standing over there because he begged me to come to ask for your help—he's my rock and angel. I wouldn't be here without him."

Darrell smiled nervously, mildly tremoring. A symptom of the agony Jay caused that night two years ago. He couldn't seem to shake it. Cat winked at him, then looked back over at the host nodding as she sat back down. Darrell's leg continued to bounce as he sat in a chair behind everyone nervously. He watched his momma, his head nodding toward the floor occasionally, appearing as if he were praying.

Cat struggled to break her relationship that she'd spent so many years building with the devil's tonic: Bourbon. She still suffered strong urges to give in. When she felt them now, she would look at Darrell and acknowledge she'd caused enough damage to his frail state already. She would mentally squash the desire, no matter how much the devil called her name.

She lost a husband and her oldest son that Friday evening, which now seemed a lifetime ago. She also lost the means to take care of her youngest, Darrell. He was just fourteen on that horrible evening and such a tortured soul. The mere flash of their past would bring instant tears to both of them.

Both experienced two hard years of struggle and were on their way to recovery from their traumas and addictions. It was a slow pace, but both were making headway. Darrell picked up a mild stammer that was more noticeable when he got anxious. Hints of her original sparkle and beauty began to return to Cat's eyes from the years the bourbon stole from them.

The fear they both lived with for so long was now starting to subside as newer happier memories replaced the harsh ones Jay ingrained in them. They felt drawn to attend the local Methodist church that Jay had forbade. Cat and Darrell began to learn what lasting grace meant and where it came. Reverend Gabriel Watkins's wife took a particular interest in them and offered them their backroom while they got their lives back on track.

"Why, honey, you and your son are welcome to stay as long as you need. It's the kind of service our loving Lord asks of us. Show mercy to those in the struggle. I can help you get right with the Lord. He has a plan for you!" She reached around them, both drawing them close into a hug, "Why that's the good news for you both!"

Cat began to learn right away what blessings could come from people who believed and practiced their faith in the Lord.

Both Cat and Darrell finished each evening before bed by reading the Bible and sharing a prayer. Their room was small and humble, but it felt surrounded by the fortified walls of New Jerusalem.

Most evenings, as they lay in their beds, they could hear Mrs. Gloria Watkins sing a hymn as she readied herself for bed. Her voice echoed beautifully and hauntingly across the wooden floor throughout the house and into their room. Her delicate voice was a crescendo of notes, like yarn weaving back and forth through itself under the power of a crochet hook.

Darrell pulled his covers up tightly around his face, leaving only his ears and the top of his blonde head exposed. Almost hypnotic, Gloria's songs comforted him. "Goodnight Momma, I love you." He would call out nightly like clockwork, just minutes before his eyelids would become too heavy to remain open. On occasion, he would quietly ask, "Do you think Poppa will ever come to find us and make us pay for what we did?"

"Now, Darrell, honey, you know your Poppa is gone for good. He's never coming back to haunt us ever again; you have my word." Cat's heart broke with sadness knowing her son was still terrified of his father, even after two years since the deadly night.

Most nights, she simply called out, "Goodnight, sleep tight…do not let the bedbugs bite." To some, it would seem like baby talk to a boy of sixteen, but Darrell had been robbed of his early childhood by a cruel father who filled him with fear. She'd been guilty in the past spending days drowned in a bourbon stupor holed up in her bedroom like a hermit. Life had been so unfair to Darrell and Billy. Yes, she now babied Darrell, but Darrell ate it up like a puppy fed ice cream by hand. She knew he would eventually pull away and become more independent. Deep in her heart, Cat needed Darrell to be the young child he was now as much as he seemed to need babying. She needed to be the loving, nurturing momma she hadn't been for so many years. Her oldest baby was gone, and she held on tight to Darrell once those instincts had awoken again.

Cat's eyes also grew heavy as Gloria's singing bounced through the wooden floors—willowy and comforting,

"Through many dangers, toils, and snares

We have already come.

T'was grace that brought us safe thus far

And grace will lead us home, And...."

12

    Billy pulled his blanket up tightly to where only his ears, eyes, and the top of his head were exposed. It was bitter cold tonight. His belly was full, but his mind became even more so. The sight of the Mason jar conjured up memories he'd pushed deep within, and now they were bubbling to the top. He saw a snowflake slowly wafting downward in a slow spiral, it lightly landed on his blanket squarely in sight, then melted into nothingness as it disappeared into the dirty cloth fibers which blanketed him.

    It seemed that snowflake represented his life as it gently glided down towards earth from high above in the darkened sky. The time it took to fall felt as quick as his life had slid down into nothingness.

    He wanted to melt back into his past, back to childhood where there were no troubles or responsibilities—but then he remembered he'd never experienced much of that. Life had been as cold as the flakes of snow falling around him. Life was frigid to the bone. It wasn't fair. Some got grace, and others got punishment—punishment for things they didn't do. But that was what got doled out to him, almost from the beginning. Grace wasn't fair. Grace was a prize. It was something you won with the luck of a wooden tile with it etched into the grain. Shake, shake—rattle, rattle, and boom! What came out was yours to savor or fear.

Tonight, beginning with the jar of peaches, then with the lone frigid snowflake landing quickly before his eyes and melting to nothingness—was a metaphor. Billy realized at this very moment; his thoughts contained one obvious outcome that should come to fruition. The Mason jar that had held fate within in the past would be reborn. People should face their judgment. They should be judged for if they were worthy or not of punishment or grace. It was his revelation, his mission.

Tomorrow he would go to work cutting the wooden tiles and etching the convictions on each tile. He felt called to do it. It was his heritage; it was in his biology.

Billy's eyes slowly closed even as his body shivered from the cold. The snowflakes slowly and intermittently continued to fall upon his blanket, proceeding to melt into the cloth.

Innocent people walked past him as he lay hidden, asleep in the dark shadows, unaware of the judgment that may be handed down to them in their near future.

13

Billy tirelessly sawed the roughly one inch by one inch by a quarter-inch thick square of wood with an old hacksaw blade he'd found while rummaging. They looked nearly identical to the ones he'd known so well. Billy was ready to test them by putting the seven pieces into the jar and tightening the lid down. He shook them. Billy shook them softly at first, then with more vigor. It sounded so familiar he felt chills down his spine. A tool to etch the punishments onto the tiles he'd carved out now needed to be obtained to complete the game.

***

Billy had never stalked anyone before in his life. Ever.

The man he walked behind was average but young. He looked like a businessman, or possibly a broker or an insurance salesman. He was probably in his mid-twenties and perhaps had a wife and maybe a family. There was a familiarity with the man he now followed. He carefully kept back twenty or so feet, walking in and out behind different people to remain in their shadows. He worked on perfecting his hunting skills. He needed to capture his prey without being targeted by either a witness or the police. He knew one wrong move could end both his freedom and his new-found purpose.

As he stared at the man's back, Billy wondered how the man would respond to the sound of the tiles bouncing on the glass sides and the metal lid. Would it instill fear? How would he feel as he saw his fate emptied onto the tabletop? The man looked as if he carried a load of sin on his shoulders as his leather shoes briskly shuffled down the sidewalk, leather briefcase clutched so tightly to his side.

With a sudden surge of excitement flowing through him, Billy returned his attention to the act of stalking instead of imagined feelings the outcome would provide.

His shifty eyes attempted to anticipate his prey's moves before they happened. He still had work to do and practice to complete so he could ensure his success. After all, he hadn't come up with the way he would subdue his defendant yet. Or how to get him to a place to dole out the verdict and sentence.

He chose to think of the subjects as defendants instead of victims. It made them fit the criminal part of the equation better in his mind, making him the decisive role of their trial. He knew they bore guilt. Everyone did in some fashion or the other. His poppa had doled out punishment for things he wasn't guilty of, but in truth, he'd also escaped punishment for some things he was guilty. It was the way of the world—the harsh coldness of it. Things evened out in the end. Now he would eventually help in the matter, once he lined his pieces all in a row.

Billy felt exuberance about his plan and preparation. Finally, he had a purpose in his life other than foraging for the day's meal.

He watched his defendant round the corner, then go up the third row of steps leading to a row-home.

His growling stomach gave him a brief thought about hunger and reminded him of his need to eat. He would head back to see Ms. Cela now he'd pinpointed the place his first possible defendant resided. He would also soon have to find a wood-burning tool or something to complete the tiles for his Mason jar.

The plan was in motion. The defendant chosen.

***

Ms. Cela's smile seemed to widen a bit when she caught a glimpse of Billy standing in line. He'd made it back in time to be midway amongst the rank and file of the other hungry. He stood prouder than when he first met her. Ms. Cela took notice of his stance too.

"Why—look at you, Mr. Billy," she said with a gleam in her eyes. "You are lookin' good t'day. A man about town with a purpose! Lookin' fine you are." She nodded her head up and down as she reached over to grab his cold hands, rubbing some warmth into them. "I for one am glad ta see you—I'd 'bout givin' up on you comin' back. Glad ta see I was wrong!"

Billy lowered his head just a bit as he looked into her eyes, "I had to come back and tell you how delicious those peaches tasted ma'am. In a way, they changed my whole mood in life. Yes ma'am, sweet and tasty!" He'd even tried to spiff himself up a bit before he had gotten in line. "I do have a question for you, though, if you don't mind me asking?"

"Why, sure enough, Billy!"

"I was wondering if there was anything for us to do—like with crafts or what-not during these cold days? Any supplies so we can be creative?

"Why yes, Billy, there sure 'nuff is. There's a community center that stays open on cold days so you can get out of the weather. In fact, on the nights below freezing, they let you stay there 'til morning. I believe they's got art supplies and games too. I wished I woulda told you sooner, honey."

"Thank you, Ms. Cela, I appreciate you treating me so kindly ma'am."

"I'll get you the pamphlet with the address, Billy. You be sure and come see me 'fore you leave, okay?"

"Yes, ma'am, I will." Billy's eyes gleamed even brighter. Not only could he stay inside in the warmth, but he could also possibly spend time on his project. He had a purpose!

***

Darrell awoke with an odd feeling inside his body. He remembered waking up several times during the night but couldn't remember why or what dream may have stirred him.

The morning light had just begun to shine outside. The sun penetrated the dust-smeared windows of their backroom and cast light, bringing shadows throughout his bedroom. A quilt acted as a wall divider between him and his mother's bed. Lying there, he listened for movement, wondering if Momma was awake yet. He heard someone quietly walking upstairs, making soft creaking sounds.

Darrell thought to himself, trying to remember what day of the week it was this morning. *Hoping it was Sunday because that was his very favorite day of the week. He and Momma would ride with Miss Gloria and Reverend Gabriel to church and spend most of the day there. He enjoyed his friends at his Sunday school class. Most of his friends from church didn't make fun of him like the ones at High school.* He tried not to worry his momma about those kids.

"Momma . . ." Darrell called out softly. "Are you awake?"

Getting no response, he quietly climbed out of bed and threw a t-shirt on, pulling his quilt back to peek into the rest of the room. He called to his momma again, surveying the lump under the covers of her bed.

She groaned a bit, "What are you doing up so early this morning?"

"I don't know, Momma. I guess I'm just excited to think it's church day!"

Cat rubbed her eyes, then stretched out her arms and legs as if she were trying to touch the walls on all sides around her. "Sunday isn't until tomorrow, honey—don't you remember what we're doing today?"

14

Benjamin Dane expected his brother at any moment, and he was unsure why this made him nervous. His fingers tapped the dining table again and again in no consistent rhythm. Eyes darted around the room, checking to see if Robert was here yet. He'd remained steadfast in his new regiment with no setbacks. Still, the thought of seeing Robert tickled the urge for him to perform his nervous quirks.

"Benny!" Robert slipped in unseen and lightly squeezed his brother's shoulders in a loving way.

"Robert, damn it, I hate it when you sneak up behind me, and I despise even more when you address me with that juvenile nickname!" Turning around, he gave Robert the stink eye as he slid his hands under the table, making them invisible to being seen fidgeting with them.

"Sorry little brother, the sight of you just brings back those youthful days. I didn't mean anything by it. How are you?" Robert leaned down, making his eyes even with his brother's while sliding into the adjacent chair of the corner table at the café. "You still on track?"

Ben locked stares with his brother, "Yes, big brother, I'm still clean and keeping right with God. Are you happy now?

"That warms my heart, Benny. Sorry, I mean, Ben." *Feeling relief to hear the words "I'm still clean" and "keeping right with God" coming from my little brother's mouth.* "I've been keeping you in my thoughts and prayers. You've passed a milestone! The urge may never leave, but it should be getting easier to battle."

"I'm battling it okay." Ben began fidgeting with his fingers, again. They moved from his mouth back down to the table. "I'm in constant quiet conversation with God, though, but the desire to feed the addictions remains. I know I have a long road—both for recovery and restitution for all the pain I've caused, but let's talk about something else."

Robert watched carefully, but tried not to look obvious or intent on noticing Ben's agitations or movements. "Job going good? Getting any new accounts?"

"Yeah, they are finally trusting me to start back in on my own a little. Thank you for standing up for me. Vouching for me as you have."

"Benny, a lot of your co-workers and bosses come to my church. They trust me, and the fact that I believe in you reassures them. You can recoup, regain trust, and get through this. The Lord has placed good people to help you with the struggles, and He watches over you."

Reaching across the table, motioning with a nod by turning his palms up and wiggling his fingers, Ben pulled his hands out from under the table and grasped his brother's hands. "Dear Father, thank you for loving and believing in my brother, Ben. Thank you, Father, for placing him with angels to help watch over and tame those temptations which try to break through and control him. Remain in his heart, continue to strengthen his faith. Thank You mostly for the grace You've bestowed on him and all of us. Without that gift, you paid the ultimate price for, we would all fall victim to the desires of this world we live in for now. Amen."

Ben's eyes remained open during his brother's prayer. He watched Robert and envied the strong faith his big brother always enjoyed. The inner strength never faltered throughout their entire childhood. He'd always been the big brother with no troubles or temptations. Watching the way his eye's remained firm under his lids and the muscles tighten in his jaws as he prayed, amazed him. It made him feel safe. As Robert opened his eyes and looked into Ben's, he drew a deep breath.

"What's wrong, Robert?"

"Just counting my blessings in having you as my little brother. You may soon be twenty-five, but you will always be my little Benny." He smiled from ear to ear, "So what are we having for lunch? Healthy or poor choice?"

"Will I ever be as strong as you?" Ben looked deep into his brother's bright brown eyes, "Will I have the faith you have, or does it take a lifetime to achieve it?"

"It's in you, Benny. Keep nurturing it, feeding it. Keep fervent with your group meetings and prayer. God wants a conversation with you, Benny. You stop talking to Him, and it won't be long until you stick Him back on a shelf and out of sight. Satan's still fighting for your soul, but you have the power of the Almighty now. 'Yea, tho I walk through the valley of the shadow of death, I will fear no evil: for thou art with me; thy rod and thy staff comfort me.'"

"Psalms 23:4. That one gets me through days I feel the world closing in on me." Replied Ben. *Knowing it came out snarky, but it was just the relationship we shared at times, competitive.*

"And there lies proof perfect that the Lord is working inside of you. Mom and Dad would be so happy—and proud, Benny. I bet they are both smiling ear to ear looking down on you right now. Remain strong in Him —and there won't be anything coming your way that you can't handle—with His help."

The thought that he had let his Mom and Dad down so many times, stolen from them, cursed them when they'd tried to intervene made his stomach hurt as a tear pushed out of each duct. "Do they forgive me? Could they ever? I know I shamed them. I harmed Dad's friends by defrauding them. How could he ever forgive me?"

Robert scooted his chair around the table so he could put his arm around his brother. "Benny, they forgive you—like it never happened. I know it. Now lay it down at the altar and let it go. It's not your burden to carry anymore. Giving those worries and your addictions to God is all that is needed for forgiveness. Mom and Dad will greet you someday in Heaven, and all will be right. No worries, little brother. No worries."

As the two brothers shared a meal by the window, they became so absorbed in their talk that neither noticed Billy slowly walk by the café peering in as he sauntered by. He'd passed several times during their conversation.

Benny must have subconsciously noticed because he mentioned a feeling of someone following him lately. "This may sound crazy, and you will probably say it's paranoia from withdrawal, but I've had an inkling this scroungy homeless-looking guy has been following me? I keep seeing him close by in different parts of the city when I walk. When I turn to look, it's like he ducks into the crowd. Am I crazy, or could someone be having me followed for some reason? Would my addiction group do that or my doctor?"

"Is there anybody you still owe money?"

Ben scratched his head in thought. He turned his gaze back to Robert, "No—I mean, I still owe people money, but I have accounts set up that I'm making installments. I'm not late on any. This guy looks homeless, I mean—not to sound like my old snobbish self, but this guy is not someone I would ever associate with, not even when I was using. I never turned on any dealers. I can't figure out why he would be following me." Scratching his hairline again and then hand combing his bangs back into place, "It must be coincidence or my imagination. Oh well, big brother—no worries, right? God has my back now, even while traveling the dark valleys!"

"Benny—Ben. Sorry, Ben, old habits! Our Savior has plans for you. I do not doubt that. I see the little brother, the one before the cantankerous one took over, inside you. You have goodness back in your heart, and it shows. I thank God daily for that rainy Sunday morning when I looked out over my congregation and saw you walk through the door. Years of prayers answered! Indeed, He has some kind of special plans for you, Ben. He let you hit rock bottom and is now helping lift you as new."

15

Billy stumbled onto a beautiful surprise. He'd been busy learning the neighborhood streets, mentally marking different areas that held either excellent spots to lay low or places which would be useful to bed down at night. This spot was perfect behind an abandoned warehouse, almost lost behind a trash pile and dirty brush. There it was, a tiny dilapidated shed. Unless you happened upon it, it was virtually impossible to see. Still standing, the small wooden shed was perfect.

Bedding down several nights without ever being disturbed gave him great comfort. It was close enough to get meals at the church but far enough off the beaten path; no one else seemed to know anything of it. He would need to be careful not to be seen coming or going into the area. *This new spot would be my home.* Shelter from the cold and a place to keep what few belongings he owned without carrying them in tow always. A newfound form of freedom.

There were big cracks in the wooden door that not only let light in but also the cold wind and blowing snow. Scrounging around, Billy found old canvas cloths and plastic. He hung them over the door and then stacked some old crates and junk close to the door, so he barely squeezed in.

Interesting how such small things in his life now felt like significant achievements. He celebrated to himself he had a "room" of his own at last after all these years.

***

Billy finally completed his wooden tiles. He had to make do with carving the words with a pocketknife, then staining the letters with black ink. The smell wasn't the same, and he missed the burnt wood odor, but they would operate just fine.

Following his "defendant" was going well. It hadn't taken long to realize people were fools stuck to the same patterns without straying much. He became interested in what the defendant carried in his briefcase. He always brought it with him by his side, clutching it tightly against his body. Billy imagined it contained a list of evil deeds, proof of sins, or stealing from people. He figured someone as young as his defendant was, and as wealthy as he appeared, was indeed performing unscrupulous deeds to achieve so much in such a short time. Guilty of many acts—he felt assured of that.

Some nights Billy laid on his newly constructed pallet of soft scraps of cloth and cardboard, his covers pulled up to the edge of his nose, bouncing between thoughts of what led him to this point in life. Electrical charges surged in his veins as he pictured being the judge, doling out punishment to the guilty. *I'll be a super-hero of sorts.* Not being able to conclude why he was feeling this energy, he curiously contemplated the root of it. *I've suffered so much in my own life. Was redemption coming? Or am I becoming a disturbed crazy person from this lifestyle?* Knowing he was lonely, could that be part of this equation?

He longed for conversation. He managed to go through a good portion of his life without it, but suddenly it felt like a drug he craved but could not obtain. The only real conversation he'd participated in for years was the short ones shared with Ms. Cela. *There was something about her that stoked the only warmth my heart seems to feel.*

"Tomorrow, I'm gonna warm the insides and outsides. It's Wednesday, and I have more than one hunger to quench." He laughed to himself. *Was that what it was down to now? Conversing with himself as if I were two.* With that, Billy snuggled deeper under the covers and drifted off to a dream-filled, restless sleep.

***

Ben felt out of his skin as he reached the top step to his front door. He reached for his key and inserted it with a twist. The door opened to a dimly lit silhouette of Gina. She was standing near the kitchen, holding a drink—ice cubes rattling in the glass. "Pour it out, Gina. I can't battle that temptation tonight," shaking his head as he closed and locked the deadbolt.

"Aw, come on Benji Baby—just an ittle wittle sip to loosen you up, or maybe some coke? You look so tense and stressed." Slinking over in her cat-like fashion, she continued, "Just because you can't handle your vices doesn't mean the rest of us should suffer."

Ben rolled his eyes, pursing his lips so tightly, he imagined the skin tearing. He knew what he wanted to say, but it wouldn't be pretty. Something tugged at his insides. He knew enough to recognize the bait that was being laid into the snare. She wanted confrontation tonight, and after it would become ugly and vulgar, she would want to make up, cuddling through the night. *After I've spent my energy ravaging her, of course.* Ben was so predictable in his past, and he knew Gina felt out of place with his newfound faith and sobriety. He knew what he needed to do; after all, he owed her nothing. They shared no official relational boundaries. The thought was on his mind lately, but he didn't know how to broach it. Maybe a bitter argument could be the catalyst to end it. *Grab the easy way out.*

No, not tonight, he decided. Tonight, he felt like it would be too difficult to battle all of his vices at once. "You do what you must, Gina. I'm going to bed—I trust you remember where the spare room is…" And he turned down the hallway without giving her a chance to respond. She didn't follow and argue, which wasn't her typical style.

Ben fell backward onto his large king-size bed without pulling the covers down or tossing the many pillows to the floor. He just let go and tumbled back, imagining what it would feel like if he committed such an act—but from the rooftop instead? He'd contemplated it many times lately.

He was teetering on the parapet, staring down at the city lights. All the people below with pretty little lives, free of all the junk pulling and tugging at them all day. Then in an instant, turning his back to it all as if to say "What the hell, it's not worth it." Quietly waving so-long to Gina as she watched blankly in a haze of alcohol and drug-induced stupor—then just unexpectedly raising his arms and falling backward. Complete. Like a light switch flicked off. No more pain, no more battling, no more Gina—but, no more Robert. And there lay the rub, the guilt.

He Pictured Robert on the other end of the phone call and imagined seeing the tears roll down his rounded cheeks. Mom and dad looking at each other from up in heaven, as their smiles melted into even more disappointment. His dad might coldly stare into Mom's eyes, saying, "I told you, Carolyn, he didn't have it in him, he never did. Success was never to be in his grip like Robert's"

Ben snapped to attention and sat up. It was like a jolt to his brain. His family robbed him of his moment of satisfaction from his torment. He remembered his conversation with Robert earlier, and the joy in his eyes hearing he was still on track. He had a hard struggle feeling his father's love. He wasn't sure if he genuinely ever thought it, but he could feel the love of his brother. He just couldn't do that to him—to stack the cruelty of a cold phone call from the police informing Robert of his death that way.

It was time again to search his heart and try to relay his internal numbness and suffering to the One he had denied for so long. Quietly, in the silence of his expansive bedroom, in the middle of a ruffled bed, he bowed his head. He couldn't get his first thought out before the salty liquid began pouring from his eyes and nose.

"Father, God, I have no right to come to you crying about how hard I have it. You know me. You know I've grown up being given everything. I've wanted for nothing…" Ben's hands let loose of the knotted covers he was clutching and folded them hand in hand near his face, looking up. "You've given and given to me, presented opportunity after opportunity, and I have either turned it away or squandered it. I have no right to come to You after I have turned so far in the opposite direction from You. Please take away these urges to fail. I don't think I want to vanish from the earth. I just don't want to hurt. Myself or anyone." Reaching to wipe away the tears, he squinted through the blurriness, "I'm afraid of failing You. My brother says that You have plans for me. What could a powerful God like You have for a worthless failure like me? I can't make it a day without almost giving in to my urges of getting high, reaching for that drink—or God forbid, killing myself." he continued to choke in sobs. "I'm giving total control to You, God. My life from this point forward is Yours to do with what You will." He sat up, opening his eyes, and cried out toward the Heavens, "If You want me to live, I will fight for it." He punched at the pillows with a determination that surrounded him. "If You choose for it to end, I won't fight it." He grabbed his chest with a pleading groan, "Please give me direction. Please take control and tell me what You want. I'll do it."

"Knock, knock Benji. Can I come in?" A quick moment passed before she continued, "I'm sorry. Do you forgive me this time? I need to hold you, baby."

Ben knew what he should do. It seemed clearer than the best vodka he used to drink. It's like God himself put the words in his mouth as he got up to open the door where Gina stood. She tried to put her arms around him in comfort. Comfort would lead to pleasure. That was the usual equation of their relationship.

Ben was a gentleman in every soft word he spoke. She continued her temptations while holding her hopes of his reprieve, but he denied her and instead drew on his inner strength. "I'm giving you this money to help you find a place of your own Gina. I'm praying that you will seek help as I have. I care for you, I do. But I can't continue with this life we're living. I'm sorry. It's killing us both—so slowly that it's hard to notice at first. Your mother is still alive, isn't she? Go to her, Gina."

Gina's tears of his rejection began to subside, and anger edged its way in their place. "You're treating me like I was your whore! I love you, Benny. I gave you everything you wanted. I can't just stop like you. My feelings don't just change like that!" She stood staring at him, silently pleading with her body language that he change his mind. She stood pouting at first and as her frustration grew, her hands began to draw into fists. Gina hit her legs with her balled up hands several times, fighting the urge to storm out.

After minutes passed and she seemed to realize that nothing was going to make him rethink his decision. She grabbed the money he'd offered from his hand, "You just lost the best thing you ever had. I hope you and God are happy together!" She left the bedroom and quickly gathered her few things. All she'd brought fit neatly in her backpack. She stopped for a moment, clutching everything she owned and fighting the tears back, she contemplated of what she'd just lost by not giving up her addictions. The only man she truly cared for, could give her up more easily than she could save herself from her own demons.

Ben heard the door slam a few minutes later. Little did he realize she would spend the money he gave her quickly and foolishly. Searching for answers in drugs and booze, other men in the clubs she worked would offer places for her to flop before she finally resorted to returning to her mother's home.

The load of weight Ben had carried for months seemed much lighter after that night, but he was still carrying stones of guilt. He knew he should let them go, but he always ached inside.

16

Billy woke up, shivering. The last thing he expected to wake up to was the frigid cold. In his dreams, he was back in Florida, wading through the ocean. These surroundings were difficult for him to reacclimate. He swore he heard the sound of waves. He found it was only the wind blowing the plastic, which loosely blocked the large cracks in his wooden door. The curtain gently flapped with each slight gust of cold frosty breeze as it entered, chilling the air in stark contrast to the warm breeze he'd been dreaming.

Billy began to change inside. Backslide. He knew deep down his world was getting darker. There was nothing to look forward to anymore. There were only two thoughts in his life at this point bringing any light or warmth to him. Ms. Cela, and the Mason jar. Two contrasting thoughts. Funny how they were tied together. He knew it sounded pathetic. If it weren't for those two things, his ideas would be drawn back to his past. He'd forced the outcome of that Friday evening back home so deep within, and it was almost as if it never happened now.

Lately, the outcome of that fateful night knocked more frequently on the doors of his suppressed memories. He was afraid to let those thoughts emerge and be mulled over too much. He knew it was dangerous and destructive. Mental torment full of feelings he never allowed himself to confront. He was far too busy fighting for survival all these years to enable feelings of his unsettled past to get in his way. He wanted the secret off of his chest, but it would inevitably end his freedom—as if the life he was living now, was one of independence.

He pictured Cat's eyes as he turned back for that last look, stepping off the bottom step, the one which quickly became unfamiliar once his feet hit the ground running. She'd had value to him at one time. She had a love for them all before the bottle became her desire. Were her tears that night for him? Or were they for the shock and fear of what she witnessed and lost?

Crawling out from under the cover, moving slowly off of his pallet, Billy mentally shoved the images of that distant day back down where it belonged. Into the deepest corner of hidden thoughts. "Won't do no good to cry about it. That world is dead, and this is the one I got left."

The grumbling of his stomach seemed loud as he stood in the familiar line, along with the growing number of outcasts who hadn't caught on to arriving early at the soup kitchen.

The warm sun felt good, shining on his cold bones. It heated the concrete walk that wound from the street to the steep stairwell leading down inside the belly of the church serving line.

Winter was entering its last days of rule, with the previous snowfall already melting into the soft thawing ground. He scanned the familiar crowd while waiting in line. He noticed how the cold this year had aged each of them. He could see it in the faces of those he knew yet seldom conversed with. He hadn't looked into a mirror for quite some time but knew his face surely must show the harshness winter had given him.

The cigarette smoke hovered in clouds above the stairwell, engulfing the stench of stale tobacco mixed with the body odor of those sandwiched together. *If I could smell it, the volunteers surely gagged from it.*

There was rarely any trouble among the ranks here. It wasn't allowed. As loving as the volunteers were toward each recipient's plight—the food line would be shut down with doors locked if any unpleasantries were to arise. It was later when you were vulnerable. While you slept was when you became the target from the face standing next to you in line. The saying "honor among thieves" was a farce. It's a dog-eat-dog fight for survival in this hellish world. You either learn to care only for yourself, or you don't live long, especially in the winter, where an extra layer of clothing was the difference between freezing to death or surviving another day to forage for food.

Everyone played well at mealtime, but the imaginary white flag meant nothing once you crossed the next block after the free meal.

Billy wasn't innocent by any means. He'd gotten rough and had to hurt people to exist. He smashed more than one pumpkin-head or choked a neck, nearly breaking it to get what he needed to survive another day in the streets of the "Big Apple." Anyone who told you any different was a liar. Hunger and frigid cold-to-the-bone temperatures made predators out of the kindest nomads.

But most smiled and mumbled in pleasant conversation as if they were good friends while standing in line for food. It was a ritual. It was the teams of two or more you needed to worry about. You were always having to look over your back and be wary of the surroundings as you headed off to your camp. If you saw you were followed, you took them on a wild goose chase to nowhere, evading them entirely before returning to your safe spot. It was a game, but it could be a deadly one.

Billy was different. From the start. Maybe it was his age or the fact he was not only homeless but also on the run—the lam. He didn't need or want to have a dependence on anyone. No reliance, no friends meant not having to make choices over alliances. Stubbornness ingrained deep within inherently. His dad never seemed like a people person either. His memory of the monster began slipping away through the years. Would he carry that tradition forward? His head slowly dropped with the thought. It wasn't shame he felt, but more of an untamed urge. His fingers closed into a fist in each coat pocket. Veins began to feel as if they would bulge from his temples. It was how he remembered feeling that Friday night so many years ago. Defiant. Adrenaline. Fear of what would inevitably come mixed with satisfaction.

The bum next to him nudged him as the gap between him, and the next one became too wide for his neighbor to handle. Billy quickly pulled his clenched fists from his pockets with a threatening glare in his eye. The man backed away with prudence, "Sorry fella, don't do nuthin' that'll make 'em shut the line down. I gotta eat, brother."

Billy was a time bomb waiting to explode today. He eased his hands back into the warmth of his coat pockets and shot a don't-fuck-with-me glare and then side-stepped towards the stairwell, closing the gap once again. Shoulder to shoulder in-tow. It was a sign to take his project farther down the road. The Mason jar, the mere thought shot an electric feeling that surged through his veins. *Yes, the Mason jar. It was time. It was time to administer a cleansing punishment to a worthy recipient. There were so many, but my first defendant with the briefcase came immediately to mind.*

***

Ms. Cela smiled as she scooped the ladle deep into the soup where the chunks of meat were thickest. "Why Billy, I've been wonderin' where in the world you been lately? You look like you sure 'nuff need a warm bite t'day."

"Yes ma'am, my stomach is talking rather loudly today. I'd also love to share some words with you later if I can?"

"Somethin' special or just some gab 'tween friends?"

"I'm just craving to hear the sound of your voice—talking to me. I've been feeling lonesome for real conversation. I mainly stay to myself out there," Billy tipped his head towards the top of the stairs. "Your voice just made me feel like home a long time ago. And I need some home today. You've been so nice to me."

"Why don't you just hang back and help me with some of this clean-up, Billy? Then we can find us some quiet place to gab and figure some curin' in this ailin' world together." She looked Billy directly in the eye and paused. She winked, shook her head a couple of times with a big smile, dipped that spoon deep into the soup, and started a conversation with the man Billy almost put a beating on. "Now ain't you lookin' handsome t'day, Tommy…."

**

The soup was good. Billy's belly was full and warm as he wiped down the tables one by one with the bleach-drenched cloth. The smell was so clinical compared to the body odors of those finishing up their meal. The smells seemed as different in comparison as the wealthy uptown and the homeless downtown. The clean and the unclean. Innocent and guilty. The world was as black and white and stark in differences as it could be. He couldn't be the only one who saw it.

Ms. Cela looked over and spoke, "Billy, whatcha thinkin' there? You look deep in thought 'bout something' that don't appear to be none too pleasin'."

"Do you ever sin, Ms. Cela? I don't mean like a bad thought about somebody or swear—nothin' that simple. I'm talking about real sin. Steal, or hurt somebody—to survive. Something where you deserve to be punished for?"

"Now that be quite a deep question, Billy. We all sinners. In God's eyes, sins' a sin, ain't no matter the size. But, as the Bible tells us, we be forgiven if we ask forgiveness and accept His Grace."

"Oh, Ms. Cela, don't go preachin' about grace to me. I've heard bits and pieces of that baloney my whole life. I'm talking about something that deserves man's punishment, no matter what your God thinks about it." Billy stopped wiping the table down and looked deep into Ms. Cela's eyes. "I know we all sin. I'm not talking small. I'm talking about something that lives so deep inside you— you got to keep poking it down when it tries to come out, or it'll eat you up."

"Do you have that kind of sin inside your belly, Billy? 'Cuz if you do, there ain't too many ways you gonna slay it. Only one I know of personally, and I just mentioned it to you seconds ago. Before you go shuttin' me down and dismissin' me, I want you to sit down and give a listen." She took Billy's arm and led him over to a corner of the room away from everyone.

As Billy walked into the small candle-lit room, the flickering shadows on the wall behind a big cross grabbed his attention first. It was a painting that covered the entire wall depicting a man being whipped by men dressed in some sort of soldiers' clothing. The pain in the man's eyes captivated Billy. He wanted to look away, but something wouldn't let him.

"You know who that man is being beatin'?" Cela quietly questioned Billy. "Do you know who the men are that are whippin' him?"

"I suppose you are gonna tell me that it's God," Billy barbed back with sarcasm.

"That's Jesus, Billy, God's only Son—did you know God voluntarily gave up his only Son, Jesus, to be beatin' and hung up on a cross? A cross much like those in front of that big wall paintin'?"

"My father was like that. Only he enjoyed doing the whipping himself."

Cela knelt beside Billy and put her long frail arms around him, "Oh Billy, I am so sorry. I'm sorry you had a father like that. But your father ain't like the Father I'm talkin' bout. He sacrificed his Son for a reason. Not for cruelty's sake. He had a purpose, and it involves even you and me. I'd be happy to do some more sharin' of that story with you…"

"Ms. Cela, I can't hear that right now. I just wanna know you are who I see you as. I can't believe you ever did anything wrong to anybody. You have what I think is actual real love inside you. I don't think love and the world can mix inside most people. Not this cruel place. What did you do to get love like what's inside of you?"

"Honey, I ain't nothin' special in this world any more than anybody else is. I have my past and stones of sin I carry inside me. I ain't no angel, Billy. I'm just a tired old woman who found Jesus, and now I try ma best to do what His Father asks of me. We's all got our pasts and sins. You right though, this old world is a cruel place without much love. But they's good news with it too. They's a better world we go to. A world full of nuthin' but the love you askin' bout and Grace too, Amen, praise Jesus!"

"Grace again, something not deserved, that's all I know. It's a gift, alright. Something you win. Something you get if you're lucky, that's all. It's just a way out of the trouble you did without getting caught. That's what I know about grace." Disdain dripped through his tone.

Ms. Cela squeezed Billy tightly and leaned into him. With her mouth close to his ear, she spoke with warmth and soft loving words, almost a whisper. "Child, it's so much different than what you're sayin'. I don't know who been teachin' you, but it ain't from the Bible, and it ain't from God. None of us deserves His Grace, and you right 'bout it being a gift. But, Billy, you ain't gonna win it. It ain't no luck of the draw neither, like a card game—it's givin' to all of us, every single soul on this earth created yesterday, today and tomorrow..."

Billy pulled back while gently but firmly pushing Ms. Cela away. "I—I don't know about what you're saying. I was just curious why you are so nice to people you don't even know. I'm glad you got what you got and that you like people. I don't have that same thing living inside me, and I don't reckon it would be welcome there if I did."

Ms. Cela stared at Billy blankly. Her heart suddenly ached for the hurt and angered nestled deep within his heart and soul. Her eyes spoke the love she held for a lost child of God's, but Billy gave her no more time to act upon it. She just quietly watched what quickly unfolded in front of her tired and frail body.

Billy got up from the chair and looked briefly at the mural on the wall and then back at Ms. Cela. "I don't know when I'll be back, Ms. Cela. I'm sorry about pushing you away, you've been nothing but nice to me, and I appreciate it. But this don't feel right, and I think I should just keep to myself."

Billy didn't look back as he exited the small room and headed for the stairwell. He was confused and moved as quickly as a scalded cat escaping from a hot water bath.

***

One of the other volunteer ladies quickly made her way to Cela. "Ms. Cela! Are you okay? I saw that man run outa here so quick! He didn't hurt you, did he?" She grabbed Cela's hands and pulled her close as she looked her up and down.

"Billy has God trying to get a hold of him, and he's fightin' back hard with everything he got," she said, shaking her head with worry. "We gotta pray right this instance for him."

Ms. Cela quickly gathered up the other volunteers into a circle and reached out her hands to the others on either side. "Dear gracious and forgiving, Father...."

17

Billy felt confused. He ran away from Ms. Cela so quickly it almost felt as familiar as the evening he'd hit the bottom step of his front porch running. It all came down on him fast. He had no time to plan how to react. It'd been a long time since he permitted his feelings and confused thoughts to bounce around at the surface and become vulnerable to someone else on the outside. He thought it was time to have a conversation with someone real, but he now knew he was very wrong. A mistake he would likely not make again.

With each step he took, he reinforced his thoughts about punishment being deserved and grace being nothing more than a game of chance. "No greater power wielded such a thing over us. We got what we got out of the life we were dealt! It's all about the luck of the draw, folks! It's who raised you and which side of the tracks you lived!" His hands flailed as he took each step. His voice grew in volume, causing the sidewalk traffic to clear a path. "That's all there was to it. Bullshit! And I thought Ms. Cela was different." He challenged the pedestrians with wild-eyed stares and jumpy movements. "Just another sucker of this hard, cold world! Another looky-loo, believing she can see the answer for us all. A gift wrapped tighter than a frogs' ass—to aid in our misfortune."

He looked around at the passing crowds who continued to give him a cautious stare as he now realized he was muttering aloud. "That's right! Bullshit! Rainbows and Goddamned unicorns. Are you a Jesus follower too?" He threw his hands up in the air and then brought them down to mimic the act of lifting the lid off of a present. "Open your gift—it's full of grace, forgiveness, and some hot soup to boot!" He laughed out loud as people moved to clear the way even wider for him. "Might be some sweet, tasty peaches in a jar too!"

He appeared to be a raving lunatic on drugs to those he passed, continuing to speak loudly and stomping down the sidewalk.

Had he finally lost his self-control along with his mind?

Rage was his Pontius Pilate, and the crowds' disgusted stares were the whips to his flesh, much like the painting on the wall depicted. Through his anger, he felt each strike piercing his skin from the people he passed who snickered under their breaths at him.

He was just another sidewalk show, a crazed street performer. Only Billy's spectacle was no rehearsed drama. He was a desperate man on the edge—an unhinged danger to anyone in his path. He was a sociopath who somehow skidded just under the radar of the authorities.

***

Benny sat on a barstool in his darkened empty apartment, stirring the ice in the glass, which contained nothing else. In his past, it would have been filled to the brim with Vavoom vodka, at $75 a bottle bearing a beautiful naked female torso rising from its glass base. He stared as if it contained his clear demon liquid. He would run the straw slowly around the outer wall causing the ice cubes to clink against each other, breaking the deafening silence of his home. Occasionally he glanced up to the shelf, which held the bottle containing his kryptonite. Miss Vavoom seemed to stare down, wantonly back at him.

He didn't want music or the television to break the silence. His will to fight his urges demanded his complete attention. Thoughts bounced back and forth from craving Gina and her affections to desiring the numbness from the drugs he once enjoyed. Or even the pure, clear visible liquid he could pour into the ice-filled glass taunting him with a need to be splashed over with alcohol.

Nights like these were not unexpected anymore. They would enter Ben's psyche in the form of small battles from out of nowhere. Yet, he had to fight. Several nights earlier, they would have just been exacerbated by the existence of Gina. She surely would have needled him to take a drink to unravel the nerves, which kept him bound.

But, he'd taken care of that part of the problem. A solution he now begrudged as he sat alone, sparring the demons in his head all by himself.

In his group meetings, he shared his anguish with the other addicts, and they and the doctor would listen and respond with what he should do.

Everyone had a differing opinion, bouncing them back and forth around the room like a new form of free-for-all tennis. Ben felt like he already knew the answer, at least, the quick and easy one. It was his brother's love and the image he pictured of his disappointed parents that kept him in line. The image of his father's knowing glare, strengthened his will to fight for another week until group meeting rolled back around again.

Ben looked around his plush apartment, all of which was given to him by his parents. Spoils from living the gifted life where all he needed to do was maintain his keeper's happiness. Ben hadn't done much of a job doing that, yet somehow still managed to live the life many coveted. *How much more natural would life be if I gave everything up and lived on the street? All I'd be responsible for was finding food and a place to rest my head.*

My brother Robert was strong enough to make his way on his own. He shunned all the glamorous gifts growing up, only taking advantage of Mom and Dad paying his school tuition. He'd done the rest without their lavish charity. His brother's home was far humbler than Ben's. *I wonder if Robert is indeed my true blood brother? We are so opposite when comparing our differences.*

Ben stirred the ice one more time shattering the silence, followed by a sigh. "Oh Gina, I want what I can't have, and I don't want what I can. I wonder. *Did you take my advice of seeking help—or did you just find another man with money and the penchant to lavish it on a beautiful play toy? You are a gorgeous girl, and tonight I miss you horribly.* He thought by saying it out loud, she would hear him and come sauntering through the door, but he kept the words internal, and of course, she didn't walk through his doorway.

He slid his briefcase closer beside him as he sat at his bar-top table and opened the tightly closed clasp on the leather flap. He reached in and pulled out the massive book his brother recently gave him. *Robert was so happy the day I opened the gift of a new NIV version of the New Testament. It was brand new to the world, the first translation to another version than King James. Robert had been sure it be would be easier for me to comprehend and therefore keep me more interested.* He thumbed through playing the game of reading wherever his finger stopped as he fanned through the thin, gold-edged pages.

1 Corinthians 10:13

No temptation has overtaken you except what is common to us all. And God is faithful; he will not let you be tempted beyond what you can bear. But when you are tempted, he will also provide a way out so that you can endure it.

"I'll be damned." Ben's eyes lit up as he finished reading the sentence. "Could it just be a coincidence?" He felt visibly shaken.

He got up to look at the city lights through his picture window. Looking above the tall building tops to the moon and what few stars shone brighter than the city, "Lord, you do have the answers! Why did I ignore and doubt You all these years? Why had I not followed the path of my brother who seemed to soak You in from the earliest day I remember?"

He was thankful he'd not answered his desire to open the vodka, but instead reached for his briefcase. Ben felt like he'd won another battle on yet another night. He wanted to pick up the phone to tell Robert, to share the good news with him what the Bible he'd given him accomplished tonight. God had spoken so clearly to his needs by simply reading His word.

But, he knew from his weary eyes the hour was much too late, and he should just turn in while he was victorious. He smiled solemnly and headed toward his bedroom to fall back into the enormous soft comfort of sleep. He knew his temptations would lie dormant alongside him, replacing the cravings of Gina.

***

Gina lightly knocked on the door, contemplating if she should be there tonight or not. She felt pain for the first time in so long; she hardly remembered what it felt like to cry. Gina realized not only did she want Benjamin Dane—her mind craved what he'd seemed to find for himself: peace within. She sniffled as the tears rolled down her cheeks and lightly knocked again, waiting for the door to open and not knowing how she would be received if it did.

***

Billy drew the curtain back as he slowly climbed into his little secret hideaway in silence. Looking behind one last time to be sure nobody saw him enter the lot. The day had turned out very differently than he expected. He was finally able to calm down after he realized continuing to create a ruckus in the streets would inevitably end poorly for him. He imagined people in Florida were still looking for him for his crime committed three years before. Murder. There was no other way to think of it. There was no grace for killing someone. There was certainly no amount of time that would pass which would ever excuse such a thing in the eyes of the law.

Somehow, he'd managed to dodge deep thoughts and memories of that night until now. Today, it all came sneaking to the surface and then exploded like a rocket taking off for the moon.

Ms. Cela had turned the conversation to grace, God, and some figure called Jesus. Things he held no belief. The only mercy he'd ever known was charity gifted from one person to another. The chosen victim only received it through the luck of the written tile.

His stomach rolled inside with the memory that entered his thoughts. *The way her eyes looked, turning to catch one last glimpse again. Wet and red full of fear and question. The way her eyes looked into mine would haunt me forever.* He snapped out of his past of that night and back to the memory of the Mason jar. A single tile shook out onto the table from the Mason jar filled with six others, each scribed with a reprimand.

He knew them well and would never forget, no matter how much time had passed.

It was now their time to rule again. Billy was ready. His latest obsession called him to set his judgment free on the world—this awful world he lived in—New York City.

My first defendant chosen and researched. Just another foolish predictable human, so self-absorbed he never noticed his surroundings. People were like sheep that could be quickly culled from the others and then brought to justice by my hand. My defendant's sin was soon to be reconciled by the Jar. It must be reconciled.

Like a lamb to the slaughter.

18

Cat knew today would be painful for her. She wasn't sure just how Darrell would react. At almost eighteen, Darrell was old enough to start facing their past. This day had been planned for quite some time now. It was the implementation she'd struggled with internally. Not sure of what memories Darrell retained from that night over three years ago left unknown questions that haunted her. She had come to the cemetery many times, which she would now lead Darrell to today. This trip would be his first time. She was always better at uncomfortable talks when approached in combination with walks. It was easier for her to control her emotions while strolling alongside the recipient of tough conversations.

Cat held Darrell's hand as they walked down the empty sidewalk to the cemetery containing the family plots. Darrell was so young and vulnerable back on that night. His shattered mind couldn't conceive what he witnessed. In the aftermath of that life-changing evening, Darrell mentally shut down. He collapsed on the porch, knowing something had drastically changed in his world, but he couldn't comprehend the ramifications of it. Darrell seemed to have no recollection of what went down that night when the officers questioned him. He wasn't able to speak much about it to them.

Cat never pressed, keeping the dark event more or less a secret from him. She knew Darrell surely must feel empty but couldn't possibly know what the void was. Little did she know while she kept secrets of what happened from him, he too had secrets locked inside his memories. She'd told him in little bits of scant details of his brother and Poppa, how they were gone and that he would never see either one again. His Poppa would never be able to hurt him again, and his brother was a hero.

She thought it would be enough at the time—and it had been until the dreams began waking him up at all hours of the night. The unknown, likely working things out of his subconsciousness as he attempted to place the pieces back in a semblance of order—an order of things that would make perfect sense at some point.

Cat feared what repercussions would come from his nightmares and questioned herself how much she should fill in the blanks. Her baby was now on the verge of eighteen, and she'd always known there would be a time when she would face this very difficult decision. She talked to Gloria, who, in turn, sought her husband Gabriel's advice. After living with them for so long, they were now Cat and Darrell's only family. She trusted their advice.

So, today she would begin to tackle the hidden truths about what happened that dark evening at the farm. She would tell Darrell why it was just the two of them and the Watkins now.

***

"Darrell honey, do you remember that I told you we were going to a special place, and I had some important things to tell you?" She hesitated briefly. "It's not gonna be easy for either of us, but with God's strength—we can both get through this. We've been through a bunch together, haven't we?"

He glanced toward her but could barely make out her face against the sun. "Yes, ma'am, I reckon I remember. This conversation is the stuff about Billy and Poppa and why they ain't neither one with us anymore?"

Cat looked over at her son. He was squinting into the sunlight ahead. He looked so handsome with his strawberry blonde hair. *She looked at the outline of Darrell's face. It looked so much like hers. She always wondered how Billy could look and sound so much like Jay, with the scratchy gruffness while Darrell was the polar opposite. Darrell took on more of her characteristics from the beginning. His softer voice and he was so much more emotional like herself. Darrell was also more closely built like her, long and tall frame, slender with less muscle-tone. Billy James was built firm and muscular. He definitely had his father's physique along with the confidence in the way he carried himself. Almost arrogant at times.*

Darrell's emotions were delicate. And now she was worried how he would react at seeing the stone in the cemetery today. She didn't hold a clue and any thoughts would be a shot in the dark.

Would it ingrain his internal grief that he'd carried all along—or enrage a feeling of betrayal and desertion? Either way, it would be an extra stressful day today for her. Even more difficult for her son, she imagined.

"It's going to be difficult, Darrell. Tough for both of us, but you can lean on me. We will be dealing with these new emotions together, okay?"

The inner turmoil in my heart makes me feel weak. I feel queasy as if weaving back and forth through a dangerous narrow mountain road aboard an out-of-control vehicle. My stomach feels every tight turn as I peer over the perilous road edge that could spill us both to our bitter end at any moment.

The urge to suddenly slam the brakes reside in my emotional metaphor, avoiding any possible unforeseen catastrophe, causing me to doubt my mothering abilities. I'm worried that maybe I shouldn't have brought Darrell on this emotional ride just yet. I'm questioning every parental decision I've ever made. Past and Present.

Drawing closer with each step, I realize that the road we are on together—at this particular moment—is far too narrow to turn the out-of-control car around even if I could bring it to a safe stop.

We have to press forward—no matter what outcome lay hidden in the next curve.

Cat gave his hand a comforting squeeze as she continued, "Do you remember the time before—before we moved in with Reverend Gabriel and Gloria?" She tried to smile as she gave him a sideways glance. *How would he respond?* She drew a deep breath, followed by a drawn-out sigh. She squeezed his hand tighter and then paused long enough; it felt uncomfortable. "Do you remember being in the kitchen the evening that things happened? Things that can never be undone?"

Darrell's body tightened as he slowed his footsteps beside her, forcing his mother to stumble.

"Momma, I think I do. It's hazy, but I remember going with Billy to see about trading for a gun with—with, um…"

"What?" She loudly questioned him as she dropped his hand to clutch her chest. Her knees suddenly felt weak and unstable as they wobbled, beginning to buckle before stopping mid-step.

"Darrell! What in the world are you talking about? What gun?"

Now suddenly feeling her analogy of the out-of-control vehicle, it felt as if they suddenly skid and leave the road. Darrell's mention of the word gun now had caused them to slide in the gravel—and rested near the edge of the drop-off in her mental scenario. The wheels teetering as they hang over the edge—any sudden movement could cause the momentum for the two of them to roll on off the cliff with an absolute dire consequence.

Darrell's response to the gun was matter of fact, void of any acknowledgement of trying to get a gun being shocking.

"I'm talking about our kitchen! When your brother and Poppa got into an argument and scuffled on the floor." Cat's heart pounded harder in her chest as she impatiently waited for his answer.

The seconds of silence between them felt like an eternity.

The look of utter surprise on his momma's face caused Darrell to stutter his first few words, "I...I...um know Momma. That's what I'm talk...talking about. The day Billy was going to kill Poppa. That's... what I'm...I'm... talking about," His eyes began to brim. His stuttered words left hanging in the air between them.

Cat's uncontrolled response through her expression was one of complete astonishment. She never saw his response coming. Darrell's answer might as well have been a speeding train smacking her from out of the unseen darkness.

She stood, her balance faltering as her words became tangled within her mouth. Unable to form any decipherable representation of the English language.

"He tried to make a...trade for...for... a gun so we could make Poppa stop." Darrell broke down in tears; he covered his eyes from her sight, he tried to continue, but his eyes became so blurred he had to stop.

"Oh! baby!" Cat couldn't make sense of what Darrell was saying. Her heart continued to tremble with fear. "Here. Let's stop and sit a minute." She pointed to the seat just ahead. Cat's legs shook as she and her son took an unsteady path toward the iron gates several steps in front of them.

As they sat on a bench at the entrance to the cemetery, Darrell continued. "We went to—to um, I can't remember his name—I'm trying. It was...Chuck...NO! It was Chad. It was Chad Price! I remember now!"

He turned to his Momma and hugged her; she hugged him back. "I remember Momma. It was Chad Price. He wanted... a dog... not just any dog... but a mean one. Billy and I looked everywhere for one." He wiped at his eyes as he struggled through his stammering. "We couldn't...we never found a...found a dog for him." He looked into his momma's eyes through his blurred vision. "Chad wouldn't trade his g...gu...gun for any...thing else. I thought the...plan...was...was done." Darrell kicked at the white chat on the ground underneath him. Pebbles shot across the path from the angered force. He looked back up toward his momma.

"Billy made me promise… not to… tell, not…not… even you."

"Oh Darrell, honey, I am so sorry. I'm sorry I wasn't there to comfort you boys. I was hiding, baby, I tried to pretend everything would be okay. I'm sorry, baby…" She pulled him tighter into her clutch as if she would never release him. "Oh, baby, I'm so sorry. I failed you, boys. I failed my two babies." She began to babble her words, making them impossible to comprehend.

Darrell squeezed her tighter. "Momma, it wasn't your fault. Billy and I were gonna fix it for all of us. But…but Chad wouldn't trade for nothin' else… I didn't know Billy was gonna kill him…ano… another way! I didn't know he got a knife—he never told me."

Cat looked shocked as she trembled. She hugged her boy as if she would never be able to again. She became flooded with emotions, questions, and guilt. Her shoulders dropped from the weight of it all. She stiffened her body momentarily before tucking her head into his shoulders. Her streaming tears absorbed into his shirt, dampening her son's neck—all of these things converging on her from a hidden place at once.

I thought my boy held no memories at all, yet somehow, he seemed to know everything plus a background I don't know about. She squeezed him again even tighter. *My boys felt so much fear and hate from what their Poppa was doing that they made plans to kill him! And all I felt was guilt for being in a drunken dulled stupor when they needed me most. Hiding from it all made me think it would be okay.*

"What have I done? What did I put my babies through?" The words fell out of her mouth as she looked up to the sky as if speaking directly to God himself.

How would I ever make it up to Darrell?

They sat on the bench for several minutes before the tears and crying subdued to sniffles.

She looked into Darrell's eyes, "Are you ready to go inside the cemetery and see his stone? We can wait until another day if you'd rather."

"Why haven't we ever come here before? He's been here all along, and he hasn't come back?" He looked at her with shock.

"Baby, I didn't know how much you remembered. I didn't want to stir any memories when it seemed you'd forgotten it all. You've remembered all along?"

"I don't know, Momma. It's all such a blur. I wasn't sure what was real and what was dreams. I remember stuff, but I just wasn't sure if it was real."

The sun seemed to brighten a bit as they stood up from the bench. They both looked into the cemetery through the iron gate and the wind suddenly seem to pick up. It rustled the leaves on all the trees making a whistling sound. It was almost like music. Eerie and haunting. The sound seemed to rise in volume as they walked through the gate and down the gravel path.

"Billy used to love whistling when we'd walk out in the fields and roads around the farm."

Cat smiled at his memory. *At least, my baby was able to retain some bright reflections despite the hard life he'd been dealt.*

Thoughts seemed to roll inside, becoming jumbled between the happy memories of Billy and the hard, painful ones left from Jay. Recollections mixed back and forth, toying with the emotions now left inside, which had abruptly changed from where our walk had begun this late morning.

Darrell asked another question as they continued walking several more minutes.

The interruption to her daydream left her answering with a subconscious response without really hearing his question. "Momma—where is his stone?"

"It's just down this path and then down a short distance on a different one to the left. We aren't far. You sure you're okay?"

"I'll be strong. I'll be strong for you too. I love you, Momma."

Cat smiled, and a tear poked out at the same time, "I love you too, son, to the moon and back. I will never let you down ever again."

They made the final turn and walked several hundred feet when Cat saw the stone. Her thoughts began to self-question again as they walked from the path and across the grass.

I'm not sure I will be able to keep my composure. The feelings still deep, and I am so conflicted. These wounds feel as if they are still just below the surface. All it would take is a slight flick to open the scabs, and I'll suffer again for sure.

But the time finally feels appropriate, and I'll try to hide my pain. I need to be strong—for Darrell's sake. But I feel a tinge of self-loathing for being so stupidly blind.

They stopped, and Cat put her arm around her son. Pointing to a short stone standing in front of a young Southern Magnolia tree, she spoke softly, "There it is Darrell. Do you want to go alone first, or do you want to do this together?"

"Let's do this together, Momma. I don't wanna be alone with him."

Cat paused, and she looked over at Darrell. *What an odd response.* Darrell tugged at her as he approached the stone slowly, and she quickly shook the thought to the side.

Darrell kneeled, and his Momma stood behind him with her hands on his shoulders as they both looked at the small faded white concrete stone. New moss grew into the chiseled lettering. There were no fresh flowers or any sign that the gravesite had been visited since the last time she had been there.

Darrell began to read aloud, "Here lies Billy James Cader…Beloved Son …."

He cocked his head to one side as Cat watched to see where his thought was going. She noticed the quick glitch in the way he moved. His head mimicked that of a puppy's. The way their head tilts to the side when they're not sure exactly what the toy they've just uncovered is. Baffled but trying to reason the answer through their slow-moving cogs inside their animal brain.

The color drained from Darrell as his hands fell to the base of the stone. "Why in the hell does it say Billy James and not Billy Jay?" He asked her abruptly. "Poppa's name should be here. He's the one who died that night, not my brother!" The hurt look of confusion washed across his flushed face as he turned back toward his momma in question.

Darrell looked up with a look of assurance as if the answer suddenly popped inside his consciousness from nowhere.

"You put my brother's name on the stone—so the law wouldn't keep looking for him!" He now smiled with the affirmation that he'd figured out her scheme. "That's real smart, Momma." He nodded sheepishly. "Yeah, I remember Momma—I saw Billy run down the steps of the porch—and the no-good sonovabitch was lying dead on the living room floor in a pool of blood…with Billy's knife stickin' out of his worthless gut."

Darrell stammered a second as if he were deciphering each movement, visualizing the night again from the horrible, but a victorious battle between his brother and Poppa.

"Yes ma'am, Momma! That was damn smart—you puttin' Billy's name on there instead of Poppa's. I bet that's kept the law real confused!"

Cat stood above her son in total shock. She had no words.

*Thinking Darrell had suppressed his memories of that fateful night, only to be surprised with the knowledge he **had** remembered, threw everything into a mental chaos. Darrell had suppressed one of the most essential facts of that evening. These three-plus years, He remembered it was his poppa who had died. He said it all when he'd said, "I saw Billy run down the porch that night."*

Her shoulders dropped, and her knees went soft, spilling her to the ground behind Darrell as he bolted up to help his momma. She crawled over to the stone and wrapped her arms around it. The dam broke as she wailed uncontrollably. She hadn't let loose since the horrible night over three years ago.

She'd come so far from where she was back then. Darrell too. Now, she was a broken mess holding what was left of the memory of her oldest son, watching her youngest boy stare blankly at her, questioning what was happening.

"You didn't know?" She sobbed as she hugged the stone tighter. "Oh, Billy, boy. My sweet, brave Billy boy. I need you now, son. We need you now."

Darrell looked down at his momma, not knowing what to do, his mind overwhelmed. *Of course, Momma was right, we both needed Billy, but he would come back someday. When everything was blown over, and people forgot. He would come back and help us both.*

Suddenly, it hit him deep inside. A fear resembling that same dread he used to feel on Friday morning, he'd wake—realizing there were only hours away before Poppa would be home that Friday evening. Looking down at his momma, he asked.

"Poppa is still alive?" He turned and ran as fast as he could back up the path they'd just walked down. He didn't wait for the answer; he suddenly seemed to know.

With no other sound than the noise of his shoes running down a chat-filled path, the air around her felt empty. Only echoes bounced through the stones and trees until his footsteps disappeared into the distance.

Cat looked away from her oldest son's tombstone to see the disappearing image of her youngest and only son left. The same memory her husband left her with as he disappeared into the darkness some three years earlier.

Déjà vu—only different.

The pain felt the same. Her heart ached like she'd not forgotten with time. There was guilt mixed with pain for ever loving the sonovabitch who did this to her boys and her.

19

The windows in the Watkins's home showed no movement as Cat slowly climbed the familiar creaky porch steps. They groaned with complaints as she climbed each one.

"Darrell..." she called out quietly when she got to the back room. She listened for a response, and she slowly pushed the door midway. "Darrell, honey..." she called out once more. No answer. She thought she heard a muffled sniffle behind the quilt serving as a doorway to the entrance of his bedroom. She carefully pulled the cover aside and peered in.

Darrell was burrowed under his covers so deep in thought; he didn't know his Momma was in the room. His world shattered once already, three-plus years before, it seemed his hopes of seeing his brother again someday were dashed. It was a dream he clung to quietly and was confident would one day happen. His brother wouldn't leave him alone forever—he knew that! He would show up someday while he and Momma were at church sitting there listening to Reverend Gabriel. He'd plotted the whole scene in his head. Darrell let the story play over and over with differing circumstances every night. His mother didn't know it, but it was how he put himself to sleep every night. Picturing his brother's heroic return.

Darrell's words came out muffled, but Cat clearly understood what she heard. It hurt her heart, but she was relieved he was home and safe and that he hadn't just taken off and run into the unknown. She backstepped to the kitchen and quietly sat down. She would sit there and wait for Darrell to come out on his own. She knew he needed time for it to soak in. She would be right there, available for him when he was ready. No matter how long it took.

Cat laid her head on the small breakfast table with thoughts of that evening, which seemed a lifetime ago. Her mind swirled as she tried to recall the events as they had happened. *Focusing on each of their faces, recalling their expressions as that last Friday night tragedy replayed over and painfully over.*

Darrell had worn a stunned and frightened face. One of shock. Billy's eyes contained hate in them—a vengeance hungered to be satisfied. Billy showed no signs of fear, only resolve—from the moment he shattered that damned Mason jar against the stove.

The look I remembered most was Jay's. The confusion in his eyes when he first opened the door and walked in. He was turning around as he surveyed the house, then seeing the insurrection in Billy's eyes. I remembered the way bewilderment swept over Jay's face, changing quick to anger and betrayal.

I could almost feel how the air in the room had suddenly grown heavy. It felt like the surge of water pulling us down in an undertow. I remember each person now, in slow motion as if it happened only yesterday. I'd pushed that evening so deep in a dark place, leaving it alone like a buried skeleton, that I was astounded it was so fresh in my mind now.

Glancing over at little Darrell, my baby, cowering in the shadow of his protective big brother, Billy, not being able to fathom what was about to happen. How could he? He was so young and vulnerable. I remembered the shame which washed over his fear. Embarrassment always overtook little Darrell when he suffered accidents. I remembered how he ran behind the table as Billy charged his poppa. It all happened so quickly, even though it felt like it lasted forever. Recollecting how quickly it all sobered me from the bourbon cloud I had stumbled into the kitchen with that evening, it somehow stirred the momma-bear inside, awakening my protectiveness. It was just too Goddamned late.

The scuffle barely lasted a minute or two once Billy and Jay collided. It was over before I knew it was going to happen. As Jay slowly rolled over and off of Billy—that's when I saw the knife buried deep. I wasn't sure Jay realized what had happened.

My instinct to protect Jay took over. I knew he needed to run. Billy was gone, not ever coming back. Jay has to leave, and I needed to make sure Darrell hadn't seen what just happened. It was like a fog in my thoughts, but my concentration was so pointed I was able to bring the blur more in focus as I repeatedly played the awful scenes over and over.

But where was Darrell, and just what could he have seen? All these years, I was certain Darrell knew his brother was dead. I had told the deputy what happened. I told him Jay had gotten up and run. I told him my son Billy was defending them from him. I don't think I mentioned to him at that time that Billy had brought the knife and attacked his poppa.

I guess I somehow blocked out what happened past that point. I assumed Darrell told him the same thing when he talked to the deputy. I just remember I smothered him with comfort for what seems like weeks. I knew day one I must stop drinking. This tragedy gave me the desire and chance. I needed to be there for Darrell, not in a fog. We were on our own now. I needed to be Momma again. Sober Momma. Responsible Momma. Loving, caring Momma.

The wooden kitchen chair began numbing Cat's bottom, and her legs ached. There was no longer any sun coming in through the small windows in their room, which meant no light was peeking through the back-room door jam. Not realizing how long she was lost in thought she pushed on the edge of the table to stand and stretch.

Darrell peeked around the edge of the doorway as the back-room door squeaked open slowly.

Cat searched for words to say to him as she walked over and took him into her arms and pulled in close. "I love you, Darrell. I'm here forever for you," she whispered. "I'm sorry I failed early as a good momma, but I'm here now."

Darrell buried his head into her shoulder and hugged her in silence.

20

Ben woke up remembering how he'd won another battle. The war still hung over him and seemed as if it always would, no matter how many skirmishes he may come out on top.

He recalled the Bible verse he'd stumbled onto the night before. The one verse that kept him from reaching for the clear naked woman's bottle of vodka; instead, he reached for the book his brother had given him. He couldn't remember the name of the passage or numbers of the verse—but he remembered the message. *The Lord will not allow me to be tempted beyond my willpower and will present an alternative way out. But was it true? Did the Lord truly open other paths up, leading opposite the temptation?*

The second thought was, of course, Gina. *Had I done the right thing pushing her out on short notice? I gave her money, and meant it to be for useful purpose—but did I make her feel like a prostitute? That was far from the way I thought about her. At one time, in the beginning, she'd been my savior.*

After a time, he'd sucked her into his addictions. She was a dancer when he met her, but she didn't do drugs when they first met. He introduced cocaine to her. Gina's mom hated him from the start. He knew she saw through him and his nice-boy ruse.

Ben didn't dare continue down this path of counting those to whom he'd wronged or baited into his web. The list was long, and he was working through making amends to those he could recall. For some, he'd just been too stoned to remember. The image of his parent's disgust of his actions and recent lifestyle appeared in his thought again.

Get up and move around. These thoughts are leading down the path to destruction. Ben put the ideas off for the moment, realizing his self-crucifying was doing no one any good. He needed to think positive thoughts and continue asking for God's grace and forgiveness. *Let the sins of the past remain at the altar.*

***

Billy awoke cold and determined. It was time. *I'll allow myself no more thoughts of Jesus or grace. I've seen how fate dealt out grace. Fate came from a Mason jar. I've lived it. Hell, I'd dealt it out. Many times, in my past. It was the power of the jar that made my two boys fear the justice I could dole out. My judgment had made Billy strong and fearless in the end!* ***I'd*** *given that power to him. And now, I was tired of hiding in the shadows. There would be no more cowering in fear more like my little girl Darrell. That boy would never grow any balls.*

The real question, though, was why was I using mine and my oldest boy's first name instead of the name I've lived most of my life answering to? Jay.

It was time. I'm tired of being bottled into something I'm not! He was angry. *Judgment and punishment were about to become alive again. From this day forward, I'll introduce myself as Jay Cader.* "I won't go another day living under my son Billy James's name any longer! I'm Billy Jay Cader! The chips can fall where they fall." He was red-faced as his anger exploded.

Blood raged in his veins. The determined ambition was reborn. Wrong or right, it was coming to one defendant very soon. He went over to the corner and dug through the cardboard pieces and debris. Pulling the hidden jar out, he held it in the light which peeked through the cracks in the wooden door. The light green tinted glass sparkled, highlighting the seven square tiles within. He lowered his ear closer to his moving hand as he shook the jar to catch the familiar sound making his heart race even more.

The cork exploded from the bottle of anger he'd somewhat controlled for these three years. His mania was now fully exposed.

Billy Jay paced back and forth, talking to himself as the dust on the shed floor began to cloud. He spoke his plan out loud, questioning, then answering himself. Jay would wait for the early evening, then watch his defendant's apartment building. If all went according to plan—he would capture him tonight. It would depend on circumstances if he escorted him to the defendant's home—or here. It mattered not about comfort. His justice could be served—anywhere.

Jay did one thing differently with these newly-prepared tiles from the old jar—the one his son smashed on the floor. In this jar, he added an eighth tile. He wasn't sure exactly how he would handle the situation if it were the tile fate chose, but it was going to be part of the equation. The new unique tile was significant. The recent addition bore the word—KILL.

***

Cat and Darrell were ready for church. Darrell was slightly upbeat because it was his very favorite day of the week. This particular Sunday, he hoped, would bring him comfort from his friends. Yesterday shattered many of his hopes and dreams of what his future might hold. The thought Billy would someday return had been something he'd clung to for these last three and a half years. Finding out it was no longer a possibility was a hard hit to the gut. It dropped him quickly to his knees, sucking for air.

He wasn't able to get much sleep, and when his eyes would drift closed, shadowy dreams invaded his thoughts. It felt like he re-lived that horrid night in his state of haze at least a hundred times.

***

It was a quiet ride with Gabriel and Gloria, Cat, and Darrell. The air felt thicker than usual, much like a moist wool blanket pulled over and tucked in around one's body. The Florida humidity mixed in, made for a feeling not befitting a typical Sunday morning ride to church. Everyone's eyes remained locked forward to avoid any contact between one another.

Reverend Gabriel and Gloria were aware of Cat and her son's struggles, especially of late. Gabriel wanted to speak up so much, but as he occasionally glanced in the rear-view mirror at Cat, he felt the nudge to remain muted. He knew God would let him know the proper time. In the meantime, it was the quietest and eeriest Sunday drive ever.

As he pulled up to his usual parking spot, he barely got the car's gear lever into park before Darrell's door swung open, followed by a quick 'clunk' as it slammed closed. He was off in a shot toward the entrance to the youth and young adult classrooms. Darrell never glanced back.

Gloria wrapped her arm around Cat as soon as they all stepped up on the curb, "It's gonna be okay, Miss Catrina. He'll be fine sooner than you know it. He's a strong boy with lots of faith. You mark my words and hang in there, honey."

"I don't know Ms. Gloria. There are so many secrets trapped up inside of him. Ones I never saw coming. Three years plus of all the ugliness bumping around in his head. I'm scared. I waited too long to start digging. I failed my baby once again." She sniffed and tucked her head into Gloria's shoulder. "I just don't know how to be the momma he needs right now. Do I coddle him, cuddle him, or let him stew a little and see what happens?"

"Well, the first thing we do, honey—is do some praising and some praying. That can lead us to the answers we seek."

"Yes ma'am, I suppose you're right about that." She squeezed Ms. Gloria, then stepped away, walking toward the door. "I have a lot of praying to do today."

***

Sunday morning for Ben brought the thought of the Bible verse as it continued to stick in his head. He felt dragged down with guilt as he battled the cure used in his past, smothering those problems in alcohol or drugs. *When temptation becomes too strong, Jesus will put another way in your path.* It was Sunday; his alternate route would be to show up at his brother's service. It would bring happiness to Robert and an escape from the lure beckoning himself to make the easy poor choice. "So be it, Jesus! I will follow your call."

Ben scrambled to shower and ready himself. It wasn't a far walk to the Church of God from his place, but he'd spent too much time this morning wallowing in self-pity.

When the usher opened the door, a first initial feeling of discomfort washed over him, like every other time. It was twofold. He felt guilt entering God's house because he'd never come to terms with his inadequacies in his faith. To top it off, looking around and realizing he was one of the very few white people in the building always made him feel flush and out of breath. He wasn't prejudiced. He was just uncomfortable around groups of people he did not know, and of course, he did not like sticking out so boldly, as his white starch skin most assuredly made him. He was always more comfortable blending into the background, and this just did not happen here, on any Sunday.

Back in the church's beginning, Robert was asked to fill in for a Sunday or two. He was between church assignments, and this church had just lost their pastor. Hearing his brother tell the story always brought smiles across his face. A starch white upper-class pastor asked to fill in at a church of dark-skinned lower-middle-class working people—in the Bronx. It was just an equation that brought smiles across anyone's face, no matter the color of their skin.

"So, I walked in through the front door, wondering if there were any Caucasian members at this church. By the way, it's a beautiful church down on East 165th Street. The door opened, and the shocked and nervous smiles told me the answer. Now, these children of God were nothing but friendly and loving to me! But I do believe someone failed to give them the entire story of who would be preaching the word in God's house that day!

"The lights went up a bit in the chapel as I made my way up to the chair beside the pulpit sitting down to wait for my cue. A praise band came from the back of the church— from a hallway near the door I'd just entered. I thought I was in New Orleans during Mardi Gras! It was beautiful! Horns were playing, and choir members were dancing up the aisles dressed in bright-colored robes with the liveliest Lord-praising music I'd ever heard. The words in the chorus were, 'We done messed up Lord, and now it's time to Clean up.'

"The congregation jumped up from their pews and were dancing and waving their arms in the air! Let me tell you. There was an overflow of the Spirit in the air filling the house. Never felt anything like it before." Robert laughed.

Robert would go on to tell how he worked the lyrics of the chorus line into his message. He said he'd never heard more "amens" and "preach it brother" in his life. He always ended the story the same way. "After my sermon was over and I shook everyone's hands and made introductions—the head of the pastor-parish committee offered me the job! She was a sweet old gal dressed in a bright yellow dress. Brighter than a fluorescent canary! That was eight years ago, and I am still a fixture here! I love every member as family, and I have earned the nickname 'Pastor Dove,' now. And I love it! I can't walk down the street or walk into a restaurant without someone yelling 'Hello, Pastor Dove!'"

Ben worked his way toward the front, where Robert expected to see him. Since his brother became the pastor, it wasn't as uncommon to see the skin of all colors come through the doors. After so many years, word of the biblical teachings of Pastor Dove spread wings and reached out amongst the entire community and beyond.

It's incredible how my brother could be so different than myself. Sometimes to the point, I wonder if we are genuinely blood-related? How could I be so introverted and Robert be so outgoing? Just another puzzle piece that somehow doesn't fit the Dane Family Tree.

"Morning Mr. Benny," a quiet voice from a cute little pre-school boy as he bumped down the aisle toward him.

Ben smiled and reached out to shake his tiny hand. His momma said, "I'm sorry, Mr. Dane, Anthony seems to enjoy you every time he sees you. I hope he isn't a bother."

"No, ma'am. He makes me feel a little more at home." He turned to see the little boy's mom. "He is quite a brave little man!" Ben smiled as he spoke.

"You look very nice today, and I know your brother will be glad to see you here again," she replied as she returned the smile.

Ben smiled and nodded as others started crowding in to welcome him. A nervous calm began to settle over him. It only seemed awkward at first, but then the warmth of the people always washed it away.

The music started from behind him as it moved up through the aisles. Ben began to smile wider as he imagined his brother sitting up in the same chair as the first time he visited here. A quick muffled chuckle escaped his lips when he noticed Robert had just picked him out of the crowd. Pastor Dove! Ben looked around with another smile as he pictured his snow-white skin standing out boldly against the sea of color around him and his beautiful and colorful flock!

21

Gina wondered, deep down, if her mom even loved her. She knew there were deep scars between them. Those very scars filled with the pain she'd caused her mother. Something Gina would never be able to take back.

She remembered the night her father walked into the Cabaret 21 Room and saw his precious little girl writhing around the pole on stage. *He stood there with the most disappointing stare as he dropped his head. When he looked back up at me, then scoured the room at all the men, I saw that pain quickly become anger. I tried to continue dancing, but knowing he was there watching made me feel so dirty for the first time. I remember stopping before the song ended. I remember the crowd of drunken men just yelling. Then they noticed my dad standing with his fists clenched. I remember seeing it all—the pitiful boozing losers who were glued to their seats, holding folded bills in their paws—just waiting for me to slink over, letting them tuck the bills neatly into my scant G-string. The anger they showed when I just stood there no longer gyrating. It made me sick. I knew how it made him sick. It angered me back then, but now the feeling was stomach-wrenching again. Like it just happened tonight.*

He loved me so much. He never said no to the help I continually asked of him.

I thought he would think differently of me once I met Ben. I didn't believe I owed my father to change my wild ways, but I thought he could forget and forgive those days with the introduction of Ben.

He'd seen right through my boyfriend the night they met for dinner at Jake's Steakhouse. I was so proud I'd finally met a guy who was something. He owned a charming row home on Morris Ave. He worked at a great job where he wore a three-piece suit. He was flush with money. Ben was somebody. Not just a bum who tried to steal a free touch as he tucked a dollar bill. I swore I'd never forgotten what my daddy said as he opened my cab door to ride off with Ben.

"Gina, this prettied-up bum will dump you when he has had enough playing with you. If you hang out in the dumpsters, you'll never find anything but rats and tomcats. Sure, they may look dressed up, but those places breed losers. That kind of bum will never be there to love and care for you in the end. He'll be just another silhouette in the distance."

It still stings—especially now after what just happened between Ben and me. It pisses me off because he always seemed to know the truth. "I hate him for it. His damned words of advice, like he's lived everything." She spoke quietly, but aloud; *I'd found better this time.* The tears rolled down her cheeks. *I knew cutting Daddy off of all communication from me would cut him deepest. I knew how to hit him where it hurt. I wouldn't let him know if I were dead or alive.*

The barrier she helped to build between them also helped destroy him. Her mom said she'd never forgiven her. "He'd be alive, Gina, if it wasn't for your damned games with him. I don't know if I want to see you again, ever."

Those were the last words either of her parents ever said to her—until her mother opened the door the other night to find her little broken girl crying at her doorsteps. Her father would never get to have another conversation with her.

Her father had gotten worried several nights after that fight about Ben. Late one evening, when he hadn't heard from her, he decided to go to The Queen's Bed, a club she'd started dancing. She listened to the bouncer yell in through the door, "POD coming through!" She immediately feared it was him. She knew all the codes. POD, which of course, stood for Pissed Off Daddy. There were acronyms for every situation. POOL stood for Pissed Off Old Lady, etc.

Gina's stomach knotted up, and that old lump in her throat swelled after she recalled her daddy getting into that ugly ruckus with a customer pawing her that night. The words quickly turned to punches thrown as she'd stood behind the curtain watching just before he was thrown out by the bouncer.

Several of the drunken regulars followed behind shouting and laughing only to return shortly after the bouncer came back inside. Her dad's lifeless body found after closing time was unceremoniously draped up over the metal fence dividing the Brooklyn Queens Expressway from The Queen's Bed Nightclub just outside the front door. He'd been beaten severely in the face along with two .22 caliber bullet holes in his head. In this particularly shady neighborhood, no one saw a thing, and the owner asked her not to come back.

Her heart ached that night until she drowned it with cocaine and booze, crying in Ben's arms and bed. Her life now bridged two different worlds. The world with Ben, her new savior, who also introduced her to cocaine that night, and there was the life of dancing for money. Dancing was something she seemed drawn to—then the drugs took control of her desires quickly—helping her justify living the seedy nightclub scene. Her daddy became a dark memory after that night. One she seldom faced. The cocaine and alcohol helped bury her dad's memory as deep as possible.

Gina moved from strip dive to strip dive, even though she'd finally stumbled into Benjamin Dane. It was a crazy and somewhat short ride between them, but she thought it was moving toward something more unique and permanent.

Now Ben hated her also. Maybe her daddy was right— she'd become just another silhouette in Ben's distance after using her up.

She'd already known her mother hated her. Gina surprised herself for having the courage to run to her mom after Ben tossed her out, and the money was gone. She was even more surprised that her mother let her stay, even with the statement it would be very temporary. No more than two nights of supervised stay and then out. She reasoned her mom must have missed the few items she'd stolen the last time she crashed her home in desperation.

Her two nights were up now. It was Sunday morning, a day that never brought fond memories for her. Gina usually slept through most of a Sunday, but not this one. Unsure where to go, without any plan in mind, she slipped out even more quietly than she'd come. Mother would not even know she was gone.

After opening the door to the bright morning sun, she slipped on her dark shades and hit the streets. With nothing but $75 in small bills and change she'd found tucked here and there in her mother's house, she stuffed it into her tight back pocket. She looked back just once, before she turned away and walked down a line of upscale Manhattan apartment homes. Gina doubted she would ever see her mother again.

22

The sun was bright, with barely a cloud in the sky. Billy, or—Jay as he'd now decided to wear his name proudly, began pacing in the morning silence around his shed.

The light shining through the cracks in the door made an eerie appearance. Shadows cut through light beams, which sliced through the dust Jay was stirring up. He continued to walk in small irregular orbits around the filthy dirt floor. Quick movements filled the tight space of his 'home'—his circular maneuvers were happenstance with no rational pattern. There was tension in the air, and Jay's gait paused then restarted in jerky movements. His mental demeanor seemed to have changed drastically over the past week.

His brain conjured up thoughts of the years spent in hiding and living out in the fringe. He had given up so much to survive these years. He was never a talkative man; the darkness made him even quieter. Jay's going underground to avoid arrest after killing his son aided in building a barricade from people. From any human connections. Along his journey, this caused a loss of himself not only to the outside world but within as well. He was becoming a real madman. At times he felt aware of his disturbance to the outside, while at other moments, it was the world that became disturbing to him.

It'd been a long, lonely haul with more than two years invested in moving from Florida to here. As Jay thought back on it now, it was a wash of misery mixed with necessity. He was astounded he had done so well, avoiding incarceration. He had scrounged his way through the darkness from eating out of dumpsters from the gulf side of Florida to the Big Apple in New York. The entirety without a single brush with trouble. It was quite an accomplishment. All those previous years being a trucker and knowing the roads and paths throughout the eastern states helped him zig-zag undetected for hundreds of miles.

A lifetime. Jay mentally divided his life into quarters to this point. The first was his rotten childhood, the few years shared with his parents, and then only his abusive dad before he ran away. His second quarter-life was scrambling on his own before being put away in prison for Ms. Pasternack's murder he didn't commit. The third quarter was Cat and the happy days. The carefree days before Darrell was born. He blamed Darrell for the fourth quarter he was living now. Darrell's rambunctiousness, mixed with cowardice, made him grow to be mean. It brought back his past when he was a young boy watching his parents fight and yell smack dab in front of him again. He didn't want that part to come back, but Darrell brought it screaming into his life.

The boy just stirred up his insides, making him crazy with anger. He couldn't wait to leave on Sunday nights, then dreaded coming home on Fridays. Seeing Cat coddle Darrell, was even begging to make Billy a weak skulker.

Billy showed nerve on that last night, though. He smiled a little, stopping in his tracks. "That little bastard finally showed brawn. Gotta admit it shook me for a moment." He laughed again out loud. "Life is shit, then ya just die. At least Billy died being a man. Darrell's probably still suckling off Cat's tits and wettin' his pants—worthless little waste of a good time."

Jay's mind was a battlefield. He was pacing to burn the steam off before the mission. He knew what he needed to do. *I have somewhat of a plan, I hope will fall into place. Catch my defendant off-guard and take him to his own home, so I can have a chance to live as the rich thieves do. I imagine the bastard's home is like something I've never seen.* He laughed again, "I know it's got a shower and a crapper. I have missed the hell out of those two things! And the food in the fridge! Every guilty punk has those luxuries!" Pacing, waiting for the day to disappear, and waiting for the sun to sink behind the ivory towers that the lucky and guilty lived. He was waiting for the time for the judgment of punishment or grace.

I hope it's punishment.

***

The day's high from his brother's church lasted through lunch and the walk back home. Upon opening his front door to the sheer quiet emptiness, the exuberance of the spirit within dissipated rather quickly. Ben immediately missed Gina's presence. *I never realized the value she gave me until she's gone. I wouldn't even know where to look for her. There were tawdry dance clubs everywhere and in all of the wrong places. The image she'd shared with me of her father found beaten and shot, stole the desire to go hunting alone for her.*

Instead, he walked over to his bar and pulled out a stool. He glanced up at the sculpted naked woman chiseled into the Italian bottle of his favorite poison. *Dare I enjoy just one shot? Or just watch as she towered over me?* Gina's taunt from not too long ago, whispers in his ear—"*Just one ittle wittle taste can't hurt. It'll settle your tense muscles."*

He got up from the stool, walked to the window and looked out, which overlooked his city neighborhood. He placed his hands on the glass window and peered outside, softly resting his forehead against the pane. It felt cold to his head and seemed to pull some of the stress he was suffering. *I've done well so far, but Mz. Vavoom is calling out to me in such a convincing voice. This roller coaster of life was never going to stop. How could others always stay at a high level with no lows? How could my brother be so damned strong, and me so weak? Did God not see fit to challenge Robert the same way?*

"Oh, these questions beg of answers. Jesus, where are you on this pre-eve of the night? Are you busy with someone of more, dire a need—or possibly testing and slightly enjoying the suffering I bring upon myself?" He gently bumped his head against the windowpane, causing the massive clear glass to vibrate against his forehead. "To drink and accept failure or fight the urge and win the battle in misery? The question of the night."

Ben spun around facing his nemesis, where she sat on the shelf behind the bar, taunting him. *The afternoon was still young. How long do I expect my will power to last? I could stop with just one drink.* He told himself as much while his mouth began to water. His conscience kept hinting Jesus would understand his loneliness and guilt about running off poor Gina into the night. *All of the pain surely justified one small shot, watered down over a glass of ice.*

He mentally made that walk to the bar ten times. He just couldn't make his legs act. He sat down in his favorite black leather chair facing the bar and buried his head in his hands. Sweat dripped from his forehead, dampening his hands and face. He felt his crisis growing with more fury and wondered when the other path from temptation God promised in the Bible verse would come? And in what form?

His will weakened as he pictured Gina's shocked, hurt face when he had told her it was over and to see her mother. He also knew her mother would surely turn her away. Tears followed the cold sweat that continued to run down his forehead.

Ben's eyes looked up one more time to the bottle of vodka on the shelf. His head then slowly lowered back down into his hands as his fingers massaged his aching temples. *Should I just crawl into a dark cocoon and hide from my troubles, my desires, and my misery. I'm ashamed I almost lost this battle with booze again. I'm scared because I know the war has only just begun.*

Grace, at this moment, was the sleep that overtook him as he buried himself deeper within, nestled into the cool leather chair, his back to the window where the sun heated the back of his neck.

***

It was dimmer in his living room when he awoke. He felt out of place in this moment of sleep and stupor, like after a night of drinking.

His headache was gone; his temples didn't pound any longer. He thought for sure when he'd sat on the chair; a migraine was on its way. Stress usually beckoned them on. Lord knew he was stress-filled lately. The headache managed to melt away through his afternoon slumber. Upon lifting his head and focusing his gaze—the chiseled Vavoom vodka-girl bottle still maintained her gaze with a tempting gleam. She and thoughts of Gina again tormented his psyche.

He didn't remember getting a cover from the bedroom wardrobe and covering up as he slowly pulled his way from its entanglement around him. As the blanket brushed by his nose, he swore he caught a hint of Gina's perfumed skin as it rolled down his chest and to his lap. He lifted it back to his nose again. Burying his face into the soft blanket, he breathed in deeply, taking in her scent with sweet reminiscence.

23

Gina felt awkward, knocking on Ben's door—again. She knew of nowhere else to go. She would change. She would do whatever she needed to do to repair her relationship with Ben. If her life of drug abuse and sleazy bars must end, then they would stop. She grew tired of the life of not knowing what was coming next. She'd gotten used to the habit of having a place to go home to each night—at least she thought of it as home. It was much different than the house her parents had provided. It was a home where she wanted to live.

She also saw what strength and value Ben quietly owned—even if he hadn't realized it himself. She admitted she deserved being kicked out of his life for continuing to be a temptation of the addictions that were killing those attributes.

With no answer at the door, the tears began to form, "Is it too late? Please, God, if you exist—one more chance if you care. If you care for either one of us?"

The door didn't open. Gina tried to peer through the peephole looking to see if any lights were on. She saw nothing. Digging in her purse to look for a pen and piece of paper to write a plea of love and regret, she stumbled onto something she'd forgotten to return, and Ben had failed to ask for. Keys.

She questioned if letting herself in would be a regrettable move. *Maybe Ben remembered and wanted to leave me a way to reach out to him?* Gina convinced herself that was undoubtedly the reason. *Maybe God is trying to help me work things out in my life?* She quietly let herself into the darkened entryway and tiptoed without a sound into his home.

Walking toward the bar, Gina noticed there were no glasses on the counter. It appeared his favorite vodka was untouched. The dim light of the early evening shined upon the face of the bottle sitting on the shelf, casting judgment on her. It appeared she stared in dismay for letting herself in uninvited.

She peeked toward the large picture window and saw the motionless body of the man she loved. He was nestled into the mold of his favorite chair and looked relaxed and free of stress. He looked content. He didn't stir.

Gina tiptoed toward him, needing to see his face more clearly than the subdued light allowed at a distance. He looked so peaceful. She wanted to drop to her knees and hold him tight, whispering how much she loved him and how sorry she was. Fear of his reaction kept her at bay. Making her way quietly to the bedroom wardrobe, she picked up the folded furry blanket and hugged it close to her, burying her face into its softness. She breathed in his scent and began to cry. They used to cuddle in this blanket. Her tears rolled down her cheek, soaking the fibers of the blanket.

Sucking in her sobs, she gained enough control over her emotions to realize it would be best not to wake him. She'd sneak back out and not destroy the chance to make things work tonight. She would reach out to him in some other way. Walking back into the living room, she carefully laid the blanket over him. He reacted by snuggling in more in-depth into the silence and comfort without even batting an eye.

The front door softly closed behind her, and the soft click of the latch snapped as she pulled the key from the deadbolt.

***

Ben picked up the blanket and buried his face into it, inhaling Gina's scent into his nose and lungs. His heart raced with the thought of her warm skin against his. Her eyes were staring intensely into his and her wet lips parting just enough for her tongue to brush across them. She was such a sensual soul. Every ounce of her oozed sexuality. He'd drank his third or fourth cocktail the first time he saw her on stage dancing.

I was immediately entranced. I, of course, knew Gina was working her magic on me with her talent, and I was no more than a payday, but I didn't care. She was more intoxicating than the drink I was holding. The only other thing I felt was jealousy every time some drunk bastard would stumble up to the stage and entice her over so he could tuck a dollar bill into her G-string. The whole scenario suddenly made his stomach wrench as he recalled how he had purposely looked into her beautiful eyes. He never tried to ogle at her scantily clad body. It seemed to excite her. *She always returned to my side of the stage.*

He never could make himself perform the money ritual on her. Instead, he mouthed the word "talk" to her. After her set, she'd nodded for him to follow her to the back-corner table of the bar.

***

The feelings he was experiencing this instant were the same feelings of jumbled nerves and longing he'd felt that night. *Why was this happening now? Was she the distraction God had given me to fight off the temptation of grabbing that bottle from the shelf and drowning my sorrow with its contents? How could the diversion work without the knowledge of where to find her? Was it help from the God my brother introduced me to—or was this torture for being so close to caving in to my demons? I'd felt so strong at times— like this morning, mere hours ago, when I sat in church. Was this all just a game? Was I only a game piece for a Supreme Being's entertainment?*

Ben jumped up from the chair and ran to his bedroom, feeling the air rush past his face. Throwing open the wardrobe and grabbing his jacket in one fluid motion, he quickly turned to go out the front door.

By God, I'll find Gina if I have to crawl on my knees inside every bar in the Bronx and Queens.

The door slammed shut without the click of the locking latch. Ben was too focused on finding Gina to worry about anything else.

Ben hit the last step from his home near a sprint. He turned south toward the bar district. The pedestrian traffic seemed heavy for a Sunday evening.

24

Jay hung back but fell in amongst the crowd as he followed his defendant. Luck must be with him tonight as he'd arrived just minutes before to see the man exit his house. The plan was now in motion.

His defendant moved quickly through the crowded sidewalk as if he, too, were on a mission. He walked with a determination, which made Jay move more rapidly than he wanted. He didn't want to make it evident to outsiders that he was following the fast-paced man in front of him. The good news was his defendant was too focused ahead ever to look behind and spot or question if Jay was following him.

Forty-five minutes later, his defendant walked into a neon-lit gentleman's club called Pink Velvet. Jay could only imagine the things that went on inside. He knew he definitely would stick out as he watched the suited clientele that walked in and out of the pink neon door.

The thought of a plan change entered his thoughts. *There was no way to get his defendant back to his home so far away— especially against his will. But if he could quickly get back to his house and get inside without being noticed, he could lie in wait until he returned. Why didn't I think of this before?* Having no idea how long his defendant would stay inside the club, he turned around and quickly started his return trip to the row-home on Morris Ave. He knew which one it was even though they all looked somewhat alike. He'd spent many hours watching and learning the layout from the street by watching lights turn on and off and studying the patterns. All people had patterns. He had taken note that the girl no longer came around. No one had come around much lately. This fact only strengthened his new plan.

His steps moved steadily as the sidewalk crowds began to thin. His Mason jar with the punishment tiles jingled in his deep overcoat pocket as his fast-paced leg bumped it with each step. His heart raced more than it ever had on Friday nights when the ritual used to take place with his boys. It was as if the whole process was entirely new for him. And yet, all he could think about was the feeling he would soon receive— that somehow some relief would come from administering judgment from the tile's decision like it did with Billy and Darrell. His thoughts bounced like a ball back to his current objective. He would need to continue his preparations once he'd entered the home.

***

Ben walked into the familiar club and looked around. He hadn't met Gina at this club, but she used to dance here occasionally after they got together. Ben could never bring himself to go when she was dancing because of the jealousy watching her brought. He felt uneasy being there now. Mixed emotions of hoping he would see her here tonight and wishing she hadn't returned to this way of life. *Wanting Gina to be at her mother's house changing her lifestyle, yet wanting to stumble into her so he could beg her to come back.* He was conflicted in thought. This process was new to him. His old procedure rarely dealt with anything but his addiction and being able to cope at work. This new edition of an addiction to a woman was much different. He was beginning to realize it was a beast of its own.

So far, she was not here. Ben sat and began watching through the rotation of girls. He felt odd ordering a Coke with nothing added. The thought of asking if Gina was working tonight crossed his mind but then decided that could set him up for troubles. There were rules in these places, and Gina wouldn't use her real name as a stage name anyway.

The barmaid smiled, "Honey, this drink won't get you where you want to be—but it's a start." She turned and intentionally rubbed her skimpily-outfitted bottom against him on her way back to the bar. A move that in his past would have reeled him into immediate party mode. Tonight, he was going to fight those urges. He would be fighting them for the rest of his life, he imagined. It was like being addicted to being an addict. He was born with those tendencies. Step one had been admitting it. Phase two and beyond were even more difficult, but he had several things backing him.

His drink quickly arrived before the second dancer finished her set. "How many different girls tonight? Trying to judge how long I stay…" He smiled and winked at her, trying to fit in more.

"It's Sunday, so it's a little slow, honey. There are three or four, and then, of course, I'll be up there last," she winked as she leaned down to let him gander down her top. "You'll want to be sure and stay for me—you may just see something you want and need badly." She intentionally rubbed against him again. He eyed her bounce toward another table to take an order.

He was enticed, and his Coke tasted bland without any kicker added. The music, the near-naked women, along with the dim lights mixed with splashy neon and mirror balls spinning above, were beginning to have an effect.

Clubs like this was what normal life had been like before his crash, his work accounts seized and his brother stepping in to clean up his messes. He knew he shouldn't be here. He wouldn't be here much longer, just enough time to make sure Gina wasn't here or didn't pop in.

He'd decided this morning in church that he wanted her back; he wanted to help fix her problems and become a team. A healed team that could help each other through their rough patches. He knew there would always be a rough-times around any corner. It was inevitable. He knew he was on the edge of one tonight, and he wanted Gina to save him. He wanted her to be that 'God-promised' distraction to keep him from the temptation that would otherwise draw him back in. It was a promise, after all.

Robert believed in it, and I will try to accept it too

It was the third dancer, and his glass was empty down to only ice. He felt a pain moving into his temples. He didn't realize he was swirling the ice cubes by sliding the glass around the water puddle on the table.

His waitress bent over, putting her lips next to his ear and giving him another full view of her naked breasts. "Honey, you really look like you need something more than a virgin Coke to knock that edge off—my boss says I can give you the first one on the house. What can I make you? You look like a shot-of-bourbon-kind of a gentleman."

"No. No bourbon for me, sweetie. You could interest me in a Vavoom Vodka on the rocks, though." He smiled wickedly, knowing that the "boss" wouldn't just give a shot of this expensive vodka away.

She leaned up slowly as she put her hand on his shoulder and lightly brushed his ear. "I'll see if we have it. That's a new flavor on me." Again, as she walked away, he watched her fleshy backside ripple back and forth with each step. She knew what she was doing. *I imagine she makes great tips.*

She came back with a glass of ice and clear liquid sitting on the tray. She picked it up and asked if she could have a sip. "My boss says you have very expensive taste and that he doesn't get too many requests for this. I like men with expensive taste."

Ben nodded, and she held the glass up to her bright red lips, slowly tipping it to her mouth, then running her tongue across the rim before licking her lower lip.

"Well, what do you think Miss…" Ben asked.

"Ginger. My friends call me Ginger. The customers here call me Sasha, and yes—it has a kind of sweetness to it. I like it. I like it a lot." She handed it to him and ran her fingers down his wrist as he pulled the glass to his mouth.

He took a drink from the same spot she drank from. He winked at her, "Yes, very tasty. It's what I imagine kings enjoy."

"A king would enjoy my show also. I'm up next. I hope to see you afterward." She turned without rubbing into him this time—a torturous kind of tease he sensed.

Minutes later, the deejay came over the speaker, "Tonight for your viewing pleasure, Miss Sasha Vavoom, dancing for any of you kings out there." The lights dimmed momentarily before a spotlight pointed to the opening in the curtain.

Ben smiled to himself as he heard the bartender speak louder than the ambient noise, so his co-worker could hear, "Ginger is reeling one in tonight. Putting all of her magic into it. She must really want this prize."

'Jamie's Cryin'' started playing as the spotlight whirled around to the curtain. Van Halen had been topping the charts for a couple of years. A lot of girls tried to strip to this song, but only a few could pull it off. The way Sasha moved from the curtains to the pole proved she was one out of a hundred. Ben couldn't take his eyes off of her as he got up to move toward the stage. Ben motioned to one of the other waitresses, and she walked over and leaned in close as Ben put in his order for the rest of the bottle of Vavoom. He reached into his wallet and pulled out a handful of ten-dollar bills, never losing sight of what Sasha was doing.

A couple of minutes later, the waitress returned with a glass of ice and the bottle of Vavoom vodka. His Italian glass bottle, which formed with the torso of a naked lady, now sat beside him at the stage bar. The sparkle in his eyes clearly stated how this evening was going to end.

With Gina not showing up to be his distraction, he continued to move towards failing what he had painfully accomplished up to this point.

He filled his empty glass to the rim with the expensive vodka, using his finger to stir the ice, cooling the sweet poison that now gained control of him. He swallowed a gulp of the sweet vodka triggering a surge of excitement. Sasha was front and center slinking on the pole, giving him slow seducing peep-shots of her fleshy body and eyeing him through the entire song. As the lights dimmed, she left the stage, grabbing his arm and the bottle, walking him back to the dark corner table where she continued to tease and tempt him until closing time.

It was a slow, crooked walk back to his home, but they made it there together. Stumbling noisily through the dark entryway of his home with giggles, they staggered toward the bedroom alcohol in their veins and sin in their hearts.

25

Jay thought he'd put together a perfect plan. He had everything lined out complete with the revolver he'd found tucked under the right side of the bedroom mattress. Jay had laid out some electrical cord cut into strips along with the Mason jar on the coffee table. The one thing he did not plan on was having a female companion come back with his defendant.

He quietly sat in the spare room closet, trying to recalculate how to proceed. Hopefully, they would be done quickly, and his defendant would send her away.

The muffled groans and screams lasted into the early morning. Jay finally heard nothing but dead silence. He sat crumpled in the corner of the closet with the hope he would be able to figure out where to go from here. He'd made no plan for a second defendant. Minutes of silence turned to a couple of hours before he finally heard someone stir.

"Oh, God, no!! You've got to leave! I wasn't supposed to…it wasn't supposed to end like this!" Ben rousted his overnight companion by pushing on her shoulder, then shaking her. "You have to leave, I'm sorry, but I have to get you out of here!"

Ginger's eyes opened wide, and she started moving about, stretching her naked body out as Ben pulled down the covers to the end of the bed. "What? What's going on? I thought everything was good?"

"I have people coming over, and it's Monday, a workday. Please hurry. I'm sorry." He reached into his billfold and pulled out some large bills. He tossed them on the nightstand. "I have to shower quickly. Please, I'm sorry, but you have to be gone when I get out."

Ginger knew she shouldn't feel the hurt inside the way she did. She'd been through this type of morning many times before. This time it seemed more than just a simple sting. She liked this guy. Or at least she thought she did before being treated like a cheap whore. She got up from the bed and began walking through the house, hurriedly gathering up her clothes.

***

Jay peeked through the louvers of the closet door, trying to get a good picture of what was happening. He saw the naked woman shimmying around the living room, grabbing up clothes and pulling them on. *It had been a long time since he had witnessed a woman with no clothing. It made him feel dirty. It gave him urges he no longer seemed to understand, urges he'd shoved deep into the recesses of his brain. She was a distraction, and he did not like that*

***.

Ginger put on the last of her clothing, grabbed her purse, and headed toward the door. She stopped abruptly and scanned the beautiful surroundings. Peeking into the bedroom, she spied the wad of cash on the nightstand. "No—well, hell…yes, I will." She quickly made her way to the nightstand, grabbing up the bills, then glanced at the light bursting through the bathroom door jamb where Ben showered. She started to say something but just a guffaw came out. Her heart raced from running around, and anger began to overtake her. She was awoken so abruptly and then told to leave from his house so rudely. "Why in the hell does this always happen to me? Rich assholes don't deserve to live!"

She turned and walked back into the living room. Scanning it over one more time, she noticed an odd jar sitting in the middle of the glass coffee table beside several lengths of electrical wires. She picked it up and saw several small wooden tiles with words etched on them. One tile, KILL, sat on top. In an instant, her heart began to race as her eyes widened with horror. *What was he planning for me?* Then she spied the beautiful Vavoom bottle on the shelf behind the bar. Rushing over, she grabbed it and ran out the front door, slamming it behind her. *What have I just escaped?* "Sick pervert!" she yelled.

Hearing the door slam, Ben came out of the bathroom, relieved that she'd left. Out of his large bedroom window, he saw the woman he'd shared the night within the drunken twist of sin and failure. She hurried down the sidewalk with his bottle of vodka sticking out of her bag. At least those temptations were no longer here. He moved his hands up to his temples and tried to rub the ache from his head.

I know I deserve pain today. There was no punishment I haven't earned. I not only let myself down last night but also my brother, my parents, my addiction group, the list went on. Most of all, I've let Gina down. I've sank to the lowest low I can remember. I am now a drunk cheater.

He thought of how yesterday began: *church, lunch with his brother, and now this. I feel the air being sucked from my lungs.* Ben dropped to the floor. "Lord, I deserve all the wrath you have. Bring it to me. I'm not worthy and far too weak to expect You to love and forgive me."

***

Jay stood in the doorway with a pistol pointed squarely at Ben's back. "Well, that was rather awkward, wasn't it?" he stated coldly, his lips tight in an evil smile.

Ben spun around, stunned. His color drained instantly in his face as he stood frozen in place, eyes scanning for anyone else. Ben saw only a scruffy, dirty man pointing a pistol directly at him. His knuckles turned white as he clutched the towel tightly around his waist to keep it from dropping to the ground. "What do you want?

The girl? She's gone! Are you her—husband, because I…I had no idea?"

"Don't know the young lady. You seem to know her pretty well, though. No, what I am is your judge, jury, and executioner of the punishment. I've been watching you."

Ben's tense body dripped sweat, and his voice stammered uncontrollably. "I…I've seen you following me…um, I mean, I thought there was something familiar. What have I done?" His eyes begged for an answer he could understand. *If the intruder didn't know the girl—what could this possibly be about?* "Are you robbing me? Take whatever you want!"

"No. I don't want your money or things." The intruder's eyes narrowed as his brows pinched together. "You, rich people sin every day and then think you can throw your money at the situation to solve it." *Money doesn't solve sin, not anymore.* "I'd say you are responsible for some guilt, like just last night and this morning. That young lady was shaken up. She seemed sorry for the whole thing. It's why I let her escape." Jay paused. "I could have killed her, you know." A full, taunting grin spread slowly across his face. "You, though, I believe your guilt runs far deeper. I think you better get some clothes on. You and I are gonna be busy awhile. We're gonna get to know each other really well. Now get dressed. Don't be long, or else."

26

Ben couldn't comprehend what was happening. *Would God have sent an angel of Satan from the depths of hell to exact payment for my sinful life? I know I've failed every promise and oath I'd made with last night's escapades, but I hadn't meant for it to happen.*

"Hurry up in there! Don't even think of trying anything foolish. I've killed before, and no one knows who or where I am."

Ben shook with fear. He prayed. *Dear Lord, I know I've failed you. I've failed many. Please, whatever happens to me, I know I deserve every bit of pain and suffering. Please—please don't let Gina or Robert stumble into my mess. I'm begging you. I am giving my heart and soul to you to do with as you may. Just please don't let anyone else suffer because of my sin.*

"Don't make me come in there. Be a man and follow my rules. We'll get through this one way or the other." Jay felt far differently than he'd expected so far. He also knew he'd moved past the point of no return. This chosen path would not only lead to the defendant's judgment but in the end, Jay's future was also on the line. Jay's future seemed to have no happy ending anyway, but he was somewhat confident his defendant's fate wouldn't fare any better. They would finish this situation together.

The door to the bathroom opened, and Ben moved out slowly, obviously nervous by the sweat dripping from his face, his color still drained.

Jay pointed toward the living room to a chair that sat ready by the coffee table. Ben noticed the table showcased a Mason jar with something in it and ropes made of wire laid out beside it. *What could all of this mean?*

The dimly-lit room caused shadows to dance across the walls from the pigeons' flying maneuvers from ledge to ledge outside.

Ben never noticed these shadows before, deeming they must be part of the event this death angel brought with him somehow. His head ached more strongly. Everything was tangled inside his thoughts as last night's poison had dehydrated his brain, causing his head to pound. His stomach growled with nausea clawing at him. Never was a previous hangover as clear and unclear at the same time. The madness was in his home in the form of an unknown and unkempt devil—one with a clouded bag of tricks that appeared to promise no good outcome for him.

"Sit on the chair, Defendant," Jay spoke with authority. "I want you to put your hands behind you, and don't you dare move unless you're told to—do we understand each other?"

Ben backed up to the chair as he struggled to clear his throat to answer. "You won't get a fight from me." He tried to see what was inside in the old fruit jar on his table. None of it made any sense. "Is it money that you want…?"

"Shut up until asked to speak!" Jay grabbed his hands, wound the wire around them together, then cinched them to the back legs of the chair. "You'll know soon enough why I'm here." After finishing with his hands, he moved to bind each ankle to a front leg of the chair. After completing this task, Jay stepped back to observe his work to see if it was sufficient.

Jay began pacing around the room, his shadow mixing with the other shadows displayed on the wall. It was a live painting of darkness dancing sporadically on the stark white walls.

As the stranger circled the room, he moved in and out of the shadows and illumination from the window. Ben sensed two separate appearances of the demon. When he would hesitate, one side of his face caught the light. He could picture a softness in his eye and humanness, showing in through his wrinkled, worn skin under a scruffy beard. Yet the dark side of his face bore murky, evil, and bleak features that appeared unable to contain any humanity. An emptiness only a demon could possess. The sight caused Ben to quiver. It almost seemed the man couldn't decide what to do next. He wanted to ask why—but he somehow knew better.

Jay seemed to read his mind. "Defendant! You can speak. I'm sure you have questions. Speak softly. Any calling out will bring reactions you do not want." Jay turned to face Ben squarely eye to eye. Half of Jay's face was lit brightly from the window while the other side remained dark.

"Did God send you here to exact punishment on me, or are you here on your own accord?" His voice quivered as he asked the intruder.

Jay thundered, "No, God didn't send me." The whites in his eyes grew, giving him a wild-eyed look of a crazy man somehow offended by Ben's question. "Religion is a carnival of smoke and mirrors." Jay retorted. "I have no personal disagreement with you. There is only one reason why I chose you." Jay began to move nervously around the room as he spoke. "I am here to bring punishment for wrongs committed. Stealing. Mistreatments of lesser people. Things of that nature."

"How do you know I've done any of those things?"

"How can you say that, knowing I was here last night and heard what you did. Adultery is a sin! Where is the other woman who used to live here?"

"Don't you say a word about her. She is none of your business here. You stay away from her, you sonova…" Ben stopped himself, not wanting to draw any attention to Gina and have this beast hurt him by involving her.

"Well then, she is still around—of sorts. And the things I heard last night." Jay shook his head, looking Ben squarely in the eye as he pointed his finger, mocking Ben. "You should be ashamed. But I'll help you with that." Jay winked along with a smirk. "My little Mason jar over there helps me with retribution. Would you like an explanation of how this will work?"

"What does it matter? You're going to do what you're going to do. I just want to know what made you pick me if it wasn't by a higher power such as God? I'll deal with whatever comes from it."

"Let's do today's round first and talk later about why I picked you. I don't want to keep you in suspense too long when you have judgment due."

Jay picked up the jar and dumped the tiles into his dirty hand. One by one, he explained the meanings of the tiles and how the Mason jar worked.

When he read the one spelling KILL, Ben dropped his head in submission. *Remembering what he had thought earlier about deserving whatever punishment God chose to dole out to him. Could my life end in this way?* Anger boiled up in his heart as he asked, "So, this is a game for you? A game of chance at my expense? You broke into my house to play some sick twisted game of 'you are better than me and without sin' so you can judge me with the luck of the draw? You're a sick coward of a man. And I thought you were some demon angel with some kind of tie to Glory." He guffawed. "You're more pathetic of a lunatic than I am as a sinner."

Jay drew a deep breath, trying to hold back his anger. "I didn't 'break' in, I merely twisted the doorknob," He snapped up the jar and began shaking it around in circles, mixing the tiles to the sound of a rattlesnake. "But I would have if I would have had to. Fate made my entry easy. The door was unlocked." Jay smiled, showing his yellowed teeth.

He concentrated on Ben's eyes to absorb his fear. He was amazed to see very little. He seemed calm and subdued— resolved to accept whatever punishment fate dealt him. Jay watched the man shut his eyes briefly when he shook out a single tile from the jar. "Here goes." Jay's lips curved into an evil smile.

The tile clattered on top of the glass tabletop. Ben opened his eyes to witness what punishment he would have to endure. He looked to see a tile with the word SLAP etched on it. Ben sighed with relief, imagining that a slap couldn't be that bad; he turned and faced his captor. "So, this game excites you? This power you get to reign over my head gives you some sick satisfaction? Sexually?" he added. Ben knew he should keep his mouth shut, but a small part inside him felt as if he truly deserved this—this whatever crazy thing it was. He couldn't explain it. A sudden calm washed over him. As long as this monster didn't touch Gina or Robert, he could take whatever punishment his captor doled out to him. Even death. He had already spent many hours thinking about that, anyway.

Jay eyed his defendant as he towered above him. His expression grew darker as he drew his open right hand back above his shoulder. With one harsh swoop, he brought his palm down hard and swiftly until it connected with the left side of Ben's face. The sound was loud and ferocious as spit flew from Ben's mouth while his head snapped hard to his right. Ben hadn't really been prepared for such a fast and solid hit. He hung his head for several seconds before lifting it back up to the sudden bite of another swift slap. This time his chin dropped to his chest with a loud gasp. His skin burned while his cheek ached deep inside even into his teeth from the harsh assaults.

"I suppose that will do for tonight's verdict. You took it very well. We'll see what tomorrow brings." Jay lightly massaged the skin of his striking hand, kneading the pain from his calloused palm.

Jay bent down, putting his lips next to Ben's ear. Ben could feel the heat and smell the staleness of his breath as he spoke in almost a whisper. "I guess this was a bit of a wake-up call for you." He continued in a tone of contempt. "This was mild punishment rolled out tonight. Must be beginner's luck," he finished with a slight cackle to which he still received no response from Ben.

Ben's head remained tilted downward; he made no sound or response to his captor. He went to a quiet place in his mind where he barely comprehended any sound, trying to mend what just happened mentally. The burning sting mixed with the ache of the aggression and his throbbing temples of the prior night's over-indulgence drove him deeper within himself.

Jay walked over to the cabinet and withdrew a glass from the top shelf. It looked like a costly crystal. He shook his head, "It must be nice living such a life, walking past people like me laying in the streets. Watching us drink to survive from your paper throwaway cups while you get drunk from booze in fancy glasses like this."

Jay side-stepped to the refrigerator, opening it to display assorted bottles of soda and fruit juices. He picked out a bottle of orange juice and filled the glass. Taking a big gulp, he turned back to the motionless defendant, "Ahhh, that is a taste I miss from my home state—orange juice. I haven't enjoyed that sweet taste for years. Thank you very kindly for your hospitality." His words dripped with sarcasm and disdain.

He sauntered into the living room, turned the television on, and sat down on the leather chair. Had he felt any satisfaction from the discipline he doled out to his kids? Made him wonder. He didn't feel what he thought he would this time. Inflicting the punishment felt bland, no real charge.

He lifted the glass of orange juice to his mouth and again took a swallow. The orange juice was tasty, as he smacked his lips from the sweet, yet sour aftertaste.

He looked back to the bar once more, and this time noticed something he hadn't spotted before. The brown leather bag that his defendant regularly wore over his shoulder whenever he had followed him. That bag was what initially triggered him to pick the one now sitting slumped over in his chair. He'd wondered what it contained. He just knew it held the secrets to this man's sins. It possibly kept proof of his thievery or lists of evil doings. He was sure it contained some form of records that should cause shame.

He thought about opening it, but he was so comfortable right now. He would open it tomorrow after letting his defendant know it was the driving force that caught his eye. That item alone made him stick out above any others who should also be brought to the justice of his Mason jar.

Jay lifted the glass one last time to swallow what was left. *This place sure beats any other place I ever stayed, including my old home with Cat, or the dirty hovel hidden in the junkyard.* His eyes felt heavy now that his thirst had been quenched. The energy he'd had was drained from his long night in the closet and doling out the first punishment. With his relaxed muscles melting into the soft leather chair, he closed his eyes for just a minute to unwind.

Ben slowly lifted his head, squinting his eyes open to spy at his surroundings. It only took a moment to see the bearded, dirty devil who invaded his home to carry out his deranged vengeance. He saw the light green Mason jar, which now evidently held his fate. *How long must I endure this calamity you see fit for me, Lord? Will I survive this, or is this the way I've earned to meet my end? Please, Lord, have mercy on Gina. Please protect her and forgive my failures of late. Give me as much strength as possible to sustain me. Amen.*

Ben's body throbbed from his wrists and ankles to the abrasions on his face. He knew he'd gotten his just rewards today. Now the residual pain was there as a stark reminder. He crawled back inside his mental safe spot where he pictured Gina snuggling into the curve of his body. It was a place he could be distracted enough for whatever would happen to him next—and when.

27

Darrell was quiet most of the day after church. Cat gave him his space but was conflicted about how to proceed. Talk or let him be? She knew she'd coddled him way too much, but she'd needed to make up for her lack of motherhood in the past. Being sober now for over three years had changed her. She was caring and protective now like she should have been all along. *I knew I would never be able to get back those first years when Jay was in the picture. I'll do my best to be whatever my boy needs me to be. He's suffered so much trauma and lost so much time he should have been loved. It's a wonder he's survived at all.*

The Watkins sat with Cat. Gloria seated next to her while her husband settled across the coffee table from them. "I'd say he's doing fine, Ms. Cader. Sure, yesterday was a big setback for him, but he knows you love him and will be with him in support." Gabriel sat tall in his chair while his eyes remained unemotional. "I do have one question we now know lays heavy on the boy's mind." Gabriel's tone growled deeper as he leaned closer in toward Cat. "Do you suspect Jay will ever show back up in these parts? Apalachicola isn't a town one could stay hidden in very well—if he did want to come back to harm—or pick up where he left off." He cleared the gravel that stuck in his throat. "You and Darrell wouldn't be difficult to find."

"I can't imagine why he would ever come back. I don't believe he wanted to be here when he ran. He always flew out of here on Sundays like a shotgun-peppered pooch." She tried to smile to lighten her statement. "Jay's love for me began to fade quickly after Darrell's birth. I don't believe he cares for his youngest or me. It seems he killed the only one of our family who meant anything to him." She continued to fidget in her chair, rolling back and forth uncomfortably in her seat. *Painfully reflecting on the iniquity he'd brought home with him every Friday.* "He turned so mean those last years—you know my story." Her head dropped, and she stared at her feet as the tears began. "I hid my drinking from the devil's bottle while my boys dealt with the devil himself."

Gloria scooted over closer and pulled Cat into her body. "Now honey, we've been through all of this. Your price paid, the Lord forgave and made you brand new again." She softly rubbed Cat's neck below her hairline with occasional pats. "Don't you let the devil back in to do damage to what the Lord's done fixed."

"Gloria knows what she's talking about Cat. We all have a past filled with mistakes, wrong choices, and sin. There ain't nobody on this earth perfect and free from sins. We need to concentrate on how the devil is trying to work his way into Darrell and not dwell on our past."

Darrell stood next to the entry into the Watkins's parlor room. He'd been listening to their conversation without their knowledge of his presence. Peeking around the corner, he showed himself rather abruptly. "Momma! If Poppa comes back around here—I'll finish what Billy couldn't. I'll kill that monster of a bastard. Don't you worry, Momma, he ain't gonna get the chance to do us any more harm. I'll see to it!" His teeth clenched, and he growled with authority and resolve. His eyes narrowed. There wasn't an ounce of fear inside his body or voice, and his hands remained firmly tucked deep into his jean pockets.

Darrell wasn't the same young boy he'd been three years ago. Darrell was changing. He was becoming the man of his family. His momma and him.

"Oh, son! I'm sorry, we didn't know you were here. You don't even have to think about doing such a thing, honey. Your poppa is long gone and may be locked up somewhere or even dead." Cat got up from the chair and moved toward him with outstretched arms beckoning him to her. "He's not coming back, son. He knows there's nothing here for him."

"I'm just sayin' if he does, I'll kill him. I'll protect us. I'm older now like Billy was." He turned and headed out the front door, bumping the screen door with his hip, hands still planted in his pockets. Cat tried to catch up with him but was too slow to see anything but his back as he launched himself off the last step. She hollered out to him, but he never turned back to acknowledge her.

Cat sat down on the top step of the Watkins's porch and looked up at the orange and pink sky. A crescent moon partially peeked out from the thin, slow-moving clouds. It was beautiful enough to calm her, letting what just transpired momentarily exit her thoughts before another reflection whispered into her heart. *God's grace is sometimes subtle but seems to be there at just the right times if you let yourself notice and accept it.*

Reverend Gabriel and his wife quietly stepped outside and sat on either side of her, letting the silence of God's beautiful creation be the conversation. They sat until the sky turned black, and the stars came out. The tiny sliver of a silver moon hung slightly crooked on its side.

***

Darrell slowed his pace to a walk as the thoughts bounced around in his head. He didn't realize that his momma and the Watkins still held all of these worries between them. Slightly angry with them that he'd been kept from knowing the truth about Billy, but couldn't stay mad long with the only three people in his world who truly loved him. *Billy wasn't coming home. Poppa wasn't going to hurt them again. Ever.* Those two thoughts remained in his brain on top of anything else he was thinking.

It was time to grow up and be the man that Billy had become—before Poppa stole him from them. I am that man, now.

***

Gina was moneyless again. She tried to stay away from drugs and alcohol, but with the people she hung out with inside the clubs, it was next to impossible. She knew she wouldn't be able to fight it on her own. *I used to be strong. I used to care for people for more than what they could give me. This lifestyle stole the real me. I want to trust again. I want to be strong.*

She thought back to Saturday when she used her key to let herself back into Ben's place. *He looked so content. He looked "cured." How could I own that look if I kept on the way I was going?*

Gina looked at her friend, who also stripped. "There is something out there, Meesh. Something you can't buy or even see. But some people possess it. Ben has it, and I want it too." Her eyes seemed to brighten as she spoke. "When I find it—I want you to have it too. It's peaceful, and you don't have to sleep with losers to make your way."

She thought about the previous night and the horrible experience she'd gone through just finding a place to bed down for the warm night. "I'm tired of being a throwaway plaything. I want more, Meesh. If I have to beg Ben to find out how I can feel the contentment he's found without snorting it, or drinking it—I promise, I'll come back and save you too."

"Whatever you talking, girlfriend, it sounds too goot to be true. I hope you find it, and I would love some too, but don't count on it. Some of us in this here world was born into nothingness. We be slaves of other's desires, and that's just the way it is." Meesh continued to ready herself for her next set. "I was born on the streets of this rotten 'big o' apple' and I been workin' them streets and survivin' off the dirty apple core the rich toss to the ground. We got no value to them, pleasure for their eyes, and sin better than their wives. That's all it is, baby girl."

"I've seen it, Meesh. It's strong too." She clenched her fists. "It has the power to change! Not only people, but circumstances also." She brought both fists down onto the powder table where they both sat. Both were seeing their startled faces in their reflections from the mirror. "I don't know what I have to do to find it, ...but..." Gina stuttered. "...but I know a man whose brother does! You ever hear of the White Dove?" She stared at Meesh in the reflection. "He's Ben's preacher brother. That's where Ben found it!"

"Girl, you saw it from a rich, white cracker! Course, he got it. Probably suckled it straight from his rich mammy's breast, who gots it from her rich mammy. Ain't no room in that equation for you or me, even if you is white. You was born on my side of the tracks." Meesh was getting worked up thinking about Gina's foolish daydream. "Sure, you want it, sure I'd take some too, but we ain't gonna get none. I'm done talkin' bout it, girl!" She rolled her eyes and slammed her locker door. "I gotta git my jigglin' booty up on stage now. Keep dreamin'. I need some big tips. My rent be due in two days."

Gina's eyes became watery again. She had almost felt like a normal person for that one minute she was with Ben. *Meesh was wrong, though. I **had** been born and raised on the right side of the tracks; I just never felt like I was worthy or fit in. I had rebel in my blood and not enough sense to fight it back then. Instead, I pushed away everything my parents did for me.*

I want it back now. Not just money and comfort. I want what Ben has found. I want what his brother had given him. "I'm not giving up any longer," she quietly said to herself as she walked out of the girl's room and through the back door, letting it slam behind her.

***

Ben imagined it must be the middle of the night when he awoke to try to move his numb hands and feet. In the shadows, the dark form on the couch reminded him of his current predicament.

"Hey! I have to use the restroom, and I can't feel my arms or legs!"

The form on the couch moved and rolled over to face his captive. He sat up quickly and saw that everything still seemed secure.

"I have to use the restroom. I need help getting there. I won't run or try anything, I promise."

Jay got up with Ben's revolver, still tucked into the top of his pants. "I'll untie you for a bit, but remember, I'll stop at nothing if you try anything."

"I couldn't run if I wanted. I can't feel anything but the ache in my face."

Jay untied Ben's feet first and then moved to unbind his hands. Ben tried to wiggle his hands and feet, but sharp tingles kept him from continuing. "It'll take me a minute, Mr...." He looked up at the dark outline standing above him. "What do I call you anyway? Judge? Or do you have a name you want to share?"

There was hesitation doused with silence for a moment. "I suppose it won't matter if you know my name. It's Jay. Call me, Jay."

Ben noticed a difference in his demeanor. His appearance was still intimidating, and he wasn't sure what might set him off, but he did seem calmer. Less frantic. He wasn't sure if it was because he'd just woken up or for some other reason, but it was there. "Well, Mr. Jay—it's going to take a few minutes before I can move unless you want to drag me over there…"

"Just, Jay. I worked for a living." He glanced at his wrists and ankles as he'd untied them. "Those look pretty swollen. It seems you got a little extra judgment doled out. Maybe your God presumed you deserved it?" His eyes sparkled a hint of sarcastic humor as his lips turned a bit upward. "Honestly, I didn't mean to leave you tied up like that in the chair all night. I…I just…."

"I know, I saw you drift off quickly once you sat down." Ben realized it would be smarter not to antagonize or cause more problems with his captor. He was coming to terms with the fact this may last a while, or it could even be the final hours or days of his life. Maybe, Ben thought, treating his captor with some form of kindness might be a distraction from the torturous notions "Jay" brought with him. He tried to remember the Bible verse he'd stumbled upon. The one about providing another path to fight off temptation. Maybe Jay needed some distraction. *Perhaps I'm Jay's other path.*

"There's a clock on the wall in the hallway to the spare bedroom. Could you look and see what time it is? It feels like the sun should be coming up soon." Ben asked.

Jay turned and walked to the clock, looking back, his hand moved to the butt of the revolver, and he made sure Ben saw it, in case he was planning on trying something. "It's four."

"No wonder the feeling is taking so long to come back to my hands and feet."

"It don't mean you are escaping any retribution from your sins later today." Jay chided. "There's no schedule, but the extra you received doesn't forgive what the future may give."

Ben noticed an emptiness in his captor's eyes this time.

"I wasn't implying anything like that. You may not have been sent here directly from God, but I have a feeling He may have a part in your being here. I realize the wrongs I've done in my past—right down to my very recent sin you witnessed." Ben's thoughts continued, *I can't believe I'm having this conversation with the invader standing over me. For some reason though, I can't refrain from continuing.* "You see, I've been made aware of many wrongs, and I have been called down on them already. I've been seeking forgiveness and attempting to defeat my desires that numb my conscience and keeps me following the wrong ways. Drugs and alcohol abuse to be specific."

"Sounds…" Jay paused, "…real interesting if I was indeed interested. If we want to get into this now, we can? Or we can just have a little small talk now and do what we have to do later?"

"I was—just thinking out loud. I'm not sure how to start a "small talk" conversation with someone I don't know and didn't invite into my home. You're the one who holds me at gunpoint and with my revolver at that. And, of course the torture. This position is all new to me. You have the edge here."

Ben added a curtness to his tone. "I have two topics right now, and they both appear connected with you. I have my guilt of things I've done, and I have my current attempts at salvation and grace from my Maker. You seem interested in the punishment part of my sins, but how about the salvation and grace part?" Ben looked down at his bluish-purple hands as the feeling painfully started working its way back into them. He then looked up at his captor, awaiting his response.

"Salvation—is that Jesus talk?" He looked Ben squarely eye to eye. There was a sourness in his question.

"It is. The act of seeking His grace for the sinful things we've done. We don't have to be burdened in our hearts and souls anymore, in His eyes." Ben meekly stared back at his captor, wondering if his point was considered at all.

"But in man's eyes, it doesn't work that way." Jay's stare became more pointed. "I'm not working for Jesus. I'm working for what's right in **my** eyes." His look then softened just a bit. "There was an old black lady at a church I eat at…and…she was trying to sell me hard grace. Or what I call snake oil." Jay snickered. "I told her I sure enough never got any grace from anyone in my life. My daddy used to whoop the tar out of my backside for things I'd never done. He didn't give any grace or talk about this God of yours having grace up for grabs." His voice grew louder, laced with agitation. "The only grace I got was the same way my boys got it—which is the same way you might get it. By chance! By the luck of what gets shaken out of that Mason jar over there. It's sort of the Cader-family tradition." His tone remained unyielding before it softened. "There wasn't anyone to dole grace out to me back when my daddy showed me his wrath." Jay's hurt in his voice became suddenly sharp, and his volume increased. "I learned to keep my Goddamned mouth shut and take it! I never let that sonovabitch see me shed a single tear. Why would I let a cheating liar like you off the hook?"

Ben responded quickly without hesitation. "Because it's not yours to call out my sins, but it sounds like your mind has already been decided. I'm presumed guilty by someone who knows absolutely nothing about me or my sins."

Ben started to get up slowly, wondering if his feet would hold his weight. "I'm going to the bathroom if you don't mind; I think I can make it now. No need to fret, I'm not trying anything." He stayed hunched over, making winces of pain, hobbling toward the bathroom. "Besides, I'm not done with this conversation just yet. What have I got to lose—right?"

Ben disappeared behind the door. Tears of pain squeezed out of his eyes when he sat. He looked at his blue and purple swollen wrists, skeptical they would ever be the same.

Ben thought of Jesus having his hands nailed to the cross after the severe beating delivered by the Romans. Good Friday.

I can't compare my situation to Jesus's at all, but I do feel like I can now understand better what He went through at the hand of the soldiers. Is my faith being tested?

Ben broke down momentarily. His heart raced, and he got light-headed. It moved to panic as his breathing became rapid. His limbs throbbed while blurred thoughts ran amuck inside his mind. *Is this a normal reaction?* Ben focused on slowing his breath, coaching himself to calm. He didn't want to show his fear to Jay. *Oh my God, I'm now calling this monster by name! Am I insane?* As his breaths became controlled, he imagined he should reappear before causing alarm to—Jay—his psychotic captor.

"I was beginning to think I'd have to come in there. I didn't want to catch another man with his pants around his ankles, though." Jay sneered. "No man wants to see that unless he has the sin of being queer." He paused for a moment, then continued, "Gotta say, as a man who has had to crap outside or in abandoned buildings for the past three or so years—it's gonna be a real pleasure taking care of business in a rich man's crapper with running water and warmth." He smiled for the first time.

Ben took notice too. "I can only imagine. I'm a spoiled city boy all the way…"

"Exactly!" Jay's voice held harsh rebuke. "That is part of my point. You big-city cons, steal and take advantage of others, all the while you live in luxury. People like me with unfortunate circumstances in our lives have to scrape in dumpsters to survive. My big crime was being born into a poor bum's abusive, uncaring world. One where he held all the power, and I was the receiver of his anger."

"I can't help where I was born, or blame that on the crimes and sins I've committed. All I can do is own them, ask forgiveness, and turn away from what caused me to stray." Ben knew he was pressing his luck, but he also was not one to keep his thoughts to himself. "You're right—Jay. I have stolen." Each time he stated his captor's name, he did it in an overtly derogatory manor. "Jay, I've stolen from clients, co-workers, family, and friends. I've mistreated and made promises to women so I could use them for my sexual pleasure. I've then discarded them without caring that they are human too. I've poisoned my body with drugs and alcohol to the point I can't seem to live without them."

Ben stood bravely without constraint before sitting down in his favorite leather chair. "Most recently, Jay, I kicked a good woman who needed help like I do, out on the streets. And last night, I failed my sobriety robustly without an ounce of remorse until I awoke to my head throbbing. To top all of that off—Jay—I picked up another less, how should I say—valuable woman and used her…I…caved into lust and cheated on the woman I now would give anything to have back. So, in other words—I'm a completely worthless, pathetic piece of shit, who deserves whatever punishment your God-forsaken jar can deal out to me!"

Ben sighed and squeezed the chair arms as tightly as his swollen and bruised hands could. "So, you see—Jay, I don't care what you do to me, Hell, you don't even need to shake it out, just pick the damn tile that makes you feel the best! Kill me. I don't care this morning. I've already lost everything that matters to me—Gina was all I had left worth living for." He leaned forward and dropped his head onto his sweat-drenched chest. "Bring it on—Jay Mr. judge, juror, and executioner who broke the fuck into my home, crying about being a living poor, unloved, fucking picture of perfection. Guiltless, my ass…" the words sadly trailed to nothing with not enough energy left even to cuss out his captor. He expected the game to begin after blurting out his rant and prepared himself mentally, best he could.

Then came the moment which changed everything. Neither Jay nor he was prepared. In the deafening silence and the blank stares between them, the tiniest sound echoed emphatically through the room—the sound of a key turning the latch, unlocking the front door.

Thinking for a moment before the thought crashed inside my brain, it was then I knew who it must be. There had been only one key given out. She still had the key, it was never returned.

Ben's stomach plummeted to a quiet sound, which sucked every bit of air from his lungs. He then looked heavenward and begged an answer from his Maker. He screamed silently inside himself. *No! She's done nothing to deserve this! Why bring Gina into my nightmare! Goddamn you!* There was silence in the room between the moment the sound echoed throughout, and the internal rage within Ben's mind before the hollow guilt rang out within his shattered psyche. *"I'm sorry, Jesus. Please forgive me. Please have mercy on Gina. Take me and enjoy your wrath."* Ben tried to lift his head and open his eyes to see Gina as she entered, but his guilt would not allow it.

Jay shot to the side of the door. A bullet couldn't have beaten him. He drew the revolver from his trousers as the door pushed open, ever so slowly.

"No, Gina. Run!" Ben screamed with every ounce of strength left in him.

But it was too late. The warning only drew Gina in, and the monster shoved the barrel of the gun into her back. He quickly slammed the door closed, blocking her escape.

Ben couldn't look at her. He failed her. Now, she was in the middle of this madness also.

"Benny? What's going on here? Who is this?"

"Shut up! I'll ask the questions around here." Jay poked the barrel further into the small of her back, producing a quick scream.

She looked at Ben for help as she was steered toward the couch across from him. "Benny, what happened to your face? Your hands?"

"Just sit down and be quiet!" Jay pushed her onto the couch, pulling the pistol around, making sure she could get a good look at it. "You aren't supposed to be here. This ain't the way it's supposed to go down." Jay rubbed his face, pulling at his scrubby beard as he paced back and forth. "Why are you here? Why now?" His eyes focused on her shocked stare. Jay punched the wall above her head, leaving a small hole, as she blurted out another short scream.

"Jay? It's okay. Just let her go. You don't need to involve her in this. Let me talk to her. I can take care of this." Ben pleaded.

"I gotta think. Just shut the hell up, everybody!"

Jay's pacing became more sporadic as he jerked one way and then the other. He began to mumble to himself, "What have I done, I've fucked this up. How do I fix this?" His voice trailed back and forth from lucid to gibberish, waving the revolver around as if he were directing an orchestra. In and out of the shadows, he resembled a demented devil dancing around his lair.

***

Gina sat frozen in desperation, unable to catch her breath as she watched in tempered silence, Benny and the madman. She began to shake; Ben watched the fear grow in her face and eyes.

Realizing no one would miss her. I have no family. No real friends—no one but Ben. Gina's head turned toward him and their eyes met, locking for a moment. For what could only be seconds, it seemed she was back with the man she loved, and she felt he returned those feelings in his eyes. *We are together.* The moment was fleeting, disappearing into reality as Jay stopped pacing and towered over them with a mixture of darkness and confusion. She held back a gasp as he waved his gun at her. The madman's searing stares from his evil eyes seemed to burn a hole in her heart. She sensed a wicked grin hiding beneath his long scraggly beard. She sucked in a deep breath to stop from crying out. His filthy odorous scent made her feel nauseous. She gagged out loud.

Jay stiffened as he growled. "I see my appearance and odor offend you?" He sneered. "Well, I reckon that's just too damn bad. You weren't invited to this party! I'm gonna have to figure out just where you're gonna fit in." Jay gave her a once-over, staring at her bare legs that peeked out of the skirt, which was pulled up high, almost exposing her panties. He shook the revolver back in forth in his hand as he forced his focus away from the distraction and back to the situation. His expression showed he despised those human urges that the other sex forced on him.

Ben cleared his throat, pulling Jay's attention back to him. "Jay. There is no reason to keep her here. This is between you and I. Let her go. Please."

Jay burst into a howl. "Let her go? Are you serious? Let her go so she can run to the cops." His smile immediately straightened as he moved directly in front of Ben and leaned in toward his face. "Do you think I'm that fucking stupid, Mr. Richie Rich? I didn't get through life being naïve, boy." His breath invaded Ben's space, and he leaned back. "Now, I'm not rich and fancy like you are, but I have achieved in a lot of ways—ways a grifter like you wouldn't comprehend." Jay straightened up and pulled back. "All of this drama has stirred my stomach. I need food—" he glared at Gina. "Woman, I bet you know your way around the kitchen. Get in there and fix us something. And don't do anything to cause me to use this," he waved the revolver in her face. "I haven't figured out what to do with you yet. You weren't intended to be on my guest list, but we'll make good use of you." He snarled, showing his yellowed teeth.

Trembling, Gina rose from the couch and slowly made her way toward the kitchen as she kept him in her sight. She avoided any closeness to the monster who directed her. She felt if she looked into his eyes, they might see into her soul.

"I wanted to enjoy a hot bath in there," Gina flinched as he brushed her arm with the gun when he pointed toward the bathroom, "but now with what's happened…" Jay growled and spat on the floor. He looked down and rubbed the phlegm into the floor with his boot.

"Let me talk to her," Ben spoke in a quiet voice as he leaned toward Jay. "She knows no one. I'm it. She has nobody to go to talk about this. I can convince her that if she just hides out, I'll get her when this is over."

"I was actually beginning to enjoy our talk, but I don't trust you—and I sure as the devil don't trust her not to run to the cops." Jay hesitated a moment and scratched a spot on his dirty head. "I'm not foolish enough to just let her go, Benny." His tone sarcastic, "That's your name?" He glanced toward the kitchen to make sure the woman was doing what she was supposed to. "I just need to sort out what's gonna happen now. You know I got nothing to lose, so you better keep your friend in check until I have a plan—capiche?"

"I will. I'm begging you not to do this jar punishment to her. Her life has already sucked. Do what you have to with me, but please leave her out of that part."

"I make no promises, Benny." He turned away, ambling his way to the bar in front of the kitchen, and sat down on a stool.

Ben's thoughts swirled as a new revelation came to him. *He's humanized me. He called me by name twice. That has to be good. I have to go slow—keep befriending him. God, please keep Gina safe. Don't leave us.*

28

As they ate, Gina dared sneak a look from her seat and caught a glimpse of Ben. She pushed her eggs around the plate.

Jay held a large clump of the scrambled eggs on his fork while biting a chunk out of the toast in his other hand. He then shoved the eggs in as he chewed the bread. He wasn't used to eating in front of others around a table.

"What did you add to these eggs?" He mumbled through a full mouth of food. "They're delicious, got a sweet taste to them like Cat used to make for me." He looked over at Gina. "You're a good cook. Bet you're hoping food is a way to my heart, ain't you?" Jay smiled wide, showing pieces of egg stuck between his teeth.

Ben looked up and agreed, giving a quick wink. "Gina, you outdid yourself! Why didn't you ever make these before?"

She ducked her head, sheepishly, "They just have a little bit of brown sugar in them. My mom used to make them this way on Sunday mornings when I was young. The only thing she ever did with me growing up—always too busy with her ladies' clubs to spend time with me."

Jay shoved another bite in, and then continued, "So that's what Cat put in 'em. These taste just like hers. I thought this was just a southern thing, not something from a New York City gal."

"My mom was from Georgia." She shrugged then looked back down to her plate. "You know—" she hesitated in a timid voice, "you would be more pleasant to eat with if you'd clean yourself up for dinner…"

"Gina! That's no way…" Ben chided, holding up his hand to stop her.

Gina interrupted, "What Benny? No way to treat a guest? Is that what he is now?" Feeling braver, she sat up straight and turned to Jay. "Maybe take a shower, even shave that wild forest on your face. Who knows what's underneath it? Maybe you'd look in the mirror and like yourself again?" She glared at Ben after speaking out. She noticed Ben give her a half-grin and nod with a wide-eyed what-are-you-doing look in his eyes? She continued. "It's amazing what a little work on one's appearance can do. I don't just wake up looking like this, Mister." She held her hands out, then brought them both down her front. She smoothed her hands down the front of her body.

Ben felt a quiver go through his body. *What was Gina thinking? Did she not see the revolver sitting beside Jay on the dinner table? Did she feel so comfortable that a weapon within a second's reach didn't remind her to be hospitable?* "What are you doing, Gina? My God, let's keep this a cordial conversation..."

"Let the lady finish, Benny. She cooked this meal for us. She deserves to lead the conversation for payment. Besides, she seems to have bigger balls than yours! I respect that." He nodded to Gina then continued, "A little honesty makes this a regular family-like meal, wouldn't you say?" Jay dribbled some eggs onto his beard with the smile that followed his sarcastic tone. "She's right. I wouldn't be catching crumbs then and looking the fool if this damned beard was gone." His eyes gleamed with his short laugh, then returned to a silent direct stare.

"You're either an audacious young lady or very foolish. You don't know who you're dealing with." Jay reached over, running his finger around the grip of the revolver that rested on the table. "I was beginning to feel comfortable with your boyfriend here before you stumbled in to our mix. I reckoned a little congeniality might make this day a little more at ease for us all." He pushed back from the table and picked up the revolver, then rested it on his lap. "You see, I haven't been fortunate enough to share a meal like this with anyone for several years. Been kinda living on my own and traveling the countryside." His eyes scanned back and forth between them as he gave another sarcastic grumble under his breath. "My plan was with Ben and Ben alone. That's changed now." His eyes widened. "I'm not a man that enjoys revision of such things. My rebound changes somewhat when surprise enters the equation." Turning his attention to Gina, he smiled, abruptly changing the subject.

"I don't suppose you have a toothpick, do you, sweetie?"

Gina cracked a smile before taking a bite of toast to squelch her from laughing out loud. "I don't understand just what the hell is going on here, mister—Jay, is it? I mean, you come here uninvited scaring the crap out of us, and then you just wanna sit around the table like a homestyle family dinner? Am I supposed to fear you or entertain you or what?"

Ben shook his head in disbelief. *My God, what the hell is happening here? Am I dreaming or lying in the looney bin being pumped with Thorazine? Wouldn't Gina anger their captor more by playing with him, or was this a milestone in the way this whole thing was beginning to play out? I know she is used to handling unruly and possibly dangerous customers at the clubs—but they had bouncers. Does she know what she's doing? We could both end up dead here.* Ben broke from his thoughts to speak out, "Can I interrupt here and suggest we change the topic? Before something unfortunate happens—Gina?"

"Seriously, Mister, you should clean yourself up with a shower. I'm looking at you up-close and I bet you'd be handsome cleaned up—especially with a little of Benny's aftershave. Keep up the pleasantness, and I might know someone to introduce you to!" she gave him a smile with a quick wink. "And brush that dribble of egg from your beard!"

Ben dropped his silverware on the plate and backed up from the table. Before he thought it through, he stated, "Look at my face Gina, look at my wrists and ankles for God's sake. He's punishing me for my sin. All the girls you know—guess what? They sin for a living! Do you hear what I'm saying?"

Gina interrupted, "Yeah, they sin for a living… and guess what…they are all pretty damn good at it…" She opened her mouth wide in laughter!

Jay guffawed, spitting out more food causing it to hang to his beard again. Gina pointed at it and laughed even harder, while Ben stared at them with a blank look and his mouth hanging open.

"I was a damn good-lookin' man back in my younger days. That's how I snagged my wife Cat. She told me that she fell in love very quickly." He puffed his chest out slightly and wiggled his body in a strangely funny way. "I had a wonderful life with her—her and Billy, my boy." His grin faded as a scowl began to form.

Gina watched the jovial gleam in his eyes start to morph into sadness. "Can I ask what happened—without being too personal? I want to know. I hate when happiness turns into sadness."

Jay scraped what was left on his plate into one last bite. "Don't wanna talk about that right now. You don't care. You're just playing me. He jammed the bite into his mouth with force. As he chewed, he spoke, his voice suddenly somber. "After we eat, I want to look at what record of sinning ole Benny boy has in his brown bag over there." He nodded over toward the far end of the bar, waving his fork toward the bag. "That bag is what made me pick you out of a sea of sinners, Benny boy." He nodded, "I'm curious. It must be something very personal. I could tell by the way you always clutched it so closely."

Gina suddenly looked as if she just witnessed the flicking off of a light switch. The atmosphere went from light to dark with one too personal of a question. *I'm scared but curious. There was pain inside his soul. Maybe more deep-seated than the pain I feel about my past life. I can't help but feel some compassion for him, but I don't know what's driving it. How can he be so terrifying one moment—and in the next, make me feel his pain and sadness? Maybe I can convince him that my desire to know more about his past is genuine? It is genuine, I think. I wish someone had shown me compassion. I wish Ben would, again.*

***

Ben wasn't sure what Jay's reaction would be when he opened the bag. At this point, it could go in any direction. He lost his appetite and slowly pushed his plate away. He glimpsed at his revolver, which was under his mattress. Its new spot was now sitting next to a man whose temper changed as quickly as a mouse scampered for the shadows when the kitchen lit up.

"Let's move to the living room and have a look-see at Mr. Ben's leather bag. How about you get it, Gina, and bring it over to the couch and have a seat? This could be interesting." He looked at Gina with a devilish grin. "Or at the least, entertaining! That's your business ain't it?" Jay grabbed the gun from the table and made his way to the black leather chair facing the kitchen. As he sat, he continued, "You clean up the dishes in just a bit, sweetie. Let's get some business done first."

Gina put the plates down by the sink and meandered over, picking up the bag. It was a bit heavy. She spoke to herself in silent thought. *I know what it contains. I also know it's no laundry list of crimes Benny had committed.* There was a feeling of uncertainty between Ben and Gina as she glanced at his face and placed the leather bag on the table. It now sat beside the Mason jar full of wooden tiles. Gina tried to be inconspicuous as she eyed the jar, attempting to read the words written on them. She managed to spy two and part of another that lay underneath. STARVE, DARK, and one ending in LL. She quickly moved to sit down on the couch beside Ben, which put them both across the table from Jay.

Full light now gleamed through the window, but the temperament in the room remained dark. The conversation was nonexistent at the moment, adding to the uncertainty.

Gina's mind drifted back to the tiles. *Trying to think of words ending in LL, narrowing possibilities down to words about punishment since being made aware of the purpose of the jar. Would I, too, be a participant in Jay's game?*

Jay had seemed to fancy me until I prodded too deep into his personal life. Would I pay a consequence for that? Had I been too brazen with him? And then a word suddenly came to mind. The air felt as if the oxygen was suddenly sucked from the room. She gasped and looked at Benny with instant fear....

Kill ends with two l's. I can't think of any other word involving punishment that did. Any humor once held or thoughts of manipulating a change in Jay's plans instantly dissipated into shattered hope. Her head dropped to her chest as if her neck had been snapped.

Ben watched as the glimmer drained from Gina, ending in what looked like total submission to fate. He rubbed his wrists as they began to ache again. The swelling had gone down, and his ankles seemed to be getting closer to normal. He hadn't hobbled from the table to the couch as much as before dinner. Ben's good thoughts digressed quickly. *But with all of that promising personal news, good feelings became short-lived hopes mirroring Gina's. She wouldn't be able to somehow sculpt a way out of this situation—even using her experience with the type of clientele she had. She'd appeared to give up, and my briefly lived reassurances faded into a slow tailspin of certain death alongside hers.*

Ben studied Jay, who appeared lost in thought. Ben's eyes fixed on the birds' shadows that painted temporary darkness on the stark white walls with each flutter of their wings. The activity rather hypnotized him with a calming mixture of black and white movement. He quietly slid his hands beside him, and he forced himself to try to relax. Convincing himself not to let his mind force him to give up. His heart rate began to slow.

Gina, too seemed to be fighting the urge to surrender and slowly moved her hand on top of Bens. She ran her fingers lightly over his. He returned the gesture by turning his hand and opening his palm, which she quietly nested her hand tightly into his. Their palms clenched together were warm and moist.

Gina, in this bonding moment, realized for the first time that his hand was soft and not one who knew manual labor. A casual and straightforward observation she had never noticed or paid attention. The polar opposite contrast to the appearance of how Jay's hands were, so rough looking, textured with callous and scars. She lightly squeezed Ben's hand in assurance, turning to give him a smile now refilled with hope. It was uncertain, but it was there.

The eerie calm and silence continued. The captor's revolver tucked close to the ready in his lap. The "family-like" dinner conversation and demeanor disappeared into the nescient silence as they sat waiting.

29

Darrell followed his nose to the aroma of fresh-cooked bacon. Opening the door to the back of Ms. Gloria's kitchen, his stomach growled. He was hungrier than he knew.

"Good morning, Pastor, where are Ms. Gloria and my mom?"

"Well, good morning to you too, young man. Care for some bacon and scrambled eggs? They're just like you like them. A pinch of brown sugar to sweeten the taste!" He held up a fork, displaying them proudly. "There are more in the pan on the stove. Gloria and your mom went out this morning. Lady talk, I imagine." He smiled, shaking his head as he scooped up another fork of eggs. "You're getting to the age I'm sure you notice lady gab? There are many times nothing concerning us is shared between women; things we don't even want to hear!" He smiled with a wink as he poked the forkful into his mouth.

Darrell laughed and grabbed a plate from the counter. He leaned over the pan and took a big whiff of bacon and eggs. "These sure are good eggs Ms. Gloria makes. Don't tell momma, but I like em better than hers. She never puts enough brown sugar in them like Ms. Gloria does." He ran his pinched fingers across his lips as if zipping them closed. "And they can keep the chicken squawking to themselves as long as they leave us roosters the eggs!"

Reverend Gabriel almost spit his mouthful out; he laughed so hard. "This conversation is just between us, young man! We would be starving if either one heard that!" He chuckled again, scooting a chair out across from him for Darrell to sit. "We men need some talking time too! Important stuff, though, like cars, football, and hunting. Man stuff." He moved some eggs around his plate.

"I think I'd like all of those things. 'Specially huntin!'" He quietly cleared his throat before continuing. "I remember this one time, Billy asked Poppa about going huntin', and Poppa laughed. He looked at Billy and me square in the eye and said, 'Only kinda huntin' I do is at the grocery store for the perfect cut of beef. I hate skeeters, and anytime I'm in the woods or the glades—I'm the one being hunted and eaten.' Anyways, it was something like that. He never did take us, not once."

"Hmm, well, I just may have to take you. It's not too long until rail season." Gabriel said.

"What the hell…" Darrell stopped short, putting his hand over his mouth for almost swearing in front of the pastor. "I meant, what is a rail?"

Gabriel gave a quick grin with a wink. "It's a ground bird. Not too big. A lot of people don't like the taste, too much like duck—but prepared the right way, it's a delicacy. Mighty tasty.

Better tasting than dove too with a little more meat." Reverend Gabriel's voice raised an octave with excitement. "I haven't been hunting for years, but with you as a partner, I might be convinced to go. They can be tricky little boogers to hit!"

"I'd sure like to try that out, sir. You have any extra chores you need to be done so I can earn going?" Darrell's eyes brightened with anticipation as he broke up the eggs on his plate. He folded a whole slice of bacon and stuffed it into his mouth.

"I'll have to do some thinking on that, Darrell." He started to get up. "I got some preparations for my Sunday message, and then I can do some chore thinking!"

"Thank you, sir. I'm glad to do anything you need."

***

Ms. Cela was working the soup line as usual as she visited and comforted those new and old to the kitchen. She always did her best to make people feel like they had worth in this world. She turned to a new volunteer who was serving beside her. "I try to stay busy, and doin' mission work seems to be the best fit for me. I just love these souls who come through here. Feel so sorry for 'em all. They's all God's children, you know."

Her counterpart nodded in agreement but said very little.

"I try to serve after volunteering here—down to the Women's Crisis Center. They's young ladies workin' horrible jobs tryin' to live. Gettin' hooked on dope and used by men. I ain't sure which is a harder place to be. Seein' this or the other. Lord, help us all." Ms. Cela shook her head with a disparaging blankness in her eyes. "Just gotta keep prayin' and servin' the Lord. I let Him use me for His good as long as my body holds out." She gave a smile, her eyes sparkling with a little gleam of hope this time.

"This city is hard, Ms. Cela. I dunno if I can be seein' all this pain and emptiness in these po folks' eyes." She turned back to scoop a big ladle full of soup and poured it into a man's bowl. His hands were shaking so badly he could hardly keep from spilling what she'd just given him.

"Ain't no long line of people to take yer place, Ms. Shanice. I'd say it gets easier, but our Saviour 'spects me to be truthful." Cela shook her head with a smile. "I say, what else I got to do other than sit on the couch and watch soap operas." She quietly guffawed and then went back to talking to those coming through the line. "You hear 'bout that new poison that's killin' these young kids. That crack cocaine? Some sorta new dope plague. No ma'am, I just don't understand. That Devil is one busy, nasty demon." Ms. Cela shook her head in wonder then looked up toward the Lord. "Help us, Jesus Almighty."

30

Jay broke the uncanny silence by flipping open the flap on Ben's brown leather bag. He slowly pulled the opening wider, "Just what do we have here?" He reached in to remove the heavy book out into the open. He shook his head in disgust as he discovered what it was. "NIV Bible. Just what does the New International Version mean, Benny? You don't mind if I call you that, do you?" His lips curled into a devilish grin.

"It's a brand-new printing of the Bible—a version my brother says makes it more understandable. You're welcome to read it." Benny said in a subdued tone.

"What's all these bookmarks for? Special parts that make the brainwashing easier?" Jay asked with a snicker.

Benny wasn't sure how to answer. "Do you have an interest, or are you just baiting me into an argument to make punishing me easier for you?"

"Oh, Benny! Do you think punishing you is hard on me? After last night?" He looked coyly at him as if he were hinting of telling Gina about Benny's recent sin. "Surely you realize I am a juror who is well aware of at least some of your sins, therefore, as the judge also…" He coughed a bit. "I have no problem with any punishments the jar pours out!"

Benny stopped tempting him with antagonizing responses. "Those bookmarks are scriptures my brother highlighted to help me with my understandings of what God wants for me—and from me."

Ben squirmed a bit and slid his hand out of Gina's. Embarrassment and fear overtook him of where this conversation might go. "I honestly haven't read them all. It's been a slow process for me. Trying to be a Christian and accepting God is not an easy task."

"Apparently not. Why don't you pick one of these brilliant testaments out and share it with us? I'd genuinely like to see what wisdom there is from somebody that can't be proven to have ever existed!" Jay motioned to Gina to come to get the book for Ben.

She got up and took the book. "Ben's brother is a preacher, Jay. Down at a black church not too far away."

"Ah, so he is a brotha of sorts." Jay mocked with a derogatory accent.

Gina handed the Bible to Ben and sat down beside him again. "Still okay if I sit here—Jay?"

Ben set the heavy book on his lap and began thumbing through the marked spots. "Do you want me to read one I have read? Or just randomly pick one?"

"You just do whichever you'd like, and Gina and I will guess if we think you've read it after hearing it." He said with a doubting chuckle. "Let's just make a game of it!" He noticed they lacked acknowledging his attempt at humor by their solemnness.

Ben flipped to the book of Titus towards the back, under the new testament. "This is from Titus, chapter 2, verses 11 and 12. 'For the grace of God has appeared that offers salvation to all people. It teaches us to say no to ungodliness and worldly passions, and to live self-controlled, upright and godly lives in this present age.'" He quietly looked up after reading, cautious of what Jay's response might be.

Jay sat still, as if trying to think how to respond, his forehead slightly wrinkled, his eyes not straying from Ben. After a minute later, he replied, "That seems like a pretty brave choice you made—Benny, knowing what we both know." He then looked at Gina briefly. "It makes me wonder if you are having a hard time earning that grace? Or, are you just a fraud pretending to play a game of believing those words?" There was a brief hush that hovered over them awkwardly. "I wonder what it means about grace 'appearing' to offer salvation to all people? He's certainly not ever appeared to provide me with any. I've always thought that book was full of false hope and hypocrisy—can you show me anything otherwise—Benny?"

Jay leaned forward in the chair, looking into Ben's eyes with a sternness he hadn't witnessed as of yet. It made him quiver. "I was beaten by my daddy from the first day I have a memory. Especially on days when I did nothing to earn those whoopings." His eyes sank deep under his furrowed brows. "Where was this grace and salvation for a young boy born into that dark hell under a man who drank his family's food money and then beat him like it was all his child's fault? Where was that God-given grace to my momma who took the same beatings when she questioned why?" He shook his head in disgust and settled back into his chair. "You got a hard sell to me, Benny. I sure as hell didn't choose to be his Goddamn punching bag. I didn't do anything to deserve, not eating regularly, and hearing my momma scream as my daddy slapped her into all hours of the night." Jay somehow let a tear sneak out from his left eye. Ben focused on it briefly before he mustered a response.

"I can't answer that, Jay. No child deserves such a harsh beginning in life. I don't pretend to know the answers to such questions." Ben put his hand down by his side, hoping Gina would touch his hand again. He needed her comfort. "I'm sorry you were born into that torment. I can't relate to that kind of torturous life. I was on the opposite end of the spectrum. I found my hell on my own and not through the cruelty of my parents."

Gina slid her hand into his again, nonchalantly and unnoticed by Jay. "May I say something?"

Jay nodded.

"I can't relate to your early experience either, Jay. My parents had money and tried to give me everything. I grew up rejecting their world and turned instead to a life I now regret." She shifted nervously in her seat. "I can't believe I'm telling you this. I've avoided the subject for years, but what the hell? What I'm hearing from you guys is—is that the darkness we fall into doesn't come from where we begin in our lives. Good or bad. It seems you came from your parent's miserable life, while Benny and I both came from lives of never really suffering. Yet, here the three of us are—all living a different life. Each of us has our struggles: Benny is a recovering addict, I am an addict who dances naked on a stage to feel like someone, anyone wants me. You? You seem like a damaged man who feels like you're owed something by people like us who you think has had it so great." She tried to look into Jay's eyes and sense his pain. "Your face tells me the pain you have, but trying to look past that, I think I see a man who just wants to get away from his painful memories. That is not anyone's fault, including those who are in this room." Gina looked at Ben and tried to smile. Ben calmly nodded back.

"It's not God's fault if He exists, and I want to believe He does." She took a deep breath. "If there is even a chance that God loves me and wants to take my sin and grief with no questions, and only asks me to believe and turn my life over to him…" Gina turned to look into Ben's eyes. "…Then I choose to believe and give Him control. I certainly have failed on my own rules. I think you should at least give it a try too. Maybe your pain will leave you? What could it hurt? It feels like we all have nothing to lose anymore." Her voice quivered briefly as her breathing quickened.

Jay sat quietly. He seemed to take in every word spoken by both Ben and Gina. Jay appeared to be searching for words to respond as he wrestled with his thoughts. "I…," he stopped. An uncomfortable length of time passed before he continued. He would start to say something, then abruptly stop. He rubbed his eyes and dropped his head for a moment. He studied the revolver in his lap, grasping the grip picking it up and then laying it back down.

Jay's actions added to the uneasiness they both felt. Had they started a reaction that they were going to dread his response? Ben and Gina both wore the question in their expressions with bated breath.

"…I don't know what to say. I came here with a plan…" Again, he stopped speaking abruptly. His legs began nervously bouncing back and forth. "… it was a plan to do you harm, Ben." He stalled. "I'll admit I think you were probably my sacrifice to help take away the guilt I carry." He struggled a minute. "I've carried guilt all of my life." The look in his eyes began to speak to the life he'd lived. "Well, not all of my life. I was innocent for many years, but that is all I can say about that for now." Jay looked uncomfortable as if he had lost control of the situation.

Ben could sense by his tone and appearance that Jay was struggling with that fact. "Like I was saying…" He continued slowly. "… I feel like I can't give that up." He wiped his eyes with the back of his hands. "If I don't finish what I came to do—then what kind of a man am I?"

Turning to glance at Gina, he kept his conversation going. "I've been a failure for most of my life. No one taught me how to avoid mistakes. I made blunder after blunder on my own, not knowing I was wrong until I was standing knee-deep in shit scratching my head." His voice went from speaking low and steady, to breaking up with obvious tenaciousness."

Gina smiled at his analogy and nodded in agreement as she thought to herself. *His personality was changing before our eyes.*

"I don't even know why I'm telling you this. Damn you for somehow sucking my purpose from me!" His voice had started to rise to his aggressive level. And then, all of a sudden, it dropped into silence. That instantaneous quiet was eerie. Both Ben and Gina waited, wondering exactly how to break back into the conversation without losing any ground that had possibly been gained. And then it broke….

"I don't know what to do now?" Another single tear edged out of the one eye that could be seen in the light. Jay again lowered his head into his hands, his elbows planted into his legs. He appeared defeated, yet the revolver remained nestled in his lap.

Gina was fearful of continuing—not being able to read his intent. *Oddly, feeling a strange warmness inside her chest.* Gina let go of Ben's hand and pushed herself up from the couch. She sidled over beside Jay. Resting her warm hand onto his filthy flannel-covered shoulder, she noticed the stains. His clothing more than likely had never seen a washing machine. It didn't matter, though. This stranger, who just mere minutes earlier had brought her fear, now begged her to show him love and compassion. Jay never spoke the words asking for her kindness, yet her actions showed that she was called to give the kind of love one could imagine God gave.

Jay didn't lift his head or move his hand toward the pistol. He just sat with his head buried in his dirty hands, tears rolling out between his weathered fingers.

Ben watched, and Gina's face met his. She saw a look in which he appeared to be thinking that he was missing his chance to overtake their captor.

Jay wailed out into a full, unraveled breakdown. He moved forward, pushing his face deeper into his hands. The revolver fell to the tiled floor with a clunk.

Jay didn't reach to retrieve it, nor did Ben jump up to overpower him.

Ben looked pale, and his eyes were blank. He just sat and watched what transpired in front of him, as a helpless spectator watching God's love defeat a demon of Satan, sent to harm.

Gina softly rubbed Jay's neck. She then moved in front of Jay, bent down, embraced him in a hug, and pulled his head into her bosom.

Jay reached up and put his hand on her back, then pulled her in close, burying his head in her shoulder.

She looked over at Ben again, slowly shaking her head in wonderment of what was happening. Tears rolled down her cheeks, not understanding what she was experiencing herself.

Out of nowhere, the sound of a telephone broke the silence. It rang twice before Jay looked up. Ben's voice suddenly sounded out, **'You've reached Ben Dane's home. I'm not available to take your call at this time. Please leave a message, and I will return your call as soon as I am able. Please wait for the tone…'**

There was a brief silence before the caller began leaving his message: **"Benny, where are you? A mutual friend who works with you told me you didn't come into the office or call today. I'm worried something is wrong. Please give me a call, it's me, your brother…"** Click.

Jay looked up, softly pushing back from Gina and peeked around her toward Ben, who still sat on the couch. "I suppose this is where I say I'm sorry and...."

Jay bent down to retrieve the revolver, holding it by the barrel and handing it in Ben's direction. "...and you go to the phone to call the cops. I won't fight you. I haven't the will or energy or even the reason anymore."

Ben slowly got up from the couch and took the few steps to accept the gun from Jay. "No, Jay, I don't have any reason now to call the police—if Gina agrees...."

Gina released her embrace and reached toward Ben. "I don't feel like we need the police here. No one got badly injured. I think we need to sit and talk over what happened and where we need to go from here. I'm just—confused, sad, happy, I just—I just don't know what I am." She gave a slight smile underneath the tears that were still dripping down her cheeks.

"It's settled, Jay." Ben reached his hand out toward Jay's and helped him up. "I don't know how to tell you this anyway. That revolver has a broken hammer spring and won't fire..." He somehow mustered a smile through all of the emotions he'd recently battled through. "...it hasn't been able to fire since I've had it." He let out a quick laugh. "I kept it just like I got it from my grandfather. I pulled the trigger years ago, and it doesn't fire. I keep it just to scare off intruders." He somehow found a way to smile again. Ben's humor helped dispel the awkwardness.

Jay took Ben's hand and was pulled into a threesome hug. They laughed and sniffled through the tears together.

After a few minutes, the circle began to pull away, and they all blankly looked at each other. No one seemed to know what to do or where things should negotiate from here. It was unchartered waters. It seemed as if they were lost at sea in the middle of the Bronx, New York.

"I don't deserve this, you not calling the cops," Jay stated.

"I'm not saying what you've done is acceptable, Jay," Ben answered. "But I'm saying that something happened here this afternoon—something beyond what is normal. I feel very differently right now. I can't explain it...."

Gina interrupted. "I do too. It feels like an out-of-body thing or something. My insides are so warm, like never before."

"I thought it was just me," Ben acknowledged.

"Me too. I still feel it. It feels—perfect. Out of this world good." Jay shook as he felt a shiver go through his body.

"I have a suggestion, and I don't want you to take this poorly, Jay," Gina said.

"What's that?" Jay questioned.

"A shower and some clean clothes, and maybe you would let me cut your hair and trim that beard?" answered Gina in a question.

"I've been thinking about a good hot wonderful shower ever since I saw it."

"I promise, Jay. You can enjoy as long a shower as you like. We aren't going anywhere or calling anyone except my brother to let him know I was—" Ben paused, "not feeling well today and apologize for not calling in."

"Okay, Ben, I believe you. I don't know why you two are doing this for me. I have a lot to fill you in about my past, though. You may change your mind about me. I hope not, but I won't blame you if you do." Jay sheepishly looked down and away from Ben.

"We'll talk, but don't worry, I'm far from perfect myself," answered Ben.

"Me too," Gina chimed in. "When you're done, we'll have some fresh clothes laid out in front of the door for you."

Jay headed into the bathroom to experience a shower, something he hadn't been able to do for several years.

31

After Jay went into the bathroom, Gina and Ben rushed into each other's arms.

Ben was the first to speak. "I'm not worthy of you, Gina. The way I've treated you, the way I've acted in your absence. But—I know one thing. I know I don't want to attempt living in this world by myself any longer. I knew it was you I needed. I know it's you I want to help get through addiction and for you to help me." He held her closer than he ever had gripped her before. "I don't deserve you, but…" He pulled back from her embrace enough to look into her blurred hazel eyes. "…I want you to be with me forever. I've never been so close to losing the chance to be with the one I love until today." He pulled her back tightly into his body, putting his lips close to her ear as he brushed her hair behind it. "It's you, Gina, God saved me today, and saved you, so I could tell you how much I love you."

She pulled his face around to her lips with both hands, giving him the kiss that sealed his hopes. She leaned back to look into his eyes. "In some crazy way, God used a man like Jay, so broken—to open the way for us to be forgiven and saved." She clung even tighter, finishing her thought in a whisper, "We received Grace today. This is a miracle, Benny. We're the recipients of a God-given miracle."

"I feel like it's our mission to help fulfill Jay's miracle also. This isn't happenstance. We're both stubborn and set in our ways. He shook us both up from our cores—to make us new for each other." Ben's heart raced and still felt warm with God's presence. "My brother will be so happy, Gina. I have caused him so much worry in my past."

"I know. I've hurt my mom too. I'm going to pray for my forgiveness for all the damage I've caused her." Gina's eyes began watering as they held each other tightly.

As she looked over Ben's shoulder, she saw the Mason jar on the table. It was the one strange item that started this miracle, which ended up saving them.

She could see into the contents of the jar, remembering the tiles she read at the top of the pile earlier, STARVE and DARK. The one she now saw had not been visible earlier. The one that sat on top in their place now clearly spelled GRACE. The jar hadn't been moved since the moment she'd first noticed it. She thought to herself, *how can that be?* She started to point it out to Ben but instead decided to keep the secret to herself as a personal message of love from the Creator, whom she hadn't known before tonight. Some day she would share the sign that God showed only her.

***

Ben held the receiver to his ear after dialing his brother, Robert.

"Hello, Robert. Ben here…" He listened to his brother's response. "Yes, I'm fine now. No, it wasn't a bug. It was more of a situation, but it's on the mend now." He listened intently for a few minutes, showing moments of anger and anguish at different intervals. He would start to respond, but then stop as if he were cut off.

Gina moved closer, trying to hear without disturbing Ben.

"Robert, that's crazy! I haven't even missed a day since all of that." He glanced up at the ceiling. "But…I…" He moved his left hand to his hairline, massaging his temple with circular movements of pressure. "No! I don't understand. I've paid almost the entire debt. I have clients that still want to work with only me! This is absurd! This was a circumstance that was totally out of my control—I couldn't—listen to me damn it! I couldn't call!" His voice rose as his anger was almost explosive. "The firm is having me fired by my brother, who doesn't even work there? That's insane! I could explain if you were here face to face. It's not something easy to do over the phone." Ben paced back and forth in quick turns to keep from pulling the phone off of the side table. "So that's it? Final? No recourse or rebuttal, just shuffle me out the door?"

He nodded while answering the questions Gina couldn't hear. She knew it must not be good news by his reactions. She suddenly felt the pain of betrayal from the Creator that she had just praised, thanking him for taking care of them. *How could God spend so much time working to get two people on the right track together, only to throw the investment away?*

"Robert! You know, in this business with what my past has been, I won't be able to work anywhere near here again. My name is more than likely being blacklisted as we speak!" He listened to his brother respond. "Rash? Don't do anything rash?" Ben laughed out loud. "I'm not going to go barging into the office! I guess what I will do—is put my house on the market and get the hell out of this town! There is nothing for me here with what you've told me. If I'm to be renegotiated down to a janitor, I'll not do it in New York City! I have one question—why in the hell did my work have you call me?"

Robert answered. "They didn't ask me, I volunteered. I knew you would take it easier from me. Remember, your boss is a church member of mine? I was afraid your faith may not be strong enough yet to accept Bill's decision of letting you go."

He looked over to see how Gina was reacting. He gave her an 'everything-will-be-okay nod. "My faith? Robert, don't even go there. I'm not the fragile damn flower you think I am. If you only knew how my faith got Gina and me through last night and up just to just minutes ago—you wouldn't question my faith! Look, I have a lot on my plate to think about. It looks like I have endless time to do it now." He shook his head no as he listened, his ear becoming red from either the pressure of the receiver or the stress from the news. "Of course, I will take my time and go through my options, Robert." He paused, cupping his hand over the receiver.

"Is it as bad as it sounds?" Gina asked as tears began reappearing in her eyes. "I can…you know…go back to danci…."

"Absolutely not, Gina! We will be fine, and I'll not have my future wife doing any such thing!"

Gina's eyes widened with astonishment.

There it was, out in the open, hovering in the air between them. We would fight this first battle on the war-field together. We were a team now and not individuals anymore. She grabbed Ben, pulling him into her arms and tucking her head into his chest as close as possible. *He does love me, no matter what. Forever. I will stand behind him through this battle and any other around any corner.*

"I've got to go, Robert. Gina is here wondering what is happening, and I have another guest to tend to." He waited for Robert to finish his words to the wise. "Yes, Robert. I will talk to you after I come up with a plan, or I should say after Gina and I come up with a plan." He turned to Gina, giving her a tight hug with his other arm. "Good-bye, Robert. Yes, I love you too, brother."

The minute the receiver left Ben's ear; Gina squeezed him even more tightly into her arms. "We will survive this, baby. God is in our hearts now. We are together to help each other through this and whatever comes next." She couldn't make herself let go of him.

"I know, Gina. For some strange reason, I feel relieved. I can walk—correction—**we** can walk away from this mess we've been in and start fresh somewhere else. I feel like it is all part of someone's design. All of this is happening for a reason. Most important, though," he pulled back to look into Gina's hazel eyes, taking them in and seeing the beauty and wonderment. "The most important thing is I have you back, and I will never push you away again. I promise. I'd rather die."

"You said..." she cleared her throat a bit. "...you used the words 'future wife.'" She smiled slightly, "was that just a slip of the tongue in the moment?"

He responded so quickly he almost cut her off mid-sentence. "No, Gina, it was no mistake or word of the moment. It's part of the future we both want, I hope. I pray."

Gina laid her head on his shoulder again. Relieved from when she'd come in unannounced and unexpectedly met Jay with the pistol in her back—to this very moment, the tension drained entirely from her body. She spoke only two words. "Prayers answered."

The two sat down on the couch together.

"A lot has happened in the last several hours, hasn't it?" she asked Ben.

"Definitely not a typical Monday. What are you doing tomorrow on Tuesday?" He turned and gave her a wide grin.

"Buying a map of the country to pick out a new place to share with you." She responded with a warm smile back.

32

When the bathroom door finally opened, Ben and Gina glanced up from the couch.

Jay walked out freshly clean, shirtless with a towel wrapped around him, and his scraggly beard was now closely shaved to his skin.

Gina and Ben stared blankly with wide eyes as they took in the artwork which covered Jay's arms and chest.

With his beard neatly trimmed, his face looked much younger, and he was very handsome. Gina tried not to stare at his chest and arms, but the tattoos covering them made it difficult. He was now a walking inconsistency of appearance. He'd been covered with a dirty flannel shirt for the entire time before. If she'd seen him earlier this morning during the frightening moments, she imagined her reaction would have been entirely different. He was such a contradiction of scary and normal. As she gazed into his eyes, they reminded her of the recent memory of the hurt and pain he brought. His eyes weren't as frightening now.

"I'm sorry, but you said there would be some clothes for me to wear at the door?"

"Oh, I'm sorry, Jay, we had kind of a moment out here after calling my brother. I completely forgot about the clothes. I'll get some. We look close to the same size." Ben got up and walked to his bedroom closet, picking out clothes he imagined would fit Jay.

The most casual thing he owned was a pair of khaki pants and a white T-shirt. He picked out a black button-down collared shirt also, in case he wanted to cover his arms. He wasn't used to seeing anyone with such artwork displayed over their bodies. It unnerved him a bit.

When he returned with the clothes, Jay held his hands out. "I think these should fit you. Let me know if they don't."

"I think this evening, we three should go out and celebrate. What do you think?" Asked Gina.

"That sounds weird, but great to me!" Ben's forehead wrinkled as he gave her a funny look. "We have a lot to celebrate, even if it came in such a—bizarre way. This day still has me in a daze. Some food and smiles will be good for all of us, and to step out of here, away from this place—well, it may be helpful." Ben headed into the kitchen. "Do you want some coffee or juice to drink?"

Gina nodded. "Just a touch of cream, please." She held her thumb and pointing finger close together.

Ben returned from the kitchen minutes later with a couple of cups, handing one to Gina. Holding his up in the air towards her, he continued, "Here's to a new life together. Unknown roads are leading to unknown places, together as one!"

She lifted her glass and clinked it with Ben's as the sound of an opening door caused them both to turn around.

"Pour yourself a cup, Jay, and come over here and share a toast."

"You people are the crazy ones. Treating me as if I'm a friend. I just don't understand why you don't want me to be locked up?"

Gina replied. "You have no idea what good this has brought to us. I realize it's hard to understand. We can't wrap our heads around it yet either. But here we are. A sort of Three Musketeers of madness!"

"We want to take you out to dinner tonight and celebrate this new-found gift of life we now share. Is that okay?" Ben rubbed his upper lip and felt dried blood. "I think I probably need to get cleaned up first. I probably look like I've been beate…" Ben stopped abruptly. "Sorry I probably look horrible."

Jay was smiling now, and his face looked completely different with his beard close-shaven. He still had wet curly long black hair with grey mixed in, but he looked like a new person. "That's okay, Ben. I deserved that." He winked. "But, forgive me if it takes a while to get used to this. I don't understand what or where it's going, but yes, I'd love to eat dinner. I'll have to try and remember the manners I've not used for a long time." He looked over at Gina. "Did you say you could try and trim this mess of my hair up, so I can look more like I fit in?"

"I would love to." She smiled. "Let me help Ben get his face cleaned up first, and then we'll go see what we can do. How short do you want to go?" They all walked down the short hallway to the bathroom. "Let me get a washcloth for you, Ben, and a couple of towels and scissors. Jay, could you grab a chair, please?"

"I didn't know you had such mothering traits," Ben responded as he grabbed the towels from the hall pantry.

Gina wet the cloth with warm water and gently wiped up Ben's face. He winced several times but kept watching Gina's eyes as she tried to be gentle. "Okay, Mister, got you all cleaned up." She motioned to Jay. "Step in here, and let's see what I can do with that mop!"

Ben backed out and headed back to his cup of coffee.

Twenty-five minutes later, they both came out to show Ben the transformation.

"Wow, you look fantastic!" As they moved closer, Ben held out his hand to shake Jay's. "You look like a Wallstreet man!" Ben smiled, but it faded when he realized that was what he was this morning, but no longer.

Gina noticed his slight mood change and rubbed his arm, "Benny, you're better than that job. Don't worry.

"Did I miss something? Jay inquired.

"We'll talk over dinner and more when we get back," Ben replied. "Gina, how about Sabino's Steak House over on 149th? It's a quiet little place where we can get a table towards the back." He smiled. "And, the steaks are excellent!" Holding his fingers to his mouth and kissing them, followed by a "Bravissimo!" he laughed. "I'm not sure it's a real Italian word, but it gets the point across that the food is fantastic and worthy of a celebration."

33

Jay quickly scooted around the table to the chair against the wall. This afforded him a view of the door. It was an old trait of any public place he went. Always keep your back to the wall and keep your eyes moving, watching. Old habits were hard to break.

Jay's thoughts began to ramble amuck. *This restaurant was too nice. People in suits. People with too much money. People who looked through him on the streets or avoided him altogether by crossing to the other side. How can I ever fit into this life?* Jay smiled when Gina nudged him as she allowed Ben to seat her next to him. Her smile comforted him momentarily. *Imagining with her old line of work that she too felt awkward in a place like this. The possibility of bumping into customers who had seen her dance naked sitting across the room pointing and talking around the table. She looked the part though in her lovely dress. If one didn't recognize her as a stripper, she'd fit right in with this upscale crowd. I, however, stick out like feathers on a snake's back.*

Ben scooted his chair close to the table and looked around the room.

Jay slowly scooted up to the table and watched Ben's demeanor. His thoughts began to ramble again. *Wondering if Ben was looking to see if any of his friends would see him here with a person like me? Am I just nervous and overthinking things? It feels very different than it did when I'd twisted the doorknob to Ben's house. As the door opened last night to a darkened home, I was vindicated in some way or another that my plan was meant to be. I knew what I had to do and set about preparing the area to complete the mission.*

Ben picked up the menu and said something to Gina.

I can't concentrate. My mind is racing. Thought Jay.

"So, what do you think, Jay?" Ben winked. "It's nice without being too pretentious."

Jay nodded and opened the menu. The first thing that came to his attention was the prices. He could eat for a week for the cost of one entre. "This is much too nice for me. I wouldn't know what to order."

"Look the menu over, Jay, order anything you like. It's a celebration among friends tonight!" Ben then turned and whispered something to Gina, their hands found each other, sliding under the table like new lovers who just found love for the first time.

Jay lifted the menu more to cover his face than to study it. It gave him the cover to slip from sight. His thoughts continued to ramble back to his past. The melancholy showed in his eyes if anyone could see them past the camouflage of the menu.

Jay wanted to be cheery like his new friends, but deep down, he knew he was responsible for his son's death along with a host of other aggressions from his past, horrible sins, both distant and recent. *I'd responded in self-defense to my son's actions against me, but in retrospect, I know my guilt. I'd spent plenty of time while on the run, time to wrestle in my mind, the actions I'd used against my family. I know I'm an intelligent man. I know I own a mean streak and resentment of life. But, I also realize my responsibilities in creating the atmosphere for what happened that Friday evening.*

Living with his actions while traveling alone with no one to consult with all week, brought its tolls. Jay had struggled daily after stepping off that last porch step to begin his fugitive run into the unknown. At first, it was worries of getting caught, but that melted into his brain's background after weeks turned into months of no interactions with the authorities. Not worrying so much about getting caught gave him more time to recount his choices in life and the effects they'd bore on his boys and his wife, Cat. *She was so beautiful and sweet when we met. I realize now that I changed her. My ignoring her and yelling at her turned her into a drunk. I deserved what little suffering for that alone. And my boy, Billy.*

Cat. She was beautiful when we first met. Then she changed my world for the better. I remember struggling with finding any value in myself to share with her. I'd never known such a beautiful life could exist. Those nights together alone. Walking along the bay, going back to that small apartment and making love until the middle of the night. Life had somehow become grand beyond belief.

After Billy came, responsibility entered the picture. So much so soon. I'd faked my way along pretty well until Darrell was born. I don't understand why, but I resented Darrell from the first minute Cat told me she was pregnant again. It was just too much to handle, I decided, especially with his neediness. I never entirely accepted that Darrell was my son. Slowly watching Cat withdraw into herself made me always figure there must be someone else in her life while I was on the road trucking.

Remembering the grilling of the boys, asking about anyone hanging around while I was gone. How pathetic those actions were, even if she was seeing someone—I hold the fault.

I knew I was slipping out of normality the first time I climbed into a dumpster behind a burger joint looking for something to eat. Not too long after running. I didn't think I lived a great life before, but after the night Billy challenged my authority and lost...life had nowhere to go but south. Hell bound.

The first mile after stepping off of my porch, the adrenaline started retreating, allowing my body to feel the pain of running. It was then I knew my reality had suddenly changed forever. Add the hour after hour of emptiness all around, and no one to converse to. What man wouldn't start to go mad?

I would wake up in the night with cold sweats and dreams of my past. I began to find it hard to remember anything other than desolation. I was drowning in solitude and painful memories—wrestling with thoughts of hopelessness and guilt. I tried figuring out any way at all in my mind to blame others for my actions.

It began to awaken my performance of pretending I was the innocent, but all I could do was suppress my guilt and transfer it to anyone else but me. Flashbacks of my father's use of a jar with punishments came back, and soon I was committing the same atrocities my father had done to me. I'd claimed my father's devil. I began taking my feelings of self-guilt out on my boys and building a legacy of fear and pain to pass on to their innocent lives as was done to me. The Cader family tradition continued. How many generations back did it go from its inception?

The night I opened Ms. Cela's bag of goodies and pulled out the Mason jar of peaches was the night I think my madness became my full-time commission—again. I knew it, I fought it, but I caved into it.

My plan grew into a calculated act of total self-destruction. I would exact my wrath on some rich selfish human. Someone with money which was the polar opposite of me, but also soulless. I would dole out my punishment until they drew the new tile of death. The KILL tile that I added to the others. After finishing their final sentence, I'd take my own wretched and guilty life.

Something powerful and unexplainable interceded my enterprise. Here I am now—sitting at dinner with my victims, as if they were best friends, struggling to understand what changed my entire being so instantaneous. It was as if I'd walked into another dimension. Who or what had conducted this—this thing? The two sitting with me were part of the same—for lack of a better word—miracle. But who believes in miracles? Why if some entity had control of such a thing—why would it waste one on me? I'm sure we all will talk about it, discuss its reasons and possibilities, but I'm certain no explanation will ever be possible.

"Hey, Jay! Yoo Hoo. Earth to Jay!" Ben grinned.

Jay looked over as his eyes refocused on the neon light shining from outside, illuminating the front glass of the restaurant. It seemed to cause a bright aura around Ben's silhouette. "I'm sorry, I guess I drifted out there for a minute." He smirked. "I'll just have the chopped sirloin with a potato."

"Jay! We're celebrating tonight." He then looked over to the waitress. "We'll have three New York Strips, all medium." He turned to Jay. "Medium okay?"

Jay nodded, still looking as if his thoughts were somewhere else.

"All medium with baked potatoes and house salads. Thank you for being so patient, ma'am." Ben looked over at Gina and gave her a wink. "The Three Musketeers of Madness! I like it! All for one, and one for all!"

Jay chuckled and leaned forward to touch Gina's and Ben's arms. As he leaned in, he caught a glimpse of himself from the mirror hanging behind Gina's head on the wall. As Jay saw his reflection smiling back at him, it hit him suddenly. He couldn't remember when he'd seen himself smile in years. He didn't recognize himself. He couldn't believe that the smiling, groomed, well-dressed man in the mirror was indeed himself. "I'll be a musketeer with you two any day of the week. I just hope you feel that way later when the new wears off, and I reveal my background. I have a hankering to get it all off my chest before I go see my wife and turn myself in for my past."

It fell silent around the table. Ben's grin straightened. Gina put her glass down, accidentally letting go as it tumbled over her silverware. The rush to grab napkins and dodge the water stream broke up the complexity of the moment.

Scampering to soak up the mess, Gina stared at Jay. "We all have pasts. I imagine mine fits in line with the ugliness yours brings to the table. I don't know much about God, and I'll be the first to admit it. But I have heard from several people throughout my life one thing in particular. He forgives all. Everything. No questions asked; no answers necessary. **All**."

"Jay, I think my brother could be of help here. He knows the Bible through and through. He knows the Lord, and he loves nothing more than to share Him with any who are willing to give themselves to Him. I'll call him. I have nothing but time right now."

The three of them sat and talked, learning little things about each other. Laughing, enduring moments of awkward silence when one didn't know what to say, and helping to steer each other towards the same direction of fellowship and friendship of new-found faith. It was something that none of them genuinely understood yet. Their hearts were all warmed again beyond normal, but none mentioned it. They just enjoyed the feeling of wonderment.

On their walk back to the house, the evening showed signs of spring. There was no wind, and the temperature was moderate, for a change. The sky held stars despite the city lights trying to squelch them into the background.

When they arrived at Ben's, they were all laughing and bumping into each other, just for fun. As the door swung open and they entered the room—Jay noticed the remnants of the night before. The Mason jar sat in the middle of the table. Ben's and Gina's eyes followed Jay's blank stare, and their gleeful expressions turned somber.

"It's okay, Jay. This just reminds us all that it was real." She touched his shoulder. "That part is over now." Gina looked over at

Ben, and his blackened eye seemed more evident. The sight of his bruised wrists brought memories of what happened just this morning.

They sat down in the living room as Ben removed the jar from the table, quietly putting it into the trash container unceremoniously.

"I apologize to you both for what I brought to this house. Ben, I don't deserve the friendship you've shown me. Gina, words can never thank you enough for your encouragement, your understanding, and compassion." He looked down at the floor. Jay felt swallowed up with emotion and the memories that had haunted his mind during the dinner festivities.

Jay cleared his throat several times before beginning the story of his past while Gina sat on one side and Ben on the other. Two hours later, they were all hugging in tears and talking about traveling together to Apalachicola, Florida.

The night came full circle from the early Monday morning, which originated it. Starting with a recovering addict's mistake the night before, then meeting a disturbed madman who'd broken into his home. An uninvited strip club dancer, former girlfriend of the home's owner, who let herself into the middle of complete unimaginable chaos. Then ending in a moment of some sort of orchestrated miracle, affecting them all in unison. Viola!

The Three Musketeers of Madness born in New York City on a Monday was anything but ordinary and one for the books.

34

The morning light poured through the window and caused Ben to stir. As he woke lying next to Gina, he noticed that both were still clothed from the night before with a blanket covering them. He remembered after he had pointed Jay to the guest room that Gina followed him into his bedroom with a somewhat awkward look across her face.

They'd talked about their future and things which had happened in their recent past. "I don't want you to think I only want you for the physical stuff. I'd rather hold off on that part of our life for a bit. Is that okay?" He'd gently touched her waist as he sat on the bed.

Gina sat next to him, looking into his eyes. "I understand what you're saying. I want you to know that I am willing to do whatever makes you comfortable. I love you." She leaned in and softly kissed his cheek. They both lay next to each other, talking about their open future. He barely remembered pulling the blanket over them before they fell asleep. He awoke clear-headed and with a smile as he turned to see Gina's face.

After mentally rehashing some of last night's discussion, several complications needed expertise he didn't personally have. Jay talked about what happened three years earlier, and his desire to make reconciliation. Whatever it took, Jay stated that he would be prepared to accept the consequences with only one stipulation. He wanted to talk to his wife, face-to-face before he turned himself in to the law, which made a sticky situation for himself and Gina. They were now harboring a fugitive from Florida, and they knew it.

Gina stirred, stretching her body before opening her eyes to see Ben, the man who recently shocked her with his plans. He was awake and already gazing at her. Life was new, shiny, and beautiful.

***

Breakfast was prepared with the table set when Jay first entered the dining room, followed by Ben shortly after.

"This meal smells delicious." Jay complimented and then continued, "I could get used to life like this!"

"I know, Jay, I consider myself one of the luckiest men alive," Ben said.

They sat around the table, passing the scrambled eggs, bacon, and toast as the conversation began to move toward the plans which lay ahead of them.

Ben spoke first. "First, I think we need to get my brother over here to help solidify our thoughts of this rather unexpected outcome. I know that's what Gina and I consider it to be, and I'm pretty confident you would agree. Nothing short of a miracle."

They all nodded.

"While this is an incredible thing that happened…" Ben paused for a moment, buttering his toast before continuing, "I want to make sure that we don't lose this feeling of His grace He has given us, and continue trying to search out what this means to our lives." Ben took a bite of eggs while Jay and Gina watched, expecting more to come.

Ben finished swallowing and then continued. "I still have struggles at the moment, I seem to have control of them, but I don't want to fall back into my old ways of dealing with problems."

Gina quickly replied. "I won't go back to the old me. I'm new, and I feel it. My heart is still so cozy warm. I can't explain it! I'll do whatever God wants me to do."

"That's my point, Gina. Like riding a bicycle, we have somehow gotten on the seat without any training. I don't want us to each crash into a different curb and return to the pain," said Ben. "I trust my brother to instruct us. His life has been dedicated to his faith as far back as I remember. I found it rather exhausting in my past, yet today, I find I want to learn more. I know it sounds crazy coming from my mouth as I say it." He smiled. "But that's the way I feel."

Jay chimed in. "I've lived my life, avoiding God and reviled such talk of faith in my past. I've seen it as smoke and mirrors at best, and a way to take advantage of people too small-minded to know better." He paused as he broke his scrambled eggs into smaller bites on his plate. "I feel drawn to this oddity of faith now. I feel a power in my life now like I've never been exposed to before.

"I've experienced people trying to push it on me. My wife tried at one time after she took the boys with her to church. I forbade it to happen again." He dropped his head. "I had dreams last night. Horrible dreams, bringing my past back to confront me." Jay cleared his throat before looking up. "I woke up remembering visions of…" he choked, finding difficulty in continuing. He cleared his raspy throat again. "… visions of each of my family's eyes at one point near the time before…" His voice cracked as he continued. "…before the world crashed in front of me—" Jay squeezed his eyes tight to stop the tears. "…by my hand."

Gina was quick to speak. "Jay, it's okay to tell us anything. Get it out and in the open. I'm not going to judge you. We're all broken in this room."

Jay's voice came out weak and low, not much above a whisper as he recalled his past life. "I remember seeing my oldest boy's eyes. I looked at them one day when he looked up; they appeared deeply inset. Almost shadowy in his face. They were closed to barely a slit as he squinted. I saw hate in 'em. Deep, dark hate." he hesitated. "I knew I'd planted this hate, the moment I saw it. But, I didn't change a thing. I didn't ask for forgiveness or nothing. I just resented him for showing it to me. I tried to tell myself I was making him strong like I was. I knew better, though.

"And then, a day or two later, I watched my youngest. He didn't know I was looking, at least he didn't show it. I studied his eyes for just a second. They were like a puppy's eyes after you smack him and rub his nose in a mess he'd just made. Filled with pain, but not knowing why. Looking up at his master in fear, wondering if he was gonna get hit again when all he wanted was to be loved. I saw weakness in my boy, and instead of changing my way or feelings for him, I scoffed in disgust." He laid his fork down and shoved his plate back, and he just talked. A certain sadness and regret filled his hollow voice.

"It shouldn't hurt the most, but when I recount my wife's eyes, the pain is unbearable." His voice caught in his throat. "She was born with beautiful golden eyes like wildflowers in a field." Tears began to form in his own eyes, and Gina reacted by reaching over and putting her hand on top of his. "When I briefly looked into her eyes on my way out the door when I ran—I saw the pain and slow death they held. It's like if you picked a wildflower and put it in a glass to savor. Instead of filling the glass with water, you filled it instead with whiskey. A flower can't live on whiskey. It'll wilt slowly at first, then more quickly in time. She'd become the wilting flower. The petals fell off from lack of my attention; only the whiskey was in the glass trying to save it. The petals that were once attached, making the flower beautiful, were now scattered in varying stages of dying—some dried to a broken skeleton. Somehow though, there was one petal hanging on for dear life. Clinging, hoping to be strengthened by the love of water instead of the whiskey." Jay broke into a loud wail, his body convulsing as he spilled the last sentence from his mouth.

"Maybe I'm that hope in her tired and dying eyes. She held onto my worthless ass down to the last moment. The flower she once was, which once raised high and happy in the field above all others." He continued, "let the last petal…" His words trailed back to almost a whisper as he grasped to catch his breath. "… fall to the ground…" Jay grabbed his napkin and wiped his dripping nose. "… knowing I'd never be the water she needed."

He cried with his head down and slowly banged it on the table as if punishing himself for his actions. He finally looked up, finishing his thought on the matter. "I did that. I killed a beautiful flower by driving her to drink…" He spoke with a new resolve. "… and then I ripped the last petal from her on my way off that damned porch." He wiped the tears from his eyes with his rough fingers before continuing. "'...Run, baby, run.' she told me. And I did. I ran away, like the cowardly bully I was. There can't be a God anywhere that could forgive a demon like me." His head dropped back down into his hands as they shot his plate across the table.

Gina looked at Ben. He stared back, neither knew what to say.

Ben couldn't comprehend where to go with what he just witnessed. He had felt pain before, and believed it to be the worst anyone could bear. But now he realized those feelings had not been close to real anguish and guilt. Compassion for what Jay lived with spontaneously overtook him.

Ben and Gina looked at each other again, realizing they were way out of their abilities to help Jay properly. Beyond being consistent, loving friends standing with him the entire journey, they knew he needed to talk to a professional.

35

Robert slowly hung his phone up. His forehead wrinkled as he shook his head with worry. After listening to his younger brother's story of his last couple of days, he came to realize how close he'd come to losing him. Not only from falling off the wagon with his addictions, but losing him in a horrible calculated way.

During their conversation, he held extreme doubts. He was a true believer in the power of Christ, but what he heard, sounded like an out-of-this-world battle between righteousness and a dark side. It drove him past his balance of reality for a moment. Ben talked about how God interceded with an evil-driven, Satanic-like man. An individual whom he was befriending? *Was he being truthful with me? Had he fallen off the wagon and dreamed all of this up in a drug-induced state? And if it was real—were he and Gina suffering Stockholm Syndrome by defending this intruder?*

Robert, himself, had frequently witnessed many examples of God's power and intercession in people's lives, but this story sounded too far from the realm of possibility. People changing overnight wasn't possible! Through the power of just one verse? Improbable, if not impossible. The thought made him question his faith. Then it struck Robert like a lightning bolt from a clear sky.

Ben is my brother, sharing this story. It's my brother who God intervened to save! This is a blessing, not a test of truth or fiction.

Seated at his desk, where his most powerful sermons usually came, Robert looked to the statue of Jesus's folded hands sitting in front of him. He closed his eyes and quietly prayed aloud, "Dear precious Savior, Father and Provider of all. I praise You for Your acts of mercy and love. Your gifts bestowed on people like myself, who are not worthy of any of it, thank You, Father. Thank you so much for the miracle You gave to my brother and those who were beside him. Please continue to open doors for them to learn and love and seek You. Father, You, are an awesome God of wonder. Forgive me for my moment of doubt. Thank you for giving each of us redemption upon asking. I praise You and love You with my last dying breath. Amen."

Robert cleared his calendar for the day as he lifted his good Book, the same one that changed his life many years ago in his youth. He gathered a few things, tucked them into his leather bag, and headed out his door.

Friends and congregants of his church greeted him along the way. He tried to keep conversations to a minimum, but when you are a pastor among the needy, you stop and spread hope.

Typically, it was about a forty-five-minute walk at most. That, of course, was if the crowd was thin and there were fewer cordial distractions. This particular trip surpassed the hour mark by at least twenty minutes before he found himself knocking on his brother's front door.

"Ben! You look like you've been run over by a Mac truck! What in the world happened to you?" Robert's concern shown in his eyes as he squinted them, moving closer to look at his blackened eye and slightly swollen cheek. He reached to touch Ben's face, but Ben's hand caught his.

"It's not as bad as it looks, but it's still sore. I'll fill you in later." He moved to the side of the doorway as he invited his brother in, the two embraced and whispered about the grace given. As they stepped toward the living area, Gina came out of the bedroom.

"Hello, Robert," she greeted. "It's been too long since I've seen you. A lot has happened since then." She smiled as she gave him a quick hug, and then headed over to the couch to sit.

"Robert, before Jay comes out, I have—I mean, we have some news to share with you." Ben walked over beside Gina on the edge of the couch. She rose and put her arm around his waist. "Gina and I have begun talking about our future. I've asked her to marry me in an unusual and…" Ben turned to look at her. "…well, a very unusual way, but I've asked her to be my wife, and she said yes before she took the time to think about it!" Ben and Gina gleamed at each other.

"I know this is a shock to you, Robert. It was a huge surprise to me also, but we both realize with all that is changing in our lives, we love and accept each other. We also know we need each other to lean on." Ben squeezed her closer to his side.

Gina locked eyes with Robert. "I know we have a short and quite frankly, rocky relationship. We both feel like a higher power has helped us realize our relationship is strong. I just hope you will accept me into the family as a sister-in-law who only has Ben's best interest in my heart." She never blinked. "I'm not speaking out of dare or authority. I love Ben." She said those three words with a resolute tone as if Robert may challenge her motive. "You have no idea what we just lived through. It brought on a big change in each of us! We are both inspired to be better—to treat each other with kindness and love…" She smiled briefly, looking from Ben and then to Robert. "…We're already one—we just want to make it official in God's eyes."

"Gina, I'm not one who holds grudges, and my concerns would not only be for my brother but also you as well. It's not mine to presume any power over Ben. I just love him and want what's best for him." Robert lightened his demeanor a notch or two. His facial muscles relaxed, allowing his cheeks to droop back to their natural state. He smiled briefly before continuing. "I see an immediate difference in both of you. God can use His awesome power to cleanse our sins and transgressions. I'm certainly not going to stand in the way of what He has opened your hearts to." He held his hands out to them. "Congratulations to you both! I know you realize there will be hard times and decisions to make in your futures. Especially now, with the sudden loss of his job."

Ben motioned to Robert, pointing toward his favorite leather chair. "Sit, brother! This day brings good news!" They all sat down, circling the coffee table in the middle.

A fleeting thought of the jar of tiles, which had held their future within its glass walls, no longer sat menacing on the table. Thankfully, that was behind them now.

"Robert," Gina interrupted, "We both have lost our jobs. I know you never approved or understood mine, but I promise to you today right now, those days are behind me. I'll work in a grocery store or clean hotel rooms, whatever I need to do. Your brother is my only desire, concern, and love. I want you to know this. I will swear it on your Bible if you would like me too."

Ben pulled Gina in closer to him on the couch. "Gina, my brother, isn't going to ask you to do that." He turned to look at him. "Robert, this is a great thing. It's not a worry. This news is the best news I've ever shared! I don't care about losing my job. It was never something I enjoyed doing. It's part of why I made bad decisions. I studied and took this job to please Dad. My heart was never into it from the beginning."

"Ben, I'm not judging you—or for that matter, Gina, either." He smiled warmly. "I'm answering a call from my brother who asked for my help. That's my only motive. Settle down, please, I'm not the enemy!"

"I'm sorry. I guess in the back of our minds; we expected the need to justify our decisions. I've grown accustomed to being scrutinized because of the indiscretions of my past. I'm thankful to be shed of all of that." Ben cleared his throat. "In case you're wondering, I left Jay in the spare room asleep. He is still reeling in guilt, and he broke down during breakfast this morning. I'll call him out after we talk awhile," said Ben.

"I must admit, I can't imagine what you two have been through, nor can I imagine what feelings I am to expect when I meet this man who brought all this to your home."

Gina and Ben then filled Robert in on all of the details they could remember, answering Robert's questions when he asked.

Robert's face contorted into many expressions as he listened to their detailed story. His eyes showed shock and disbelief at many times. He'd never moved so much in a chair, not being able to be comfortable in any position for very long. Finally, he sat still and stared blankly at the two of them as he appeared to be searching for the right words to reply.

Robert spoke methodically and carefully. "Ben, do you remember back about six or seven years ago..." He paused as his index finger nestled into the corner of his mouth briefly. "...the headlines in every paper were reporting a story from Sweden about an escaped convict hold up with hostages in a bank?" He reflected in thought momentarily. "I can't remember the fella's name, but that's not important anyway. He held several hostages—bank employees, customers, and such..." Robert stirred in his chair, seeking to change to a more comfortable position. "...he yelled something like—'The party has just begun, in English,' but this was happening in Stockholm, Sweden. They thought he was a madman. The whole event played out for four or five days as..." He studied Ben and Gina to view their demeanor. "...if I remember correctly, four or five people were held in tight quarters within the vault of that bank."

Gina sat quietly, nestled into Ben's side. Ben listened intently, his body not moving a muscle.

Robert continued. "It seems that being held captive by someone who threatens to harm or kill a person..." Robert cleared his throat. "...but never bringing any harm to them, and allowing them to eat, get up and walk around—if I remember correctly, one of the women had claustrophobia, and he allowed her to walk outside the vault..." He shook his head momentarily and grunted. "...he allowed her to move around with thirty-foot of rope tied around her neck like a leash." He chuckled a bit. "In case he needed to jerk her back inside if she strayed too far!"

"So, where are you going with this interesting story?" Ben questioned as he shuffled briefly around on the couch.

"These hostages, even though they were indeed hostages who had their lives threatened by their captors—became emotionally attached to them. They never got hurt, and their captor gave them the necessities of life and they in return, began to see them as the good guys. It became known as the Stockholm Syndrome." Robert sat up straight in his chair. "A few years later, similar circumstances happened here with the Patty Hearst and her S.L.A. captors." He cleared his throat again.

"Could I get you something to drink?" Gina asked.

"Yes, thank you. Maybe a glass of water, please."

"So, what does this have to do with Gina and me? Are you comparing our situation with those two incidents? Are you claiming we have succumbed to the Stockholm Syndrome?" Ben's voice tightened with sharpness. "You weren't here, Robert! I would think that as a preacher of God's Word, you wouldn't try to put this off as us being bamboozled and possibly be more receptive as us receiving a wonderful miracle from God—that is what you preach, isn't it?" Ben's voice bore a snarkiness to it.

Gina walked back toward Robert with a glass of ice-water. "Settle down, sweetheart. He's just suggesting that there are instances of such things and to be aware…" She handed Robert his glass, glancing down at him. "…aren't you? There are no accusations attached, are there?"

"No, of course not! I just care about you two and want to make you aware that our minds can formulate safe zones and circumstances which help us deal with the unknown to comfort us—and can be false comforts. That's all." Robert squirmed in his chair after taking a sip of his water. "I haven't even met this person you've told me about, and I'm by no means a professional therapist. I just thought I should remind you that these things can happen to perfectly normal people under the right circumstances."

"Okay, we've been made aware. I'd like to move on from here and talk about Jay's future." Ben took a big breath, letting it out slowly and controlled before continuing, "Jay wants to see his wife face to face before remanding himself to the authorities. I know that I am probably in jeopardy because of Jay's likely fugitive status." Ben threw his hands up. "The fact is—I made a promise to help him to the end of this. I promised his meeting with his wife would take place first if I can make it happen."

Robert leaned in close toward the coffee table, separating them.

Ben mirrored his brother's move and leaned forward also. "I intend to keep that promise." He sat back as if he'd won his brother's physical challenge. "The other concern we have is the fact we don't want him to fail, spiritually speaking. Gina and I have each other. We have you and, of course, our desire to continue seeking God." Ben's hands came together, fingers gripping into a double fist. His elbows moved to his knees, and he then placed his chin upon his fist. "You see, I know in my heart Jay has that desire also, he has shown us that…" He looked at Robert with unwavering eyes. "… but what he doesn't have—is a support system. We don't want to see him fall back into his depression and guilt. He has turned to the Light as if the switch was flipped. I'm afraid without us as his support, that switch could be flipped back to the darkness."

Gina spoke up. "He has true value." She smiled at Robert. "I know you, above all, believe people can be redeemed. He's astute. He sometimes speaks as if he were a poet. He was born into a complete and horrid disaster, being mistreated and neglected from his very beginning. I'm sure he has seen things the three of us can't even imagine." She acted as if she were an attorney, making a closing plea for her client. Gina sighed. "What happened that night in his home was not planned. He reacted to his son, who attacked him with a concealed knife. He knows he is responsible for his son dying." Her voice paused, and then in a louder tone, she continued. "Jay is repentant. He's consumed with his guilt. It's what's driven him into this entire dark scenario."

Robert was utterly taken in by their recounting of what transpired over the last couple of days. He would lean in at times, as if he were a fish on a line, swallowing the bait then being reeled toward the fisherman.

"He had found Grandpa's revolver…" Ben held back a smile. "…you remember it, don't you? The one that the firing mechanism was completely rusted. When he pointed it at me—I knew it couldn't fire, but I, of course, never let on."

At other times, Robert

quickly sat back into the leather chair, as if he were a fish de-hooked and thrown back into the water. His eyes portrayed every reaction he felt.

"I see you smiling as if there is humor to be found in this…" Robert shook his head. "…the man had a weapon and wanted to harm you! I don't see any humor about that at all!"

"I see it now, Robert. I didn't see it then…" Ben grinned and glanced at Gina. "…but a lot has happened since then!" He chuckled to himself, not able to control it.

"You're suffering sleep deprivation and the collapse of tension. It's not funny, Ben."

Gina shook her head in disbelief. "He hasn't been like this until now." She looked at Robert. "You're completely correct. None of this was funny."

"I'm sorry, and you are right. None of this was funny. It was scary as hell, and I don't know why I'm laughing now." Ben's mouth fell from the upward curve to a straight line. "Jay was scary and crazy at moments. No doubt…" He leaned forward. "…and in the next moment, he'd go from yelling obscenities to being reflective of his past, to complete sadness. He could turn on a dime." He looked at Gina to concur, and she nodded. "But since we started talking about God—there has been none of that scary back and forth mania. It's like that part of his personality has been…" he looked up and, with one hand, acted like he grabbed something out of his other and tossed it away. "…deleted. Unbelievable, I know."

"I must admit, in all my years of listening and counseling couples and individuals who have suffered all kinds of problems and events in their lives…" Robert leaned forward, his hands clutching the Book containing the Word of God. "This has my mind in a complete quagmire." Robert shook his head. "This man, Jay, obviously is a very tormented and disturbed individual." His tone became deeper with a sharper terse force. "You two, I would think, are still in peril if he should suddenly regress. He needs professional help, and then there is also his guilt to be determined about his family situation in Florida." Robert sat back in his chair, trying to get comfortable with the whole situation, but struggled to wrap it around his brain. "I know you both want to help this suffering man, but neither of you would be prepared to do this in a safe environment with help nearby if this man flipped and became violent again."

"I see how you could feel that way, Robert, I do. I want you to understand, I've already made a promise. Surely in your position, you've at times needed to act on your faith in God alone?" Ben asked in a quiet voice.

Robert sat in pause for a moment, mulling the question over carefully. He opened his Bible, turning it to Proverbs. "I'm going to read you a verse from Proverbs, chapter 12, verse 15." He pulled his glasses down his nose a bit, eyeing Ben over the top of them, before continuing. "I am not trying to provoke you with this, mind you; it's food for thought." He looked back down, "'The way of a fool is right in his own eyes: but he that hearkens unto counsel is wise.'" Robert looked up again at his brother. "I don't read this to provoke anger. I read this because you have sought counsel, and now counsel has been given. What you do with it now is upon your shoulders."

Robert closed his Bible and rose to go toward the kitchen to refill his drink. "You are no fool, Benny. I know your heart is calling out for you to show compassion. You've done that. To trust this man may no longer be a danger may be true or not, but it is an area in which you have no expertise. This can be the foolish part you need warning or counseling on." He put his hand on Ben's shoulder. "I love you, brother, and I don't want you or your fiancé to be foolhardy and suffer the consequences. You can be of help without taking control of the situation on your own." Robert filled his glass with water. "I'm anxious to meet this man. Do you have any other thoughts or questions before bringing him out?"

36

Jay quietly slipped into the bathroom to clean up a bit upon hearing voices and assumed Ben's brother had arrived. He turned the faucet on, cupping his hands underneath, he filled them up. Leaning down, Jay splashed the cold water across his face, clearing the blurry sleep from his eyes. After toweling, he spied the black bottle of cologne he used last night. Using the fragrance gave him a feeling of a man with stature. He picked it up, holding it to his neck before misting himself.

He finger-combed through his newly shortened hair and buttoned up his shirt before tucking it into the khakis he still wore. Looking back into the mirror, he leaned in close to study his eyes and face. His skin seemed as if it had aged a decade over the last three years. The eyes staring back at him looked hollow, yet a hint of hope sparkled in his dark pupils, which blended into the dark green irises. He now wore wrinkles and grey hairs mixed into his eyebrows and scalp. His close-cut beard now looked more like manicured stubble instead of the thick long, wild facial hair he'd had before trimming it.

It was the first time he studied himself. He'd caught glimpses in reflections of glass before, but not inspected himself under bright light and a clear mirror. He wondered what Cat thought of him? *Was*

I gone from her mind and written off as dead? Would there be forgiveness if I promised I was a new man—or was she with someone else? And what about Darrell...?

He shook himself back to the present and then cleared his throat. Getting to the next step of trying to get back to Cat, he first needed to prove his worthiness to Ben's brother. *Can I pull it off? Could I be convincing? This new faith seemed to conquer my demon along with the residual hate.* Looking up again at the mirror he smiled at himself. *I am a new man on the outside, but more importantly on the inside, aren't I God? Is it possible for You to change me?* He nodded at himself in the mirror with confidence or at least attempting to convince himself first.

He turned away from the mirror and stepped out to meet the day's challenge. Wondering how this man would test him? *I wonder if I will be believed and forgiven?*

"Here he is, Robert! Our new friend and fellow redeemed child of Christ." Ben got up and walked toward Jay as he entered the living room.

"Are you feeling better now? You look rested." Gina got up to greet Jay. "Maybe a bit nervous? Don't be, no one here to be uneasy about," Gina said quietly.

"I'm still kind of tired from napping. It's not something I usually do. I'm usually awake and out looking for food by now," answered Jay.

"Sounds like you had a hectic evening with my brother and Gina." Robert responded quickly with intention.

It was warm, and Jay didn't know if it was the actual heat or his nerves, but he rolled up his sleeves, not thinking about the artwork on his arms.

"It takes a special type of person to sit and take that kind of pain—doesn't it? And of course, money. I hear they're not exactly cheap!" Robert again shot jabs at Jay.

For a brief moment, Jay sat in pause and nervously crossed his arms with one sleeve up and his sleeved arm covering it as best he could. Jay remained calm and relaxed. "I see what you're trying to accomplish. You want to see if you can rile me into a fit of rage…" Jay looked directly into Robert's eyes without blinking. "…I thought that was something shrinks tried to do—and preachers of God's Word tried to forgive and offer His love and aid?"

Robert smiled briefly. "Well, it does look like you have some interesting ink …" Robert continued. "I'd love to study it better and hear you tell me about the meanings—they look like they contain a lot of demons and hostility. Do you think any of those demons still reside on the inside?" Robert looked squarely into Jay's eyes. "This is my family that you are staying with. I'd like to make sure they're safe today and not unsafe like the recent past." Robert sat up tall in his chair. "Fair enough?" He nestled back down. "I would like to hear about the tattoos and a little history of what made you become such a full canvas of artwork."

Ben and Gina sat with their mouths dropped.

"I've had enough of this badgering Robert! My God!" Ben got up from the couch. "He is a guest now in MY home. I asked you over to help—not try and bait Jay into some sort of trap…."

Gina interrupted. "This is wrong. This whole line of…this harassing and…this antagonizing our friend…." She was starting to shake from frustration and anger. Her words just got tangled and unable to exit her lips in the way she intended.

Jay watched the theatrics play out before he calmly re-entered the conversation. "You're judging me?" He calmly asked. "It doesn't appear that even normal people…" He held up his hands and used his fingers as quotation marks. "…have some problems being rational. So, I'll be glad to get back to answering Robert's question about my artwork." He remained calm and sat until everyone gained self-control, and silence filled the room. "These are tats that were gotten a long time ago—way back when I was younger. I was incarcerated when I was sixteen years old." Jay paused. "I'm sure you've heard it so many times it becomes a pointless blur—but I didn't do what I was convicted of." Jay lifted his covered arm and rolled up his other sleeve and stretched his arms out before crossing them again.

Robert leaned forward in the chair, "A story you'd like to share?" His voice firm but mixed with sarcasm.

Jay shook his head and then looked into Robert's eyes, "Honestly, it was an entire lifetime ago. I'd like to leave it behind me and not relive it." His voice was calm, but with a tone as if closing a book. "I've been told that when you receive grace from God—you should leave old baggage at His feet..." He spoke with quiet reserve. "... I'm guessing that doesn't mean a thing in this world with people now 'days—does it?" He unfolded his arms, leaning forward, then propping his elbows on his knees.

"Again, I have my brother and his fiancé to be concerned about. I've heard what the night entailed, and I can't just turn my cheek to see what happens. I know as a man of God, that this is to be expected of me..." Robert sighed. "...but I'm human, Jay. And I have relevant questions about you."

"Oh, I understand you have questions..." Jay smiled with a hint of disgust in his eyes. "...I have questions too. I experienced something amazing inside of me the other night. Inside my heart." He looked at Gina and Ben. "I—I should say, we received something none of the three of us can label." He looked back at Robert. "Ben told me that you were the one he trusted to go to—to search out and explain what we all experienced." He pointed to Ben and Gina. "They are the ones who should have questions about my authenticity. They are new at this whole Faith thing like me."

Jay returned his gaze to Robert. "But instead, you choose to turn your back on your ministry to doubt and bait me." He dropped his head for a moment as if he were collecting thoughts before looking up at Robert again. "I'm sorry, but this feels like I'm being interrogated, and by a man of God at that." Jay's anger bubbled up a little, but he looked as if he was handling it with control. "It just doesn't give me much hope for the future that He's promised me, does it?" Jay started to hoist himself up off the sofa as he finished, "Feels to me like you've already made judgments in your mind that are set like concrete—and I'm sure feelin' the sentence coming head-on like a racing truck barreling down on me." He was on his feet facing Robert, looking down from his standing position. "Yes sir, I can feel the heat from the headlights. Just moments before the collision." Jay turned and looked at Gina and then Ben. "I won't be hanging around for the calamity that's soon to follow." Jay started toward the front door.

"Robert! This is not why I invited you over here! I asked for your help, not your condemnation and arrogant attitude. Where did this come from?" Ben scolded Robert with a frown. "Jay, wait!

Don't leave, please!" Ben looked back at his brother. "My brother will be leaving, not you. Please come back and sit down."

Gina quickly stood up and moved between Ben and Robert. "C'mon guys. This is crazy. You need to just settle down and stop puffing up like buck roosters, or whatever. There's too much testosterone in this room right now!" She reached for each of them. "I thought we were past this now that we all have a relationship with God." Gina was near tears as she wiped the moisture from her eyes. "I want God to be a good thing inside of me. He's liable to see us failing this soon after accepting Him, and move on to someone else." Sobbing, she grabbed onto Ben and tucked her head into his shoulder.

The room went silent except for Gina's muffled lament.

Jay turned around and returned, falling into the sofa with his hands covering his face in shame.

Robert held one hand up to his head as if he were battling a headache. He turned to Gina, "I'm sorry. I am not acting like a Christian at all right now." He turned toward Jay and continued, "I apologize, Jay. I speak from the pulpit almost every Sunday, condemning us for being smug and judgmental, and I have been the harshest hypocrite I know today." He wore a sincere demeanor. "You're right for questioning me, Jay." Robert shook his head as he stepped toward him. "I did try and bait you into a trap so they could see how your rage could take control of you. I had no right. I judged you from before I even saw you." After walking over to the couch, he held out his hand. "I'm truly sorry. If you can find a way to forgive my actions—I'd like to start fresh."

Jay stood up and offered his hand in return. "I can forgive and also ask for the same. I know what we went through is unbelievable. I wouldn't have believed it if someone offered up a story like ours." Robert took Jay's hand and pulled him closer into a quick hug. He then turned to his brother, who was already now standing close with Gina in tow.

Holding his other arm out with a slightly wet face, he pulled Gina and Ben into his arms, "Please forgive me. I'm just a worried overprotective brother right now who let his foolish pride get in front of the man I pray to be." He hugged them briefly, then stepped back and faced them. "I've set the poorest example ever and disgraced my faith by treating and questioning you the way I did. I'm a preacher of the Word, but as imperfect as any living creature. I fail like anyone else."

Jay sighed and reached around the larger frame and, with one hand, patted him on his shoulder. "Truth is— what I've done in my past and to your brother—I deserved your lack of trust. But I sure appreciate and accept your apology." He studied each of their eyes as they stood facing each other. "I would sure love if we could just drop this sack of rocks right here at the Lord's feet..." He looked down for a moment then scanned them once more. "...and move on to the next steps of my making amends to my wife and son..." Jay sniffed then rubbed his nose. "...before, I turn myself in to face my mistakes in Florida."

"Do you feel like telling me that story of your past? I'll do my best at taking it in the way I should have from the beginning." Robert asked.

Jay was quick to respond. "Sir, I AM innocent of what the state of Florida tried and convicted me for when I was only sixteen. I have no idea who robbed and killed Ms. Lila Pasternack, but it sure as hell wasn't me. That sweet old woman took me in, off the streets. I ran away from a dad who beat me for no reason other than his enjoyment, and I was alone. She fed me and gave me a warm bed to sleep in." Jay spoke softly, almost a whisper as he reflected his past aloud. "She was more of a mother to me than my flesh and blood momma. I'd sooner it was me lying dead in that house than her." Jay sank back onto the couch. "Ten years of my life when I was just sixteen, were stolen from me. Somewhere out there is the guilty one who not only robbed and killed my friend but stole every dollar I'd been saving from hard work so I could make something of myself." His words were calm and deliberate, spoken with the integrity of a Deacon.

Robert sat back down slowly into the leather chair. "I believe you, brother Jay. And I am sorry life dealt you such a hardened hand so early in life. Indeed, I am truly sorry. Please forgive me."

Robert's judging overtones, which were so aggressive earlier, were now missing from his voice and manner.

***

After an hour or so of discussion—friendlier and more to the point of helping Jay instead of convicting him, Ben broached a different subject with his brother.

"I know you won't approve, but Gina and I have been talking. We are planning on moving out of the city." He searched Robert's eyes to see his reaction. "Things will be tight until the house sells, but thankfully I still have some reserve cash in my account. I'd like you to reassure your friends that I will continue to make my restitution to them. I won't skate out on my obligations. Thankfully, our father paid off this place, so when it sells, and I expect it will sell quickly, we will have the money to start fresh."

Robert responded, "You have proven yourself to be worthy of your word by action. Mother and Father would be proud. I know if they are looking down, watching, they are wearing smiles of relief and happiness." He smiled. "Do you have any ideas of where you will settle?"

"We are almost to the point of closing our eyes and putting the finger on a map. Then again, if our plan to take Jay to Florida works out, we may look around there. Warm weather sounds fantastic. I've always heard a lot of New Yorkers move down to Florida to retire, not that I could do such a thing at such a young age!" He laughed. "But we have no idea. We just feel like our stay here has concluded, for now, at least."

Robert asked, "What will you do for a living?"

Gina chimed in. "Start over in that area also. I'll find something to help out while Ben decides. He's smart and resilient! If we get established and can afford it, I'd like to go back to art school. I don't know why I ever threw the opportunity away that my parents offered me." She looked over at Ben, pulling his hand close and cupped in her lap. "It feels like the world is just now opening up, displaying itself to us for the first time. At least that's how I feel. It's incredible!"

"I'm happy for you. I'm thrilled and thankful for this revelation in all of your lives. God can do wonderful things and open magnificent doors to those who love and give him control." Robert started to get up. "I'll be praying extra for each of you. Jay, I make myself available to you anytime you need." He reached over to shake his hand and then pulled him up into a hug once again. "I need to run now. I've got others to visit. Keep me posted and Ben, I've got a good friend who is a great real estate agent. He'll get you the best price possible."

"Thank you, Robert. I appreciate that."

Robert moved over to pull Ben and Gina up. "Gina, I'm happy for you two. I did have my concerns about your intentions back in the past—those reservations are washed away clean. Welcome to the family, and I will help in any way I can."

Ben grabbed Robert after all the hugs and good-byes, then walked his brother to the door.

Robert leaned in close, speaking softly, "Congratulations, brother, and welcome to the world God planned for you. Call me soon; I have some news that will surely help you. I think I should share it on a more personal level than in a group." He winked, leaving Ben to shake his head sideways, giving his brother a curious smirk.

"We'll talk soon, Robert, that I can promise." He closed the door, wondering what his brother meant? "Well, this was an interesting morning," he mused. "Rough start, but good finish!"

They all looked at each other and then smiled. "I'm glad that's over!" Gina said.

Ben chimed in. "You are! I was the fish in the sushi roll! You were merely dessert left to watch the main course get eaten alive!

Gina giggled. "Yes, the attention did seem to be on both of you. But guess what? We survived, and he didn't even complain about you moving!"

Ben nodded. "Yes, I've got some things to wrap up before we can leave." He pulled Gina close and gave her a peck on the cheek. "I'm going to run for a couple of hours—you two be okay while I'm gone?

Gina pushed him on his chest. "We'll be fine. I'll get Jay's help picking out something to cook for dinner tonight, and we'll go get it at the market." She smiled. "Don't be running off without me!"

Two and a half hours later, Ben hadn't made it home.

Jay kept hearing a loud car horn. It was almost like a pattern. Honk, honk. Silence. Honk, honk, honk, and then repeat. He got up from Ben's leather chair and went over to the large front picture window. "Well, I'll be a sonova…!" He cut his sentence short, trying to work on cleaning his language up. "… Gina! You gotta come see this!" He continued peering out at a big white convertible Caddy with bright red seats. It was no warmer than thirty-five or thirty-six degrees outside. There was Ben, with a huge grin, sitting behind the wheel of a huge Cadillac Coupe Deville and with the top down and a big scarf wrapped around his neck! He was waving as big as he could and honking the same pattern over and over. It was one loud tri-tone, beautiful sounding horn. It screamed comfort and class! It kept burgeoning the excitement in Jay, and he couldn't stand it any longer without jumping up and down like a little kid getting a new toy! "Gina! Come out here. You have to see this!"

Gina finally opened the door to the restroom. "What? What's all the excitement! Who in the world is making the racket outside?" She hurried to the window to see what Jay was so hysterical about. "Oh my..." she turned to Jay with her hand cupping her mouth, "...that thing is a land yacht! It's bigger than our bathroom!"

"We better get out there before he runs the battery down, honking the damn horn!" Replied Jay. They both raced to put on their coats and headed out the front door.

Ben got out and shut the door as they came rushing down the steps to him. "What do you think? A 1969 Cadillac Coupe! It's got everything in it. 471.653 cubic inches of torque and speed! I've always wanted one but no real need or anywhere practical to park it. But we aren't going to live here anymore, so I splurged! She's low-miles and in great shape, ready to head out on the highway, southbound!" His grin was as wide as the white beast's footprint.

Gina just stared at it from front to back and then back to front. "We could deliver a busload of kids to school in this boat!" She laughed.

"Jump in Musketeers! Let's go for a spin around Manhattan!" Ben opened the passenger door and folded the seat forward. "Jay, climb in there and spread out!" He folded the seat back up. "Sweet Gina, your ride awaits you! My name is Benjamin Dane, and I'll be your chauffeur for your riding pleasure today, Miss." He closed the door with a deep clunk and skipped over to the driver's seat. "I'll crank the heat up, it's not going to help much, but it'll be a beautiful view today, kids!"

The classic white monster growled to a roaring display of power as Ben pulled quickly into the lane, then sped off up Morris Avenue.

Ben checked the rear-view mirror, spying a grin across Jay's face as his eyes darted back and forth, viewing the city from a different perspective for the first time in his life. Gina scooted across the seat and swung her arm around Ben's neck. They roared off out of sight into the blur of New York City's people, buildings, and lights.

On the drive, the three chatted and made plans on how to get to Apalachicola and when they should go. It was the main topic of discussion, and nothing held them back.

The sunset was beautiful, and it was an awesome sight to drive under the skyscrapers with the top down, watching the pink, orange and yellow reflections in the tall buildings glass windows. When the sun began to drop behind the buildings, it became too chilled to continue riding in the open air.

Ben rolled up to the curb to call it an evening. "Can you two be ready to go in the morning? We can get you two some clothes once we get down the road. I am ready to say good-bye to this Big Apple."

Gina asked, "Can you take me by the Alibi Room so I can talk to Meesh before we leave? She was feeling down about the world, and I told her I wanted what you'd found, Ben—your relationship with God." She playfully pushed him as she continued, "I told her if I found it; I was going to share it with her." She shivered from either the cold or excitement. "I want to show her it's out there. I want to tell her what all it brought me and what it can do for her. Can we?" She stared at him with her hazel, puppy-dog eyes.

Ben looked over and smiled. His heart surged a beat with the reminder of what God had indeed given him. "Sure, we can, sweetie. We'll stop on our way out. I probably ought to call Robert and let him know too."

Gina cooked a wonderful meal while Ben dialed his brother to let him know they were leaving for Florida in the morning. "Hey, big brother, how are you?"

"I'm living the dream and tending the flock." He chuckled. "You sound good tonight!"

"Yes sir, life is grand, and that is why I called."

"Yes? Should I start worrying?" asked Robert.

"Nothing like that. I just wanted you to know that I picked up a used car, and the three of us are headed out for Florida in the morning."

"I had a feeling I'd be getting this call soon. No negative signs of setbacks, are there? Jay is still doing okay and on track?"

"He is doing incredible, no worries, we'll be fine. I just wanted to tell you the house will look tiptop, and your friend is welcome to show it anytime he likes. I'll call and check in to see if I need to come back and sign anything or do any paperwork. We'll keep in touch and keep you informed. It's not a disappearing act, I promise!"

"I know that now, Ben. I'm comfortable enough to share what I wanted to talk to you about—if you like and have a minute?"

"Oh yeah, I'd forgotten. I'm surprised because it sounded so clandestine!"

Robert laughed, "Well, I'm not sure you ever really knew that Dad and Mom left us some money in our inheritance. Dad had written stipulations in his will—and don't be upset. These were his decisions, not mine."

"Yeah, it's okay, just spit it out. I won't hold you responsible. I was the problem child during their last days. I'm sure they gave anything to one of Mom's charities or clubs that they were going to leave me."

"He left yours in a trust, and left me in charge of managing it, until, in his words again, 'He's ready to grow up and not waste it on drugs and women every night.' I see significant changes in you, Ben, and I know Dad would agree you are ready and responsible."

"Robert, I'll have the money from the sale of the house. We'll be okay. I'm not mad if you needed to use it or donate it."

"Ben, listen to me, brother. I'm telling you that you have an account that holds your inheritance—all of it. I never touched it. It's been safe and growing equity."

"Okay."

"You don't have to be in a hurry to sell your home if you don't want to. Your account is quite sizable."

"For crying out loud, just tell me. How sizable?"

"Are you sitting down?"

"I'm sitting in my favorite chair. The one you always grab when you visit. So, how sizable?"

"$876,948.78, as of yesterday."

Ben's phone was silent. It was quiet for 36 seconds, and some change according to Robert's wristwatch. "Are you still there, Ben?"

"I'm here. I—uh. I'm—speechless. I didn't know they had that kind of money? I—I also can't believe he or they would want me to have this—kind of inheritance after everything I did."

"Ben, they loved you. They were worried that you would either end up dying before they did, or you'd squander it if they left it to you in the shape you were in back then. Dad set this trust up with explicit directions to take care of you, and if you pulled through your irrational lifestyle, to make sure you knew they wanted you to be cared for."

"I thought they hated me, Robert. I would have deserved it if they did." Ben's eyes welled up with tears. "I never meant to hurt them with my foolish actions or to put them through the hell that I did. It hurts they didn't get to see me change before they...."

"They know Ben. I know it. They're up in Heaven overflowing with pride. They know you've come home—the Prodigal Son returned, and the money is the fatted calf. Now just promise me you're going to be all right and be safe. I love you, little brother."

"I will and Robert—thank you for not giving up on me. Thank you for being there for me, big brother. I love you, more than you'll ever know."

"Keep in touch, Benny. When you get back or if you get an address, let me know, and I'll get you all the paperwork you need. Hold off on the house for now?"

"I'm sorry, Robert, but if we do come back, I don't want it to be here. List it. We'll talk again soon."

Click.

37

Ben lay in bed next to Gina, staring at the ceiling, too wide awake with the news his brother told him, along with the excitement of tomorrow's trip.

"Gina, I have to tell you something."

She rolled over to face him, her lips inches away from his. "You can tell me anything, Baby. Anything."

"Robert gave me a rather surprising bit of news tonight."

"I was wondering when you were going to say something. You've been aloof all evening. Even Jay picked up on it at dinner."

"First off, I have a confession."

"You don't have to do this. Remember what Robert said? Jesus has forgiven all of our sins, and we should leave them at His feet."

"Jesus forgives, but I also want your forgiveness and understanding." Ben sighed and looked away for a moment. I'm a recovering alcoholic who fell off the wagon the night Jay showed up at my house. I'm an addict who will struggle my entire life." He looked back at her again. "I've been a horrible womanizer as far back as high school." He moved his hand over to clutch her arm.

"Gina, I brought a woman to this house that night I fell off the wagon. I woke up knowing I betrayed myself, and more importantly, I betrayed you...."

"Ben, you ended things with me. We weren't a couple. I wasn't innocent after I left, either. I came back though, because I saw you change before my eyes. I wanted what you seemed to have and what I saw in you. It certainly stings but I forgive you, and I hope you forgive me too. My heart is already yours, forever."

"But, I'm what the oddsmakers would call a risky bet. I'm sorting through so much baggage. Are you sure you want to tie yourself to such a living hazard like me?"

"Benny, I knew before that you were all of those things, and I know life is still going to push us both to the limits of temptation. I suffer most of the same struggles you wrestle with." She moved her hand to touch his and clutched it tightly. "There is a big difference since then. We're new in spirit. We have the highest power in the universe on our side now. Jesus will be with us to see this journey through—together."

"I love you, Gina. I am so sorry for the things I've done and the words I've spoken to you—for tossing you out when I wanted someone to blame. Will you forgive me? Completely?"

"I forgave you the afternoon I let myself in and saw you sleeping in your chair. I wanted to wake you up and hold you, but I was afraid. I wanted to warm you by lying beside you, but you looked so peaceful. I covered you with a blanket and sat crying on the couch, watching you sleep in a peace I wanted so badly to share. God answered my prayer. I love you, Benjamin Dane. Through good and bad, healthy, and not. To the end, Benny."

He looked into her teary eyes through the blur of his own. "Gina, the minute we get out of town, I want to find a beautiful church and make you my wife. Will you marry me?"

"Yes, a million times over."

38

The Cadillac was warmed up and loaded, ready to try and find Meesh, so that Gina could say good-bye.

Jay also asked a favor. "Could we stop by the Woodycrest Methodist Church on west 166th Street? I want to say thank you to a woman I know. I need to let her know I'm okay. She's a sweetheart who helped me without me understanding at the time. It's a food kitchen down in the basement of the church. She feeds us homeless folks and gives hope." He paused. "She tried to tell me about Jesus, and I got angry and stormed out. I want her to know it sank in finally, and I found Him."

Ben pulled onto the street and headed toward 166th Street.

Jay sat back in the plush seat, a smile on his face mixed with a bit of apprehension. He looked up front and saw Ben's eyes looking in the rearview mirror and responded with a wink, "All for one, and one for all. The Three Musketeers of Madness!"

They all smiled, and Jay reached up to touch each of their shoulders.

Ten minutes later, the Cadillac pulled up to the side of the road and parked. As Jay looked around, he saw familiar faces in the line. "I can go alone if you like. I know it's probably uncomfortable if you've never been here."

Gina turned to look squarely at Jay. "Absolutely not! We go in together. We're this close," she said, showing her thumb and pointing finger about an inch apart. "Not gonna lose you in the crowd when we're this close. Come on, show us around. I want to meet this wonderful angel of a woman!"

They climbed out of the car and headed over to the shrinking line of people.

Ben gazed into the eyes of those he passed and those in front of him looking back. The pain and despair in their eyes spoke loudly. Some wore thin coats while others just wore layer after layer of clothing, probably every stitch they owned. Their frosty breaths were noticeable as they shivered standing in line.

Some grouped, looking like birds on a wire, chatting quietly back and forth as if old friends meeting at the usual spot. Others stood in silence as if they were lonely islands sprinkled about in an ocean of desolation. Hope was absent in many of them in their cold and gray faces. Some bore facades, anxious to give an illusion, the deception they were strong and in control of their circumstances—despair in the middle of this chaos-filled world.

Gina had once experienced small moments of what she was seeing in front of her. She was homeless in a different kind of way in her recent past. Some of these faces struck her at the core.

Ben's eyes showed the shock and lack of understanding of how people could survive in these conditions. His eyes opened to this dark side of humanity for the first time. His happiness for what his future held, mixed with the emptiness he saw. He sensed a pain that felt different, standing amid the lost and forgotten. Ben was seeing them up close and personal for the first time. The news stories he'd watched never stirred his compassionate side as it did today.

Gina looked closely at Ben and mustered a smile across her face. "It's not the world you and I are accustomed to seeing, is it?"

"My God, Gina, it makes me wonder why God allows this to happen?"

Ben continued side-stepping in line down into the stairwell of the church where one could smell the delicious aromas. It was enticing, and his stomach called out in a growl, even though he'd just shared a meal among friends.

As Jay moved close to the open door at the base of the stairs, he peeked in around the corner. Looking between the bobbing heads of those being served a meal, he tried to spy Ms. Cela on the volunteer side as she doled out meals. Jay didn't see her. It would only be a couple of minutes before all three would be well inside the building where he could move around the room and look for her.

Ben continued to study the different people as they sat around the table eating the meal they'd received. He noticed families with small children up to middle teens. He turned to Gina again. "I'm just sick. There are so many, and the children…"

Gina responded. "I know. The world is a harsh place for a lot of people ever since they started cutting the funding for mental health and putting it on the states. They talked about this at the Women's Crisis Center a couple of months ago. It's sad." She looked around, "Did you see where Jay walked off to?"

"No, I wasn't paying any attention. Too busy looking around with my mouth hanging open. He's probably found his friend and is talking someplace quiet." He pointed to a table in the corner. "Want to go sit? I'll try to see if I can get a couple of cups of coffee?"

"I'll be there in a minute. I'm going to go look for Jay."

"Don't run off." He winked and smiled.

She smiled and rolled her eyes as she turned and meandered across the room, looking through doorways.

Jay walked around the corner toward the kitchen, where he spotted his dear friend. "Hey, Ms. Cela!"

She turned and looked Jay's way, "Hello there, young man. What's yer name? I haven't..." She squinted a bit as she walked up to him. She acted as if she'd lost a distant memory of whom he might be. She looked him up and down. "I feel like I should know you, but..."

"It's me, Billy... Billy Jay! I kind of ran out on you a week or two ago. You pulled me into the chapel and started trying to tell me about Jesus."

"Oh my, Mr. Billy! You shaved yer beard and cut yer hair! You sure 'nuf clean up mighty fine!" She gave him a toothy grin and reached to hug him. "I been wonderin' whatever became of you?"

"I've been busy praying and asking for forgiveness, Ms. Cela. Jesus gave me a miracle! I mean a real honest to goodness miracle! And I owe a good part of it to you, ma'am."

She pulled him in tight and squeezed him as she whispered in his ear. "I knew I saw somethin' special in you, Billy. I've been prayin' for you, and I'm so happy yer soul is safe. You keep up with readin' a Bible. I got extry if you need one."

"That would be special, ma'am if you have an extra. I'm headed back to Florida with some friends to finish up some healing of damage I've caused. I suppose I can put all my past at His feet after I ask forgiveness from my wife and boy." He pulled back from her so that he could look at her dark, wrinkled, and sweet face. "I would love a Bible to remember you by every time I open it up. I'd also appreciate some more prayers, too. I know I'll be needing them."

"I sure 'nuf will pray for you. I'll go git that Bible and a jar of my sweet peaches for the road." She smiled at him as she turned to head back through the doorway.

Jay cocked his head for a minute at the thought of that jar of peaches and quietly said to himself. "I don't reckon I'll be needing those anymore." *Those damn peaches she gave me in that Mason jar the first time brought a sudden desire that I thought was dead. Lord, help me bury those memories—and the urges that still come to me at times. Make me strong to fight off those feelings.* His fingers drew into a fist, squeezing each with all of his strength. Jay willed his muscles with calming thoughts to release his fists before anyone noticed.

As he waited for Ms. Cela to return, he heard Gina cry out.

"No, that can't be!" A burst of sobs came through the doorway where Ms. Cela had just walked.

He and Ben met at the same time to look through the door. Ms. Cela was on her knees at the end of the hallway, comforting a bawling Gina who was practically sprawled out on the floor, sobbing uncontrollably.

Ben ran and squatted down to hold her. "What in the world is wrong, Gina? Are you okay?"

She continued crying, bursting louder at times.

Ms. Cela turned to Ben. "I told her I was sorry 'bout Meesh, a friend of hers. I'm sorry, I had no idea she didn't know." She shook her head as she rubbed Gina's back. "Gina, sweet darlin', I'm so sorry, child. She's in a better place now. It's gonna be alright, honey."

Gina looked up. "But I didn't get to tell her I found what I was talking about," she sobbed. "I wanted her to have it too. I found Jesus, Ms. Cela. He's given me so much in such a short time." She dropped her head into Cela's lap and broke into tears again. "I wanted her to come with us…with us to Florida." Ms. Cela dug a hanky from her pocket and handed it to her. "I knew I could make her see what I had now if she went with us."

Ben ran his fingers through her short black hair. "I'm so sorry, Gina. I don't know how to make this better?"

Jay squatted down and touched her back. "I'm sorry, Miss Gina. I know it's hard. Losing a friend is something I don't know much about, the only person I know about losing is my oldest boy. I know it's different, though. Can we all hold hands and pray? That's what we should do. Isn't it, Ms. Cela? God helps us in times like these, through friends."

Gina looked up with a weak smile beneath the dripping tears. "That's completely right, Jay. And I am with my very best friends right now." She sat up, wiping her face with her coat collar. "Let's pray together, all of us." She said as she held her hands out, grabbing Ben's in one and Jay's in the other. Ms. Cela completed the circle by holding their other hands and began to pray aloud.

"Lord God almighty, You and you alone got the power to bring good out'a the bad. Help us understand the meaning of these losses we suffer as your children. We know we be like the patches in a massive quilt. We can't possibly see or understand what each patch chosen will hold in the end. But we can rest for sure knowing You got the plan. A plan that ends in a beautiful piece of work, with Your purposes fulfilled all across this world. We pray in our final time; You will reveal to us Your love and meaning. Until such time for each of us, please comfort us and cover us with Your undying love and precious grace. Praise God! Amen."

Gina opened her eyes and gently spoke aloud, "Ms. Cela, that was the most beautiful prayer I've ever heard anyone pray. I know Meesh heard it too. I know she's sitting up there with God, looking down on us right now with a smile." She hugged Ms. Cela tightly. "I'm going to miss you, and I couldn't have heard the sad news about Meesh from anyone but you. Thank you. Thank you for helping her and all the others with their addictions and problems."

Gina let go of Ms. Cela and introduced her to her husband-to-be and her new friend Jay.

"Oh, my goodness-gracious, I know this one here, Ms. Gina" she said as she reached over and squeezed "Billy's" hand. "This one had me prayin' extra, day and night!" She smiled at him so big, her gold tooth shined bright. "You kids take care of each other. God knows what he did when he put us all together t'day. We's a part of his quilt patch together!" Ms. Cela smiled clutching Gina and Billy Jay. She looked at one then the other. "You two are friends in Jesus…what 'bout that?" She shook her head. "What 'bout that!" Ms. Cela looked sternly at them a moment. "There's mean stuff on these streets today. You hear the words crack cocaine, and you run, you hear? It's killin' lots of my friends here."

"Ms. Cela, you don't have to worry about that with us. I promise." She reached over one more time for another hug. "I'll never forget you, Ms. Cela."

Ms. Cela said, "Hold on there, Mr. Billy…" She walked around the corner and reached into a cabinet. She came back with a beautiful worn brown leather NIV Bible. "This is one of my Bibles, Billy. I underlined my very favorite scriptures, along with some scribbles of my thoughts, 'bout how they affect us. You read this, and you'll be wearin' God's armor. Protection from the evil of men's hearts." She put it into Jay's hands and then cupped her hands over his. "You're a special man, Billy. Don't you forget it? God's got a plan for you in that beautiful quilt He's creating every day."

Billy Jay reached over and pulled her into his arms. He hugged her as if his life depended on it. "I love you, Ms. Cela. You helped turn my life around. I'll have you in my heart every day."

As they left, the three walked through a sea of suffering souls who Ms. Cela fished in every day of her life. Her nets were always ready to cast out to save as many as she could pull in.

Gina looked over at Jay. "Billy? I didn't know you knew Ms. Cela. More of the miracle, Jay. What more proof should we need?"

"I know Miss Gina, and yes, my first name is Billy—same as my oldest boy's was. I was using his name, but Jay is what everyone else knows me as."

Gina shook her head. "Too crazy for just coincidence."

Ben grabbed Gina's hand. "I'm sorry about your friend. Are you okay?"

"I'm with best friends now, I'm good." Answered Gina.

Gina and Jay both looked back at the same time to catch one last glimpse of Ms. Cela. She was already back at her usual way, helping and loving the lesser fortunate of the world as if she'd never missed a beat.

Ms. Cela was the Big Apple's Mother Teresa. She died of a massive heart attack three days later in the basement of the church she served every day without ever missing. Some of the folks that witnessed her passing swore they saw angels carrying her soul upward to the heavens—passing through the ceiling as if it weren't there. Other's say they heard the sounds of Gabriel's trumpet playing.

Gina and Jay didn't hear the news of her passing.

39

The mood was different in the car as Ben found his way to I-95, crossing the Harlem River into Morris Heights and then across the Hudson River. It would be their last sight of Manhattan Island.

They didn't have a schedule to maintain. Ben figured it would be close to nineteen or twenty hours of drive time. It would be a trip of leisure—a chance for the three to get to know each other in conversation and grow their oddly-conceived friendship.

Jay turned back to look at the disappearing skyline of the Big Apple. His face showed a reflective mood, and Ben wondered what he was thinking, but didn't feel comfortable breaking the silence to ask. He knew Gina was hurting from the news of her friend's passing. Ms. Cela told them Meesh was found in the parking lot near the club where she worked. Her arm still held the dangling hypodermic needle. Her body turned blue by the frigid night temperature. It appeared she had passed all alone.

Jay gazed at the back of Gina's head while she stared out through the window, watching the city disappear into a blur from the past.

After several minutes of the deafening quiet, Ben reached up and adjusted the volume before turning on the radio. "How Deep is Your Love" by the Bee Gees was playing. Ben slowly turned the volume up to blank out the whine of the road. Neither Jay nor Gina showed any acknowledgment. They both continued to watch the world go by, as the broken white center lines continued to roll beside the Cadillac as it roared on down the highway.

Ben's thoughts were amuck also. He'd never ventured out of the city much except for vacations as a kid with the family. There were seldom business trips as he already lived in the heart of the nation's finance world.

He thought about his father. He pictured his face. It was amazing that between his brother and him, he looked most like his dad. Robert was always more stable, like their dad, but he looked more like mom, or mother as she preferred to be called.

He was torn from his thoughts when Gina broke the silence.

"Are either of you guys thirsty?" Gina's voice seemed to shatter through the barrier of solitude that had formed in the car since they'd climbed in.

"We can stop and get something. Are you two feeling okay?" Ben asked. "We need to liven up this trip. This trip is supposed to be our last hooray…" He knew he shouldn't have said it that way the minute the words left his mouth. He knew Jay must have mixed emotions about the trip. While it hopefully would bring him back to meet with his wife and son, it also meant facing his past and his running. The previous record of prison time and the circumstances would surely be hanging over his head heavily. The courts would not see the present-day version of Jay, which Gina and he saw blossom into a new man. They would see a dangerous repeat offender. A short-fused menace, but he most certainly was not that image any longer.

Ben shook his head a little with his thoughts as he flipped the blinker on and pulled off the toll exit for Woodbury Heights, NJ. Turning toward the town, he pulled into the parking lot of a small hole-in-the-wall looking café.

Once parked, Ben turned to face them, "I know this whole thing is crazy. We will get through it all. Jay—the fight for you isn't over with us once we get there. Gina and I will find you an excellent attorney. It's going to work out. God hasn't brought you this far to let you wither up and disappear." He reached back and grabbed his hand. "If we can come this far together in such a short time, we can face and endure what comes next—together. Okay?"

"Pray for me. That's all I ask. I don't deserve it from you, but I'm thankful." Jay smiled, and his eyes lit up slightly brighter than the second before. "I could sure use a Pepsi right about now, though!"

"Me too, Jay, me too." Gina and Ben responded, almost in unison.

Sitting around the table, all three sipping from their drinks, Jay opened a topic for conversation. "So, Ben—when are we gonna get there?"

Ben looked up, straw still in his mouth, "You've got to be kidding me…"

Gina shot Pepsi through her nostrils as she snorted out a laugh.

Jay smiled ear to ear. "Never gets old, does it?"

Ben replied, "Actually, it could—and rather quickly with only two hours under our belts!" He smiled, followed by the same from Jay and Gina.

"Just thought I'd attempt to lighten the mood!" Jay joked. "It looks like I succeeded." After they settled back down, he continued, "Seriously, this feels odd, but to me anyway, it feels—I don't know, seasoned."

Gina added, "I know what you mean. Like a favorite pair of shoes that you put on, but you realize they can't be that comfortable because they're brand new! Yet they are."

"Never started a friendship like the way this one got started!" replied Ben. "This friendship feels special. It's indescribable and surely unbelievable to anyone we would tell! My brother may be the only one that ever gets it, and even he struggled at first!"

"I wish he were with us to help me understand the scripture in this book," Jay said as he lifted his Bible from the table. "At least it has Ms. Cela's underlines and added thoughts."

Back in the car and on the interstate, their smiles and conversation continued. The awkward quiet passed for the most part as they continued their talk about God, their experience with Him, which drew them together, and how to continue to seek Him further.

"I say we stop at a church this Sunday, no matter where we are on the road. Let's visit the first one we come to." Gina suggested.

"We have a day and a half. Let's look at the map and guess where we'll be," answered Jay.

The bond between the three grew tighter with each mile. Sometimes Gina sang aloud with familiar songs on the radio, begging them to sing along. At times, all three broke out in song laughing together, mimicking school children on a playground during recess.

***

Darrell lay in bed with his quilt curtain pulled closed. The realization that his father was out there in the world somewhere entertained different scenarios in his mind. The questions seemed to dominate his thoughts. Sometimes fear, but other times he wondered if the evil somehow had withered and died inside of his poppa.

His mother did her best to try and comfort him at moments, yet give him his space at other times. It felt like he was a pin being juggled in the middle of a circus ring. All eyes were watching to see if he would fall to the ground where they would be ready to run and quickly pick him up before the crowd noticed.

He suffered a hard time concentrating on his schoolwork and some of the less friendly classmates who picked up on his internal strife. High school was already a change he'd struggled with. Battling off those who took joy in picking on him, made the days more difficult to manage. He found it difficult to hide those challenges from his family. Being seventeen in a small town with people who remembered the "incident" was no picnic. The whispers he'd grown up hearing, the looks of shock he noticed when out shopping in the small-town market, and all the collateral damage caused by that "event." Now to realize he held hope for the last three years for something which would never be possible, added more pressure to the balloon in his head already overfilled with helium, ready to burst.

***

"So, do you think there is a lawyer out there who can help me?" Jay asked. "I'm expecting to be locked up for a long time. I know I may be there for the rest of my life."

"When we get there, I'll start looking for the best attorney there is. I'll call Robert and see if he can get a good referral from those he knows. We're not going to give up. Don't you dare give up either! As I said, I refuse to believe the Lord put us all together under the circumstances we came through, just to take away everything and leave you dangling. We have to keep praying and listening for answers. Keep our faith in Him." Ben spoke with assurance.

Gina reached back for his hand. "Do you want me to sit back there with you? Or would you rather sit up here?"

Jay stared at the back of her head, momentarily. Thinking to himself. *She sure does seem to want to touch me a lot.* He thought back to some of the times she had rubbed his back or cupped his hand. His body began to react to where his thoughts led. Jay responded abruptly. "No, I'm fine, just have these nagging thoughts and fears jumbling around in my head." He held her hand and looked at it uncomfortably. "I keep picturing Ms. Cela's face. It gives me comfort, knowing she thinks God has special plans for me. Maybe it's to be a speaker of God's word to fellow prisoners?" Jay tried to concentrate as his mind wandered back. *Her hand is so soft, softer than I remember Cat's being. Picturing Gina running her fingers up and down his back as she sat in the back of the Cadillac—Ben still driving and oblivious to what they were doing. She ran her hand over the top of his lap, brushing his belt buckle....*" J

Jay snapped back to reality as Gina said, "Stop! You doing this to yourself isn't going to help." Gina squeezed his hand tighter and smiled. "No matter what, your piece of the quilt will be beautiful. Like Ms. Cela says, someday His plan will all make sense to us. Your portion of the quilt is surrounded by mine, Ben's, Ms. Cela's, and the Lord's. You're surrounded in love. What may feel like a scrap right now is becoming a part of a beautiful creation. That—is what Ms. Cela was talking about."

"I know, it's what I heard too, but my fear is what I feel. Which is stronger—hearing—or feeling?" Jay pulled his hand away as nonchalantly as possible from Gina and picked up his Book, which Ms. Cela gave him. *Mixing feelings of God and the feelings Gina is putting in my head makes me struggle.* He began thumbing through the pages, reading bits and pieces of phrases. "Such a large book. Ms. Cela says it is full of wonderful stories that will give us answers. She also told me many times, the verse she needed would be pointed out to her. Do you think that's possible?"

Gina replied, "I now believe after the power and warmth I felt the other night, and the change it's made inside of me—anything is possible."

Ben agreed. "Jay, you remember what was in your heart and soul the night Gina let herself in? You'd made plans of possibly killing me. Remember the strangely quiet and warming calm in the room after you asked about the verse I read?" He glanced back at Jay in the rearview mirror. "Do you still have the feeling of hate inside of you?"

"No, Ben. All of those ugly feelings are like they were washed away in one big wave." Jays mind drifted. *I'd lied just now to my friend. I did remember those feelings when Gina showed up. I'd fought urges then to take her into the bedroom and have my way with her while Ben was tied up in the living room. Those feelings are supposed to be gone now. Why aren't they? I love Cat—but with Gina—the way she touches me—her touches make the feelings very different. Dangerously different. They are feelings like I'd had in my past. My past no one knows anything about—that past I buried under the surface. Hopefully, to stay.*

"Exactly! A miracle for me, for Gina, and most assuredly for you," replied Ben.

"Maybe the answers are all in this book? I may have the time coming up to read it front to back." Jay replied. Again, Jay fought with his thoughts. *My mind is suddenly bouncing back and forth. Why is this happening to me? I haven't had urges like these for years. They make me feel dirty like I did in the closet when Ben brought that girl home—the one he did nasty things to through the night.*

Gina retorted, "Jay, that's the devil mixing in with God. You, Ben, and I should take the time to read it. Don't have yourself locked up in prison before that time possibly comes." She reached back and patted his hand in assurance, ending with a quick rub. "That time may not come. Who knows the future in this car? I would never have seen myself here with you two in a Cadillac, headed to Florida!"

The men agreed.

The conversation quieted down while the road noise lulled Gina into a nap. Jay read through Ms. Cela's Bible, while Ben looked as if he were lost in his thoughts. He looked straight ahead as he steered the big beast steadily down the road.

About an hour later, Jay looked up to see Gina's head nestled against the window, using her coat as a pillow. Ben was listening to the radio, glancing ahead down the highway.

Jay scooted forward and leaned on the front seats back. Ben barely acknowledged. Jay looked over at Gina. Her blouse had come unbuttoned, leaving her cleavage exposed. Jay glanced back at Ben to see if he'd seen him look. Ben still stared straight ahead. Jay looked out of the corner of his eyes, trying to see down her shirt further. He noticed part of her lacy brassiere, and his lower body reacted. Jay quickly looked away, feeling as if he'd been caught in the act. He scrambled to retrieve his previous thoughts.

"This book is hard for me to follow," Jay said quietly to Ben. "I don't know if it will become clearer with the more I try to read it, or maybe I'm just not smart enough to understand?"

"My brother says it takes time and commitment to understanding it. He has told me God will open my mind to the understanding of His Word. But I know what you are saying. Every time I try to read, I find myself going over the same sentence over and over."

"I've found some verses I like. One, in particular, I am going to try to remember, word for word. It's from Phillippians Chapter 4, verse 6. 'Do not be anxious about anything, but in every situation, by prayer and petition, with thanksgiving, present your requests to God.' I hope He answers my prayers and takes my fear away about seeing my wife, Cat."

"You said she told you to pack quickly and run, didn't you? That must mean she still held feelings for you," answered Ben.

"I've made so many mistakes. How could Cat remember the good times we shared when we first met? The evil inside overgrew and took control. How could she trust me again?"

"Those are questions I can't answer. Keep praying. God knows your heart."

Gina began to stir, her eyes slowly opening. "The sunset is beautiful! Look at those colors with the puffy clouds." The sun was fading, and there was a beautiful skyline ahead. "What city is that, Benny? It's pretty." She looked down and noticed her blouse unbuttoned, looking over toward Jay, leaning on the backrest. She rebuttoned her shirt, noticing Jay was peeking from the corner of his eye.

"Richmond, Virginia. I thought we would pass through it, then look for a motel on the other side. Sound okay? I'm ready to take a break for the night!"

"I can drive too, Ben. I drove a semi-truck for years!" replied Jay, glancing back to Gina with an out of place devilish grin.

"I know, Jay, but I don't want to chance you getting pulled over before we get there."

"Probably a good idea, I just feel bad not contributing anything."

Ben pulled off the interstate into Petersburg, VA, thirty-five minutes later, and found the Hotel Petersburg. He got two rooms for the night.

***

Gina lay on the bed, watching Ben get undressed. Curling her short hair around her finger, she posed the question tugging on her heart. "Are you sure you love me enough to marry me?"

"What kind of question is that, Gina? Of course, I do!"

Gina thought to herself how Jay seemed to be paying more attention to her than Ben was. She thought about how she'd caught him watching her button her blouse back and wondered how long he'd been watching her before she woke. And that wicked grin he gave her after saying he could drive too. Was that some kind of sexual innuendo, or was she just used to picking up on that kind of bar talk at the clubs from men?

"I was just wondering. It seems like you try to avoid me at night. I just worry that's all."

"Gina, I love you. I knew almost immediately after I asked you to leave," Ben sat down on the bed beside her. "I'm not avoiding you. I just want to put this part of our relationship on hold until we get married. I know it may seem foolish since we've had a past concerning sexual relations, but I want it to be right this time. I want our love-making to be blessed by God."

Gina pulled him in for a close squeeze, "You just made me love you that much more, Benny." She let go as he climbed in under the sheet. "I have a rather uncomfortable question, too," she paused.

"Yes?"

"Do you ever notice Jay looking at me? You know—in ways that maybe he shouldn't?"

Benny rolled onto his side so he could see her. "I have, and sometimes it makes me uncomfortable. I assumed it was just me being jealous."

"I guess I shouldn't be so—you know, me. I mean, I'm naturally a hands-on person. Partially from my job—but mainly because it's just the way I am. I don't mean anything by it. I hope he isn't taking anything from it." She laid her hand on Ben's side and lightly ran her fingers down his ribs. "Now, with you, Mister! I mean something by it!" She giggled.

"Maybe just try to slow down a bit. I haven't seen anything out of line yet—you are something to enjoy looking at!" Ben winked wickedly. "Different subject, Babe…you know, I never told you the news Robert shared with me?"

"I didn't want to push. I knew you'd share when you were ready to. It doesn't matter to me what it is, good or bad. You're stuck with me!"

"Oh, it's good." Ben beamed. "It's going to help us get an excellent attorney for Jay too."

"Well, now, you have my attention. Are you going to share?"

"My father left me an inheritance I knew nothing about. He instructed Robert to put it in an account until he felt I was capable of being responsible." Ben pulled back to look at Gina. "The amount is kind of amazing. We don't have to worry about the future if we act wisely." He winked. "And when the house sells, well…" Ben stopped and watched for Gina's reaction.

Her eyes wrinkled up as she held up her hand, motioning him to stop. "Benny, you don't have to tell me. It's yours, and I don't need to know. I'm not with you because of the money or your house. I'm here because you give me hope about the important things in life now. Not those other things. I'll still love you if we have nothing but each other." She reached over and pulled him back into her arms. "I hope you know, deep in your heart, as I do."

"$876,948." He whispered into her ear. "Not including the house."

Gina didn't know how to respond. A feeling of numbness began to come over her, but she pulled Ben closer, and they fell asleep with him under her arm. They nestled together like spoons.

40

Gina fell asleep, exiting reality and entering into a surreal world. Her eyes were jerking quickly back and forth like a very swift-paced metronome.

Her semi-consciousness melded into the dream she began living—just as she'd discreetly entered into Ben's home uninvited.

In reality, Ben lay quietly asleep beside her, experiencing occasional heavy breaths and sighs just barely audible over the whir of the ceiling fan above them.

Back within her illusion, she'd just unlocked the door and moved toward the living room, where she was startled by a hard object pushed into the small of her back. Quickly assuming it was the barrel of a gun, she felt the heat of someone's breath readily mixed with the dankness of their scent, causing her to wretch. She quickly understood the danger she'd put herself into by trespassing.

For a moment, she recognized Ben hog-tied in a kitchen chair that sat out of place by the living room coffee table. On the table sat a jar with something inside it. It was visually impossible for her to make out the object within. Her glance at the situation did not allow.

Ben's head was slumped motionless and appeared to have blood dripping from his chin.

The intruder shoved the blunt object deeper into her back, speaking in chopped up words—"Bedroom, now, shut up"—which pointedly rolled over her left shoulder in a mist of pungent odor. She obeyed what she was told. She peeked down the hallway toward Ben one last time before being shoved through the doorway and into the darkness of the bedroom, lit only by a glint of a streetlight fighting the darkness to shine through the window. The curtains were quickly jerked shut.

Gina stood shaking, afraid to turn around or move until she was ordered to do so. Her nipples pressed hard against her shirt from the cold and fear that caused her to shiver.

"I hadn't expected such an enticing sight tonight! Makes for a serendipitous occasion, wouldn't you say?" The stranger quietly chuckled to himself in a low, raspy voice. "I don't normally appreciate surprises, but I'll happily deal with this one." He lightly dragged the barrel of the revolver down the small of her back. "And now, I'm gonna ask you to start taking your clothes off—real slow. Kind of like you're at the club—just for me, okay, sweetie?"

Gina could feel his eyes scrutinizing her as she began to slowly lift her shirt over her head, exposing her lacy, transparent bra. She'd worn rather scant and naughty undergarments, hoping to entice Ben tonight. She now thoroughly regretted her decision.

"It's okay, honey..." his low rough voice made her skin crawl. "... I don't think your boyfriend is gonna mind." He paused as he watched her slowly bend over to unstrap her heels. "He's kind of—tied up at the moment." He snickered at his shot at humor and then drew a deeper breath with a moan. "You are a sexy thing. I believe we need to add some light to this show to appreciate your fully—shall we say— attributes." He had to adjust himself before he walked over toward the wall, feeling for the switch and then flicking it up, bringing a harsh light that forced them both to cover their eyes until they adjusted.

Back in reality, Gina stirred in her bed and moaned quietly. Not the moan that was brought on by pleasure, but one that spoke of terror and regret. She tossed back and forth as Ben lay motionless in sleep next to her, oblivious of the terrorized state she was experiencing.

"Aw—that's perfect..." The intruder's eyes were glazed over, drunken with lust as he directed her naked body to crawl across the bed and position herself on her back. His trousers bulged even more as he unbuttoned his shirt, displaying the readied anticipation of what was to come. As he dropped the shirt to the floor, it revealed a human canvas of inked paintings showing darkness and evil goblins covering his chest and arms.

Gina was terrified and shivered profusely. The only thing covering her body was the thick tension of fear surrounding her.

"Please don't do this…" she quietly begged as she turned away from him, but he continued to remove his belt. "…please don't."

The tattooed captor let out an evil laugh as if calling out to the other predators of his victory. He unzipped his pants, letting them fall to the floor—and stood silently like a hawk on a towering branch of a tree. He scouted for his prey. His eyes locked as he finger-combed his long greasy hair back, mocking the feathers ruffled on a hawk. Like a bird of prey that just spied his meal from above, he launched his descent onto the foot of the bed. The intruder made his way up the mattress, and instinctively engaged his target's most precious and vulnerable region.

The musky scent that filled the room began to overtake her senses. In her past, she had been the stalker. The customers sitting around the stage were her victims, drunk and boisterous. She was used to filling the room with an atmosphere overflowing with lust. She would move her body seductively around the pole and stage enticing her prey as she would play peek-a-boo with her fleshy body rippling to the music.

But she always got to call the shots and draw the line when to stop. Armed and muscled bouncers were still nearby to protect her. She didn't have that advantage tonight. She was the caged animal who had to perform, hopefully, to save her life. A huge quiver rushed through her body, causing her stomach to rise and fall as her back arched up from the bed.

"The anticipation is making you jumpy, isn't it?" His rough hands were running up each leg from her ankles moving north.

The muskiness turned to the smell of sweat and soured clothing; the closer he moved toward her face. She fought the urge to vomit even though her stomach begged her to concede with the rumblings deep within.

His hands moved all the way up to where her legs met her torso and then suddenly stopped. His thumbs pressed harder on the insides of her inner thighs, edging very close to her private region.

Gina bristled.

Closing her eyes tightly, she silently pleaded for Ben to break free and save her. She knew deep down it wasn't possible. She pictured the way Ben had looked as she was quickly rushed past him before being forced into this chamber of rape. Gina wasn't even sure Ben had seen her or knew she'd been forced into the bedroom.

She wanted to fight but knew that her struggle would only excite her captor even more. She instead lay as still as possible, showing no emotion, which her assailant could interpret as pleasure. If this was going to happen, she wanted it over as quickly as possible.

She knew since she was a stripper—he probably assumed she had no problem with having sex with whoever performed it on her. It was the cost of the job. A job that was full of assumptions by men pent up with urges but couldn't get dates without paying.

She was just an object of lust to whoever had charge.

Tonight, that was him.

Strippers were just presumed an economical means to satisfy men's deviant sexual pangs of hunger and fantasies. We were objects to tuck dollars under our panties, affording them cheap brushes of our flesh with their roaming fingers. This monster was likely a regular customer at one of the clubs she danced in. If she were alive when this was over, she'd find this bastard and have him killed. She knew guys that would do this for her.

She imagined he probably shared a dirty, broken-down apartment with a homely wife filled with snot-filled kids who knew nothing of his illicit evening's activities.

The captor's hands moved down each leg this time until they were just above her knees. He forced her legs apart and in the same fluid movement, pushed them upward, leaving her treasure fully exposed for his view.

Her stomach rolled again, and she convulsed and quickly wrestled the act of vomiting.

Her movement drew her attacker in closer as if he deciphered her wrenching as desires.

He inhaled her scent through his nose, catching a sweet smell of cherry blossoms mixed with her body's dankness. "Hmm, cherries! How did you know that was my favorite perfume? Especially when it's mixed with a lady's smell." He laughed with an evil growl.

In her mind, she desperately searched for pleasant memories to distract what was about to happen to her. She quickly drew from memory from when she was five or six. She sat motionless on a swing in the church playground. It was where she and her mom and daddy attended. She remembered she wanted to swing high, but wasn't able to get started; not knowing exactly how to move her legs correctly to get forward momentum. Suddenly growing frustrated, she thrashed in the seat—making any wild movements trying to start the back and forth motion.

The movements in her mind mimicked the actions he made as he began violating her, thrusting back and forth inside of her.

In her subconscious hideaway, she remembered looking up to the top of the church steeple, noticing the cross sitting brightly in the sun. It was the first time she'd been enticed to pray on her own. She prayed to God to bring her mommy or daddy out to help her swing and low and behold—the door to the church opened, and her daddy walked toward her. He'd seen the frustration in her eyes and actions and came running over to comfort her. He kissed her on her forehead and pulled the chains of the swing as far back as he could, then slowly releasing her to swing forward. Upon her return back, he gently pushed her forward again to a continuous and gentle rhythm of sliding back and forth through the air. She remembered looking at the tree branches above and wishing she could swing high enough to reach out and, with one hand, touch them. She hollered "Higher Daddy, Higher!" as she leaned forward then backward with the motion and momentum. She looked over her shoulder toward her daddy with a smile as wide as the blue sky.

She lost herself in that moment, shutting out everything else from her mind.

The intruder stared down at her, sweat dripping as he maintained his rhythm in sync with the movements of his victim. He was clueless to her mental escape into the memory she was reflecting on, trying to avoid the feelings of his violation. Her eyes were tightly closed as she rocked back and forth with him.

"That's right, baby-doll..." He glared at his victim, moving back and forth as he thrust himself harder and deeper inside her each forced shove. He didn't care if she wasn't enjoying him, but with her pushing back, he assumed she was. "...give it to me. That's right. Ohhhh...."

With a sudden tightening of his muscles throughout his body, followed by a slow, drawn-out groan of completed pleasure— he collapsed on top of her, his sweat pushing out between their flesh.

He lay there, catching his breath as she quietly cried, tears streaming from her eyes. She suddenly realized she'd been so caught up in her mental escape, helping herself get through the trauma that she'd been parroting his movements until he finally collapsed on top of her, spent and empty. He'd probably imagined she was enjoying her rape.

She wasn't. Gina only felt pain and filth: betrayal and fear, now trapped like a turtle on its back.

But what would he do now? Would he get rid of the witness to his crime? Were there other intruders in the house waiting their turn?

His head was nestled between her breasts as he quietly let out a snore periodically. She couldn't move his dead weight as she tried gingerly to push him over.

The bastard had fallen asleep on her. With each wiggle and attempted roll, her assailant stirred as if he would awaken.

Her body was numb, and her nerves and muscle began to prickle with each movement. The tingles felt like needles stabbing into her skin. Her pelvis felt as if it had been repeatedly kicked. She'd never hurt down there like this before; it throbbed with a deep burning ache.

Through her shame and pain, she worried about Ben.

Was he still alive? She lay still in silence, attempting to listen for any movement outside the bedroom she lay captive in. Nothing. Dead silence.

Tears rolled once more as she realized her prayers for God to intervene between her and this demon were left unanswered. How could she believe in an entity that could neither be seen and also had ignored her desperate pleas for help, but instead left her suffering and trapped?

The rapist slept sprawled on top of her. His manhood now lay limp, nestled in the same spot, touching her now spoiled gift she was giving to Ben. The gift he'd just violated, making her used and dirty, stealing her precious value.

Ben and she were making their gifts brand new again, waiting until they were bonded together in marriage. They were saving that part of themselves for each other through God's love in marriage. Would Ben even want her now? Now that she was even more tainted than she had been before? Was this the price doled out to her by God for coming over tonight, to try and tempt him?

She lay crying and ashamed. Her mind was searching through scattered and torn thoughts.

Gina had no concept of time. Her panic now overcame her rationale. There was no safe place left to go into mental hiding anymore. She needed air. His stench choked her along with his massive, hot, and sweaty body, which lay relaxed on top of her in a clump. It was almost worse having him asleep on her than the desecration he'd performed. All she could do was lie there—hopeless as she felt his demon seed oozing from between her legs with every movement, no matter how slight.

She panicked again. A new horrible thought suddenly overtook her.

What if this beast impregnated her with his evil spawn?

She pushed against him with all of her strength in a sudden burst of energy. She drew from every ounce in her body and focused it on shoving him over.

In Ben's reality, at that exact moment—he was flipped onto his side and abruptly awoken wide-eyed and in shock. As quickly as he began to get his bearings—a closed fist met his face, followed by a sharp scream.

Still deep in sleep, Gina pushed her rapist from her body, and as he rolled onto his side—she planted her fist into one of his eyes. He reached for a knife he'd left on the bedside table, but before he could grab it—she nailed him with her other fist.

Awake now, Ben touched the side of his face with one hand, feeling the pain under his eye—when another flailing fist suddenly hit him.

"Gina! What the hell!?" Ben rolled over and sat straight up in bed. He looked over at his fiancé, who had eyes streaming with tears and streaked mascara across her face with a look of horror.

"Jay was on top of me…I…I…couldn't…" she struggled to breathe, "…couldn't catch my breath…he rape…raped me, Ben!" She rolled up into a ball on the bed and broke into hysteria.

"There's no one here…Jay isn't here…it's just me…" He laid his hand on her side gently, afraid he might set her off in another barrage of fists. Ben didn't know what just happened, but he knew his fiancé was shaken to the core as she trembled next to him in the fetal position.

"Daddy…I…thought you'd…I…you came to save me…or push…I…the swing." She sniffled. "You pushed me …really…high…and…he came at…me…."

"It was just a dream, sweetie. It's okay now. I'm here with you. Nobody is going to hurt you." He curled around her and continued to gently whisper assurances as he lightly stroked her side with his fingers.

Gina mumbled through the jerky gasps. "He was…horrible…like a monster…."

In the adjacent hotel room, Jay lay wide awake, staring at the ceiling fan, which rotated in slow hypnotic circles. A small squeak chirped in rhythm every ten to twelve seconds. He knew this because he laid on top of the covers, unable to sleep, timing the sound, counting the seconds in his head.

The first night away from the Big Apple had brought consequences to each of them in entirely different ways.

    CHIRP.   CHIRP.   CHIRP.

41

It was nine a.m. before either Ben or Gina stirred once they'd both fallen back asleep. It would have been Ben's first full night of complete rest if it hadn't been for Gina's nightmare. He still didn't know the whole story of what she'd dreamt.

Gina wasn't ready to talk about it. It was not a particularly restful continuation of the night for her, either. She tossed and turned throughout the rest of the early morning hours.

Ben thought if she dreamed of anything that it would be because of the money he'd told her about, not Jay or anyone else attacking her.

The first thing Gina did after waking was to check Ben's side of the bed to make sure he was there. When he wasn't, she panicked for a moment, especially after she heard noises in the bathroom.

"Ben?" she called out, but her voice cracked in fear. "Ben…" she called again.

The door opened with Ben smiling at her, "Yes, my love?"

She jumped out of bed and quickly ran into his arms, again in tears.

"Gina, honey..." He wiped the rest of the shaving cream from his face. "It's okay, sweetie—I'm right here, and I'm not going anywhere!" He held his arms open, then wrapped them tightly around her as she snuggled in close to him.

"You left me. You were interested in every other woman, but me," she said with tears rolling down her cheeks. "It was all because Jay raped me. You kept telling me you had money and didn't need or want a whore like me anymore..." she was beginning to shake as she nestled in tighter.

"You were having another nightmare, Gina. I'm not leaving you. I promise. You're my world, and I couldn't live in it without you." He looked puzzled. "Why the sudden nightmares, sweetie? Are you okay?"

Gina leaned back, looking into Ben's eyes. "You promise the money won't change anything between us? I don't want any part of it if there is even a slight chance."

"I'm not losing you, Gina, I'd give it all away before I'd let that happen."

"Well, I want you to keep an extra close eye on Jay." She looked up at Ben. "I know you'll say it's just in my head and only a dream—but something's been different about him." She tried to muster a smile, but Ben seemed able to see through to the worry that was behind it.

"I'll watch him closely, sweetie, but we can also continue to help him. He is all alone in this world. I've been there too, and Robert was my only saving grace." He squeezed her tightly. "We are all he has in this world. He's probably going to be locked up for a very long time. Can you hang in there until it's over? I'll be beside you with my eyes wide-open." He moved his head back to look at her. "I promise, sweetheart—you'll be safe with me."

"I know. I realize now it was just a dream, and we are out in the real world for the first night together." She looked as if she were thinking her sentence through cautiously stating it, taking her time, and speaking at a slower pace. "Maybe it has just been harder on him than us. His situation has got to be scary. I guess—looking for your estranged wife after three years on the run." She nodded in agreement with what Ben had just spoken about—his prison possibility. "You're probably right. It's possible I've been overreacting and seeing things that aren't there."

Ben agreed with a nod. "I'm glad you see this nightmare as just that. It's just in your head. It's the stress of what we went through. You're letting it get under your skin. I'll watch, though, I promise." He rubbed her back and then kissed her forehead.

"On a different note." He pulled back, looking at her with a huge grin. "We can, however, take our time finding the perfect place in this world for us! The pressure is off!" He moved his hands to both of her arms and lightly squeezed them with affection. "If we spend sparingly and wisely, we can make life a little slower and have more time spending it together! You and me! Maybe we could start a business together? We're an open book, just waiting to write our story!" He watched her face light up and thought to himself. *I'll ask her later for the details of her dream. I don't want to spoil the good mood she's moved into. The poor girl had a rough night, and my face still hurts where she smacked me. Twice.*

He let go of her arms and hugged her again, reaching up to his upper cheeks to lightly massage his mildly red and swollen face.

***

Jay had stayed up late reading his Bible. He concentrated on things Ms. Cela underlined, along with her notes and explanations. One place she'd written on the margin next to a verse, stuck with him well into the night. The verse ran in a loop through his thoughts as he'd laid awake, unable to close his eyes. James 2:14-26. Her words were poignant but straightforward, and to the point of the verse, it was written next to. Her handwritten understanding was the narrative that had baited the hook, which tempted his nibble. For some reason, he was drawn to Ms. Cela's renderings of God's Word as if it were the nourishment that gave him life.

He couldn't reason or rationalize a motive why, but he also failed to refuse his muse either. Her handwritten scribbles seemed timeless to him. He read her particular adaptation countless times throughout the late morning hours.

"One MUST submit themselves to the Lord and not try to fool him with dishonest games of belief. VERY IMPORTANT! I seen many goin' through the soup line simply playin' the game for temporary nourishment of their body and not infinite loaves of the bread of life that will provide their minds and souls."

After an hour or so, he reached over and set the book down. His eyes and mind too weary of reading.

At three a.m., the chirp of the fan had finally burrowed into his head, but it was too hot to turn it off. So, he lay there thinking—then counting the seconds between those damn chirps from the fan.

He reached to the book on the nightstand again as if it were an addiction that he was unable to abandon. He opened its pages and read the actual verse aloud. The one beside Ms. Cela's version scribbled in the margin.

"Anyone of this world can say they believe in Christ Jesus. Satan himself believes in God, he just doesn't bow down or acknowledge him as his Lord. To be a true believer, one must do more than speak it. One must submit themselves to Him and live it in their outward actions of God's love for others."

This statement stood out boldly to him. He knew Ms. Cela was a Christian because she lived what she believed—selflessly.

Inside his mind, he knew as he read her translation of what believing was, that he wasn't the saved Christian he'd first thought. Did he want to live as that believer in Christ from now on; or simply play the game of deceit for the temporary nourishment? It was an honest question. It was a genuine query into his psyche. He felt a thirst for learning and becoming more like her, but he also hadn't defeated the desire to dole out retribution and consequence to others. The act of merely believing in Christ was leaving more of a hollow feeling inside with each minute. He wanted others to see God's reflection through him, but was it through doing mission—or through wrath? His fear of God seemed to melt away as his desire to quench that thirst for his knowledge grew stronger. *Maybe I am to be more God-like than I am to be disciple-like?*

Before he realized just what he was doing—he fell to his knees beside his bed, hands folded, forehead resting against them. In the quiet of his hotel room, he cried out for forgiveness and acceptance of his heart, mind, and soul. Inside his mind, it merely felt like the actions of a game. The act of rolling and shaking the Mason jar around—waiting for the answer to tumble onto the table, revealing him what actions to take.

He stayed on his knees in prayer beside his bed for several minutes before he was startled back to reality by a knock on his door.

"Jay! It's me, Ben." He tapped again on Jay's door. He glanced toward Gina, smiling, "Wonder if he's still asleep?"

The door opened slowly to reveal Jay, disheveled, and teary-eyed.

Gina started to reach out and touch his shoulder before quickly stopping and retracting her hand. "Are you okay? What happened?" She hoped he hadn't noticed how she'd held back from touching him.

She tried looking him in the eye, and he quickly darted his eyes to Ben. Thinking it odd, she wondered if he somehow knew she'd noticed him checking her body out lately—or worse yet, could he possibly know about her dream?

Jay perked up, "I think I just received another miracle or something. I stayed awake all night reading my Bible, and God called me down on my knees. I talked to Jesus in prayer." His mouth curved into a widening grin. "I confessed and asked him to take control of my life! Everything is good. My worries are gone!"

He'd just told a bold-faced lied to Ben. He knew deep down he was selling snake oil to the weak and needy. He was somewhat confused by the entire events of late—but he wasn't desperate, and he sure as hell wasn't stupid. He smiled again, for their benefit, but—to satisfy his growing wickedness on the inside was the real reason. To see if he could pull it off. He was talented at acting. He knew just when to push and when to back away. He'd needed to survive by reading other people and learning how to play them into his own hands. He might well be a little confused, but he hadn't lost the art of deception. He'd started calculating his surroundings from the moment he'd climbed into the back seat of the Caddy for the trip. He quietly laughed out loud. *Caddy...just like catty. I'm a shrewd one, as nasty as need be in the moment or as calm as a kitten to seduce the feeble-minded!*

After checking out of the rooms, they loaded into the big white convertible. Jay took the front seat, and Gina sat behind him in the back. Off they went, heading out on day two.

Gina felt more comfortable sitting behind Jay. It would make it more difficult for him to study her as tightly as she'd thought he'd been doing. Catching Ben's eyes in the rearview mirror, Gina shot a quick wink followed by a kiss with her lips. She turned her gaze over to the side window before turning forward, looking at the back of Jay's head, studying the hair she'd cut just a day or so ago. *I wonder if he could feel my eyes upon him?*

Jay quickly turned his head and smiled at her.

Gina's stomach turned queasy for a moment. *Maybe Jay could sense things?* Suddenly she felt violated by him like in her dream. It felt real. *Am I going crazy?* She knew it wasn't possible, but she felt the same burning ache between her legs that she'd experienced in her nightmare. She quickly turned back to the side window, gazing at the scenery that was forming a blur in the distance to the sounds of tire noise on the highway and the music of Cyndi Lauper, "Time After Time."

Ben lowered the vinyl top to the Cadillac about four hours later as the weather turned much warmer. Close to Hamer, South Carolina, they stopped at "South of the Border," just past the North Carolina border at a tourist trap.

They climbed the "Sombrero Tower," ate Mexican food, and played miniature golf at "Pedroland Park" before purchasing matching T-shirts. Even kids stared in amazement at the trio. They were having laughs and making fun acting silly. All three were sure they left the employees with several funny stories of their antics to retell.

Gina played along, trying to pretend everything was as it was a day or two ago. She knew Ben wouldn't believe what she was thinking. He'd had her persuaded it was all inside her head. *But was it? Or was there something evil locked up inside Jay that he was somehow able to hide it from people he wanted to?* She'd witnessed the miracle brought to them all in Ben's living room. *Was it real, though, or was Jay some evil incarnate able to expose bits and pieces to some while obscuring those same bits to others?*

She shook her head, playing it all off when asked why she was so quiet. "I think it's the Mexican food or maybe the climb to the top of the Tower? I'll be okay." She forced a happy look and then laid her head back on the seat. The wind blew her shorter dark hair straight up at times as it occasionally blew under her dark shades, which concealed her eyes from both the sun and any scrutiny from the two in the front seats.

Several hours later, past sundown, Ben pulled the car in front of the River Street Inn. It sat in the historic district of Savannah, Georgia. It was a beautiful old hotel on the bank of the Savannah River. After checking in, they took off on foot down a cobblestone road and stumbled into Vic's on the River–a restaurant in an old cotton warehouse. They ate outside under the centuries-old live oak trees. It was a beautiful evening to walk along the river and see the Saturday evening nightlife of Savannah under a bright almost full moon.

Jay walked beside Ben and Gina, who were walking close, hand in hand. He looked over, "Only about six hours away from home! Can we go to church before we leave tomorrow? I think I need to feel the warming of my soul before crossing into Florida."

"Of course, we can," replied Ben.

"I imagine there are some gorgeous old churches here. This place is beautiful!" Gina looked up at Ben, winking. "Might be a place to consider living, huh?"

Ben chuckled, "You never know! Looks pretty inviting and romantic!"

Jay's mind quickly reeled backward in time to when he first met Cat on the oceanfront boardwalk. He wondered what she was doing now and if she ever thought of him at all; in loving ways.

His mood change was noticeable enough for Gina to look over at him in question. "You doing okay, Jay? You look like you're deep in thought about something."

"I'm okay. Just thinking about the early evening that I first met Cat while sitting on a boardwalk bench in Apalachicola. It was alongside the picturesque bay with placid waves rolling in. The moon had risen just above the horizon as the sun was beginning to sink." He looked up to the evening sky. "Just thinking…and wondering if Cat ever recounts happy thoughts of back then?"

"As a woman who loves a man, I would guess she does."

"I sure hope so—I pray we get the chance to relive some of those memories. I know it's a lot to ask. I'm not counting on it, but it would be wonderful." Jay looked over at Gina and winked.

It was a wink that couldn't be categorized. Yet something about it made Gina feel awkward. She again tried not to make anything of it other than acknowledging her sixth sense.

"We'll pray for you. No matter the outcome, both of us are with you," replied Gina. Ben nodded his head in agreement.

***

Jay sensed his trial coming quickly. Three and a half years from when he'd left everything, running to save his neck. He was running away from an unforgivable mess he'd created through years of his selfish acts of meanness. Those years now seemed as if they were a lifetime ago. In many ways, they were.

He gave up that life not only when he ran, but when he handed that life over to his newly-found Savior. He'd looked forward to his chance to ask forgiveness and make atonement. Now, as time was racing past, his feelings were in turmoil. He struggled with the things he was fighting inside his head. He knew there would be a price of some kind to repay. No one gets off scot-free from crimes. Especially the ones he'd perpetrated. Was part of that repayment the internal torment he was battling? Tomorrow was another new day, only this tomorrow—would be like stepping back in yesteryear.

Walking back toward the River Street Inn, where Ben again graciously took care of his expenses, giving him another night inside a fabulous room, reminded him that he should give thanks for real friends.

It was something he wasn't used to experiencing. He looked over toward a shop window and caught a glimpse of the three of them in the reflection. He took a mental snapshot. A picture to remember this trip at this particular moment with friends, and how fortunate he indeed was. He might need this memory, he thought to himself, in case he would need to draw on this moment in his future if it took a deserved turn for the worst.

He was the third wheel in this event. They never asked for any of this to be stacked upon their shoulders. Still, they stayed by his side. They never pointed out his intrusion upon them. Not even when he had violently held control over their lives. Why did God create such people? So forgiving, so loving, even after all he'd done to hurt them.

Jay quietly shook his head in wonder as the conversation never seemed to break enough for them to notice his retrospect. They were almost back to the hotel when he felt the urge to turn and run back to the window front, to see if the image was still there. Knowing it would be impossible, he let the notion slip away from his mind. Instead, they crossed the threshold into the front lobby.

No long goodnights tonight at the doorway. Jay would let his loving friends have the dessert of the evening together, alone to enjoy themselves. Jay said his goodnights and headed to the hotel bar to have a nightcap. Something he rarely did.

Ben and Gina were so lost in themselves; they didn't notice the direction Jay walked.

Jay sat down at the bar. The stairwell was within his vision through the openness of the hotel's bar to the foyer.

He watched Gina cling to Ben's hand before his gaze moved to her bottom. It gracefully moved with each step she took upward. The way the silk of her skirt clung tightly to her ass, allowing the jiggle of each cheek to perform its symphony of sexuality. He knew she'd surely not even worn panties, there were no panty lines. Lust. He despised the feeling even though it made his mouth water as the barkeep walked over to see what he wanted. He knew what he desired before she reached the top step and turned toward their room. He thirsted with lust tonight. He knew whiskey would have to suffice.

"I think I'll have a Jack Black on the rocks. What the hell, make it a double, I'm feeling it tonight!" He laughed aloud. "Yes, sir, I am feeling it tonight."

A minute later, he was tipping the glass to his lips, sipping at first, before shooting it down fast and ordering another round.

I'm gonna let loose a little tonight. I deserve it. I'm suffering from watching that tight body and not being able to do anything about it. I like Ben and all, but I bet he doesn't even appreciate what she can do. He probably has a difficult time making his mechanics work properly. He grunted out loud, ending with a snicker. *I could ride that merry-go-round all night long until the motor smoked and ceased from overheating.*

He sat up straight when his second round got slid in front of him. His eyes blurred for a moment before he held the glass up to his lips again. *I just wonder what three and a half years has done to Cat? There were nights when she was boozed up that had been fun.* He shook his head as he remembered coming home from the road. Punishments doled out, and kids put to bed. There were nights he had to bury her head in the pillow. Cat could be a screamer. *I wonder if Gina is?*

He guzzled the last of his drink and slowly made his way up the steps. He stumbled several times, once almost dropping to his knee. He wasn't used to drinking. Four shots were a lot for a man with no penchant for alcohol. He never liked to be out of control of himself. He'd watched Cat become addicted and sleep her life away when she wasn't slurring her words, pissing him off with nonsense.

But tonight, I need it to help me battle my demons.

He stopped in front of Ben and Gina's room. He stared at the door as if he tried hard enough; he'd be able to see through it. He imagined how she looked as she undressed and readied herself for him. He didn't even want to say Ben's name tonight. He tried to imagine himself lying there, watching her move and imagining her, touching herself softly in her seduction of him, instead of Ben.

He was lost in his daydream, not noticing the younger ladies walking past him. They looked down below his belt and giggled to each other at the sight they saw as they walked past him, both turning to see it again.

"You fine…lad…ladie…ezz… see somthin' ya like? He tried to make his words work to no avail.

They continued to giggle as they scurried down the hallway.

As the door to his room closed, he almost immediately sobered, as the cover to Ms. Cela's Bible opened without hesitation. The sounds of the Riverwalk pedestrian traffic drifted in through the slightly open window along with a refreshing breeze. Cooling and calming as he lie on the bed, reading under the nightlamp above. His other urges gone. For some reason, he tried to continue to read.

***

Ben lay next to Gina, the breeze and night sound blowing into their room as the bright moon filled the walls with shadows. He felt desires to be with her, only to be squelched with the promise he'd made to himself, her, and God. He knew she was a gift given to him to be respected and treated as such. His mind began to fill with the possibilities of their future. He smiled to himself as he closed his eyes, giving thanks for being spared in so many ways.

He rolled over to his sleeping side.

***

Gina snuggled against her man, her heart feeling warm even though the light breeze felt brisk against her shoulders. She was thankful for what the Lord was providing. Her happy thoughts mixed with the regret that her past caused her mom and dad. She would always live with the guilt of her father's death. She knew her mom would always hold her to blame for losing the man of her dreams. She was realizing her dreams not long after she'd contributed to stealing her mom's.

She fell asleep quickly. She drifted off, asking God to forgive her and to bring happiness back into her mom's life. She'd also asked for guidance on how to handle her new feelings about Jay. She didn't want to put the blame where it may not be due. She knew he had a hard life in his past.

***

It was early Sunday morning in Savannah, Georgia. The cool breeze brought only a quiet chill into their rooms. The cobblestone street was silent, almost haunting.

Ben found the address and service time for the Trinity Methodist Church. He'd called Jay's room, and he was almost ready, dressed in his best clothes to attend before hitting the interstate again.

Ben headed down to the lobby to check out of the rooms. He noticed Jay's bar tab on the bill and thought it odd. He hadn't seen or heard of Jay being a drinker, although he was surprised. He shrugged the charges off, smiling to himself. *I can't fault him for needing to unwind with all the tension on his plate.*

Ben struck up a conversation with the hotel manager while he waited for Gina and Jay. "So how far is Trinity Methodist Church? He asked.

"Are you driving or walking?" asked the manager.

"Is it too far to walk to?"

"No, no. It's about a ten to fifteen-minute walk. It's a nice stroll through the old district, especially on a beautiful morning like this."

"Could you write down the streets we take to get there? You are right, and it is beautiful outside!"

"Yes sir, I can, Mr. Dane, I would be glad to, sir."

Ben looked at the name tag the hotel concierge was wearing, "David, my father was Mr. Dane and a sir at that; please call me Ben!"

"You bet, Ben. I hope you enjoyed your stay and will come back to see us soon." He continued to write directions while pointing to the paper and explaining some of what they would see. "I think you will love the service at Trinity. My mother and father attend most Sundays there. Reverend Wilkes was the man who married my wife and me, just last year. There is a beautiful, enormous pipe organ; the pipes fill the entire wall behind the altar. Sounds awesome too!"

"Is it okay if I leave my car in the lot while we attend?"

"Yes sir, not a problem at all. I hope you enjoy your morning!"

"Thank you, David, I hope you enjoy your Sunday." Ben slipped a couple of folded fives into his palm.

Gina and Jay stepped off the elevator. Jay looked sharp, and Gina was fabulous. He motioned for them to walk towards him. He admired his woman as she strolled his way, wearing a gorgeous form-fitting mid-length, light blue sweater dress. She wore a white scarf around her neck with a beaded belt around her waist. She moved toward him with a warm smile, and he pulled her into his arms and whispered into her ear. "I am the luckiest man alive. You are the picture of elegance. I love you more today than yesterday."

Ben explained the plan to walk as he waved to David and led them out through the lobby door.

The streets and sidewalks were relatively quiet this Sunday morning. It looked nothing like the busyness they were used to experiencing in the Big Apple. Fifteen minutes later, they were in front of two massive stone columns that stood guard in front and on either side of the massive wooden front door. A greeter opened it wide for them as they climbed the four stone steps up to the entrance.

They entered the sanctuary, seeing two matching stone columns standing in front of the multiple sized organ pipes running vertically up the wall behind the pulpit and choir chairs.

Gina leaned in to whisper in Ben's ear, "I would marry you in here. I would marry you today in this beautiful church."

Ben looked over at Jay and winked. "Maybe we should stay another night and check out getting a marriage license tomorrow? One more day, okay with you, Jay?" Ben chuckled.

Jay nodded back and then glanced at Gina.

They found seats about midway in the sanctuary. The sounds of people talking echoed throughout the large room, sounding almost like the stock exchange floor he occasionally visited, back in the Apple.

Once the service began, the three listened intently. The church was a relatively new thing for Gina and Ben but was literally the first time Jay had ever stepped foot in a church to hear God's Word. The message was on God's forgiveness. The disciple Judas Iscariot, who betrayed Jesus, was mentioned. Reverend Wilkes spoke about how Jesus forgave Peter, another one of his disciples, even though Peter denied Him three times. He talked about how it was never clear whether Judas was forgiven in the Bible. The reverend said that he believed Jesus would have forgiven him had he shown interest in being forgiven. He did suffer guilt over what he'd done, to the point of throwing the blood coins on the floor of the Temple and running off to hang himself.

"The point I am trying to make is…," continued Reverend Wilkes as he slapped his hand on the pulpit, "is being sorrowful for your guilt is not enough to be forgiven. You must repent of your sins to God to be forgiven. You must come to him humbly and acknowledge your sin, asking to be forgiven in His name." Reverend Wilkes finished his message with the following, "Any of us can be forgiven for anything we've done. Speak to God, acknowledge He is your Father, and you wish to turn your life over to Him. Ask Him to enter your heart. Amen."

Jay's eyes were moist as he got up and side-stepped out to the aisle. He ambled down the aisle to the altar rail to the right of the pulpit, where Reverend Wilkes still stood. He kneeled, bowing his head as he continued to sob. Reverend Wilkes motioned to someone behind Gina and Ben and continued with the closing prayer.

A man and woman walked up from behind and knelt beside Jay, one on each side of him, putting a hand on each of Jay's shoulders.

Gina glanced up at Ben, tears pooling in her eyes as she grabbed his hand and squeezed. "I feel horrible now, I've been accusing him of faking his faith…," she quietly whispered, "…and look how brave he is to kneel publicly and confess." She looked up at Ben. "Am I a horrible person?"

Ben shook his head no. "You're not horrible. You're rebounding from some horrible circumstances…," his voice cracked, causing him to look around to see if anyone noticed, "…you're looking for explanations of what you see…you are not a horrible person."

After Reverend Wilkes finished the prayer and dismissed the congregation, he walked over and knelt in front of Jay. Facing him, he spoke softly while putting his hands on each shoulder.

Ben and Gina quietly walked up to the front pew and sat down. The preacher and the two congregation members were with Jay for another few minutes before he got up and hugged each one.

Gina leaned in toward Ben and whispered in his ear. "Let's wait, I know you were going to talk to the preacher, but let's wait. I don't want to trespass on Jay's day. We can make wedding plans another time." She squeezed his hand.

Ben looked at her with a knowing look and a nod. "See? You're not a horrible person." He said in just a whisper.

They took a leisurely walk back to the hotel parking lot and climbed back into the big white beast to head on to Florida. It was quiet again as they wound through the beautiful neighborhoods on the way back to the interstate. As they merged back onto I-95, Ben mashed the pedal down, roaring quickly down the road towards Apalachicola–a town that unknowingly held Jay's atonement.

<u>42</u>

It was seven p.m. when they finally rolled into Apalachicola, Florida.

Jay's mood was a mix on this last leg of their trip, as was Gina's. Ben frequently gave him encouraging words, especially the previous jaunt across the state on I-10 out of Jacksonville.

Ben was tired as he pulled onto US-98 East out of Port St. Joe, Florida, for the final blitz of the journey into Apalachicola. The conversation was much quieter the closer they got. But it was dead silent as he pulled into town and stumbled on to the Gibson Inn. It was across the street from the Franklin County Courthouse.

"Is this okay, Jay, or should I look for another place to stay?" Ben asked.

"There isn't much else around. It'll be okay. I'll stay out'a sight as best as possible. Whatever happens, is going to happen." He spoke quietly. "I don't know that a lot of people knew who I was anyway. We lived out away from town."

"I'll get our rooms. You and Gina stay in the car for now." Ben got out and walked up the stairs and then through the front door.

The next morning Ben called Robert to see if his brother could find a suitable lawyer for Jay in Florida and to let him know they'd arrived safely. "All is well, Robert. I can tell Jay is nervous about being home, but he's been reading the Bible daily, and it seems this new life is sticking with him. Thank you for all you've done to help us, even though it seemed crazy."

"I'll make some calls and see what I can do. You be careful and keep me posted. I'll leave a message at the desk of the Gibson for you if I find anything. Love you, little brother! You seem to be a new man yourself. I'm happy for you. I'm happy for Gina too."

Ben hung up and went to knock on Jay's door.

He returned to his and Gina's room. "I knocked but no one answered? Have you seen Jay this morning, Gina?"

"I wonder—there could be two places I would go if I were him." She looked at Ben with a quizzical glance. "Either to see his wife or the cemetery where his son is buried."

"We need to try and find him before somebody recognizes him. We've got to get him an attorney to get started researching his case." Ben said with a serious tone.

***

The Chestnut Street Cemetery still looked the same to Jay. He'd never really spent much time in it, but he'd been there with Cat a time or two to visit her dad's gravesite. He thought he'd start there first. He was confident Cat would have laid Billy to rest near her father if she could. He thought he'd remembered her say they owned several pre-paid plots for the family so that they could be together in the end.

He roamed around, trying to recount which paths they'd taken in the past. He remembered there was a tall, sprawling live oak tree close to Cat's dad's headstone. Large branches were reaching out over many gravestones. Some large, massive tree limbs with bends near the ground sat on pedestals underneath, holding the weight as they then turned upward, growing back toward the sky again.

Jay's mood was very melancholy while he lingered up and down the white chat paths, glancing from tree to stone. He talked to God aloud, trying to clear his conscience as much as possible for the reason which brought him here—his son's death by his hand. He replayed that Friday evening in his mind like he had many times in the past. This time, it felt different. He wasn't hundreds of miles away now. He was here in his first boy's final probable resting place.

The breeze was light, but would occasionally build in a burst of air which blew like a furnace vent shooting hot, humid air through his hair. It was years since he'd felt humidity and heat like this. The smell of saltwater from the bay mixed in with the sultry breeze. He'd missed it in a way. The summers of New York were nothing even close to the end of winter in Florida.

He looked up abruptly as one tree seemed to stand out among the others. It was the one where Cat's father's stone lay, and he was sure as he hurried toward it. He first noticed the taller stone. It was Cat's father's resting place. His eyes looked to the right where two empty plots lay. On the third plot sat a smaller stone peeking up from the earthen grass. It was newer, not as weathered as the other. It had a small bouquet of wilted flowers neatly laid in front, resting against the stone with a delicately-tied ribbon around the dried stems. There it was. The words across the top. Here Lies Billy James Cader, Beloved Son.

Jay approached it slowly and with reverence. His legs and hands both shook as the tears poured from his eyes, rolling down his cheeks. He knelt on one knee and placed each of his hands gently on the top of the small headstone. "I'm sorry, son." He started quietly, in almost a whisper. "I can't expect you to forgive me, boy. I don't deserve it. What father torments and brutalizes his flesh and blood? And to the point it makes them look to kill their poppa? I'm sorry, Billy. I'm sorry for what I did to you, your momma, and your little brother, Darrell. It should be me in the ground, not you." He spoke louder now, as he confessed his guilt to the place where his son's body rested. "I'm sorry I ran and left the mess for your momma and

Darrell to live with. I don't know how I can expect God to forgive me ever when I can't get your forgiveness—now—or ever."

He looked upward toward the puffy morning clouds drifting by. "God, I know you exist now…" he sniffed, his nose was running full bore. "… I don't know why you saved me. I don't know why you gave me angels from your heaven…" his eyes were blurry as he searched for words. "…angels like Ben and Gina." He wiped his sleeves across his moistened face. "You'd be better off striking me with a bolt of lightning from this blue sky to punish me for what I've done. The lives I ruined." His voice grew louder.

"The sins I've committed! Hell! I'm lusting for the woman of the man giving me everything…!" His voice was rising indignantly. "…How can you forgive a man who has done so much damage to others for so long and still begs to do more harm?" Jay yelled for an answer from God. No such answer came to him as he laid his head on top of the hands that gripped the stone. He just whimpered and sobbed. "Goddamn me, Lord. Strike me down right now!" His words were yelled in a challenge. "I'm tired of being a damn puppet—my strings pulled between you and Satan!" His hands slid from the stone to the ground. His head dropped to the grass, and he sobbed with no control. "I killed my only boy…that…was like…me…" His words jumbled together as his voice dropped to placid weeps

***

Cat woke early, feeling somber for some reason. Her son Darrell was having hard times ever since she'd taken him to the cemetery. She felt comfort in the times she visited, but she saw the pain and confusion it brought to her youngest son. She realized too late he was not yet ready to know the outcome of that fateful evening.

She walked around Gloria's yard, picking some of the flowers which started to show signs of diminishing and mixed some of the prettier, newer ones with them. It seemed right to take some of each and help make the dying ones more pleasant by combining them with the fresher, more colorful ones. She needed to walk today and decided she might as well replace the bouquet on Billy's grave that she'd left last time. Her heart was yearning for Billy more these days. She knew to get up early, and going alone was best. She could let her heart cry more with Darrell absent from her on this trip. As she got a block or so away, she looked back toward the house, making sure he wasn't tagging behind.

Meandering down the path at the cemetery, she looked over all the different stones which rose above the ground. Some stood staunchly upright, while others leaned one side or the other from age and lack of care.

She wondered what had ever happened to her mother. She knew where her daddy was, but after her momma left, she'd never heard another word from her. Cat blamed her mom, in a way, for her daddy's death. He was as broken-hearted after momma left as she was when Billy died, and Jay ran. Her daddy only had his princess left; his queen vanished, leaving the king banished to his castle alone with only his princess. Her daddy always called her princess, very seldom Catrina.

Cat concentrated on the path ahead as she made her way through the cemetery. She soon became lost in her thoughts of the past. She hadn't looked up and failed to notice the stranger kneeling beside her son's gravestone. Neither did she see Darrell following her in the shadows of the trees and stone markers.

She suddenly stopped, feeling something amiss, queasy from the immediate butterflies in her stomach. Her eyes darted toward the big tree. Yes, this is the right spot, but who was that man? Her breath immediately became labored as her eyes focused in on the strange man kneeling at her family plot.

The chiseled chin on his profile and broad shoulders keenly looked familiar. "Jay?" she blurted. Her hand immediately covered her mouth in a gasp, intuitively trying to silence the name which escaped her lips. Her heart racing, feeling as if it would pound through her chest.

He turned, searching to find the voice he recognized but hadn't heard in so long. Upon seeing Cat, he slowly rose, pressing against the stone with his hands to help his weary legs straighten. He turned to face her.

Cat stopped dead in her tracks, dropping the bouquet from her grip. All color drained from her face as her eyes widened in disbelief. "Jay? My God! What are you doing here? What…?"

Darrell ducked behind a tall stone, keeping himself hidden while his heart raced. A flash of memories surged through his consciousness of the monster who killed his brother. There stood the same monster who shook the damned jar filled with his rage. He froze in place as he watched the man walk toward his momma. Anxiety gripped his soul as the same old fear crept up his spine. The warmth from his bladder filled his shorts and filled the air with a strong urine odor. His heart wanted to rush over and protect his momma and attack the demon that returned uninvited. But his legs wouldn't work; he couldn't make himself move. Darrell stood frozen from the same fear that locked him in place every Friday evening so many years ago. Darrell thought of the times he heard the sound of Poppa's diesel truck pulling up the driveway. The growl of the motor and the sounds of tires crushing the gravel in the drive. The memory overtook his mind, and suddenly, he was again terror-stricken from his past.

Jay walked toward Cat with outstretched arms. Tears poured from his eyes as indiscernible words came from his lips.

Cat couldn't move. What was happening? She wasn't prepared for this moment. "No, Jay, it's not you! You're gone. You left us. Billy is dea…" She couldn't wrap her mind around this scene unfolding before her. She reached for her chest, pressing against the sharp pain she felt.

He now stood less than two feet away, staring into her eyes. "Cat, I'm so sorry. I don't know where to start…" His words faded into silence while his eyes remained fixed on hers. He held his arms out again, inching slowly nearer until he was close enough to wrap them around her slowly.

Cat's legs began to buckle as the light of day rushed from her vision. She reached forward as her sight became a bright light racing away from the tunnel of darkness she was experiencing. She suddenly fell forward.

Jay stepped up to her in time to catch his estranged wife before she had the chance to stumble to the ground.

As Darrell watched, he saw it as an attack. He didn't know what to do. He forced himself upward onto his legs and peeked around the stone one more time. It appeared that his poppa held onto his momma as she struggled to break free. On instinct, he ran—but not in his momma's direction. Darrell ran from the cemetery, and he would get help. He'd get Reverend Gabriel.

Cat slowly lifted her arms up and gradually put them around Jay's torso. It felt awkward, but her instincts brought back the habit she'd trained herself to do to keep him happy. To keep her from being reprimanded for things she never knew were coming. She wasn't in a cloud of bourbon-induced stupor anymore, yet she suddenly felt as if she were. Everything moved in slow motion as if she were dreaming. She suddenly snapped back to the present and pushed back on his sternum, "No! I won't do this, Jay! No! You are out of my life, and I won't let you back in just like that."

He stepped back a step or two as Cat instinctively covered her face, expecting to be smacked for being disobedient.

"Oh, my Lord, no, Cat. I'm not that man anymore," he said as he watched her recoil in fear. "Cat, I don't want to hurt you. Not ever again. That man is dead. I understand your fear, and it makes me sick." He spoke softly. "I've got the Spirit of the Lord inside me now. I'm saved."

She slowly lowered her hands with caution and looked deeper into his eyes as if trying to decipher his words and check them for truthfulness. "Why are you here? You'll be arrested if they see you."

"I know. Some friends brought me here to make amends for what I've done. I asked them first to let me see you and Darrell before I turn myself in."

"He won't see you, Jay. He just recently realized it was Billy who died that evening instead of you. He'd always prayed Billy would come back for him…for us."

Jay dropped his head. "I don't understand how the Lord can forgive me if my family can't find a way to do so. I know I don't deserve it." He looked up at her again. "You're still beautiful, Cat. You've gotten younger looking. More beautiful than I ever deserved. I'm sorry I lost my sense and treated you so horribly."

"It wasn't me, Jay. It was our boys. You made them want to kill you. It's my fault too…"

"Cat! It was never your fault. Ever!"

"Jay, I poured my heart and soul into a bottle of booze and let this all happen."

"You have no blame, sweetheart. I don't know how the devil got into me so bad. I have no excuse that's ever gonna be good enough, but I do know you have no blame. You were just trying to escape the demons inside of me." Jay began to sob. "Those demons were inside of me until my friends got me to listen about God. I was gonna hurt them too, but God intervened and saved me." He began to bawl even louder, and then his legs gave way, dumping him to the ground.

Cat stared at him for several moments before she kneeled, daring to put her arms around his neck and talk into his ear. "I prayed you would change Jay. I loved you the night I told you to run. I didn't want to lose you. I hated you, but I was in love with you…" She stuttered a bit, "I—I can't explain it." She shook her head at the dichotomy as tears began to blur her vision.

"Cat, I think the memories of you are what kept me alive… until finally, I'd just given up to the madness in my head." He drew his eyes upward. Jay looked out across the cemetery blankly. He scanned the stones protruding from the ground until his gaze met Cat's dad's stone that rose above Billy's. He looked back in Cat's direction but solemnly dropping his head toward the ground. "I own no explanation good enough to ask for your forgiveness. No words could ever repair the damage done." He glanced up at her, the sun causing him to squint from its light. "The only thing I can speak of is what I've been through since I ran. It's been hell." He kicked at the dirt. "I know it doesn't compare to how I left you with the mess I made, but it wasn't a picnic I've been clawing my way through either. I made it up to New York City. It was cold—I'm talkin' the kind of cold that makes a man suffer and think about mistakes he's made."

"I realize it's probably not been easy for you either, Jay, but you gotta understand it ain't just you here and me. You might as well have killed Darrell too that day. His insides have been practically dead all of these years." She reached over and pulled his chin up so she could see his face again. "He's been a walking dead soul for over three years, Jay. After I got myself cleaned up from the bottle—I've had to raise him back up from toddler stage practically. He still calls me Momma for God's sake. I've had to baby him back to reality."

"I gotta ask, Cat. I know it's gonna bring the anger on, but I have to know…."

"I swear he's yours, Jay." She looked away for a second before turning back. "I know you've doubted it since he practically fell from the devil's tail…" she chuckled. "…as rambunctious and noisy as he was—he's yours."

Jay stared into Cat's eyes. "Then, I'm going to make it as right as I can with him."

"He's not going to let that happen," she shook her head in disagreement. "I think he'll hate you 'til the day one of you dies. He's not the same boy he was when you left. He's crawled down deep inside himself." She strained her neck to see Jay's eyes again after he looked away. "He will hardly talk. He'll open up for me every once in a while, but since he found out that Billy isn't coming …" she hesitated. "…he's lost to himself even more so. We've lived with our preacher and his wife now for most the time you've been gone." She nodded her head and pushed out a subtle grin. "It's been good for him. Reverend Gabriel has been a male figure he could look up to. Ms. Gloria has been so much help to me, too."

"Sounds like there's no opportunity here with what you got going on."

"It's a hard pill to swallow, you just showing up like this." Cat replied.

"Before you just shut me out…" Jay sniffed as his tears began to return. "…I was hoping to introduce you to my friends, Ben and Gina—the couple who brought me here. They've helped me make changes. They've helped me fight my demons and meet my Maker, so to speak." He wiped his face with his sleeve. "I'd like you to at least meet them if you would. They opened my eyes to God. I…we, all three experienced a miracle. A life changing-miracle. Would you meet with them? We're staying at the Gibson."

"Right there across from the courthouse? Are you crazy, Jay?"

"I'm ready to turn myself in and do whatever time they give me. I just wanted to see you and Darrell first. I needed to tell you how sorry I am and beg for your forgiveness." He reached for her hands. "I couldn't do time without knowing I at least tried to get your forgiveness. I can't run anymore from my past. I have to own up to it." He squeezed her hand slightly. "I'd like to try and talk to Darrell too, after all, he's my only son I have now." He looked into her eyes with a feeling of deep sorrow.

"I'll take you home to see him. But I can't guarantee he will ever come out."

Jay started to follow Cat over to the flowers she'd dropped on the pathway earlier. "I'm just asking to try; I'll not force anything on anybody."

She turned around to him because of a sudden urge to hug him, and she stepped closer.

They embraced, pulling each other tightly like two old friends who hadn't seen each other for years. Neither seemed to know when to let go and step back.

After a long embrace, they began to walk. Cat told him how she hoped Darrell would give him a chance of reconciliation he wanted. Then it became quiet. The breeze seemed to die the minute they passed through the gate of the cemetery and onto the road. Not too many minutes later, they neared the front steps of the Watkins's home—her and Darrell's home.

43

Darrell quickly ran up the steps of the Watkins's home. His heart pounded fiercely while sweat oozed from every pore of his body. Running to the Watkins's bedroom, he hurriedly made his way to the back corner of the large walk-in closet. There, leaning against the corner, hidden behind Reverend Gabriel's suit coats, sat what he came looking for. The double-barrel side-by-side shotgun. The same one he practiced with when Reverend Watkins had taken him to shoot for hunting.

He backed out of the closet, gun in hand, purpose in his heart. He was going to save his momma from the monster who killed his brother and was now attacking her. He knew he must finish what Billy had failed to do. He rummaged through the dresser, looking for the shells. The third small drawer down, as he ripped it open, caused the sound he looked for. Shells rolling to the back of the drawer. He quickly grabbed up a handful, shoving some into his shorts pocket as he slid the action lever, breaking open the shotgun, exposing the breach. He fumbled several times, trying to push a shell into each barrel. Frantic, he took a deep breath, letting it out as slowly as he possibly could. He looked down, noticing the dark stain still on the crotch of his pants, but he had no time to change. He poked the second shell into the barrel and snapped the breech closed.

He had a monster to kill, his momma's life depended on him.

***

Ben and Gina were in the lobby, getting directions from the manager.

"The quickest way to the Chestnut Cemetery is to go out here on 4th street, the manager pointed toward the door, "about two blocks to Highway 98, then turn left for about four blocks. You can't miss it."

"You wouldn't know where I could find a Miss Catrina or Cat Cader—would you?" Ben asked.

"Are you asking as a reporter or something, fella? That incident has been over for the past three years." The manager's mood suddenly changed, and a scowl formed across his brow. "That is something this town would just as soon forget."

"No, sir, we're not reporters at all. We're friends of a friend who asked us to check up on her to make sure she is doing okay. There will be nothing put in print, sir. We aren't here to stir up any story."

Gina looked over at him, knowing very well the story was going to break. It would come back to the surface shortly as soon as Jay turned himself over to the authorities.

"All I can say is, I've heard the boy, and she is staying with Reverend Watkins and his wife. He's the pastor down at First United Methodist Church on Live Oak street. Just before you reach the cemetery if you were on Highway 98, with that, I'd say good day, sir. I have things and other guests to attend to." He turned, scratching his head and huffed back to his office.

Gina pulled Ben close and whispered, "I believe you struck a hornet's nest. I wonder why the attitude about something over three years past? And, by the way, we are going to stir the past back up with bringing Jay here. You do realize that, don't you?"

"Yeah, I know, but no reason to let the facts out while we're asking for help to find out what we need to know," he whispered back as they walked out the front door. "Walk down Highway 98 first to the church, and then over to the cemetery? Or vice-versa?"

"I think Jay would go to the cemetery first to clear his chest and deal with what he did in the past while he's alone. Let's head to the cemetery," she replied.

***

Cat and Jay kept a slow pace while they shared what their lives had been like in the shadow of what happened over three years ago.

"I don't drink at all anymore, Jay. I go to AA meetings weekly, and Darrell and I attend the Methodist church, which Reverend Watkins leads." She kept her eyes straight ahead.

Jay responded. "The first couple of years, I rarely spoke a word to anyone other than to myself. I stayed away from all outsiders in fear I'd be recognized and locked up. I did speak aloud to myself, though, so I'd maintain the ability. I was my only friend and confidante. I'm not telling you this to seek sympathy—just painting the portrait of what life was like when I left the porch that night." He fidgeted as he continued, walking to the side and picking up a blade of grass to chew. "My world priorities flipped in an instant. I never talked a lot anyway with my job being a trucker through the week, but the aspect of life changed dramatically on the lam. I saw everyone as either an enemy or a target to survive."

"Our lives changed also. Honestly, a lot changed for the better. Fear had overtaken all three of us in those years. Those years your love faded as it became replaced with anger. That anger seemed to kill the person I fell in love with. Billy and Darrell only saw you as the threat who came home and doled out punishment—unjust, cruel punishment." She looked at him and stared. "You had evil inside of you. I don't know if we caused it or what? We were all terrified of you."

"I know that now. If I could take it all back, I would. I'm sorry about it all. It's unforgivable. I know you probably wish you would have never sat down beside me that day on the boardwalk, so long ago." He stared down at the ground.

They were almost in front of the Watkins's home, although he didn't know it. Jay stopped and turned to face Cat with his back to the house. He put his hands on her shoulders and gazed into her eyes. "I wish I could have the time to show you the changes God is making in me…"

"Jay! Look out!" Ben yelled as he ran towards him, Gina following close behind.

***

As Ben and Gina walked toward the cemetery, they noticed Jay and a woman standing side by side on the sidewalk. He looked at Gina. "That must be Cat?" He had no sooner spoken than he saw the young man with a shotgun behind Jay and the woman up on a porch. The two were so intense in conversation; they were oblivious to everything else.

Darrell flew out the front door with the shotgun in hand, prepared to protect his momma. Almost to the first step, he saw his poppa clutching his momma with both hands. Darrell stopped, lifted the shotgun, and pulled the two triggers back to firing position. He pulled the butt of the gun to his shoulder, lining up the end of the barrel toward Jay.

***

Ben yelled again as he got closer to Jay. "Jay! Watch out! He's got a gun, up on the porch!"

Hearing Ben's frantic voice, Jay wasn't sure what was happening but sensed immediate danger. He turned, looked up to the porch, and seeing a gun, pushed Cat abruptly backward. She tripped over her feet and fell to the ground.

Darrell's entire body shook as his finger searched for the front trigger.

Ben dove and tackled Jay as he was throwing himself towards Cat to cover her.

As Ben and Jay fell to the ground, the silence was shattered by a loud bang and the immediate sound of pellets hissing as they flew beside them. Both rolled over onto Cat, shielding her from the flying shot. Another loud bang shattered their already deafened ringing ears. Again, the sound of spattering pellets whizzed all around them; only it was muffled and much quieter this time, their ears pained and hollow.

It was dead quiet for a moment. The birds scattered from the trees and were circling above out of harm's way.

The blasts brought Reverend Gabriel running through the door from his upstairs study, where he was preparing Sunday's sermon. Ms. Gloria followed close behind him, running down the stairs. She'd been working on a quilt just before a loud bang almost caused her to jump out of her skin. The sound forced her to rise and run to the window of her sewing room. She saw people on the ground while others circled them and then heard the second blast.

The front screen door slammed shut behind Reverend Watkins as he stood in stunned silence at the scene before him. Darrell dropped the shotgun the moment he saw Reverend Watkins staring at him with a questioning look.

Time froze for a moment before Ben rolled over off of Jay, who was still lying on top of Cat. There were red splatters of blood soaking tiny spots in Ben's shirt.

The screen door slammed closed again. Not knowing what just transpired in their front yard, Ms. Gloria hollered, "Oh Lord, please be with us!" She glanced at Darrell and saw fear and confusion as he stood over what appeared to be her husband's hunting gun.

Gina, who stood in shock of the entire episode, tried to filter in her mind what had just happened and looked over to see the woman she presumed was Cat—not moving. She ran to her, knelt on the ground, and nudged her shoulder.

"She's not moving!" Gina cried out, but then she saw Cat begin to sputter and cough as if she were coming to.

Jay moved to touch her face and look into her eyes. Holding her soft chin in his hand, he whispered, "Cat, baby, talk to me."

Cat looked him over, slowly responding in a faint voice. "Jay? There's blood on your shirt." Still stunned and in shock, she hesitated. "What happened? You're not here, are you?"

Gloria and Reverend Gabriel quickly rushed to survey the injuries. He called back up to Darrell, "Call the sheriff, son, and tell him we need medical help—hurry!"

Darrell's first thought was to run. Run as his poppa did. But then he saw his momma lying on the pavement. He ran inside and dialed the sheriff.

A few minutes later, Darrell came back out on the porch and hollered to the reverend. "Sheriff and an ambulance are on their way, sir."

Jay heard his boy and looked up at the porch to see him standing staunchly, but bewildered. He couldn't help but notice the wet area on the crotch of his shorts. Jay turned his head back to the boy's momma. He'd heard Darrell say the word sheriff and knew his moments of freedom were short. He cupped his wife's face and bent down close to her ear, whispering. "I'm so sorry, Cat. I didn't think anything like this would happen. I love you, and I'll not cause you any more pain. I'm turning myself in without any trouble to the sheriff when he comes."

Cat looked up, tears rolling, and responded in a raspy whisper. "I still love you, Jay. Darrell didn't mean anything. In his mind, he was protecting me."

"I know. I don't blame Darrell. I just hope he can forgive me." He moved enough to lean in and kiss her on her thin lips before he rose and turned to Darrell. Jay slowly walked to the porch steps and began to climb them toward his boy. He felt sharp pains in his left leg and the side of his chest and arm. His clothes were stained red, scattered with tiny holes throughout. He reached the top step and looked at his son standing firm in the doorway, eyeing him with a mix of menace and fear.

"You done what you needed to do, son. I'm proud of you. I deserve so much more for what I did to our family, to your brother Billy, your momma, and especially to you. It's unforgivable. I don't expect you'll ever be able to grant me any grace." He winced a little as he continued, a stream of salty tears beginning to roll down his dirty and bloody cheeks. "I have something I need you to hear from me, son." He hesitated, searching for the right words. "I was wrong all this time, Darrell. Grace don't come by chance—it doesn't come from being shaken out of a damned jar by a man with the devil inside him. It comes straight from God himself—and from loving family and friends who believe in Him." He reached out with his right hand and put it on Darrell's left shoulder, gripping it slightly. "You're one of those good people who believe, that's what your momma tells me. Well, the Lord has control of my soul now. I gave it over to him of my own free will." With his left hand, he touched his chest in the area of his heart. "He gave me a miracle I don't deserve, and I have to make my reparations for all the sins I committed."

The sounds of distant sirens moved closer. "I'm gonna be gone again, son, so you don't have to fear me. I just hope one day you can find it inside your heart to try to forgive me. I was broken—but now God is mending me and taking me under His wing of His grace and love. Take care of your momma, son." He turned and began walking down the steps from the porch and towards the sheriff's patrol car rolling up to the curb. Ambulance sirens blared not far behind.

He held his arms in front of him, wrists up, as he approached the sheriff. "I'm Billy Jay Cader, sir. I believe I'm probably the fugitive you've been looking for."

The sheriff hesitated with a confused look as it worked its way across his face. He pulled a set of cuffs out and snapped one side around Jay's left wrist, pulling it around to his back, then pulling his right arm back to attach the other cuff to his right wrist. As Jay was loaded into the back seat of the patrol car, he looked at Cat as the ambulance technicians began to examine her. She glanced back for a moment, their eyes locking. He saw the same face he'd seen three and a half years earlier when he turned back for one last look again. Her eyes held beauty in them, even though they were also filled with the pain that he'd brought.

It was like déjà vu.

"We'll get a good attorney, Jay! No worries, Gina and I aren't leaving until we get this worked out." Ben yelled.

Gina put her hand on her heart and then pointed her finger to him as a deputy pulled the car slowly away from the scene.

Jay dropped his head and began a prayer. "Dear Gracious Father, thank you for your mercy…" He looked up again and stared at Gina as she looked back at him. He took a mental snapshot of the way her clothing clung to her tight young body. Her breasts were pressing firmly at the fabric of her top. He winked at her and then returned to praying. "… Thank you for being the difference in my life this time. Thank you for being beside me no matter what lies ahead. Take care of my family. Please help me know the truth about Darrell and the fact if he's mine. Forgive me as you have—if it is in Your will. Amen." He searched his mind for answers to what had happened just now with this whole scenario. *Who in the hell were these people and how did they rattle my head up so well? I don't know what is going on inside my brain, but I intend to come through it with an understanding: one way or the other Lord—one way or the other. Lay on me what you will. I'll survive it.*

The ambulance crew continued to check the injuries of Ben and Cat as more police pulled onto the scene, both local and state.

Cat came out virtually unscathed physically. Mentally, surely was another story. She stood weary-eyed, her face pale as Ben touched her arm to draw her attention to himself.

"I'm sorry to meet like this. I'm assuming you're Jay's wife?" Ben knew but wanted a way to start a conversation with her. "It looks like you got away without being too injured?"

"Yes, sir, it appears so. I guess you and that lady are the new friends Jay was telling me about?" Cat brushed the dirt from her clothes caused by the tumble. "Your lady is quite pretty. Jay been leaving her alone?" She cocked her eye and waited for his answer.

Gina overheard the question and took a couple of steps toward her to introduce herself. "Hello, I'm Gina. This guy you're talking to is my fiancé. And to answer your question—after a kind of rough start between us all—Jay has been a gentleman and a friend." She scanned Cat's reaction briefly. "Should I have been expecting otherwise?"

"Well, I, of course, never had any proof, but..." she gave a bit of a crooked smile "...I always thought Jay had an eye for the pretty ones. I can't say for sure he ever cheated on me, but he was away from home all week, every week. He can be quite a lady's man when he wants to be." She looked over at Ben. "Looks like your man got pretty lucky that it was only birdshot my son fired. He was just trying to protect me." Cat smirked. "Long story, one you probably don't want or need to hear. Especially since it looks like Darrell just caused you some superficial wounds, probably have to get that shot picked out from underneath the skin, though before an infection sets in." She pointed towards Ben's face.

"Looks like they just missed your eyes! I'm glad for that." She looked up at the porch, where the sheriff was talking to her son. "I better get up there and make sure Darrell doesn't say something wrong to Sheriff Burks. You know young boys—always tryin' to own something before they know what they're buying." She gandered back at Ben as she started walking towards the porch. She turned back when she reached the steps. "He's a good boy, Mr. Ben. He was just protecting his momma. You understand that, don't you?" She didn't wait to hear his answer before she walked up and grabbed her boy's shoulder, protectively pulling him into herself away from the sheriff.

The medical personnel wanted to load Ben into the ambulance and take him to the hospital, but he refused treatment, stating he would seek it soon. He wanted to see the incident wrapped up first and answer any questions.

Gina comforted Ben, carefully hugging him, not knowing exactly where all his wounds were. "You should take that ride. I want to make sure you're in tip-top shape!" She smiled brightly after kissing him, boldly stating, "Benjamin Dane—if I can find a suitable place here in Apalachicola, Florida—will you marry me here?"

Ben returned the grinned and kissed her back. "Yes, ma'am, I will. I'm yours until the end of time. But, no! I do not need to go to the hospital! The young man missed all of the important parts!" He patted himself below the belt as if making sure for added humor.

Gina giggled and then leaned in close to his ear. "Pardon my French, but wasn't that some strange shit the way Jay's wife was reacting and talking to you and me?"

"I'm sure it was the shock from all of this. The whole thing hasn't turned out exactly as I saw it in my head," Ben replied. "In New York, there'd be cops everywhere after a shooting like this."

Reverend Gabriel and his wife had walked down from the porch. They were standing close enough to hear their discussion and leaned toward them, clearing his throat, "Ahem, I'm Reverend Gabriel Watkins, and this is my beautiful wife, whom I married right here in this town twenty-six years ago. Right over there," and he pointed to the beautiful bright white-sided Methodist Church across the yard to the left of them.

"It's beautiful, Reverend. I'm Benjamin Dane, and this is my beautiful fiancé, Gina Rae Elkins. We're good friends with Jay. We've all helped each other through some hard times. We're kind of new to being Christians, so we are learning every day and trying very hard to get it right." He paused. "Does every new visitor get the customary shotgun welcome?" He knew he shouldn't have said it, but it slipped out before he could stop.

"Well..." Gabriel chuckled nervously and cleared his throat again. "Ahem, No—no—that doesn't happen for everyone, and I'm thankful for that." Gabriel looked back at his wife. "Well, welcome to the family of faith! If there is anything I can do to help, you let my wife and I know." Gabriel reached to shake Ben and Gina's hands. "Miss Catrina and her son Darrell have been staying with us for some time. I taught him to shoot." He grinned sheepishly at Ben, not knowing if his humor would be received very well.

Ben directed attention to his shirt with his hands. He pointed to all the little red, moist spots throughout. "You taught him well, Pastor. Are you teaching him to be a preacher too? The boy managed to make my shirt pretty holy." Ben coyly peeked up at the preacher, and after an uncomfortable moment, he cracked a grin.

"You got me there, son." He looked back toward the porch and noticed the sheriff still talking to Darrell. Turning his attention back to Ben and Gina, "Let me go back to the reason I cut in earlier before I dig myself into a hole I can't climb out of." He chuckled. "I couldn't help but overhear your discussion a couple of minutes or so ago. Did I hear you two wonderful people are wanting to get married here in the area?"

Gina laughed and grabbed Ben's arm. "I'm trying to nab this one before he changes his mind!" She paused for a moment. "…Or maybe gets himself shot and killed…" She smiled and continued, "…or since he's already been shot with a shotgun…we've completed most of the shotgun-wedding already, haven't we?"

The group of them all chuckled as Ben pulled Gina next to himself.

Gabriel grinned a moment, putting the tips of his fingers on both hands together and lightly bouncing them, "You know, I'm a licensed and ordained minister capable of doing such beautiful occasions! You just let me know when we can get together and talk through the details, we'll leave the shotgun upstairs—if you are so inclined!"

Ben winked at Gina, turning to the reverend, "Oh—we are so inclined, without the firearm, though!"

They all smiled, and Ms. Gloria cut into the conversation. "I don't want to be a spoiler, but Darrell is looking pretty bewildered up there with the sheriff, Gabriel."

Darrell lifted his head, looking at his momma, eyes full of tears, and a wrinkled forehead showing signs of fear and confusion. "Why do I gotta go with him, Momma? Poppa was hurtin' you! I stopped him!"

She pulled him in tighter, glaring at Sheriff Burks. Her eyes were becoming full of the salty burning mix of perspiration and tears. "Sheriff Burks, why the hell does he have to go? Can't we just settle this here and now?"

"Ms. Cat—There was a shooting in which your boy was involved. I reckon I'd look pretty derelict of my duties if I didn't at least take the boy in for questioning. I'm not arresting him this evening, but he by golly is gonna make an appearance at the station."

Sheriff Burks side-stepped Cat and walked Darrell down the stairs, without cuffs. She followed behind him and her boy as they walked to his squad car. The sheriff pushed through the Watkins's, Ben and Gina. He was losing his patience. "Ms. Cat, I'll call you when you can come down to the station and see him."

"See him? Don't you mean pick him up and bring him back home?" Asked Cat with an intent look in her eyes.

Sheriff Burks opened the back door and ushered Darrell into the back seat. He briskly walked around the car, and as he opened his door, he tipped his hat. "I'll be seeing you, ma'am, I'm certain of that." He started the car as soon as he got seated and slapped the gear-shift lever into drive.

Darrell's eyes showed fear as he watched his momma and the Watkins's faces as the squad car pulled around them and headed down the street.

Ms. Gloria pulled Cat in close and whispered, "It's gonna all work out, honey. Trust in the Lord. He's got everything in control."

The Reverend stepped next to his wife and consoled Cat, patting her back and softly speaking.

Ben leaned in toward Cat and the reverend. "I'll pay for an attorney. We need to get one down to that station quick before they question either one of them. Darrell may not know to say nothing without representation!"

"I got a few lawyers that are members of my church. Follow me, Ben."

Ben and Reverend Gabriel climbed the stairs to his office to begin calling friends of his who either were reasonable attorneys or possibly knew of someone.

Ben's body began to show the sting and ache of his scattered pellet wounds. As adrenalin decreased, the reality of the birdshot under his skin awakened his senses.

Gabriel noticed him squirming and moving carefully. "You need to get that taken care of—praise the Lord, I only had light birdshot shells, and the shotgun was only a 20 gauge. Could'a been a lot worse." He looked at Ben and then to the statue with a cross with Jesus's body hanging on it. "I'd say there were a few miracles today, yes, sir."

Ben nodded in agreement. "He's been pretty busy in my life lately. My brother is a pastor, also."

"Tell me more about your brother, Ben. I'll keep checking my address book for a good defense attorney." Gabriel pushed his old wire-rim glasses back up the bridge of his nose, and he thumbed through his Rolodex file.

"My brother is known by his congregation in the Bronx as the 'White Dove'…."

44

Every question Sheriff Roy Burks asked Darrell, he sat silent. He sat in his chair with his head down, staring at the tabletop.

"Son, I realize you are scared. I have a feeling you may have had a good reason for the action you seemed to have taken, but I need to hear the story from your perspective and your mouth." He paused for a moment, not expecting any response after he overheard the advice given from his phone call to his mom. "What all did your father do to you and your brother growing up? Do you remember anything about the day your brother expired?"

Darrell looked up at the sheriff with a glare of meanness in his eyes. "First off, my brother didn't 'expire.' He died. He was murdered. My Poppa stabbed him with a knife." He dropped his head back to where it had been. "As soon as my mom sends a lawyer over, that's when maybe I'll start answering questions. Until then, I ain't sayin' nothin." He lifted his hand and formed his finger in a defiant vulgar, suggestive action.

Sheriff Burks jumped from his chair, ramming the table hard, which jarred Darrell's hands that propped his head up. "Get up, son. I'm gonna have to put you in a holding cell until I hear from that lawyer then." He walked him through the door of his interrogation room and down a short hallway filled with framed law enforcement personnel photos, which seemed to stare sternly.

It succeeded, making Darrell nervous as Roy continued to walk the young man past a couple of cells and purposely paused for a moment in front of the cell holding his dad.

Roy looked over at him, "Jay—why'd you drag your sorry ass back here after all this time? Did you just want to bring all this mess back here to my town? To your boy and your wife?"

Jay lifted his head from where he sat on the cot. "I came back because I'm tired of my life the way it was. I know you don't care, but I want to make things right. I've been blamed all my life for things I didn't do. I might as well try paying back for the ones I did. Surely making amends and asking for forgiveness is a good thing, isn't it?" Jay shook his head at the question. "I'm admitting my guilt for what happened to Billy—ain't that enough retribution from my family without draggin' the boy into it?" He sneered.

"You know, if I could believe you, I'd answer yes. But now that you've even gotten your son involved—that's just a damn shame." He nudged Darrell to move on down the hallway to the next holding cell. "Make yourself comfortable, son. I don't suggest talking to your ole man." He shut the door, locking it before he returned down the hallway toward his office.

Roy returned to his office and, upon sitting in his chair, kicked his black cowboy boots up onto his desktop. He leaned back, tilting his chair as far as it would recline. "Those two motherfuckers are real pieces of work. Florida's finest swamp-trash!" He grinned a vile grin as he reached into his shirt pocket, pulling out a large cigar and poking it between his teeth. Reaching on top of his desk, he snagged a book of matches and withdrew one. "I'm gonna feed the damn gators this Cader trash..." He dragged the match up the side of his pants, sparking a smoky flash, then drawing it to the fat tip of the stogie in his mouth. He sucked long and hard, extracting the freshly lit tobacco smoke into his mouth. Upon expelling the cloud, he chuckled again with a look of pride that could swallow the canary. "Just what the hell did that pretty little Catrina see in his worthless, cartooned up ass?"

***

The room was quiet and humid. The onset of spring was early, making it steamy in the small town's Police station. It stayed hot and quiet for hours, each detainee wondering if the other was going to speak first.

Finally, Jay spoke up, asking a question. "Did you know the sheriff before today? I only ask because I was wondering if he was always this way, or is it just me and the situation I brought? He seems to lack certain civility to be holding a public office."

Darrell didn't respond.

"I can't imagine what you're thinking about, now that I've come back. Your momma said you remembered things differently that last evening." Jay wasn't sure how to start a conversation with his son if he was his son, but he couldn't just sit there silent any longer.

"Darrell, I'm sorry. I don't know how to tell you any other way than what happened. Your brother dying was an accident. I came home, and he just ran at me. I didn't even see the knife he held." He stopped talking, deciding to let what he just said settle in.

Jay closed his eyes and leaned back against the wall weighing the breadth of the circumstances. *I Wonder what tile of punishment I'd receive from the luck of the Mason jar roll if that were the way they did it? No matter what, I'll take it like a man. I wouldn't be pissin' my pants like the bastard child callin' me Poppa—sittin' there whimpering in the next cell.*

45

"It was late 1948, an elderly woman, a Lila Pasternack was found murdered and robbed. Neighbors say she'd let a young Billy Jay Cader live in her spare room after she spotted the young sixteen-year-old digging in a dumpster for food." Attorney James T. Bollard replied to Ben. "The thing is, they nailed two escaped cons about a year into Billy Jay's prison stint for a couple of crimes with identical circumstances up the road in Vicksburg and West Bay, Florida. They finally admitted to the Pasternack robbery, rape, and murder six months later. These two were some bad players."

"Nothing was ever cross-reverenced through the state's case against Billy." The attorney leaned in closer to Ben and Gina. "Jay finished the roughly eight and a half years of his sentence that he should have been released from—for a crime he didn't commit. The two escaped cons' confessions never came to light with Billy's case."

"You've got to be kidding me! That can't happen, can it?" Ben asked. "He truly was an innocent boy, convicted of a horrendous crime. No wonder he turned dark like he did, given his dad was abusing him also." He looked at James Bollard with eyes of sorrow, then with piqued curiosity. "Surely, that will speak volumes to the prosecutor in what goes forward with this case?"

Mr. Bollard sat up straighter. "If we can get his son and wife to speak to the fact that Jay's older boy provoked the attack when he died in that conflict between the two of them—I think he's got a good chance to have any case against him dropped."

"How did you find out about the Pasternack case? I mean, it seems like someone wrongfully—and possibly even knowingly withheld evidence after the fact…" Gina asked as she sat on the edge of the guest chair in his office.

Ben nodded in agreement, then asked the question again. "How did you find out about the two escapees and their confessions?"

Mr. Bollard leaned back in his chair with his arms folded across his chest. "I have the best investigative team in Florida. That costs a lot of money, but it pays off for the clients I represent." He smiled before continuing, "It makes it easier to justify the cost, when the evidence presented back to the D.A. is so overwhelming in our defendants' innocence in their cases."

Ben responded. "Worth every penny, sir."

"Mr. Dane, it's certainly not a guarantee—but his case looks pretty rock solid. I think the only thing they could prosecute him on is spousal and child abuse, but that would be shaky without evidence on their part, especially so many years ago. Will the wife and son testify on his behalf? Or against?"

Gina replied. "His wife still loves him. I think she wants to help him. His son? He could be another story."

***

Cat sat across the table from Darrell. "Looks like you will get to come home soon. The attorney has convinced the prosecuting attorney to allow you home under house arrest until they come up with a trial date."

"I was defending you, Momma. How can that be assault, when I saw him grabbing at you? He'd already killed my brother!"

"I know it looked like he was grabbing me, Darrell, but it wasn't exactly like that. We were talking, and he was apologizing for all the wrongs he did in our past. He was sick, honey. He was doing what was done to him by his daddy." She reached across the table to hold his hands.

Darrell pulled his hands back abruptly. "Sounds like you're picking him over me, Momma. He's a murderer. He used to beat us—have you forgotten?"

"No, Darrell, I haven't forgotten."

Darrell gave her a look of disgust. A look he'd never given his momma before.

"Maybe you just don't know 'cause you was drunk all the time?"

He knew he'd drawn a sword and made a very painful stab, plunging it into her heart. He sat back quickly and retreated.

"Oh, honey, no." She tried to lean closer across the table toward him. "You have every right to call me out, but I know you don't hold that against me now. You love the same Jesus I love. The One who tells us He doesn't hold our sins against us forever if we ask for forgiveness." She reached across the table again, attempting to touch his hands. Darrell didn't retract them this time, but he also didn't respond to her touch. "Jesus wants us to try and reflect the love He shows us. It doesn't mean you have to accept being hurt again, but if it's a genuine act of asking for forgiveness…" She lifted her left hand to wipe away the tears forming. "We have to forgive. Your poppa didn't set out that night to take your brother's life, Darrell. Jay acted in defense; it all happened so quickly! Billy fell into his knife in the scuffle. Your poppa didn't set out to cause his death. I know that in my heart. I knew it that night. I saw the pain in his eyes." She teared up again, beginning to sob. "I don't want to lose my entire family, Darrell. I can't. I know you may never trust him. I wouldn't blame you, son. But you can forgive him and accept those horrible accidents happen in the heat of altercations. Your brother was trying to kill him. I saw it in his eyes before your poppa came home. I saw it when he threw that jar as hard as he could and shattered it." She squeezed her young son's hands. "He donned wrath in his eyes, Darrell. Your poppa didn't know what he was walking into."

Darrell looked down at their hands; his momma's rubbing his as tears rolled down both of their cheeks.

"I can't live without you, Darrell. All of this has been a horrible tragedy. I know it was born of the meanness in your poppa's heart. But it doesn't excuse our actions after. We have to live the way Reverend Gabriel and Ms. Gloria have spent teaching and nurturing us to live. God's way, sharing God's love with all who seek it."

The deputy walked in and cleared his throat, announcing he was there. "I'm sorry, ma'am, but it's time to wind down and get ready to go. Visiting time is over."

Cat got up and looked to the deputy, "Can I give my boy a hug, please?"

"Yes ma'am, I don't suppose that would hurt."

She walked around the table as Darrell stood. She wrapped her arms around him, tucking her head onto his shoulder. Cat squeezed him in, taking in his scent, the smell of her baby. She whispered into his ear, "Think about what I've said, Sweetie. It's an important decision you have to make. Life-changing for all of us. He's not the same man he was. I know that." She kissed his cheek, and the deputy pulled her arm, forcing her to step back.

She slowly followed the deputy out as another deputy began to take her son back to his holding cell.

"I love you, Momma. I'm gonna pray about it." The door closed, and Darrell watched her walk away through the small horizontal window in the door. For a brief moment, he was allowed a parting glimpse of her until she became a blur of color in the distance.

The deputy was much more agreeable to Darrell than the sheriff had been. Darrell was glad the deputy allowed his momma to hug him. He felt very alone locked away in the drab muggy cell. Especially at night, knowing the man that was supposed to love him, was instead the man whose dark shadow lurked on the wall across the hallway, back and forth against the stark white background.

"Did you get to see your momma, son?" asked Jay.

Darrell lifted his head, turning to where the voice came. "I don't like it when you call me that."

"I'm sorry, Darrell. You came from my seed, so it just seems natural. If it bothers you, tell me what you want me to call you?"

"Why did you even put the tile with the word GRACE written on it? I don't remember you getting any satisfaction when that tile fell out onto the kitchen table."

Jay's mouth paused as he mulled the question over in his mind. He squinted to himself as if the question caused pain, but he slowly answered, "I had a war going on in my head. I know how you felt, and that's the excruciating part for me to accept. I was in your shoes when I was young. Most of the time, my daddy didn't bother with the jar. He just smacked me around when his angry side was disturbed. At least with the jar," he hesitated a moment. "I had a chance of getting GRACE." He finger-combed his hair, which was now getting greasy. "I guess maybe that's why. It made the punishments have odds. You may have thought I got pleasure from punishing you boys—but you couldn't see what was going on inside me. I never derived any joy from it. It just seemed to satisfy the devil's thirst that was living inside of me…" Jay was glad Darrell couldn't see him. He was certain inside his mind that if Darrell could see his face—he'd certainly know he wasn't exactly honest with him. "…the devilish heart given me from the evil my daddy gave me." He paused for dramatic effect. "Now that sonovabitch—**he** enjoyed it. I could see it in his eyes when I was brave enough to peek at 'em." Jay believed parts of what he was telling his son, but those feelings his dad had driven into him were long since dead. He was confident they had no lingering effect on him now. "I don't think even God would waste his time trying to reach inside my Daddy's wretched soul." He rubbed his face with both hands and then got up to use the toilet. He unzipped and began to relieve the pressure in his bladder.

Jay felt no pride getting in his way of exposing or relieving himself anywhere—no matter where he was or who may be watching or listening. The fact was, he hardly even thought about it.

It was just a natural function. He knew he was just an animal in this world.

Darrell could hear the monster's venom splattering against the stainless-steel toilet as it left his body. He shivered as he imagined how his poppa looked with his shirt off, and those horrible ink carvings etched into his skin as he stood emptying his bladder.

Those tattoos would come to life as he moved. Darrell remembered how terrified he was of them. The images gave him nightmares on Friday evenings when it was bedtime. He would see the lady with the scales imprinted on his chest with the bloody knife embedded in her heart, bright red liquid dripping down into his belly button. His arms inked full of skulls and scary goblins. He was the devil to Darrell, and he knew Billy feared him also.

"You still awake, Darrell?" Jay growled in a low voice.

There was a silence that lasted a lifetime before he mustered up an answer. "I'm awake. I was thinking about how your ugly tattoos gave me nightmares after the Mason jar—when it was bedtime. I was too scared of watching them dance on your body as you punished me from what the tile said." He shook a little, like a quiver from a quick cold breeze across his back. "How is a child supposed to sleep after that Poppa?" Calling Jay Poppa caused his stomach to wretch. "How in the world were you able to go to sleep afterward? Did you know we would lay awake in fear, thinking you might come back again?"

Darrell lay on the cot, waiting in the sullenness for the answer to his question. He asked another quickly before getting a reply back. "What did you do or say to Momma afterward when you were lying in bed with her? Did you kiss her and say I love you?" Again, he waited for some kind of justification from his poppa.

Darrell waited in silence for a moment and then continued, "Do you know how many times I killed you in my daydreams? How many different scenarios I played out in my head to make it happen?" Darrell's body began to shake, and his hatred showed in the curtness of his voice. "I hate you, you sonovabitch. You stole my life, my Momma's will, my hope for the future, and the only brother I had…" A single tear snuck out of his left eye, and he wiped it away quickly. "…and you have the Goddamned balls to come back here begging for my understanding and forgiveness—when all we hoped for was you found dead and rotting…."

Jay's rebuttal finally bounced off the hallway wall and back into Darrell's cubicle.

"Son, you're asking questions I can't answer. I know it seems like a coward's way to deal with it, but I honestly don't remember. That demon has left me, and with him went most of my memories of it. Maybe it's been the years running, or the reality of losing something valuable I was supposed to love and care for. I just don't know, son." He paused a moment before continuing, "I'm not comparing pain with you because I don't have that right. All I can say is while I don't remember specifics anymore, I do remember the lack of any kind of love inside or around me. I don't think I knew what love looked like."

He took a deep breath, letting it out slowly as he leaned against the concrete wall, the droplets of sweat sliding down his skin that held the demons in ink. He drew another breath, then spoke. "That night, Billy and I took that mad tumble to the floor—I'll never get to say I'm sorry to him. That's a horrible loss. That'll be my hell for the rest of my life. All I can do is tell you how sorry I am—and that I'll never hurt you again in those or any other ways. It'll be up to you if I keep your hell with me to the end also."

The veins bulged from Darrell's temples, throbbing from the anger building from sitting in the cell next to his nemesis he'd recently thought was non-existent. "I hope you choke on my hell every single day, you worthless piece of shit. It's my turn to pass the verdict—the sentence—and punishment…" Darrell rolled to his side, shaking from the tension as he finished his last words. "…and I don't need no fucking jar to do it." He laid there knowing his Savior was disappointed in his words, but he felt relief getting them off of his chest.

Jay's body felt utterly drained. The questions were challenging to deal with. His answers lacked any kind of elegance as if elegance could have offered any saving grace in the conversation between them. He now knew where he stood. He'd seen now that Darrell too contained courage within himself. Maybe he was from his seed? Jay rolled from the wall onto his back and stared at the stained ceiling above his cot. He breathed in a long deep breath through his nose, smelling the musky damp odor of urine and body odor. It reminded him of the first days of prison life so many years back when he was just a lost child. *There is no beauty in this world of God. That's the God's truth.*

***

Cat walked to the Gibson Inn to talk to Ben and Gina.

Ben asked her if she would be willing to talk about Jay and her feelings. About what happened between Billy and Jay that night so long ago.

She knew the time would come after this latest incident between Darrell and him. The phone call from Ben had sealed it.

"Hello, Mr. Dane, Ms. Elkins." Cat held out her hand to shake theirs.

Ben said hello, and Gina reached out to hug her.

"It's nice to see you again, Ms. Cader," replied Gina.

"Y'all don't need to be so formal. We're just regular people here in Apalachicola," Cat responded. "And the Ms. part ain't even correct, I reckon. I never divorced, so technically—it's still Mrs."

Ben motioned over to an empty banquet room for them to meet. "I'm Ben, it's nice to see you again, Cat? Right? Is it okay for me to call you Cat?"

"Certainly, I insist."

"Jay's attorney is supposed to meet us here any minute. I hope that's okay?" asked Ben.

"That would be fine. I assumed he probably had some questions about this whole ordeal," replied Cat.

"Well, Jay has become very special to us. I know he has a past that is not anything like the Jay we have grown to know recently," stated Ben. "I don't know if Jay mentioned anything about us or not? I know Gina and me are not aware of a whole lot of his past with you and Darrell. He's shared some pretty horrible things that he is ashamed of doing in his past and hoped to seek forgiveness." Ben paused and cleared his throat. "I'm hoping you can explain some of those things to his attorney, Mr. James Bollard. He's been working on Jay's defense with not only the horrendous incident involving your oldest son but also a case that landed him in jail many years back." Ben led her and Gina to a table just around the corner from the door. "I don't want to delve too much into it before Mr. Bollard arrives, but I did want to give you an idea of what the discussion will be."

Cat nodded. "Ben, I just want to say, I don't hate Jay. I never really did. I don't know why I don't. He caused the boys and me extreme hurt over the years. I'm not seeking any retribution from that." She fidgeted a bit in her chair, crossing her legs one way, then the other. "I can sense he's changed. I'm stuck in the middle between a man I loved, and the only son I have left, whom I love with all my heart. My oldest has been gone now for over three years. I've never entirely gotten over that. I probably never will; I think of him daily." Cat's eyes had tears beginning to fall. She reached up and wiped them away with her hand. "He was such a brave young man at seventeen to try and protect Darrell and me as he did—it cost him his life. He was always lookin' out for his little brother. He took Darrell's punishment along with his own every time he could." She reached up with her hand and carefully wiped each eye's tears away, again. "He begged Jay to give him the harsher of the two, every single time." She teared up again, and Gina reached over, putting her warm hand on Cat's shoulder. "I don't know how anyone comes out a winner in this. I know Darrell probably holds the most memory of hurt from Jay. Jay never treated him like he did Billy. I think he disliked Darrell from the moment we brought him home, maybe even from the minute he found out I was pregnant."

Someone tapped on the door as it slowly opened. Mr. Bollard peered in. "Am I interrupting?" He edged into the room. "I am sorry, I'm late."

"Come on in, Mr. Bollard." Ben motioned as he rose from his chair. "Sit down. I've just been filling Ms. Cader in on what we would be discussing."

The four sat around the round table and reviewed what the investigator had uncovered. They followed up with details of the deadly event between Jay and his oldest son.

"So, in finishing up on that night, Ms. Cader, your statement would agree with Billy Jay having no preconceived idea or any way to foresee what Billy James had in store for him that night? He was truly acting in self-defense, with the whole conflict lasting less than a couple of minutes? Correct?" asked Mr. Bollard.

"Yes, sir." She looked directly into Mr. Bollard's eyes. "That night, when Jay opened the door, he was clueless he was about to be attacked by his son carrying a knife. I'm not saying he didn't deserve Billy James's wrath that night, but he was not the one doing the attacking—it was our son."

"And you don't mind or feel forced to sign a statement such as this discussion or testify if this proceeds in court?" asked Mr. Bollard.

"No, sir, I don't mind signing, and yes, I will testify if need be."

"Now, onto the matter of your youngest boy and what he witnessed." Mr. Bollard continued. "You stated that up until a month ago, he remembered the night as his poppa being the one which ended up deceased? And not his brother?"

"Yes, sir, Mr. Bollard. He mistakenly, and unknowingly to myself, misremembered the event. He was young. I wasn't sure how much he'd seen or understood. He was only thirteen and a very distraught boy at that. He'd grown up being punished weekly because of the outcome of that damned jar. The one Billy James smashed against the stove that night." Cat's weary eyes and drained color in her face showed the difficulty of reliving the stories. She bravely continued. "Darrell was terrified before his poppa ever got home, just by his brother's actions." Cat appeared tired as she tugged on the necklace that held a cross with Jesus nailed upon the silver charm. It was the gift Ms. Gloria had given to her on the day she accepted Jesus as her Savior. She also had added a tarnished silver heart-locket to the chain, the only keepsake she had left from her mother. Inside were tiny pictures of her two sons, Billy on the right, Darrell on the left. It was her most precious treasure and never left her neck.

Her creased forehead from the wrinkling of her brow painted the hurt caused by the conversation. She sought comfort by touching the cross and locket, everything of value at her fingertips. It gave her comfort in moments of difficulty, like the present.

"I don't believe we will need a statement from your youngest boy, ma'am. He wouldn't be a credible witness with his memory being incorrect for so many years, along with his young age at the time. I think we can surely persuade the prosecuting and District attorneys to withdraw any charges with what we have. The horrendous mistake the State made with the Pasternack case will only add to our favorable position for dropping all charges. I hope to keep your youngest away from any of the court proceedings if possible, ma'am."

Gina was the first to acknowledge the news, "That is great news, Mr. Bollard! I have one question, though. What about Darrell? In this whole mess, we don't want him to end up coming out the worst." She looked at Cat and Ben, then returned her attention to the attorney. "Will Darrell be charged for shooting at Jay? It was self-defense, correct?"

Cat added her perception. "He surely won't be held of any account, will he? He saw Jay's hands on me and with our past…" Her voice was pleading. "…he naturally assumed I was in danger. His brother died trying to do the same thing!"

"I will be talking with his attorney later this morning. I know Mr. Dane won't be pressing any charges, nor his father either. I will suggest if they won't drop the aggravated assault charges, they reduce them to reckless endangerment. With no previous record and the extenuating circumstances—I would think some probation would be a worst-case scenario. I think between all of us involved here, we would all like to see Darrell's record remain untarnished."

Cat let out a sob so loud, it made everyone in the room jump. Fighting her emotions, she began to speak again. "I can't…believe…believe it's…it's over," her voice cracked. "I don't know how to thank each one of you. Life for me has been…I can't even…" She dropped her head down and cleared her throat. She looked at each one of them. "I don't want to complain about my life anymore. I'm glad you may be able to vindicate some of my husband's past. It will never begin to excuse the other things he's guilty of with my boys, but I have a better understanding now of why. I thank God He used each of you to bring us all to this point." The color in her face became brighter, and the wrinkles in her forehead smoother. "While I don't see my family ever being what a family is supposed to be or what ours was meant to be in God's eyes—each of you has been part of His hands in bringing about new possibilities of change. Change for the good. I just want to say thank you, and God bless each of you." Her head dipped back down as her breath heaved several times before beginning to slow into long deep breaths.

Ben, Gina and Mr. Bollard quietly looked at one another, giving Cat her space. Each reacted differently.

Gina walked around the table to where Cat sat and hugged her with a womanly understanding. She rubbed Cat's back, but spoke quietly—Ben or James could hear nothing but a murmur.

***

Apalachicola was a small town, a close-knit community tucked in between the Apalachicola River and the Apalachicola Bay. The locals there knew just about any news about any other person in town or the outskirts from it. The community lived and breathed the old small-town life. It was a great feeling most of the time, but there were town secrets that some felt should be left alone. Tucked somewhere deep where the outer world needn't hear about them.

The day Billy Jay Cader and Darrell Lee Cader walked out of the Apalachicola Courthouse; a small-town secret of the past became something all of Florida would hear about. It would come back to light overnight and then talked about in the nooks and crannies of small cafes, gas stations, and any other places people congregate.

Reporters from Panama City, Pensacola, Tallahassee, and as far away as Jacksonville showed up at the courthouse steps. Cameras filming, interviews of locals recorded, microphones poked in front of unwilling faces. News from the old story was rehashing and spread like wildfire through water-starved, dry timber.

The look on Sheriff Burk's face was stern and unpleasant as he led the way in front of the Cader family, clearing a path for them to make their way to their futures. The cameras caught his ugly glare, and the film clip was repeated over and over for days to come. Questions were asked concerning the Sheriff's demeanor, but answers were not immediately found, and conjecture would abound. "That might just be a story for another time," some would say, chatting in small local gatherings.

Once the story slipped into the past, the days in Apalachicola slowly slid back into a slow normal rhythm again. Steady like the tiny waves of the bay, slapping quietly onto the rocky shoreline.

***

There remained some questions and turmoil between Jay and Darrell and would always seem to be present when they were together. Either sitting quietly in the corner of the shared space or more boldly in their sharp snippets between each other.

Darrell resented how his poppa had gotten off scot-free from justice. He was bitter, and the day he walked out of the courthouse, it was apparent to anyone who saw his face that there was hatred in the young boy's heart.

Jay had stumbled into some new questions about the bloodlines in Darrell once again. On the jaunt through the police station, he'd noticed photographs on the walls of deputies and past sheriffs. Jay spotted an old photo of a much younger Roy Burks, when the sheriff was a fresh new young officer. The old photo caught Jay's eye enough that he stopped briefly to study the face. It had a strong familiarity with it. The eyes and jawline were unmistakably recognizable. He just knew he'd finally realized he'd been correct all those years back. He hadn't been crazy in his assumptions. His intuition had been spot-on.

The little bastard walking in front of him through the courthouse door wasn't his at all—Darrell was trailing behind his true father, Sheriff Roy Burks, and neither one held a damned clue about the other. The big-headed uniformed asshole in front, leading this freakish parade was in fact Darrell's Goddamned father, and trailing behind us all —was his cheating momma, the last liar in the procession.

Justice had not yet been served to the one most deserving.

Cat had lied to all three of us. She'd made us all her fools.

Jay looked over his shoulder at her as they climbed into the cars that would whisk them away from scrutinizing cameras and microphones, and that one quick look into Cat's eyes, he could see the guilt hiding in full display for all to see. The cameras caught it on film and broadcast it across all the stations, but, were too focused on the forest to see the crooked tree.

I was the only one who was on to Cat's twisted lie. She would pay though, in good time, she would pay.

46

Ben and Gina finally met with Reverend Gabriel and set their plans for marriage. The ceremony was small, attended by their close network of local friends that quickly became family. Robert came to be Ben's best man, while Cat became Gina's best friend and bridesmaid. They were married in Reverend Gabriel's United Methodist Church on a hot summer day like any other in Apalachicola, Florida.

They bought a home that overlooked the Apalachicola Bay. It was small and humble but came with an extra couple of bedrooms in case they decided to grow a family. The two planned to open a restaurant called The Big Apple on the Bay and included Jay as a full partner.

Cat and Jay occasionally went out for dinner and conversation. Jay kept his secret of knowing the truth about Darrell's true father. Their continuing relationship was his ruse. Many times, they would end up on the bench down by the docks to watch the sun go down. Their relationship slipped into the slow casual rhythm of the area, taking life on the slack and easy, each pretending to reacquaint themselves to each other. There was no real depth between them as far as Jay felt.

He continued to battle his internal demons between playing the game of faith and trying to buy into it for real truth. The knowledge that Cat had indeed cheated on him all those years back—and then adamantly denying it—continually haunted him. He thought about forcing a paternity test, but that would merely open up motive if anything ever would happen to her or Darrell. He indeed wrestled within, playing various scenarios of vengeance in his thoughts.

He wondered if the ignorant Sheriff Roy Burks would ever get a clue that Darrell was his son. It just supported his knowledge of what an ignorant asshole Roy was. Jay scoffed each time he was reminded of the fact when he would spot the uniformed cheater, acting high and mighty in his one-horse town.

***

The church was every Sunday, a staple for all involved. It was just what people did in the remote little town hidden in the past.

Darrell was slowly trying to heal, but accepting his past was not easy. He grew into his maturity more each day. Cat noticed more smiles got caught up on his lips as the days fell into nights, piling into the past. Some were forced, but some showed authenticity. He'd become close friends with a couple of the neighborhood boys, which helped ease her mind. Those same friends had grown her boy's vocabulary with words she did not approve—but those were wars she'd not yet chosen to battle over. She was just glad her boy had a shot at being normal after all he'd been through. He was finally becoming a more outgoing young man, instead of a boy that needed coddling.

Jay could be found almost every evening out on the fishing pier. He sometimes had a pole in his hands, but a lot of times he just stood at the end of the pier, staring out into the bay and lost in thought.

Many times, Reverend Watkins brought Darrell out to the pier with him, poles in hands. His motive was never a hidden one. He tried to be the bridge of faith between a father and a son who were both broken, but in his mind, not beyond repair.

Some days the conversations between Jay and Darrell out on the pier made it feel like the scars were healing. Other days it looked as if a corner of the scab had been intentionally bumped, opening unhealed flesh and filling their odd relationship with an agitating pain. A pain that needed a little extra salve to aid regrowth. Reverend Gabriel tried his best to be that salve.

Nobody knew the real truth behind Jay and Darrell's strained relationship. The two would share untrusting looks between each other through the corners of their eyes, each appearing to have dark thoughts and suspicions of the other. There were dark secrets shared between them left unstirred for the most part.

Reverend Watkins slipped food for thought and words of encouragement that seemed to come from out of the blue.

"Worship the Lord your God, and His blessing will be your food and water."

"Words to live by!" Jay would agree. He knew he no longer bought into it, but he played the game biding his time, trying to decipher the voices in his head.

Some days the only words spoken were those of excitement when one of their poles would form that grand bend as the reel would squeal and click—hollering to the other to "bring the net!' to assist in the catch.

Sometimes Reverend Gabriel just couldn't let the quiet stay silent any longer. He would grin a toothy smile and holler out a favorite quote, "Fishing just seems to be God's tool to heal the heart! That's why Jesus chose fishermen for disciples. Cast your nets, you sons of Zebedee, and catch men instead of fish!"

Gabriel would smile, either missing or ignoring the seething undertones beneath the Cader family's veneer.

Those nuances still lurked just beneath the stormy shadows, as dangerous and unpredictable as an unseen bull shark lying beneath the murky waters froth. Hungry and ready to bite and thrash without hesitation or warning.

TO BE CONTINUED WITH BOOK 2

THE SPARK OF WRATH

About the Author

Eli Pope lives with his family and two dogs in the heart of the Ozarks. He is currently working on several writing projects that includes upcoming additions to The Mason Jar Series along with a thriller being co-written by one of his sister-in-law, Kendra Nicholson, author of THE CLIMB.

His love of writing is his escape from the everyday grind of working full-time in the real world of paying the bills and providing for his family.

This is his passion along with painting and creating.

Proud member of the Springfield Writers Guild.

Visit **elipope.com** to keep up with upcoming books and projects. Eli makes available to purchase paintings and artistic creations occasionally and lists them on his website.

3 dogsBarking Media LLC strives to bring you as the reader the very best quality of entertainment. Please let us know if part of our product is not up to your level of satisfaction as a loyal customer. Contact us at:

3dogsbarkingmediallc@gmail.com

Works in progress

FATED INCEPTION
By Eli Pope

AVAILABLE NOW

THE CLIMB
BY Kendra Nicholson

THE WANING CRESCENT
By Steven G Bassett

Please leave reader reviews with

Amazon.com and Goodreads.com

This helps the author immensely.

ELI POPE

CPSIA information can be obtained
at www.ICGtesting.com
Printed in the USA
LVHW090733040221
678262LV00018BB/609